"What are you insi
pull the plug o
family, toss me
agree to come b

"I prefer to think of it a   marriage a fair shot before we rel   story books. You come back to me, w   and make it work, I pull Carmichael out of its financial difficulties before it becomes a footnote in the list of great American dynasties. It's a *win-win*."

A win-win? Angelina stared at Lorenzo, disbelieving. "You would really hold that over my head?"

"You didn't play fair when you walked out on me, *tesoro*. You just cut and ran. So, yes, I will use whatever means required to make you see the light. To do the right thing."

"I asked you to go to counseling. I begged you to. I tried to save our marriage and then I left."

"You expected us to solve things overnight. It doesn't happen that way."

Her fingers curled tight around the delicate stem of her champagne flute. "Putting the two of us back in a marriage where we'll destroy one other is *not* doing the right thing."

"We're both older and wiser. I think we can make it work."

She shook her head. "That's where you're mistaken. That's where you've played the wrong card, Lorenzo. Because I will never become your wife again."

She turned on her heel and left. He let her go, because he knew she'd be back. He'd never gambled on a deal he couldn't win.

Jennifer Hayward has been a fan of romance since filching her sister's novels to escape her teenage angst. Her career in journalism and PR, including years of working alongside powerful, charismatic CEOs and travelling the world, has provided perfect fodder for the fast-paced, sexy stories she likes to write—always with a touch of humour. A native of Canada's East Coast, Jennifer lives in Toronto with her Viking husband and young Viking-in-training.

Books by Jennifer Hayward

Mills & Boon Modern Romance

Reunited for the Billionaire's Legacy
Tempted by Her Billionaire Boss
The Italian's Deal for I Do
The Magnate's Manifesto
Changing Constantinou's Game

The Billionaire's Legacy

A Deal for the Di Sione Ring

Kingdoms & Crowns

Carrying the King's Pride
Claiming the Royal Innocent
Marrying Her Royal Enemy

The Delicious De Campos

The Divorce Party
An Exquisite Challenge
The Truth About De Campo

Visit the Author Profile page at
millsandboon.co.uk for more titles.

A DEBT PAID
IN THE
MARRIAGE BED

BY
JENNIFER HAYWARD

All rights reserved including the right of reproduction in whole
or in part in any form. This edition is published by arrangement with
Harlequin Books S.A.

This is a work of fiction. Names, characters, places, locations and
incidents are purely fictional and bear no relationship to any real
life individuals, living or dead, or to any actual places, business
establishments, locations, events or incidents. Any resemblance is
entirely coincidental.

This book is sold subject to the condition that it shall not, by way of
trade or otherwise, be lent, resold, hired out or otherwise circulated
without the prior consent of the publisher in any form of binding or
cover other than that in which it is published and without a similar
condition including this condition being imposed on the subsequent
purchaser.

® and TM are trademarks owned and used by the trademark owner
and/or its licensee. Trademarks marked with ® are registered with the
United Kingdom Patent Office and/or the Office for Harmonisation in
the Internal Market and in other countries.

First Published in Great Britain 2017
By Mills & Boon, an imprint of HarperCollins*Publishers*
1 London Bridge Street, London, SE1 9GF

© 2017 Jennifer Drogell

ISBN: 978-0-263-92514-2

Our policy is to use papers that are natural, renewable and recyclable
products and made from wood grown in sustainable forests. The logging
and manufacturing processes conform to the legal environmental
regulations of the country of origin.

Printed and bound in Spain
by CPI, Barcelona

A DEBT PAID
IN THE
MARRIAGE BED

For my dad—a gifted surgeon, teacher, woodworker and master of anything trivia, you were also the greatest father I could have hoped to have.

There is a piece of you, Dad, in every hero I write, because you were larger than life. I can't imagine a world without you, where I can't ever pick up the phone again and pick your brain on a storyline. I only know if I live a life half as courageous and remarkable as yours I will be happy. xx

CHAPTER ONE

"Sɪʀ."

Lorenzo Ricci pocketed his phone and lengthened his stride, pretending he hadn't witnessed the appearance of his portly, balding, middle-aged lawyer in the hallway behind him. Fifty minutes back on US soil, the last thing he needed was to discuss the fine print of the complex acquisition deal he had been negotiating, a subject bound to make his head ache even more than it already was.

Tomorrow, after a shot of his favorite whiskey, a steam shower and a face-plant into the Egyptian cotton sheets his housekeeper had procured for his very comfortable king-size bed, would be soon enough to endure that brain-throbbing task.

"Sir!"

Dio. He pulled to a halt, turned and faced the man doing his best to catch up to him on short, stubby legs, his outward appearance the very antithesis of the pit bull he was in the boardroom.

"I've been traveling for sixteen hours, Cristopher, I'm tired, I'm in a vile mood and I need sleep. Trust me when I say tomorrow is better."

"It can't wait." The edge to his lawyer's voice commanded Lorenzo's full attention. Not once in five years of completing difficult and sometimes downright antagonistic deals together had his legal counsel ever looked this rattled. "I need five minutes of your time."

Expelling a long sigh, his stomach souring at the thought of attempting to interpret the finer points of legalese when what his brain officially needed was sleep, Lorenzo waved a hand toward his office. "*Bene.* Five minutes."

Cristopher followed him into the sleek, black-and-chrome offices of the Ricci International executive team. Gillian, Lorenzo's ultraefficient PA, gave him an apologetic I-tried look. He waved her off. "Go home. We can go through everything in the morning."

She murmured her thanks, got to her feet and started gathering her things. Cristopher followed him into his office, hovering in front of his desk while he dropped his briefcase beside it and shrugged off his jacket. The apprehension skittering up his spine deepened. His lawyer didn't hover. *Ever.*

He walked to the bank of floor-to-ceiling windows framing a magnificent view of a dusky, indigo-lit Manhattan—one of the perks of being CEO of his family's international Italian conglomerate, a shipping dynasty he had evolved into a diverse empire that included hotel chains, cruise lines and real estate arms. He loved the view, but tonight, it barely penetrated the fatigue clouding his brain.

Turning, he leaned back against the glass and crossed his arms over his chest. "All right," he said, "give it to me."

His lawyer blinked behind gold-rimmed spectacles, flicked his tongue over his lips and cleared his throat. "We have a…situation. A *mistake* that's been made we need to rectify."

He frowned. "On the deal?"

"No. It's a personal matter."

Lorenzo narrowed his gaze. "I didn't invite you in here to play twenty questions, Cris. Spit it out."

His lawyer swallowed. "The legal firm that handled

your divorce made an error with the filing of the papers. An *omission*, actually…"

"What kind of an omission?"

"They forgot to file them."

A buzzing sound filled his ears. "I divorced my wife *two years ago*."

"Yes, well, you see…" Another long swallow. "You didn't actually. Not in the technical tense because the papers were never filed with the state."

The buzzing sound in his head intensified. "What are you saying?" He asked the question slowly, deliberately, as if his brain was having trouble keeping up. "Just so we're clear?"

"You're still married to Angelina." Cristopher blurted the words out, a hand coming up to resettle his glasses higher on his nose. "The lawyer who handled your divorce had an insane caseload that month. He thought he'd asked his clerk to file the papers, was sure he had, until we went back to look at the specifics after the conversation you and I had recently."

When it had become clear Angie was never going to touch a penny of the alimony he gave her each month.

"My wife announced her engagement this week. To *another man*."

The lawyer pressed a hand to his temple. "Yes… I saw the piece in the paper. That's why I've been trying to track you down. It's a rather complicated situation."

"Complicated?" Lorenzo slung the word across the room with the force of a bullet. "How much do we pay that firm an hour? Hundreds? Thousands? To *not* make mistakes like this. *Ever*."

"It's not acceptable," Cristopher agreed quietly, "but it is the reality."

His lawyer squared his shoulders, looking ready to be verbally flogged to within an inch of his life, but Lorenzo had lost the power of speech. That his short-lived marriage to his wife, a disaster by its ignominious end, had, in fact, never been legally terminated was too much to take when heaped upon the other news his father had delivered today.

He counted to ten in his head, harnessing the red-hot fury that engulfed him. *This* he did not need as he attempted to close the biggest deal of his life.

"How do we fix this?" he asked icily.

Cristopher spread his hands wide. "There are no magical solutions. The best we can do is hope to expedite the process. But it could take months. It will still mean— I mean you'll still have to—"

"Tell my wife she can't marry her boyfriend so she doesn't commit *bigamy*?"

His lawyer rubbed a palm across his forehead. "Yes."

And wouldn't that be fun, given Angelina was set to celebrate that engagement in front of half of New York tomorrow night?

He turned to face the jaw-dropping view, blood pounding against his temple in a dull roar. He was shocked at how much the idea of Angie marrying another man repulsed him even though he had once convinced himself if he never saw his wife again it would be too soon. Perhaps because her vibrant, sensual, Lauren Bacall-style beauty haunted him every time he thought about taking another woman to bed… Because every time he tried to convince himself he was ambivalent about her, he failed miserably.

The conversation he'd had with his father before leaving Milan filtered through his head like some sort of cruel joke, had it not been of an entirely serious nature. The chairman of Ricci International had fixed his impenetrable, ice-blue stare on him and dropped a bombshell. "Your brother Franco is unable to produce an heir, which means it's up to you, Lorenzo, to produce one and produce it soon."

His dismay for his younger brother, his bewilderment Franco hadn't told him this the night before over dinner, had evaporated under the impact of his father's directive. *Him marry again?* Never happening. Except, he conceded with bitter irony, he was apparently *still* married. To the woman who had walked out on him and said he had no capacity to love. The woman who had stolen the last piece of humanity he'd possessed.

"Sir?"

He turned around. "Do you have any more bombshells to add to the pile or is that it?"

"That's it. The deal is fine for the moment. We're still negotiating the smaller points and you need to clear those last couple of tricky items with Bavaro, but other than that we're on track."

"Bene." He waved a hand toward the door. "Go. I'll take care of Angie."

His lawyer nodded. "Do you want me to file the papers? Get the process started?"

"No."

Cristopher gave him a stupefied look. "Sorry?"

"I said leave it."

His lawyer left. A wise decision. He walked to the bar and poured himself a whiskey. Padding back to the windows, he lifted the glass to his mouth and took a sip. Began to feel vaguely human as the spirit warmed his insides and smoothed out the raw edges—raw edges that had been festering ever since one of the clippings in his daily press briefing had buzzed about his former wife…*current* wife's betrothal plans to a prominent Manhattan lawyer.

He had pushed the news of Angie's engagement aside. Refused to acknowledge how it sank its claws into his skin, dug into his insides—inspired dark, inexplicable thoughts he couldn't have identified if he'd tried. Angie had ended a marriage that had descended to the very deepest depths of acrimony, a marriage many would have left for dead. So why did it still sting so much?

Why was he still so angry, still so damn angry it was like a disease inside of him, eating away at his soul? He *itched* he was so angry.

Why hadn't he asked Cris to file those papers? Ended something that should have been ended two years ago?

He stared out the window for a long time, sipping the whiskey, watching night fall over a light-strewn Manhattan. Considered his duty to the Ricci line. The fifteen-billion-dollar acquisition deal in front of him—a deal that required every bit of his concentration—that would make Ricci the top luxury hotel chain in the world if he landed it.

The solution to his predicament, when it came, was shockingly, simplistically clear.

Why wasn't there any air in this room?

Angie took the glass of champagne the bartender handed her, turned and leaned against the lit glass surface, surveying the cocktail-dress-attired crowd mingling in the elegant, whitewashed art-gallery space. Shimmering light from the antique chandeliers cascaded onto gleaming black marble floors, while directed lighting spotlighted the stunning artwork on the walls. A perfect, sophisticated backdrop for her and Byron's engagement party, everything they'd envisioned to celebrate their upcoming nuptials. Why then did the room seem to have drained of oxygen as the night wore on? Why this restless pull in her veins she couldn't explain?

She *should* be ecstatic. She had the career of her dreams as one of New York's most buzzed-about new jewelry designers, the freedom she'd always craved from life as a Carmichael and a wonderful man waiting in the wings. What more could she ask for?

And yet something still felt…missing.

It did not, she told herself firmly, have anything to do with the man who haunted the edges of her happiness. Who had shown her what having everything looked like, then taken it away in the next breath. Because she knew now that kind of an adrenaline rush was for fools. What went up must come down, and in her and Lorenzo's case, had come crashing down.

A searing pang throbbed in her chest. She took a deep breath of the nonexistent air. Perhaps that's what she needed—oxygen to clear her head.

Byron engaged with a business colleague across the room, she seized the moment. Winding her way through the buzzing crowd, around the live jazz band to the elegant staircase that led to the second level, unused tonight, she climbed the stairs and headed for the small terrace that opened off the upper level.

Hot, thick summer air hit her like a wall of heat as she stepped outside. She walked to the edge of the beautifully landscaped space, rested her elbows on the railing and drank it in. The frenetic activity in the street below as cabs and pedestrians battled for supremacy on a sticky Manhattan night was a familiar refrain that soothed her senses.

Another sensory impression seeped in. Spicy, masculine, it was imminently familiar. *Disturbingly, distantly familiar.*

Cold fingers clamped down on her spine. Her heart a drumbeat in her throat, she turned around. Her brain flatlined as she took in the tall, dark-haired, olive-skinned male dressed in an exquisitely tailored suit standing in front of her. She lifted her gaze to his hard, dark eyes, as treacherous as black ice. Moved them down over Lorenzo's prominent Roman nose, the day-old stubble lining his jaw, his beautiful, sensual mouth that knew how to wound and pleasure in equal measure.

For a disturbingly real second or two, she thought she'd conjured him up. That he wasn't actually here, but was a product of the strange, restless mood she was in. That, in this fantasy of hers, he'd heard about her engagement and come here to stop it. That he still cared about her, because once, during the stormy complexity of their marriage, she'd sworn he had.

A panicked pulse echoed through her. What if he had? What would her answer be? She was terrified she'd cave like a ton of bricks.

She pressed her champagne glass to her chest before her shaking hands spilled it. Before she allowed herself to start conjuring up the fairy tales she'd always had about this man. That maybe he'd wanted *her* when he'd married her. That what they'd had in the beginning *had* been magic, instead of the reality that had materialized like a harsh slap to the face.

That he had married her for political expediency, to secure his heir, and when she'd lost their baby he'd lost all interest in her. *Shattered her.*

She took a deep breath, shifted her weight to both feet in an attempt to gain some equilibrium. "What are you doing here, Lorenzo?"

His lethally handsome face twisted in a mocking look. "No 'Hello, Lorenzo'…? 'You look well, Lorenzo'…or even a 'How are you, Lorenzo?'"

Her mouth tightened. "You've crashed my engagement party. I hardly think pleasantries are in order. We abandoned those at about month six of our marriage."

"Did we last that long?" He crossed his arms over his chest and leaned back against the railing. She forced herself not to follow the ripple of muscle in that powerful body. To acknowledge how he seemed to have hardened into an even more dangerously attractive version of the man she'd known.

He lifted a shoulder. "My apologies for showing up out of the blue, but I have business we need to discuss."

"Business?" She frowned. "Couldn't we have discussed it over the phone?" She flicked a nervous glance toward the door. "Did Byron—"

"No one saw me. I blended in with the paint. I did get a chance to listen to the speeches, though. Touching as they were."

She stared at him, horrified. "How long have you been here?"

"Long enough to see you clearly have *Byron* roped and tied, as my rancher friend, Bartlett, would say. Fully enamored with your considerable charms…ready to let you run the show. Is it everything you ever dreamed of, Angie?"

Her blood heated, mixing with the panic fizzling her veins. "I never wanted to run the show. I wanted equal billing in our relationship—something you, in your arrogance and chauvinism, refused to give me."

"And our good friend Byron does?"

"Yes."

"What about in bed?" His eyes glittered with deliberate intent. "Does he satisfy that insatiable appetite of yours? Does he make you scream when you wrap those long legs of yours around him and beg? Because he doesn't look *man* enough to me, *cara*, to deliver it the way I know you like it. Not even close."

Lust slammed into her hot and hard. An image of Lorenzo's beautiful, muscular body imprinted itself on her brain, filling her, pushing her to the limits of her pleasure, his voice a hot whisper at her ear, demanding she tell him if it was good, not satisfied until she'd begged to let him know it was, until she'd screamed, because yes, he *had* made her scream.

Blood rushed to her cheeks, her stomach contracting in a heated pull. She'd been so desperate for his love, for his affection, she'd taken whatever crumb he'd been willing to throw at her. In the end it had been all they'd had.

She sank her teeth into her bottom lip. Lied. "I have no complaints in that area, either."

His eyes hardened, a dark glimmer stealing across their ebony depths. "Too bad it just isn't going to work out."

A frisson of apprehension swept through her. "What are you talking about?"

"Well, you see, there's been a…hiccup in the paperwork for our divorce."

"We *are* divorced."

"So I thought. The firm handling the paperwork failed to file the correct papers with the state. The error was brought to my attention yesterday after I asked them to review the document."

Her knees went weak. "What are you saying?"

"We're still married, Angie."

The floor gave way beneath her feet. She grasped the railing, wrapping her fingers around cool metal to steady herself. Blinked as she tried to work through the fog enveloping her brain. *Married?* She and Lorenzo were still married?

She swallowed past a paper-dry throat. "I'm marrying Byron in three weeks…in St. Bart's. We're eloping."

His stare was bold, aggressive, like the predator he was. "Unless you plan on committing *bigamy* that would be impossible."

She struggled to get her brain in working order. "You need to *do* something. *Fix* this. It's your firm's fault. *They* should fix it."

An indolent shrug. "There's only so much they can do.

These things move at a snail's pace. It could take months to push it through."

"But you *know* people. You have influence in all the right places…you could make it happen."

"Perhaps."

Her blood ran cold at the hard, unforgiving lines of his face. "But you don't plan to use it."

"No. It would be an unnecessary calling in of favors."

Unnecessary? A red mist descended over her vision. "I am getting *married* in three weeks. It's all planned. How is that *unnecessary*?" She shook her head, pinned her gaze on his. "Are you still angry with me? Is that it? You want to punish me for walking out on you? For God's sake, Lorenzo, you knew our marriage was doomed. You knew it was never going to work. Let me move on."

He stepped closer, six foot three inches of far too intense male vibrating just centimeters from her. His expression, when he looked down at her, was full of leashed aggression. "Our marriage was not *doomed*. Our marriage failed because you were too young and selfish to realize that marriages take work. *Effort*, Angelina. Instead you put all your energy into rebelling against what I asked of you. Into ignoring what *I* needed."

She lifted her chin. "You wanted a perfect society wife without a mind, a *purpose* of her own. You should have hired a beautiful robot to fill the role. It would have been the perfect match for you."

His eyes flashed. "Don't be sarcastic, *cara*, it doesn't suit you. I liked your mind, you're well aware of that. I offered you all sorts of chances to get involved in the charitable efforts Ricci supports, but you didn't have any interest in them, no matter how challenging." He pointed his glass at her. "As for being my society wife, you knew what you were getting into when you married me. What the reality of my life was."

Had she really? Twenty-two, pregnant and wildly in-fatuated with her husband, she'd had no idea she'd been exchanging one lonely existence for another. That instead of finding the love she'd craved, she'd be giving up the very independence she'd been searching for, the dreams she'd had of being a jewelry designer. That she'd be fol-lowing in her mother's footsteps in falling for a man who had no capacity to love—the one mistake she'd sworn never to make.

She lifted her chin, chest tight. "I thought you, of all people, would understand my need to pursue my passion. My need to *be* something."

"I did understand it. You had a fledgling online busi-ness. I helped you nurture it. What wasn't going to work was to play start-up with a boutique that would take up the lion's share of your time. Our life was too busy."

"*Your* life was. It was never about *my* life. Yours was more important."

"That's not true."

"It damn well is." Champagne sloshed the sides of her glass as she jabbed it in his direction. "All you wanted was for me to stay in line, to look the part…to warm your bed. And even then, I was a possession to be enjoyed and discarded according to your whims."

His jaw hardened. "Our intimate relationship was the one thing about us that didn't need fixing, *cara mia*. Don't sully it with your sharp tongue."

"Didn't it?" Her mouth twisted. "You never truly let me in—not in bed or out of it. Emotional intimacy was simply not on the table with you."

A glimmer of something she couldn't read passed through those dark eyes. "You are right," he agreed in a clipped tone, "that I, too, bear responsibility for the break-down of our marriage. We *both* bear responsibility for it. Which is why we're going to fix it together."

Her jaw dropped. "Wh-what?"

"Franco cannot produce an heir. That responsibility falls to me now. Since we are still married, it leaves me with only one option."

Oh, no. She backed away from him. "That's insane. *You* are insane. I'm sorry for Franco, but I am engaged to be married."

"I've just explained why that's impossible."

She absorbed the hard set of his jaw. *My God, he's serious.*

"Lorenzo." She adopted her most reasonable tone. "It can't work between us. We've been through too much. We want different things. I have a life I've built, a career. I'm not giving that up."

"I'm not asking you to give up your career. We'll find some middle ground on that. But I do intend to have my wife back, that part is nonnegotiable."

She bit down hard on the inside of her cheek, the salty tang of blood staining her mouth. Once, she would have given anything to hear him say that—that he wanted to fix what they'd broken. In those first few weeks after she'd left, terrified she'd made an irreversible mistake, it had been *all* she'd wanted to hear. But she knew from experience people didn't change. You couldn't heal them no matter how much you loved them. People broke your heart over and over again.

"I won't do it," she said quietly. "You can drag the divorce proceedings out as long as you like, but you're crazy if you think you can just snap your fingers and I'll come back to you and deliver you an heir. I'm engaged, Lorenzo. I'm in love with my fiancé."

Lorenzo absorbed his beautiful wife's lie with the confidence of a man who'd had enough practice reading her reactions to know it was exactly that. A woman didn't pronounce her love for another man and mean it while she ate you up with her eyes like she'd been doing with him. When he could tell he had every nerve in her curvaceous body on edge.

The thought of her offering *that* body to another man made his blood burn. *Watching* her make that toast to her fiancé when she was technically still his. When she would *always* be his.

He dropped his gaze to the thrust of her breasts beneath the delicate silk of her dress. Down over the swell of her hips…the length of her amazing legs atop stiletto heels. His body throbbed with a need that had eluded him for so long his skin went tight at the intensity of it. The injustice of it. *Always Angelina. Never anyone else.*

He returned his gaze to his wife's face, studied the heat that stained her cheeks with a savage satisfaction. "You think," he drawled, "that if I touched you, I couldn't make you forget about him in about sixty seconds? Because you know I could. There's this thing that happens between us, Angelina, that is undeniable. Pure biological chemistry."

Her mouth tightened, a layer of ice settling over her face. "I'm not playing any more of these games. Byron will be looking for me. I'd advise you to go ahead and have your lawyers fix their mistake or I will sue you and your law firm for incompetence."

A smile twisted his lips. "The thought crossed my mind, too. Then I realized it must be a sign we are meant to fulfill the responsibilities we assumed three years ago."

"You *are* crazy." She spun and walked toward the door. "Get out, Lorenzo, before anyone sees you."

The antagonism in him darkened. She had walked out on him at one of the lowest moments of his life, left him to face a firestorm of Manhattan gossip, to break the news to their family and friends while she'd gone vacationing in the Caribbean. Left their marriage in ashes…

She would not walk out on him again.

"Oh, but I'm not finished." His quiet words stopped her in her tracks. "You didn't think I came here empty-handed did you? Without some bargaining power?"

His wife turned to face him, blue eyes apprehensive.

"The Carmichael Company is bleeding money," he told her. "Has been for quite some time. I've given your father two large loans to keep things afloat."

She blinked. "That's impossible."

That had been his reaction when Angie's father had come to him for help. That the Carmichael Company, an over two-hundred-year-old textile dynasty, an American icon with its name on the main campus of one of New York's most prestigious design schools, could be in the red, *deeply* in the red, had been inconceivable to him.

He watched the color drain from his wife's face. "If you bothered to go home, you would know. So many countries are in the mix now, producing high-tech fabrics. Things haven't been good in some time."

She shook her head. "If this is true," she said faintly, "why would you help my family?"

His lips curled. "Because I am loyal to the relationships I form, unlike you. I don't run when things get rocky. Who do you think is underwriting your studio?"

She frowned. "*I* pay the rent on my studio."

"You pay one quarter of the rent. It's my building, Angie."

Her mouth slackened. "I hired that real estate agent. Found the space…"

"You found what I wanted you to." He waved a hand at her. "It made me sleep better at night knowing you were in a safe part of town."

Her face crumpled as realization set in. "What are you insinuating? That you will pull the plug on the aid you're giving to my family, toss me out on the street if I don't agree to come back to you?"

"I prefer to think of it as *incentive*. We owe our marriage a fair shot before we relegate it to the history books. You come back to me, we try and make it work, I pull Carmichael out of its financial difficulties before it becomes a footnote in a list of great American dynasties. It's a win-win."

A win-win? She stared at him, disbelieving. "You would really hold that over my head?"

"You didn't play fair when you walked out on me, *tesoro*. You just cut and ran. So yes, I will use whatever means required to make you see the light. To do the right thing."

"I *asked* you to go to counseling. I *begged* you to. I tried to save our marriage and then I left."

He ignored the stab of guilt that piece of truth pushed through him. "You expected us to solve things overnight. It doesn't happen that way."

Her fingers curled tight around the delicate stem of her champagne flute. "Putting the two of us back in a marriage where we'll destroy one other is not doing the right thing."

"We are both older and wiser. I think we can make it work."

She shook her head. "That's where you're mistaken. That's where you've played the wrong card, Lorenzo, because I will never become your wife again."

She turned on her heel and left. He let her go, because he knew she'd be back. He'd never gambled on a deal he couldn't win.

CHAPTER TWO

ANGIE RETURNED TO the party, shaken to her core. Palms damp, heart thrumming in her chest, a frozen numbness paralyzing her brain, she made a beeline for Abigail. Mouthing an apology to the well-known philanthropist her sister was speaking to, she extracted Abigail from the conversation and pulled her toward a quiet corner of the room.

Her sister eyed her. "What's wrong? You look like you've seen a ghost."

"Lorenzo is here."

Abigail's eyes widened. "At your *engagement* party?"

"Someone screwed up our divorce papers, Abby. We're still married."

"Married?" Her sister's jaw dropped. "What do you mean 'screwed them up'? Who?"

"Lorenzo's legal firm. They forgot to file the papers with the state."

"Is he fixing it?"

She closed her eyes. "He won't."

"What do you mean 'won't'?"

"Franco can't have a baby. Lorenzo needs to produce an heir. He wants me to do my duty and put our marriage back together. Give him a baby."

A gasp escaped her sister. "That's outrageous. You're engaged."

"Am I?" Panic skittered up her spine. "If I'm legally

married to Lorenzo, what does that make Byron? My *illegitimate* fiancé?"

Her sister looked dumbfounded. "I don't know… Regardless, we'll sic our lawyers on him. This has to be negligence."

"He's angry," she said quietly. "So angry at me for leaving."

"You did what you had to do. Lorenzo wasn't an innocent victim in all this. You both had a role to play in what happened."

Angie pushed a hand through her hair. Fixed her gaze on her sister. "Is the Carmichael Company in trouble? Is there something you haven't been telling me?"

A guarded look wrote itself across her sister's face. "What does that have to do with this?"

"Lorenzo says he's given Father two loans. That he will bail Carmichael out of its financial problems if I try and make our marriage work. *Incentive*, he called it."

Abby's eyes turned into hard, bright sapphires. "That bastard."

"Is it true? Did he give father those loans?"

"Yes." Her sister's admission made her stomach plunge. "At first it was the need to switch over equipment to compete with other high-tech manufacturers. But Carmichael never really recovered from the new technologies taking over the market."

Angie's breath left her in a sharp exhale. She'd been hoping against hope it wasn't true.

Abigail's lips firmed. "You aren't doing this. Father's been burying his head in the sand for years. He didn't want to see the writing on the wall. It's his problem to fix, not yours."

"Why didn't you tell me?" She swallowed past the lump swelling her throat. "You promised you wouldn't carry the load alone."

"You needed time. You were shattered when you walked away from Lorenzo. The last thing you needed to know was that your ex-husband was bankrolling the Carmichael Company."

Blood pulsed against her temple. "And Mother? How is she handling this?"

Abby frowned. "Ange—"

"Tell me."

"She's become more unstable since the financial difficulties began. It—" She waved a hand. "It may be time to check her into a program. She doesn't want it. She swears she won't go, but I got a call from Sandra last week while they were on a girls' night out. I had to pour her into bed."

Emotions she'd long held at bay welled up inside of her, causing her throat to constrict and the knots in her stomach to twist tighter. "What was it this time?"

"Gin."

She closed her eyes. She'd distanced herself from her family for her own self-preservation—because picking up her mother again and again had left her in a million pieces. Because she just couldn't do it anymore while she'd been trying to pull herself back together after the demise of her marriage. But the guilt surrounding the difficult decisions she'd made was always there in the background, impossible to escape.

It wrapped itself around her now—tight, suffocating. For when Della Carmichael started sliding down her slippery, alcoholic slope, the bottom came fast and furious.

"Angie." Her sister's firm voice brought her head up. "I won't allow him to do this to you. This is not on you."

But Angie knew her sister was wrong. The only solution to this was *her*. Her convincing Lorenzo this was insane, that it would never work. Because she knew tonight hadn't been the end of it.

* * *

Her dilemma was still raging in her head as she put down the phone the following evening having assured Byron she was fine—that the headache she'd pleaded to extract herself from the party just before midnight was gone. The same headache that had made her slide out of her fiancé's kiss and leave him on her doorstep, a frown on his face.

Dammit. She gave up on the idea of work, pushed to her feet and walked across her bright studio space to stand looking out at the street. SoHo at night was still busy with foot traffic, the city thick with tourists at the height of the summer. A good thing for the boutique she ran below the studio that featured her work. The bell announcing visitors had been ringing all day.

The purple awning bearing her name whipped in the breeze below. *Carmichael Creations.* It rankled, more than she could say, to know this studio she loved, that she was so proud of, had been contaminated by Lorenzo's powerful reach. She'd wanted—*needed*—to prove so badly she could do this by herself. To follow her heart and forge a successful career as a designer after Lorenzo had dismissed it as a hobby, when in fact, self-expression was as necessary to her as breathing.

She watched a group of young girls walk by, laughing and jabbing each other in the ribs as they pointed at a slick-suited handsome male in front of them. Her heart gave a painful squeeze. She'd been like that when she'd met Lorenzo—desperately innocent, utterly swept away by his powerful aura.

The memories flooded back, tumbling one over another in painful succession until she was standing by the pool at her parents' legendary winter party in Nassau clad in the sexiest silver lamé gown she owned, butterflies in her stomach knowing the gorgeous, ruthless corporate raider Lorenzo Ricci would be in attendance. Her father had been doing friendly business with Lorenzo rather than serving as one of her husband's hostile take-over targets, but Alistair Carmichael's directive had been clear to his daughter—*leave Lorenzo alone, you're way out of your depth*.

And she had been. But smarting from an argument with her father, needing to escape her miserable, lonely existence for just one night, she couldn't resist. Every woman had wanted to catch Lorenzo, the most desirable widower in Manhattan, perhaps because none ever had. She'd taken her best friend Becka's dare to ask him to dance and shockingly he'd said yes. That dance had led to a kiss in the garden and a hot, heated assignation that had shaken her innocent foundations to the core. She'd gotten her one night with Lorenzo Ricci plus way more than she'd ever bargained for.

She closed her eyes, an ache pulsing low in her chest. She'd thought she could be *the one*, the one who could make her husband love again because what they'd had had seemed earthshaking to her twenty-two-year-old self. That by offering him her unrequited love, she could help him get over his late wife, Lucia, who popular consensus had said he was still hung up on. Until Angelina had learned love was an emotion her husband reserved exclusively for his late wife, an emotion that would never be on offer to her.

Blood throbbed at her temples. She couldn't change the past as much as she wished she could, but she *could*—would—fight Lorenzo on this.

She could postpone the wedding until her divorce came through. Move to a cheaper studio space. But that still didn't address the financial difficulties the Carmichael Company was in. The responsibility that lay on her shoulders.

A chill crawled through her at the thought of the cold,

hard stranger she'd faced on the terrace last night. Lorenzo had always been tough, carved by his experiences, shaped by the cutthroat scion of the Ricci family, Salvatore Ricci, but last night she'd seen a whole new lethal side of him.

Had her walking out on Lorenzo made him this heartless? Or was that just the man he'd become?

Guilt fought a battle with anger. Anger won. She'd been right last night—too much had passed between her and Lorenzo to ever resurrect their marriage. He needed to see reason.

She stalked to her desk, pulled her purse out of the bottom drawer and headed for the door. She was not letting Lorenzo bully her, steal her happiness. Force her back into a life that had nearly destroyed her because he needed an heir for the illustrious Ricci dynasty. She had grown too strong over the past couple of years to let him ride roughshod over her.

Her husband was about to find out just how much she'd changed.

Lorenzo was easy to find. Another hot, steamy Manhattan night bathed the city in a smoky heat as Angie stepped through the doors of her husband's Park Avenue building. The doorman's face lit up when he saw her. Federico's gray brows rose just a fraction before he lowered them back into place and ushered her into the private elevator.

Lorenzo didn't bat an eyelash when the doors opened on the top-floor penthouse. He waved her in as he talked on his headset. As if he'd been expecting her.

Dressed in black jeans and a T-shirt, he looked less corporate shark tonight and more deadly male, the jeans riding low, hugging his lean hips and muscular thighs, his black T-shirt skimming rock-hard abs he kept in premium condition at the gym where he pushed himself as hard as he did everywhere else.

Hell. She banished the frisson of sexual awareness that pulsed through her and walked past him into the luxurious dark brown and chrome space. Lorenzo in casual clothes, which made him look like a mere mortal rather than the deity Wall Street painted him as, had always been her weakness. Perpetuated her belief he had a heart when in fact he did not.

Eyeing the bottle of wine and two glasses that sat on the marble bar, she wondered if he'd been that confident she would show up or whether he'd been expecting someone else. Her stomach contracted into a tight ball. Bringing her back teeth together, she walked to the bar and looked for a bottle of sparkling water in the fridge. Lorenzo covered the microphone and told her to open the wine.

She did. If only to give herself something to do other than absorb the pure physicality of the man pacing the room. She poured two glasses of wine, picked up one and took a sip. Lorenzo rattled off a series of instructions for whoever was on the call and ended it.

"Scusami," he murmured, as he pulled off the headset, tossed it on a chair and walked toward her. "I'm in the middle of negotiations for a company we're looking to acquire."

When wasn't he? "You didn't know I was coming," she said, holding out a glass of the expensive French red he'd provided to put a physical barrier between them. He noted it with an amused twist of his lips.

"I apologize if you were expecting company."

"I was expecting you." Instead of taking the glass, he wrapped his elegant, long-fingered hand around hers and drew her to him.

Her heart slammed against her chest. "Lorenzo…"

He dipped his head toward hers, a dark glimmer of intent in his beautiful eyes. "We forgot our manners last night. Perhaps we should start again."

Her breath caught in her throat. He was going to kiss her. She opened her mouth to protest, to say *absolutely not*, but his firm, sensual lips landed on her cheek instead. Lingered just a little too long for civility's sake…

An electric current charged through her as he repeated the gesture on her other cheek, little pinpricks of heat exploding across her skin. Thoroughly flustered, she stepped back. "I'm not here to accept your proposition."

He lifted a brow. "So you are here to…"

"Talk reason with you."

"All right," he said calmly in the placating tone he'd always used to soothe her like some high-spirited racehorse he'd paid millions for. "Over the wine, then. I've had a hellish day."

Was she allowed to find that secretly enjoyable? She handed him the glass and followed him to the sitting area, where she sank down into one of the chocolate-brown leather chairs she'd always loved to read in.

"What company are you acquiring?"

"The Belmont Hotel Group." He lowered himself into the sofa across from her, splaying his long legs in front of him.

The Belmont? One of the world's most historic luxury hotel chains, it boasted boutique properties in some of the world's most glamorous, exotic locations.

"I'm shocked it's for sale."

"It's not."

"*Ah.*" She took a sip of her wine. "A hostile takeover, then."

"More like a reluctant bride that needs to be brought to heel. She wants to be there but she can't bring herself to admit it."

She eyed him coolly. "Isn't it all the same? It's your specialty, after all. Find a vulnerable company, strip it of its assets, then relegate the rest to the scrap heap. Symbolism, tradition, be damned."

He cocked a brow. "Is this you setting the tone, *cara mia*? I thought you wanted to keep things civil."

She lifted a shoulder. "I don't care for what you do."

"You didn't always feel that way. You used to think it was hot, the power I wield. It was an *aphrodisiac* for you."

Heat stained her cheeks. "And then I grew up. I saw the hundreds of people you put out of jobs. How you relegated iconic companies to the history books if you could profit from it. It was always about the almighty dollar."

"Most of the companies I acquire would eventually fail. It's only a matter of time. In Belmont's case, they have lost sight of what the luxury traveler is looking for—their profits have nose-dived. Call it being cruel to be kind."

"A wolf in sheep's clothing is still a wolf..." She pointed her glass at him. "The question is, when is it all going to be enough, this obsession you have with owning the world?"

He rested his glass on his thigh. "What would you have me do? Rest on my laurels? Tell my shareholders I've proven myself—'so sorry, but that's all the profit you can expect this year...'"

She set her gaze on his. "You could try addressing the demons that drive you."

His dark, spiky lashes swept down. "We aren't here to talk about the past. We're here to discuss our current situation."

"Oh, that's right," she murmured, "that subject is off-limits. I forgot the rules of the game."

His jaw tightened. "Stop baiting me, Angelina, and tell me what's going on in that head of yours."

"Your proposition is outrageous. To expect me to dissolve my engagement and come back to you, simply to ensure the continuation of the Ricci line…"

He shook his head. "I told you, it's about more than that. It's about both of us putting the effort into this marriage we should have in the first place. About living up to the vows we made."

"You *divorced* me."

"It was a mistake."

Her heart skipped a beat. "What do you mean 'a mistake'?"

"I mean you like to run from your problems, *cara*. And maybe I was running, too. But given the current circumstances, given we are still married, technicality or not, we need to rectify that mistake. I did not intend on marrying twice. I certainly don't intend on marrying a third time."

She came back to reality with a crashing thud. "You don't want me," she said flatly, "you know that. You want a nice little Italian wife your mother will love who will host your dinner parties, charm your business acquaintances and greet you at the door every night in sexy lingerie. *That* would be your idea of perfection."

An amused glint entered his gaze. "I'm fairly sure I would be bored with an obedient wife after you. But you are right on the lingerie—that *would* be my idea of perfection."

She said a very bad word in her head. "You don't even know who I am anymore. I'm different. Changed. Not the woman you married, nor will I ever be again."

"Then I look forward to finding out who that woman is." He gave her an appraising look. "I'm prepared to make concessions to make this work. Your career is a case in point. You've clearly become very successful. You've worked hard to get where you are. As long as it doesn't interfere with our important commitments, we'll make it work."

We'll make it work? Heat rose up inside of her. He had no idea what her work meant to her. The sanity it had been throughout her rocky life.

"As for my mother," he continued, "she had certain… *preconceived* notions regarding our marriage you never dispelled with your behavior. You also never made an effort with her. If you do so, I expect you'll find her a different woman."

Her fingers curled into a fist. "She thought I deliberately trapped you into marriage."

"Not an unreasonable assumption when our one night together resulted in a pregnancy. I did, however, make it clear that the responsibility lay on both of us."

"How big of you." A red mist of fury wrapped itself around her brain. "What other *concessions* are you prepared to make, Lorenzo? Are you prepared to let me beneath that impenetrable layer of yours? Talk to me instead of shutting me out? Confront our issues instead of pushing me to the outer fringes of your life until I cease to exist?"

"Yes." The low rumble in his voice vibrated through her. "I understand I was distant at times…emotionally unavailable if you like. I recognize that as a fault of mine I need to work on. But let's just be clear, Angelina, you locked me out just as surely as I ever did you with those cast-iron defenses of yours."

After the big chill had begun. Because eventually it had become too painful to give and never get anything back.

Hurt contracted the muscles around her heart. The wine warming her blood, loosening her inhibitions, made her reckless. "If we're going for the brutal truth here," she growled, "if we're not going to pull our punches, then let's get all the skeletons out on the table shall we? The real reason our marriage failed was Lucia. Because you would have preferred to stay in your cave, pining for your dead wife. Instead you had to marry me."

The color leached from his olive skin. His face tightened, cheekbones standing out like blades. The cold fire that engulfed his dark eyes told her she'd gone too far this time. "It was *your* obsession with Lucia that you wouldn't let go of, not mine."

Her chin lifted, heart pounding in her chest. "Tell yourself that enough and you might even start to believe it."

The silence in the room was deafening. Chest tight, she pushed to her feet and crossed to the floor-to-ceiling windows that framed a magnificent view of Central Park lit up at night. Hugging her arms around herself, she took a deep breath and attempted to regain her equilibrium.

"You aren't this heartless," she said after a long moment, turning to face him. "I don't believe you will let the Carmichael Company fail. You like my father too much."

His eyes were a purposeful, dark velvet cool. "Then don't make me. I meant what I said, Angie. I want you back. I want us to give this marriage the shot it deserves. You come back to me with your heart and head fully in it and I will ensure your legacy survives."

The confusion swirling in her head deepened, thickened. She wrapped her arms tighter around herself, struggled to contain her emotions, but they spilled outside of the edges of her barely shored-up walls. "Wasn't it enough for you?" she asked, voice trembling. "Every second, every minute of those last excruciating months together? We couldn't even be in the same room without tearing each other's throats out. And when we did, it didn't feel any better...it felt worse."

He got to his feet and prowled toward her. "We lost a baby. It was painful, Angelina, it *hurt*."

A rock climbed into her throat. "And here we are hurting each other again."

He stopped centimeters from her. Her body reacted to the heat of him, the familiarity of him, vibrating with an internal memory she couldn't control. She pressed her fingers to her cheeks, trying to hold it in, trying to stop the insanity midflow, but he saw it, read her as he always had, eyes darkening with heat.

"The point is to get past the pain. To deal with what we should have dealt with years ago."

"No," she said, shaking her head, fear bubbling up inside of her like magma, threatening to push her on a course she knew she'd regret. "I'm engaged, Lorenzo. I love him."

Fire licked his gaze. "You know that's a lie."

"It's not a lie. It's the truth."

"You are my *wife*." Curving an arm around her waist, he drew her to him. She swallowed as her vibrating body swayed perilously close to the wall of heat that drew her like a moth to a flame. She flattened a palm against his chest, but her feet wouldn't seem to take her anywhere and her eyes locked on his. "Kiss me like you don't belong to me," he said huskily, "and I might reconsider."

"No." Her sharp response sounded as panicked as she felt. "Why are you doing this? Why are you being so cruel?"

"Because I should have stopped you the first time you walked out. Because the thought of you with another man drives me insane...because you *haunt* me, Angelina, every time I'm with another woman. All I can see is those beautiful blue eyes of yours and those vows we recited..." He cupped her jaw in his hand, fingers closing possessively over her skin. "Because we are not over, *mi amore*. We never will be."

Her heart stuttered, an ache enveloping her that seemed to go soul-deep. "You can't do this to me," she said hoarsely. "Throw threats at me one minute, then say these things the next and just expect me to—"

He lowered his head, breath mingling with hers. "Prove

you feel nothing for me. Prove what I'm saying isn't true and I'll walk away."

"No." But even as she said it, his mouth was covering hers in a whisper-soft caress that switched on every cell in her body. She closed her eyes. *Just do it, Angie. Prove it to him, then walk away.*

He slid a hand up her back, flattened his big palm against her spine. Warm, possessive, his touch seeped into her senses, stroked a wounded, jagged part of her that had never healed. Warning bells went off in her head, a blaring, unmistakable cautionary signal she should stop this now. But she had to convince him it was over.

Slow, infinitely gentle nudges of his mouth demanded a response. She held herself rigid, determined to end it. Tightening his fingers around her jaw, he tilted her head back and took a deeper possession of her mouth. The alarm bells in her head grew louder as the sweet intoxication of his kiss melted her bones.

"Lorenzo—"

He slicked his tongue across her lower lip. Erotic, intimate, it sent shock waves of pleasure rocketing through her. Her mind blanked, stomach clenched, fingers curling around a handful of his T-shirt. He did it again, stroking soft, vulnerable flesh with a deliberate possession that made her quiver.

When he flicked his tongue along the seam of her lips and demanded entry, she obeyed, lost in a sea of sensation. He rewarded her with a hot, toe-curling caress that made her moan low in her throat, grab hold of him more firmly.

He brought her closer with the palm of his hand at her back. Swept it down to cup the flesh of her buttock. The kiss turned needy, desperate, her hips arching against his burgeoning arousal. Thick, hard, he was so potently virile he turned her blood to fire.

Reality slammed into her like a bucket of ice dropped

over her head. She shoved a hand against his chest and pushed back. Breathless, her mouth bruised from his kisses, she stood staring at him.

How had that happened? How had she *let* that happen?

"I hate you," she breathed. "I really do."

His mouth twisted. "That makes two of us. Sometimes I really hate you, too, *tesoro*. It's the rest of the time that messes us up."

She shook her head. Backed away from him. Turning, she snatched her purse off the chair and walked out without looking back.

What had she done?

CHAPTER THREE

New York Daily Buzz
Society Shocker!

Word has it the engagement of up-and-coming designer Angelina Carmichael and district attorney candidate Byron Davidson is off after a flashy soiree to celebrate the couple's betrothal just two weeks ago.

The buzz about town is the prominent lawyer is clearly devastated at the split, perhaps suggesting it was Angelina who called it off?

One can't help but wonder if the reason for the break comes in the form of none other than Angelina's ex: sexy corporate raider Lorenzo Ricci. The two were seen dining at Tempesta Di Fuoco last week, conjuring up images of the couple's tempestuous marriage that offered this column a regular supply of juicy news over its fiery but short duration.

Given the much lusted-after Lorenzo has been curiously devoid of a woman on his arm since the split, suspicion is running rampant that Angelina could be the cause.

The question on everyone's lips is…are the Riccis back on?

OH, FOR GOODNESS' SAKE. Angie tossed the salacious tabloid on the coffee table in her studio, blood heating. Did those people not have better things to do with their time? Her heart sank as she imagined what Byron must be thinking. *Feeling.* How he was coping with the barrage of gossip that had spread through town faster than a forest fire eating up dry timber.

She hadn't talked to him since the night after her confrontation with Lorenzo, when she'd given him back his ring. Since that *kiss* with her husband had made it clear she couldn't marry her fiancé. Even if Lorenzo had miraculously changed his mind and offered to expedite their divorce, she still couldn't have married her fiancé. Not after everything she'd done to prove she was over her husband, that she didn't care about him anymore, had been exposed for the lie it was.

Her mouth turned down. *That* was why she'd felt so off the night of the engagement party. Because she'd been trying to convince herself she was in love with her ultraintelligent, grounded fiancé, that she wanted the opposite of her roller-coaster ride of a marriage, when in fact she had never truly gotten over Lorenzo—the man who had made her feel as if her emotions were out of control.

The movers, currently emptying her apartment above the studio of her possessions, stomped back in to take the final load of boxes out to the truck parked on the street. The ball of tension in her stomach grew as she witnessed what was left of her carefully constructed existence disappear before her eyes.

A conversation with her father had provided no alternatives to her husband's proposition, only a suggestion by her father to repair the marriage she never should have left in the first place.

Potential investors were too spooked by Carmichael Company's recent performance to touch the once lauded company, nor would her father's pride allow him to hunt other offers of assistance. Which meant, as she'd feared, she was the only solution to this problem if her brother, James, who would someday soon run Carmichael Company and her sister, Abigail, were to have anything left of the company to inherit.

She picked up her coffee, taking a sip of the steaming brew and cradling the cup in her hands. Allowing Abigail to bear all the responsibility for her mother was also something she needed to fix. She had her life together now. She was strong. It was time to start assuming some of the responsibilities she'd been shirking so her sister could have a life, too.

Which didn't negate the fear gripping her insides. The anger keeping her awake at night, tossing in her bed, leaving her hollow-eyed in the morning. That Lorenzo was forcing her into this reconciliation, using her family as leverage, made his intentions very clear. This was a power play for him like every other he executed on a daily basis. He wanted her back, needed his heir, so he'd made it happen.

It was not about his feelings for her. Or lack of them... About a sentimental, real desire to give what they'd had a second chance. It was about him repossessing what he felt was his. Staking his claim.

She set down her cup in its saucer. If she was going to do this, she needed to do it with her eyes wide-open, naïveté firmly banished. On *her* terms. She wasn't going to allow him to take control, to overwhelm and intimidate her as he had the first time around. She wasn't sacrificing the independence and freedom she'd carved out for herself and she wasn't letting her husband break her heart again. Those were her *rules*.

Defiance drove her back to her worktable when the movers left, where her anger fueled a furious burst of productivity. By the time she finished up a couple of pieces for Alexander Faggini's Fashion Week show, her watch read 7:00 p.m. *Oops.* She was supposed to be home having dinner with Lorenzo right now—their first night together again in the penthouse. Unfortunately, she was going to be at least a half hour late.

"How's the deal going? Still mired in legalese?"

"Sì." Lorenzo cradled his mobile between ear and shoulder while he poured himself a drink in deference to the end of the week. "There's a few small points Bavaro and I have to work through. He's been a bit of a wild card."

"Bene." Amusement danced in Franco's voice. "I love watching Father on this one. To make Ricci the largest luxury hotel chain in the world is an accomplishment even he can't match. It kills him to think of you surpassing his achievements."

Lorenzo smiled. His father, retired now and serving on the boards of other companies, had an endless thirst for competition. That included the one he had with his sons. It had made the bonds between him and Franco even tighter as they had united to combat their father's powerful personality, with Franco running the shipping operations out of Milan, while Lorenzo oversaw the rest of the company from New York.

"He needn't worry he'll be forgotten. He has more than his fair share of achievements." Lorenzo lifted the whiskey to his mouth and took a sip. "So," he said, as the fiery spirit burned a soothing path through his insides, "when were you going to tell me about the IVF? I have to hear it from the old man?"

A low oath. "I should have known he'd jump the gun.

We didn't get the results on the latest procedure until today. I was waiting until we knew for sure before laying that on you."

"I figured it was something like that." He paused a beat, searching for the right words. "So what was the verdict?"

"It didn't work. Likely never will."

A knot formed in his throat. "*Mi dispiace.* I know how much you and Elena wanted this."

"It is what it is."

The raspy edge to his brother's voice gutted him. It always hurt to be so far away but right now it felt like the sharp blade of a knife. "How is Elena taking the news?"

"Not well. She's claiming it's her fault even though I've told her it could just as easily be me."

He closed his eyes. He didn't know the pain of being denied what he'd always assumed to be his, but he did know what it was like to lose a baby. How deeply it had cut when just a week after being given a clean bill of health, Angelina had inexplicably lost their child. How you didn't know how much you wanted something until it was taken away from you.

"Be there for her," he said quietly. Do what he hadn't done.

Franco exhaled. "We might adopt. I don't know…it's a big step."

"It is. Take your time with it."

A pause. Franco's tone was wary when he spoke. "Your reconciliation with Angelina… The timing is…"

"It's not because of this. Yes, there is that, but it's become clear to me Angelina and I have unfinished business between us."

"She walked out on you, *fratello.* How much more finished do you want it to be?"

Lorenzo winced, pressed a hand to his temple. "I bear

responsibility for the demise of my marriage, too. You know I have my ghosts."

"*Sì*. But she changed you, Lorenzo. You shut down after she left. You don't trust like you used to—you aren't the same man."

No, he wasn't. His wife had taken a piece of him with her when she'd walked out that door on the heels of the loss of his child, his fledgling trust in life and love, his half-built bond with Angelina vaporizing on a tide of bitterness so thick he'd wondered if he would ever move past it. But with time, as his grief over Lucia had subsided, his own faults had been revealed. It would be delusional of him to lay the blame solely at his wife's feet.

"Angie was young. She needed time to grow. I intend for our marriage to work this time."

"Or you will take the house down around you as you try." A wry note stained his brother's voice.

Lorenzo asked about his mother's upcoming birthday celebrations. They chatted about that for a few minutes before his brother signed off. Lorenzo leaned against the bar and nursed his drink while he waited for his wife to deign to appear.

The thought that he would have to produce the Ricci heir no longer evoked the violent reaction it had when his father had lobbed that grenade at him. Instead of feeling *roped and tied*, he felt strangely satisfied. As if his father's directive had been the incentive he had needed to rewrite a piece of history that hadn't gone down as it should have.

Two years after the death of Lucia, he had still been without a taste for women the night he'd met Angelina in Nassau. Plagued by demons, if the truth be known, over the wife he hadn't protected. Until Angie had walked out on the terrace while he'd been talking to one of her father's associates and he'd felt as if he'd been struck by lightning.

All it had taken was one dance, his hands taking purchase of her lush curves, before he'd found himself in an isolated part of the gardens taking over the seduction, driven by a need he couldn't name. His libido had woken up like a five-alarm blaze by the time they'd made it to his luxurious room on the Carmichael estate. Somehow, in the haze of his still ever-present grief, Angie had brought him back to life.

His mouth twisted as he brought the whiskey to his lips. Little had he known that the passion they shared would devolve into the plot from *The War of the Roses*. That the only place he and his young wife would be in sync was in the bedroom, where they'd solved every argument with hot, burn-your-clothes-off sex.

The clock chimed seven thirty. His good mood began to evaporate. The elevator doors swished open a couple of minutes later, his wife breezing in dressed in black capris and a sparkly, peasant-style blouse. Her hair pulled back in a ponytail, face devoid of makeup, she was still the most exquisite woman he'd ever known.

"Long day?" he drawled, leashing his anger.

Pink color stained her cheeks. "It was. I had to finish up some pieces for a show. I'm sorry I'm late."

No, she wasn't. But for the sake of their fresh start and given everything he'd thrown at her, he cut her some slack. "Go change." He cocked his head toward the bedroom. "Constanza unpacked your things. She left dinner in the oven. It'll keep while we have a drink."

Her eyes darkened at the order. Firming her mouth, she dropped her purse on a chair and swept by him.

"Angie?"

She swung around.

"Put your wedding rings on."

She lifted her chin. "Is this how it's going to be, Lorenzo? Just like old times? You firing orders at me? Expecting me to run and do your bidding?"

"Married people wear wedding rings." He held up his left hand, the elegant, simple gold band she had given him glittering in the light.

Her face tightened. Turning on her heel, she disappeared down the hallway. When she returned, she was dressed in the comfortable black leggings she favored and a cream-colored tunic that fell just below her curvaceous derriere. *Unfortunate*, he decided. He'd have to fill in that part from memory.

"Drink?" he asked, walking to the bar.

"Mineral water, please."

"It's Friday night."

"I'd still like mineral water."

And the battle lines were drawn… He poured it for her, added a slice of lime and carried it out onto the terrace, where Angie had drifted. Strategically placed lanterns lit up a thirty-five-million-dollar view of the park.

He handed her the drink. Noted she wore her sapphire engagement ring and wedding band. "Which show?"

She blinked. "Sorry?"

"Which show are you designing for?"

"Oh." She wrapped her fingers around the glass. "Alexander Faggini's Fashion Week show."

"That's impressive."

She lifted a shoulder. "A friend of mine introduced us. He thought my designs worked well with his. It's an honor for me."

"I'd like to see the collection."

"Would you?" She turned those beautiful blue eyes on him. "Or are you just making an effort to appear interested?"

"Angelina," he growled.

"It's a fair question." Her chin set at a belligerent angle. "I am, after all, *playing at a start-up* business that has somehow, magically, found success."

He rested his gaze on hers. "Three-quarters of new businesses fail in this city. They don't even last until their second year. You have done something extraordinary with yours. I'm proud of you. But at the time, it seemed like a long shot."

"You didn't think I had the talent? Not even with you *nurturing* me?"

There was a distinctly wounded edge to her eyes now. He blew out a breath. "I could see you were talented. But you knew I wanted my wife at home. We were having a baby."

"You were like that after we lost the baby. When I desperately needed something to occupy my brain."

His mouth flattened. "I could have supported you better, there's no question about it. I *should* have. But someone had to run our life. I needed the sanity of you at home."

"And I needed the sanity my work provided me." She turned her gaze to the lush canvas of green spread out before them, Central Park in full, glorious bloom.

He studied the delicate line of her jaw, the stubborn set of her mouth, silhouetted in the lamplight. *Defensive. Protective.* It made him wonder about all the pieces of his wife he hadn't known. Didn't know. Had never attempted to know.

"Sanity from what?"

She shrugged. "My life. All of it."

He frowned. He understood what being the offspring of a dynasty meant, because his family was as much Italian aristocracy as the Carmichaels were American royalty. Understood how the pressure of the relentless press coverage, the high expectations, the *rules* in their world could weigh a person down. What he had never understood was what about it his wife reacted so violently to.

"Why do you hate it so much," he asked, sweeping

a hand through the air. "This world? Why has being a Carmichael been so difficult for you? I could never figure it out. I know you have a combative relationship with your father and that having his affairs plastered across the media couldn't be easy for you…but it always seemed like it was more."

A cynical light shone in her gaze as she turned toward him. "Did it need to be more? Those affairs devastated my mother, cut her so deeply she never recovered."

"No," he agreed, "it doesn't. My father worships the ground my mother walks on and rightly so. I can't imagine how painful it must have been to watch your father disrespect your mother like that when she has stood by his side the entire time."

Her dark lashes swept over her cheeks. "You see what everyone else sees. The glittering, perfect world of the Carmichaels. You don't see the dysfunction on the inside."

"So tell me about it," he countered. "Help me understand."

"They are private family issues. I would be betraying confidences if I did."

"You are my *wife*. You can confide in me."

Her mouth formed a stubborn, straight line. An oath left his lips. "This is one of those areas we need to fix, Angelina. How can we make this marriage work if there are big pieces of you I don't know?"

"Like those big pieces of you I don't know?" Her eyes flashed, a storm rising in their gray-blue depths. "You can't press a button and summon emotional intimacy. *Trust*. It doesn't work like that. It takes time and effort. If you want that from me, you have to lead by example."

Heat seared his belly. He knew she was right. Knew he'd been operating on automatic pilot in the years after Lucia's death, cauterizing his emotions, refusing to feel. But it wasn't the easiest thing to admit.

"Bene," he conceded harshly, opening his arms wide. "Consider me an open book, then. No subject is off-limits. Anything is fair game. But we *are* going to learn how to communicate—in ways that do not involve the bedroom."

The stare she leveled at him rattled every nerve ending. Made him ache to resort to tried-and-true methods. But he wasn't going there. He was making good on the promise he'd just given her.

"I think," he said evenly, deciding a change of subject was in order, "we should host a party in the Hamptons over the long weekend. Marc Bavaro, the CEO of the Belmont chain, has a place there. I'd like to try and soften him up a bit. Get a few outstanding issues resolved. It would also provide an ideal opportunity to formally announce our reconciliation given the gossip that's running rampant."

She muttered something under her breath. His brow lifted. *"Scusa?"*

"I *said* to put your stamp on me. That's why you want to have this party."

"I already did that," he murmured, eyes on hers. "Why would I need to make a public display of ownership when we both know the truth?"

A flush stained her cheeks. "Go to hell, Lorenzo."

"I've already been there, *cara.* At least this time there will be a great deal of pleasure along with the pain."

Her eyes locked with his. A long, loaded moment passed as they took a step into uncharted territory. Lashes lowered, his wife studied him, as if deciding whether to continue the charge.

Her chin dropped. "Everyone's calendars will be full on the Labor Day weekend."

"They'll be doing the rounds. What's one more stop? Speculation about us alone will pack them in."

She gave him a pointed look as if to say that was exactly the issue. "I have to finish the pieces for Alexander so he can match them up with the show. If something doesn't work, I'll need to come up with an alternative."

"It's one weekend. There's nothing pressing between now and then. Work around it." He pointed his whiskey glass at her. "This is where we learn to compromise, Angie. You give, I give—that's how it works."

Her mouth flattened. "Fine."

"Good. Gillian will plan it, you will contribute your guest list and the staff in the Hamptons will execute. All you need to do is show up."

Her expression remained frozen. He sought the patience he was not known for. "I expect you to invite your family. Whatever's going on between you and your parents, you need to fix it. This will be a good opportunity to do so."

"No." The word flew out of her mouth—swift and vehement. He lifted a brow. "I went to see them last week," she explained. "They aren't in the Hamptons much anymore in the summer. There's no point in inviting them."

"I'm sure they'll make the effort to come. It will look strange if they're not there given I do business with your father." He took a sip of his whiskey. "Speaking of parents, mine will be visiting the week after the party. They'll stay at their apartment, but we'll host them here for dinner. Decide on a date with Gillian that works for you."

Her face fell further, if that was possible. "What did you tell them? About us?"

"That we've decided to make this marriage work. That we made a decision in haste at a time when we were both in pain and now we are rectifying it."

"So you chose to leave out the part where you're *bullying* me into becoming your wife again?"

"I prefer to think of it as a mutually beneficial arrangement. *Motivation* for us to make this marriage work." He leveled his gaze on her combative face. "We made a deal, a commitment to each other, Angelina. I meant it when I said your heart and soul have to be in it, but I'm not so unfeeling that I don't understand you need time to adjust. After that settling-in period, however, I expect an *attitude* adjustment, because this is not how it's going to be."

An attitude adjustment? Angie was still fuming after she and Lorenzo had shared a tense, mostly silent dinner on the terrace, where she ate little and talked less. It had been so *generous* of him to concede she needed time and space after what he'd done to her. *Clearly* she should be falling into line, looking forward to spending more time with his PA than she did her husband.

Her mouth twisted. *I meant it when I said your heart and soul have to be in it.* He didn't even *have* a heart… or a soul for that matter. What would he know about it?

Lorenzo was ensconced in his home office to finish some work, so she elected to have a hot bath and go to bed. Constanza had unpacked all her things in the light, airy master bedroom, with its gorgeous vistas of the park, the housekeeper's usual ruthless efficiency putting everything back as if she'd never left.

It was eerie to pull a nightgown from a puddle of silk in a drawer and untangle her hair with the pearl-backed brush that sat on the dresser in the exact same place it used to be. On edge, her nerves in disarray, she headed for a rose-scented bath in the Italian-tiled en suite, immersing herself up to her ears in hot, cathartic bubbles.

All sarcasm aside, she was relieved with her husband's acknowledgment they needed time—that he didn't expect her to jump into bed with him as seamlessly as her brush had landed back on the dresser. But clearly, she thought, stomach knotting, given that her things were where they were, he expected her to share that bed with him. The thought made her search desperately for something else to focus on, like why he had rose-scented bath bubbles in here.

Either Constanza had been thoughtful, as she was wont to be, or they had belonged to one of his lovers. Because surely, the tabloids couldn't be right? Surely her highly sexual husband, who'd thought he was divorced, had had other women?

You haunt me, Angelina, every time I'm with another woman... Her heart sank, a numb feeling settling over her. He'd pretty much admitted he had. Lorenzo wouldn't have spent two years pining after her as she had him. Going dateless until Byron wouldn't take no for an answer.

The thought of her husband with other women lanced her insides. She sank farther into the bubbles and closed her eyes. They had been so happy in the beginning. That's what hurt the most. What *might* have been.

After Lorenzo had accepted the consequences of what a broken condom had produced, he'd submitted willingly to her mother's ostentatious society wedding—what he'd considered a politically advantageous match, she suspected. She'd been too crazy about him to care.

They'd spent the first months of their marriage in a pheromone-induced haze, tuning out the world. In Lorenzo's arms, her worries about why he'd married her had faded to black. He'd hungered after her with an intensity that had made her feel as if she'd been the most important thing on the planet to him, their addictive obsession with each other inescapable, unassailable. The wounded pieces of her, the parts that had been convinced she was unlovable after a childhood devoid of emotion, had begun to heal. For the first time in her life, she'd felt whole, as if she was *worthy* of love.

And how could she not? Having her husband focus on her, choose to engage, had been like having the most powerful force in the universe directed at her. Suddenly all the pieces of her life had been falling into place and happiness had seemed attainable after years of wondering if it even existed.

Until reality had interceded—one of Lorenzo's big, flashy deals had come along, he'd immersed himself in it and their cozy cocoon had become her husband's insanely busy life.

She'd learned being Mrs. Lorenzo Ricci had meant wining and dining his business contacts multiple times a week, their social schedule so exhausting for a pregnant Angie she'd barely been able to keep up. She'd begun to feel as if she was drowning, but Lorenzo hadn't seemed to care, was too busy to notice.

It had all come to a head when they'd lost their baby. Her increasingly distant husband withdrew completely, rendering him a virtual stranger. He'd descended into the blackness, whatever hell had been consuming him, and they'd never recovered. But, apparently, she thought bitterly, it was *her* obsession with Lucia that had crippled their marriage—not his.

The water cooling, a chill descending over her, she got out of the bath and got ready for bed. Slipping the silk nightie over her head, her eyes were half-closed by the time she stood in front of the beautiful, chrome, four-poster bed.

Too many memories crowding her head, a burn in her chest so painful it was hard to breathe, she fought back the hot, fat tears that burned her eyes. *I can't do it.* She could no more get into that bed as if the last two years hadn't happened than she could convince herself that coming back to Lorenzo hadn't been a big, huge mistake.

She padded down the hall to the guest room. Done in soothing pale blues and yellow, it evoked none of the master bedroom's painful echoes. Pulling back the silk coverlet, she slid between the sheets. Peace descended over her. She was out like a light in minutes.

She woke to a feeling of weightlessness. Disoriented, half-asleep, she blinked against the velvet black of night. Registered the strong arms that cradled her against a wall of muscle. *Heat.* The subtle, spicy, familiar scent seduced her into burrowing closer. *Lorenzo.*

Lost in the half-awake state that preceded full consciousness, bereft of time and place, the dark, delicious aroma of her husband seeping into her senses, she flattened her palm against the hard planes of his chest. Reveled in his strength. Registered the rigid set of his body against hers.

Her eyes flew open, consciousness slamming into her swift and hard. The taut line of Lorenzo's jaw jolted her the rest of the way to full alertness. Cold, dark eyes that glittered like diamonds in the dim light.

"Wh-what are you doing?" she stuttered as he carried her down the hallway and into the master bedroom.

He dumped her on the bed. "You can have all the time you need but you will sleep in here. We are moving *forward*, not backward."

She pressed a hand into the mattress and pushed herself upright. "I—" She slicked her tongue over her lips. "I couldn't get into this bed. There were too many memories, too many things I—"

"What?" he responded harshly. "Too many things you want to forget? Too much backstory you'd like to erase instead of facing it?"

She blinked, her eyes becoming accustomed to the light. Anger pulsed in his face—a living, breathing entity that made her heart tick faster. "Why are you so angry?"

"You weren't in bed," he said tersely. "I didn't know where you were."

He'd thought she'd left. Again. The realization wrote

itself across her brain in a dazed discovery that had her studying those hot, furious eyes. She'd known instinctively that walking out on Lorenzo hadn't been the right thing to do, but she hadn't been equipped with the emotional maturity at twenty-three to handle the destruction they had wrought. Instead she had left Lorenzo alone to face the fallout of their marriage while she'd spent a month in the Caribbean with her grandmother. She'd never quite forgiven herself for it.

"I'm sorry," she said quietly, reminding herself he had things to be angry about, too. "For leaving like that. I didn't handle it the right way. I did what I thought was necessary at the time. I needed to find myself—to discover who I was. But it wasn't right. I know that."

He reached for the top button of his shirt, eyes on hers. "And did you succeed? Did you find what you were looking for?"

"Yes." She laced her fingers together, eyes dropping to the sapphire that blazed on her finger. "I found me."

"And who is she?"

"The true me," she said quietly. "The one who spends her evenings with a sketch pad beside the bed, who gets to get up every morning and make those ideas into reality, tells a story someone might find beautiful. That's what I love, Lorenzo. That's when I am at peace."

He stared at her for a long moment, then finished unbuttoning his shirt. She told herself to look away as he stripped it off, but her sleepy, hazy brain, her senses, still filled with the scent of him, the parts of her that still craved him like a drug demanded she watch. Absorb every lean, cut line he exposed, angling down to the V that disappeared into his belt line.

Heat lifting to her face, she lay back against the pillows. It didn't matter how many times she'd seen Lorenzo naked, it still had the ability to fluster her beyond reason.

Seeking to distract herself, she voiced the one question her still unguarded brain needed to know as she lay staring at the ceiling. "Those women you talked about... did you sleep with them?"

Lorenzo balled up his T-shirt and tossed it in the hamper, struggling to get his anger under control. A part of him, the bitter, wounded part that hadn't been able to enjoy the one woman he had taken to bed during their time apart, while she had apparently found her fiancé more than satisfactory, wanted to see her flinch, *hurt*. But something stopped him. He thought it might be the knowledge that if he followed through on that desire, it would haunt them forever.

Setting his knee down on the bed, he joined his wife. "I don't think we should go there," he said softly. "I said, forward, Angie, not back."

Her face crumpled. "I want to know."

A knot formed in his chest. He drew in a breath. *Dannazione*—he was not the injured party here.

"One," he said evenly, "and no, I won't tell you who she is."

"Why?"

"Because you don't need to know."

She closed her eyes.

Heat seared his belly. Blood fizzling in his veins, he threw a thigh over his wife's silk-clad body and caged her in, forearms braced on either side of her head. "Angelina," he murmured, watching as her eyes fluttered open, "you asked. And while we're at it, let's not forget about our friend Byron."

Her lashes shaded her cheeks. "I didn't sleep with Byron. We were waiting."

He rocked back on his heels. "Waiting for *what*?"

"Until we got married."

Incredulity that any man would marry a woman without knowing whether they were sexually compatible warred with the infuriating knowledge that she had lied to him.

"And yet you deliberately let me think you'd bedded him," he murmured. "'I have no complaints,' was how I think you put it."

Her eyes filled with an icy blue heat. "You blackmailed me back into this marriage, Lorenzo. If you think I'm going to apologize, think again."

What he *thought* was that he had no idea what to think. Knowing his wife remained his and only his satisfied him on a level he couldn't even begin to articulate. That she might be as haunted by him as he was by her...

He traced his gaze over her lush, vulnerable mouth. Across the enticing stretch of bare skin the askew neckline of her nightie revealed, down over the smooth flesh of her thighs where the silk had ridden up...the dusky shadow between her legs. *Unbearable temptation.* Hard as rock, he ached for her.

"Get off me." His wife drew his attention back up to her flushed face.

His lip curled. "What's the matter, *mia cara*? You afraid I'm going to penetrate those defenses you cling so desperately to? That make you feel so *safe*?"

A defiant look back. "Just like yours do?"

"Ah, but *I* am promising to open up." A lazy smile twisted his lips. "I'm a caterpillar poised for transformation. You get to come out of your cocoon, too, and try your wings."

"Very funny." She pushed at his chest. *"Off."*

He dropped his mouth to her ear. "An open book, Angelina. That's what you and I are going to be. The brutal truth and nothing but. We might just survive this little experiment if we can offer each other that."

He levered himself off his sexy, furious wife and headed for the bathroom. It occurred to him, then, as he stepped under a hot shower, his emotions a tangled mess, that he might have underestimated the power his wife still held over him. That both of them might end up getting burned before this was over.

CHAPTER FOUR

ANGIE SPENT THE WEEK leading up to the Hamptons party attempting to avoid any further confrontations between her and Lorenzo. That combustible scene in their bedroom had convinced her engaging with her husband was not a good strategy. Avoidance was. And with Lorenzo immersed in his big deal, it hadn't proven difficult. It was almost like old times.

Except it wasn't. She had been working long hours, too, at the studio getting Alexander's collection ready, with Lorenzo's support. Her husband, however, had insisted they share dinners together, even if they had to work afterward. He was intent, it seemed, on making this marriage work. They talked, shared things about their day, managed, for the most part, to be civil. But soon afterward, Lorenzo retreated to his office to work, not coming to bed until the early hours, ensuring her strategy had worked perfectly.

Tonight, however, she conceded as she watched a perfect East Hampton sunset stain the sky, there would be no escaping—not from her combustive relationship with her husband, nor the past she'd worked so hard to leave behind. Tonight they would host the toast of high society for cocktails at their sprawling waterfront estate, an event that had the gossip hounds frothing at the mouth and her insides curling in an intense, visceral reaction that begged her to retreat.

But it was too late. It had been too late ever since Gillian had sent out the cream-and-silver embossed invitations via courier and the RSVPs had started flooding in by the dozens, proving Lorenzo's point that a helping of titillating gossip would always command the day.

She watched a graceful, forty-foot sailboat navigate past on the gray-blue Shinnecock Bay, the high waves and white foam a perfect mirror for her churning insides. She adored the peace and tranquility of this exclusive enclave, the ability to escape a tourist-infested, muggy Manhattan and enjoy the cool breezes that tempered the island. What she didn't enjoy was the microcosm of Manhattan society the Hamptons were at this time of year. Taking part in the requisite social circuit, forging the right contacts through her and Lorenzo's recreational activities, *being seen with the right crowd.*

"You might as well be at work," her entrepreneurial friend, Cassidy, had once said, referring to the intense networking that went on here 24/7. "At least in Manhattan, you can disappear into your town house, plead a prior engagement and no one will ever know. In the Hamptons, *everyone* knows."

Her mouth twisted. And the cliquishness? The competitiveness? The feckless alliances that changed with the wind? She had seen the devastation they could wreak, had watched her mother shredded by their vicious bite and yet Bella Carmichael had, unfathomably, always gone back for more because headlining an American dynasty wasn't something you just walked away from.

Her mother had learned to grit her teeth and smile as all Carmichaels did, even when her world was falling apart, pretending the gossip chasing through the room about Alistair Carmichael's infidelities, which of his "assistants" he was sleeping with now, didn't faze her in the least. That her husband's predilection for twenty-five-year-old blondes and the power that came along with his ability to command them was par for the course in the world they lived in.

She smoothed clammy palms over her cranberry-red silk dress, praying her father's indiscretions would not come up tonight. She'd already briefed the waitstaff her mother was not to be served alcohol under any circumstance. Watching her go off the rails in front of the upper echelons of Manhattan society was the last thing she needed.

"I like this dress." Lorenzo materialized behind her, his hands settling on her hips. "Although," he drawled, turning her around, his inspection dipping to the plunging neckline of the dress, "I'm not sure I'm going to appreciate every other man in attendance tonight enjoying the same view."

Her pulse fluttered in her throat. Heat radiated from the light spread of his fingers to forbidden places, *dangerous* places, warming her insides. She took a step back, putting some distance between them.

The dress *was* provocative—the flesh revealed by the low neckline leaving a hint of the rounded curves of her breasts bare. It was more than she would normally put on display.

"It's one of Alexander's designs. He insisted I wear it tonight."

"I'm not surprised. It was made for you."

The sensual glitter in his eyes sent a skittering up her spine. Or maybe it was how good he looked in a silver-gray shirt and dark trousers that set off his spectacular dark coloring and beautiful eyes.

Her gaze dropped away from his. He curved his fingers around her jaw and brought it back up to his. The appraising look he subjected her to made her feel like glass—utterly transparent and far too vulnerable. "You've been off all day. What's wrong?"

She pulled free. "Nothing. I'm fine."

"No, you aren't." Irritation clouded his expression. "There's this thing that happens when we socialize, Angie. You turn into a plastic version of yourself. Aloof. Unreadable. Why?"

"That's hardly true."

"Every time, *cara.*" He shoved his hands in his pockets and leaned back against the sill. "You can tell me or we can keep your parents waiting. It's all good with me."

Heat sizzled her blood. "Perhaps because it's always about a goal, a *business* transaction, rather than us enjoying ourselves. I was graded on my ability to accomplish those goals. Romance a partner of yours, flatter his wife, impress a potential target with my impeccable lineage..." She waved a hand at him. "Tonight it's Marc Bavaro—what's the goal with him? What would you like me to *be*, Lorenzo? Amusing? Intellectual? Cultured? Flirtatious?"

His gaze narrowed. "Not in that dress, no. And here we are getting somewhere, *bella mia. Communicating.* Because I had no idea you felt that pressure. *I* enjoy the thrill of the chase, accomplishing something by the end of the evening. To me it's us being a team. But I would *prefer* for you to be yourself...for you to be the woman I have always appreciated that never seems to show up on these occasions."

She leaned back against the sill, fingers curling around the edge. "And which woman is that? I'm intrigued despite myself, since I never seemed to get it right."

"The vibrant, spirited woman I met that night in Nassau who didn't seem to care what anyone else thought of her. Where has she gone, Angie? Where has that light gone?"

She blinked. Who did he think had snuffed out that spirit by asking her to be something she wasn't? By shutting her out when she displeased him? By constantly making her aware she wasn't measuring up?

She lifted her chin. "Why this sudden obsession with what makes me tick? It never seemed to concern you before."

"Perhaps because I'm realizing the woman I thought I knew has all these vulnerabilities lurking beneath the surface, vulnerabilities I think might be the key to why she is the way she is, and yet she won't let me near them."

"I think you're overthinking it."

"I think I'm not." He scowled and pulled his hands from his pockets. "I had some things to work through before, things I *have* worked on. It has proven illuminating to me. I would like to learn from it."

Things like Lucia? Her heart beat a jagged rhythm in her chest. To allow herself to believe that, to believe he truly cared, that he wanted to know her, *understand* her, that he truly wanted this time to be different between them, threatened to poke holes in the composure she desperately needed as she faced her old social set tonight. Not to mention her parents, who were waiting for them downstairs.

"We should go," she said quietly. "My parents will be waiting."

He pushed away from the sill. "We'll continue this later," he warned, setting a hand to the small of her back to guide her from the room. His warmth, his undeniable strength, bled into her skin. She swallowed hard. Somehow in the midst of all the chaos in her head, among all the conflicted feelings warring inside of her, his touch anchored her as it always had. Perhaps that was why it had hurt so much when he'd taken it away.

The poolside terrace was lit with flaming torches as they joined her parents outside, the lights from the sprawling, Italian-inspired villa reflected in the infinity pool that served as the star attraction of the space. Sleek waitstaff dressed in black hovered at the ready, the marble-and-brick bar stocked with rows of the perquisite champagne on ice.

Della and Alistair Carmichael were already holding drinks, listening to the local band they'd hired to play. Angie gave her mother, who was looking her usual elegant self in a powder-blue cocktail dress, her silver-blond hair a perfect bob to her ears, a perfunctory kiss on the cheek. Her gaze slid down to the drink her mother held as she drew back, the tightness in her chest easing when she saw that it was sparkling water.

"You look beautiful, Mother."

"Thank you." Her mother gave her a critical once-over. "Faggini?"

"Yes." A wry smile twisted her lips at their practiced small talk. It was how they'd learned to coexist after their fiery relationship during Angie's teenage years, when her mother's alcoholism had emerged and everything between them had been a war of wills. Their practiced détente still didn't quell the pain of losing the mother she'd once had, before Bella Carmichael's disease had devastated her, but at least it was a norm she knew how to maneuver within.

"Lorenzo." Her mother turned her attention to Angie's husband, the feminine smile she reserved for handsome, powerful men softening her face. "It's so lovely to see you." She kissed him on both cheeks. "Although," she said in a pointed tone as she drew back, "I think we've seen you more than our daughter over the past couple of years. Perhaps your reconciliation will remedy that."

"We're counting on it," her father said, stepping forward. Tall and distinguished with a hint of gray at his temples, his eyes were the same slate blue as his daughter's. That was where their similarities began and ended.

Eschewing the embrace he knew Angie would reject, he shook Lorenzo's hand. "Angelina knows how thrilled I am to see her back where she belongs."

Back where she belongs? A surge of antagonism pulsed through her. She wouldn't be in this situation if her father hadn't allowed his arrogance to blind him to the business realities staring him in the face. He was using her as a pawn and showed not the slightest conscience about it.

Lorenzo read the tension in her body, his palm tightening at her back. "My parents are in town next week," he said smoothly. "Perhaps you can join us for dinner? It would be nice for us all to reconnect."

Angie's back went ramrod-straight as her mother gushed on about how lovely that would be. It wasn't lovely, it was the worst idea ever. To put Saint Octavia, Lorenzo's supremely dignified mother, in a room with her own, given Della Carmichael's loose-wheel status of late, was a recipe for disaster.

Thankfully they were saved from discussing it further as the first guests began to arrive.

Hand at his wife's back, Lorenzo greeted the arrivals. Guest after guest arrived in cars piloted by drivers who would spirit them from party to party that evening. His wife grew stiffer and stiffer with each new arrival and the open curiosity about their newly resurrected relationship. By the time Marc Bavaro, the CEO of the Belmont Hotel Group, arrived with his beautiful redheaded girlfriend, Penny, Angie had perfected her plastic self.

Lorenzo's inability to understand what was happening to her, as his need to connect on a personal level with Bavaro pressed on his brain, made his impatience boil over.

"That's Marc Bavaro and his girlfriend walking in now," he murmured in his wife's ear. "Can we try for happy just for the next few minutes? Less like you're facing the executioner being by my side?"

Angelina pasted a smile on her face. "Of course," she said sweetly. "Your wish is my command."

Even without her real smile, his wife captivated Marc Bavaro. The CEO's leisurely once-over of Angelina's red dress, despite the stunning date at his side, made his wife's cheeks redden. So Marc Bavaro did have a roving eye, as advertised. Lorenzo couldn't necessarily blame him, given Angie's ability to mesmerize any red-blooded male with whom she came into contact.

He tightened his fingers around her waist. "Great that you could make it," he said to Marc. "Good to get out of the boardroom."

"Agreed." But Bavaro still wore the cagey expression that had been making Lorenzo mental as they debated the last few points of the deal.

"Your necklace is beautiful," Penny said to Angie. "Is it one of yours?"

"Yes. Thank you. It's one of my favorite recent pieces."

"I love your stuff." Penny threw Marc a wry glance. "I've given him lots of hints on what he can buy me for my birthday."

"Perhaps you'd like to come in to the studio and I'll design something for you?"

The redhead's eyes widened. "Would you?"

"Of course." Angelina slid Lorenzo a glance that said she was playing the game for now. "Why don't I introduce Penny around while you two talk business?"

Penny agreed and the two women set off through the crowd. Bavaro's eyes trailed after Angelina. "That's quite a dress."

"It is," Lorenzo agreed, amused. He didn't doubt the connection he and Angie had. It ruled out any other male as a threat. He was content to play the waiting game when it came to bedding his wife. Figuring out what was going on in her head was another matter entirely.

He nodded at Marc. "Let's find a quiet place to talk."

* * *

By the time Angie had introduced Penny around to anyone the real estate broker might have found interesting or useful, she'd had enough of this party for a lifetime. She hated small talk with a passion, had always dreaded the legendary Carmichael parties she'd been forced to attend, not to mention the fact that all roads seemed to lead back to her and Lorenzo's unexpected reconciliation in the sly side conversations she was drawn into.

"I thought maybe there was a baby in the works," joked their next-door neighbor. "But clearly that can't be true. That dress is *amazing* on you."

After the last, thinly veiled attempt to pry the story out of her, she returned Penny to Marc. The Belmont CEO asked her to dance in turn, and Penny didn't seem to mind, so Angie accepted, eager to get away from prying eyes. Marc was a good dancer and conversationalist. He was charming, despite Lorenzo's depiction of him as a shark.

They danced two dances before Lorenzo cut in. "I'm not sure if I should lock you up or use you as a weapon," he murmured as he took her in his arms. "Bavaro is like a puppy salivating after a bone."

"Ah, but I don't have a purpose tonight." Sarcasm stained her voice. "I'm just supposed to *be me* in all my glory. The woman you *appreciate*."

His lips curved. Bending his head, he brought his mouth to her ear. "I do appreciate you in that dress. It screams 'take me,' *mia cara*. Too bad we are still learning to communicate *verbally*. The timing is all off."

Fire licked up her spine. He pulled her closer, a possessive hand resting on her hip, his splayed fingers burning into her skin. A slow curl of heat unraveled inside of her. She'd enjoyed her dance with Marc—he was handsome by any woman's standards and equally charismatic.

But being in Lorenzo's arms was a whole different story. Dancing with her husband was...*electrifying*.

Her nerve endings sizzled as her hips brushed against his muscular thighs, erotic tension in every muscle. The masculine warmth of him bled into her, heating her blood, weakening her knees. She took a deep breath to center herself, but it was his dark, delicious scent that filled her head, heightening her confusion.

She stepped back, putting some distance between them, heart thudding in her chest. His ebony eyes glittered with a banked heat, moving over her face in a silent study. "Thank you for offering to design the piece for Penny. You didn't have to do that."

"It's fine." The husky edge to her voice made her wince. *You hate him, remember?* He had just turned her life upside down.

"Perhaps we will make that superior team," he suggested on a speculative note, eyes holding hers. "If you manage to move past that anger you're holding so tightly to."

Her gaze dropped away from his. She focused on the other guests, sticking determinedly to her vow to keep her shields bulletproof when it came to her husband.

A high-pitched laugh stole her attention. The blood in her veins turned to ice. Whipping her head around, she found her mother in the crowd, talking to a well-known society columnist, a glass of champagne in her hand. Oh, no! She'd found someone to enable her.

Panicked, she scanned the crowd for her sister. Abigail was all the way across the terrace in a group of people. She looked back at her mother, champagne sloshing from her glass as she laughed at something the columnist had said. It was not her first drink.

"Your mother is in fine form," Lorenzo said mildly. Her brain frozen, she just stared at him. When the music ended, she slipped out of his arms. "Keep socializing," she said, nodding at Marc. "Abigail's just waved for me to go meet someone."

He frowned at her. "Are you okay?"

"Perfect. Back in a minute." With as blasé a smile as she could manage, she set off through the crowd. Approaching the group her sister was in the middle of, she caught her eye. Abigail disentangled herself and came over. "You okay?"

"It's Mother. She has a glass of champagne in her hand. It's not her first."

Abigail frowned. "I've been watching her all night. She's been drinking sparkling water."

"She found someone to enable her." Angie's stomach lurched. "She's talking to Courtney Price, Abby."

Her sister's face grayed. Leading the way, Abigail wound her way through the crowd, Angie on her heels. Her mother had drained the champagne and procured another glass by the time they reached her. Her loud voice penetrated the din of the crowd, drawing glances from those around her. Angie's heart plummeted.

"You grab her," Abigail muttered. "Get her out of here. I'll do damage control."

Angie nodded. Heart in her mouth, she headed toward her glassy-eyed mother. Her mother glared at her. "Oh, look!" she declared in that far too loud tone. "My daughters are here to cut me off before I say something I shouldn't. I haven't, have I, Courtney? We're just having a nice conversation."

Courtney Price had a half fascinated, half horrified look on her face. *Brilliant column fodder.* Angie reached for her mother's arm. "Actually I have someone I'd like you to meet."

Her mother yanked back her arm. The force of the movement sent the champagne flying from her glass, splattering the dress of the woman beside her. Paralyzed, Angie stared at the silk dress, then lifted her gaze to the woman's bemused face. She was the wife of one of Lorenzo's business acquaintances.

Oh, hell.

Gasps rang out around her. The shocked sounds spurred her into action. Grabbing her mother by the arm, she propelled her through the crowd, people gawking at them as they went. Angry and humiliated, her mother kept up a verbal barrage the whole way.

"It was *your* fault that happened, hauling me out of there like that."

Angie kept her mouth shut. Nodding her thanks at the butler who opened the patio door for them, she marched her mother inside and up the stairs toward her parents' suite, keeping her mother's weaving steps on course. Where the hell was her father? Somehow this just never seemed to be his job.

Guiding her mother inside her suite, she flicked on the light. Her mother stared at her belligerently, hands on her hips. "All I wanted was to have some fun," she said, her speech slurred. "All I wanted was to be *happy* tonight, Angelina. But you won't even give me that."

A lump formed in her throat. "You're an alcoholic, Mother. You can't drink. *Ever.*"

"I am fine." Her mother put her arms out as she lost her balance and weaved to the side. "I would have been fine. I only had a couple of drinks."

A lie. Angie had heard so many of them, about the drinking, about the pills, about every secret her mother had wanted to hide—it had become her normal state of being.

Her mother headed toward the bar in the lounge. Threw open the door of the fridge. "There's nothing in there," Angie said quietly, stomach churning. "You need to go back for treatment, Mother. You know that."

Her mother swung around. Fear pierced her hazel eyes. "I told Abigail I won't go back there. *Ever. Never* again."

"You need help. Professional help."

"I won't go."

"Yes, you will." Rage vibrated through her. "You will not destroy all of us in your quest to annihilate yourself. Abigail needs a life. *I* need a life. You need help."

"You," her mother said, fixing her with a vicious look. *"You* who don't care. You who turned your back on me and walked away."

"Because I couldn't stand it anymore. Because you were taking me apart piece by piece, Mother."

Her mother's gaze darkened. She pressed her fingers to her mouth. "I don't feel well."

Angie moved fast, sliding an arm around her and helping her to the bathroom. When her mother had upended the contents of her stomach multiple times, Angie cleaned her up and put her to bed.

"I'm sorry." Her mother started to cry, her transformation from angry to sad happening with its usual rapid-fire swiftness. "I'm so sorry."

Heat burned the back of Angelina's eyes, the pieces of her heart she'd finally healed shattering all over again. "I know." She clasped her mother's hand in hers, hot tears escaping her stinging eyes and sliding down her face. "I am, too."

For everything. For all of it.

Turning off the light, she let herself out of the room. Tears blinding her vision, knees shaking, she slid down the other side of the door until she sat on the floor, hands pressed to her face.

She couldn't do this again.

CHAPTER FIVE

"ANGELINA?" LORENZO PULLED to a halt when he saw his wife sitting in the hallway, legs drawn up, head in her hands. Her quiet sobs tore loose a piece of his heart.

He squatted down beside her. "What's wrong?"

No response. He tipped her face up to his. "Angelina," he said more urgently, "what happened?"

Her beautiful blue eyes were red-stained, unfocused. Heart jamming in his throat, he cupped her jaw. "*Dio*, Angie. Talk to me. What's wrong?"

She shook her head as if to clear it. Lifted a hand to push her hair out of her face. "I—" Another tear streaked down her cheek.

He cursed. Slid his arms beneath her knees and back and scooped her off the floor. Carrying her down the hallway to their suite, he shouldered the door open and set her on the sofa in the sitting room. Her beautiful red dress was wet, stained with something. Champagne, he assumed, from the story he'd heard.

He sat down beside her. "What the hell happened out there?"

She frowned. Rubbed a palm over her brow. "I'm so sorry about Magdalena's dress. Did Abigail smooth it over?"

"Magdalena's dress will survive. What the hell happened with your mother, Angie?"

Her gaze slid away from his. "She had a bit too much to drink."

His brow rose. "She was drunk. *Blotto.* She could hardly stand up. I'd say it was more than a bit too much."

She bit her lip. "So she was drunk. It happens. I apologize for the scene she caused."

"I don't care about the scene." A flash of heat consumed him. "I just found my wife crumpled in a ball in the hallway crying her eyes out... *Dio mio,* Angelina, what is going on?"

Her chin dipped. "It's nothing. I'm just...emotional. It's been a tough night."

He pulled in a breath. Counted to five. "You can either tell me why you've been such a disaster tonight, what is going on with your family, or I will go outside and ask Abigail. In the spirit of making our relationship work, I'd prefer, however, if the truth came from *my wife.*"

She stared at him for a long time. He held her gaze, ready to follow through on his threat.

"My mother is a functioning alcoholic," she said finally. "She's been that way since I was fifteen. We've managed to keep it from being public knowledge, have taken her to rehab twice, each time thinking it would be the last. This recent dry spell lasted two years. She started to slide backward when the money troubles began."

A red tide swept through him. "You were carrying this around with you our entire marriage and you didn't tell me?"

"My mother swore us to secrecy. It was the only way she'd agree to go for treatment. It was decided it would remain locked within the walls of the Carmichael family vault. If we didn't speak of it, didn't acknowledge it, it ceased to exist."

He frowned. "Who *decided* this?"

"My father."

"I'm assuming your sister's husband doesn't know, then, either?"

A flush swept her cheeks.

"*Dannazione*, Angelina." His hands clenched into fists by his sides. "Why didn't you feel you could trust me with this?"

She waved a hand at him. "You have the perfect family, Lorenzo. I was worried you would look down on us. You have such a disdain for a lack of discipline."

Heat seared his skin. "I would have *helped* you, not looked down on you. That's what a husband and wife do for each other."

"And we had that aspect of our relationship perfected, didn't we?" Her eyes flashed. "I never felt good enough for you, Lorenzo. Appreciated by you. *Ever*. Not after those first few months when you started tuning me out. Treating me like an afterthought. At least when you wanted me, I felt I had some value. When you lost interest in even that, it *decimated* me. Why would I tell you about my mother? Air my family's dirty laundry? All that would have done was make you regret your decision to marry me even more."

"I did *not* regret my decision to marry you. *Ever*." He stared at her, stunned. "Is that what you think?"

No response.

Confusion warred with fury, the red tide in him winning. "You are so off base, Angelina. *So* off base. I might have been distant, we agree that I was, but do you really think I would have thought any less of you because of this? That I wouldn't have supported you?"

Her mouth pursed. "I don't know."

His breath hissed from his lungs. His marriage was suddenly illuminated in a way it had never been before. What the cost of his emotional withdrawal had been on his wife. What he should have *seen*. He didn't like what he saw.

He took hold of her hand and pulled her to her feet. Turning her around, he reached for the zipper of her dress. She jerked away from him, eyes wide. "What are you doing?"

"Putting you to bed."

"I can't go to *bed*. The party's still going."

He moved his gaze over her face. "You're a mess. You can't go back down there. Things are winding down, anyway. I'll go finish up."

He turned her around and slid down the zipper. She pulled away, arms crossed over her chest. "I can do the rest."

He headed for the door. "Did Abby talk to Courtney Price?" she called after him. "She can't print this in her column tomorrow."

He turned around. "She pulled her aside. I saw them talking."

Her face relaxed. "Abby will fix it. She always does."

Abby will fix it. She always does. The words rang in his head as Lorenzo went back to the party. Is that what Angelina and her sister had spent the past decade doing? Fixing their mother's lapses before they made it to the tabloids? Preserving a family secret that was tearing his wife apart, a secret he hadn't known about because he'd been too caught up in himself, in his own stuff, to see the warning signals?

The tension that had always lain between his wife and her parents, the distance she'd put between herself and them this past couple of years, his wife's refusal to ever have more than one or two drinks no matter what was put in front of her—it all made sense now.

Anger at his own blindness fueling him, he found Alistair Carmichael and ensured he went and checked on his wife. What kind of a man was he to leave it to his daughters to pick up the pieces? To ignore what was clearly a cry for help from his wife?

Perhaps, he thought, the same kind of man *he* had been during his marriage. A man who had simply not been there.

Angie willed herself to sleep after Lorenzo left, curling up into a ball under the cool satin sheets and squeezing her eyes shut. But the scene with her mother kept replaying itself over and over again in her head.

You who don't care. You who turned your back and walked away.

A knot tied itself in her stomach. She *had* walked away. Because going through what had happened tonight again and again, never reaching that place inside of her mother that was in so much pain she couldn't heal, had taken a piece of her soul.

She burrowed into the pillow, an ache consuming her insides. Lorenzo's anger, his *fury*, twisted the knot tighter. Perhaps she should have told him. Perhaps she was as guilty of holding things inside as he was. Except it was difficult to communicate with a brick wall and that's what he'd been near the end.

She hugged the pillow tighter. Tried to force herself to sleep, because it hurt too much to be in the here and now. But she couldn't settle. She was still awake when Lorenzo came in just after one, stripped off his clothes, showered and came to bed.

He smelled so good, so achingly real and familiar, she had to fight the urge to beg him to hold her. Closing her eyes, she curled her fingers into the sheets. Lorenzo sighed, reached for her and turned her toward him. Feeling utterly exposed with her tearstained face and puffy eyes, she closed her eyes.

He ran a finger down her cheek, making her lashes flutter open. "Angie," he murmured, "*mia cara*. Things between us have to change. You have to learn to trust me. I have to get better at reading you...at knowing when you need me, because clearly I am terrible at that."

She searched the angular shadows of his face in the moonlight. "You're serious about this."

"You think I would have done what I've done if I wasn't? I want you back because you are meant to be with me, Angie, not because I have some cruel desire to make you suffer. I *married* you because you are beautiful and intelligent, because you were what *I* wanted in a wife, not simply because you were pregnant. Because for the first time since Lucia died, I felt alive. *You* made me feel alive."

Her heart stuttered in her chest. If she had sensed that this was the case, felt that intense connection that had bonded them together, he had never once verbalized it. When he had begun to shut her out, she'd convinced herself she'd imagined it, that she was delusional and hopelessly naive where he was concerned. But this, *this*, she didn't know how to process.

His fingers traced the edge of her jaw, commanding her attention. "If we had disagreements about how our relationship worked, it didn't mean I found you *lacking*— it meant we had issues to resolve. To say we didn't do a very good job of that is an understatement."

She bit her lip, the salt tang of blood filling her mouth. She'd been convinced he'd wanted her because she'd been a politically viable Carmichael, as a wife who could open doors for him in alternate social circles. For what he'd *thought* he'd been signing on for. If it really had been more than that, if he had wanted her for *her*, what did that mean?

Had she walked out on a marriage that had been reparable if she'd just stuck? It was an overwhelming, earth-shattering prospect to consider. She sucked in a deep breath and lifted her gaze to his. "Every time you withdrew I felt it as a rejection. It hurt, Lorenzo, badly."

"I know. I realize that now."

A long moment passed. His fingers slid to her cheek, thumb tracing over the tracks of her tears. The ache inside her grew until it was almost all-encompassing. The need for everything they'd had. Everything they'd never had. For this to be different this time as he was promising it would be. But she didn't know if she could trust him, wasn't sure she could go through another of his Jekyll-and-Hyde routines. Didn't know if she could trust her *own* instincts anymore.

Fear invaded her, coiled its way around her insides. She pushed a hand into the mattress to move before she did something she would regret. Something she wasn't ready for. Before she *did* beg him to hold her. Lorenzo hooked an arm around her waist and tucked her into the warmth of his body before she could, her back nestled against his chest. "Go to sleep," he murmured, brushing his lips over her shoulder in a fleeting caress. "Tomorrow we'll deal with what happens next."

Except she couldn't relax. Couldn't slow down her brain. Not with him so close, clad only in the sexy hipster briefs he'd added to his routine in deference to their *adjustment period.* Not when tomorrow would mean deciding what to do with her mother. Convincing her to go back to the treatment facility in California she swore she wouldn't return to.

Silent tears slid down her face. She reached up to brush them away, shocked there were any left. Lorenzo muttered an oath. *"Don't,"* he murmured, shifting so she lay back against the pillows. "We're going to solve this—I promise."

She should have protested when he set his mouth to

her jaw. As he kissed and licked away her tears, working his way up one cheek, then down the other. But the erotic, soul-searing comfort he offered eased the ache inside of her. Lit her up in a way only Lorenzo could.

A low sound escaped her throat. Her eyes locked with his in a hot, heated moment that held time suspended. Murmuring her name, he closed his mouth over hers, taking her lips in a slow, sweet kiss that drove everything from her head but him. How much she missed this. How much she missed everything about it.

He captured her jaw in his fingers, held her as he dipped deeper into her mouth, his tongue sliding against hers. The taste of him exploded through her, dark and dangerous as she tangled her legs with his, a tight fist of need forming in her stomach. She twisted closer, seeking, *needing* the oblivion he could give her because this, *this* had always been right.

She rocked against him. His obvious arousal, covered only by the thin cotton briefs, sank into her softness, the delicate material of her panties no obstacle. She gasped as he moved against her with possessive intent, the friction turning her insides molten.

"Lorenzo..."

He threaded a hand through her hair, held her still as he lifted his mouth from hers. "Angie," he murmured softly. "No."

No? Her eyes flew open.

"You will hate me tomorrow, *cara*. I guarantee it. You're emotional. I won't take advantage of that."

Her brain right-sided itself with a swiftness that made her dizzy. She pushed a hand against his chest, humiliation and confusion flaming through her. Lorenzo levered himself off of her. She scrambled to the other side of the bed, pressing her hands against her cheeks. "You started it."

"I wanted to comfort you," he said softly. "It got out of hand."

She turned her back on him and curled up in a ball.

"Angie." He laid a hand on her shoulder.

"Leave me alone." She took a deep breath as her fractured breathing slowed. She had no idea what she was doing. Thinking. Nothing made sense anymore. Everything she'd thought was true was now a massive gray area she had no idea what to do with.

Pain throbbed at the back of her eyes, her heart a rock in her throat. Lorenzo was just as much of an addiction for her as the alcohol her mother consumed. Just as dangerous. She would do well to remember that before she started making life-changing, potentially disastrous decisions to sleep with him again. Her husband was right in that.

She closed her eyes. This time sleep came swift and hard with the need to escape.

CHAPTER SIX

ANGIE WOKE THE next morning heavy-headed and bleary-eyed. Apprehensive about what lay ahead, confused about what had happened between her and Lorenzo last night, she dressed in jeans and a tunic, threw her hair into a ponytail and headed downstairs to the breakfast room, hoping it would be empty so she could spend a few minutes composing herself over coffee.

Her wish was not to be granted. Her husband sat by himself in the sun-filled room that overlooked the bay, the morning's newspapers spread out in front of him. He looked gorgeous in jeans and a navy T-shirt, his thick, dark hair still wet and slicked back from his shower. It was utterly disconcerting the way her heart quickened at the sight of him, as if it had a mind of its own.

He looked up, gaze sliding over her face. "You slept in. That's good. You needed it."

She took a seat beside him at the head of the table, even though her brain was screaming for distance. It would have looked churlish to do otherwise.

"Constanza made your favorite," he said, waving an elegant, long-fingered hand at the freshly baked banana bread on a plate. "And the coffee's hot."

"Thank you." She poured herself a cup of coffee. "Where are my parents?"

"Your father went for a run. Your mother's still in bed."

And would be for a while, she figured, taking a sip of

the hot, delicious coffee. His brow furrowed. "Your father, he is always this...*distant* when it comes to dealing with your mother?"

"Always. He thinks she is weak. That she should be able to conquer this addiction. When she slips it infuriates him."

"That's no way to get to the heart of the problem. Your mother needs support above all things."

She eyed him. "You were the king of distancing yourself when I displeased you."

"Yes," he agreed, dark gaze flickering. "And we've talked about how I'm going to work on that."

Right. And she was just supposed to take that at surface value? Forget the big stretches of complete alienation that had passed between them when he'd retreated into that utterly unknowable version of himself? How every time they'd made up in bed she'd thought it would be *better* just like she'd thought it would be better every time her mother promised to stop drinking, only to discover nothing had really changed.

She twisted her cup in its saucer. "It's always been that way in my family. We are the exact opposite of the Riccis—instead of expressing our emotions we bury them. Instead of talking about things we pretend they don't exist."

He frowned. "Ignoring an addiction, continuing to perpetuate an illusion that everything is fine when it isn't, is inherently damaging to all involved."

"I told you my family is dysfunctional."

The furrow in his brow deepened. "You said your mother started drinking when you were fifteen. What do you think precipitated it?"

She lifted a shoulder. "She always had the tendency to drink to cope with all the socializing. But I think it was my father's affairs that did it. Ask her to represent the family three or four times a week—fine. Ask her to do that when everyone is talking about who my father is screwing that week…to suffer that humiliation? It was too much."

"Why didn't she leave him?"

"She's a Carmichael. Image is everything. A Carmichael never concedes defeat. *Ever.* If we don't get her help, she will drink herself into the ground proving she can make this marriage work."

"That's nuts."

She arched a brow. "Didn't you say there's never been a Ricci divorce? It's what our families do."

He sat back in his chair, a contemplative look on his face. "That's why you don't like this world. Why you hate parties like the one we had last night. You hate what they represent."

"Yes."

"So you decided to leave me so you would never end up like your mother. You crave independence because you need to have an escape route in case our marriage falls apart like your parents' did."

Her mouth twisted. "That's far too simplistic an analysis."

"Perhaps, but I think your experiences drove your thinking with us. My withdrawal from you evoked shades of your father. Leaving you alone to cope while I went off to manage an empire. Except my vice wasn't other women, it was my work."

Her lashes lowered. "There may be some truth in that. But *saying* you're going to be more present and doing it are two different things."

"True," he conceded. "We can start with your mother, then."

"That's my issue to handle."

"No," he disagreed. "It's *our* issue. Like I said last night, we are going to handle this together. As a team. The way we should have the first time. You are not alone in this."

She shook her head. "It gets messy with my mother. It will be awkward for you."

"Exactly why I should be there." His jaw was a stubborn, unyielding line. "I saw you last night, Angie, crumpled on the floor. You were a wreck. This isn't going to be easy for you."

She pushed a hand through her hair. "You want to solve this like you want to solve everything, Lorenzo. Snap your fingers and *poof*, it's fixed. But it's far more complex than that."

"I know that. That's why the power of two will be better than one."

She exhaled a breath and stared out at the water, sparkling in the sun like the most electric of blue jewels. "We need to convince her to go back to the treatment facility in California. She's refusing to go."

"I may have an option. I called a friend of mine this morning. He had a brother in a facility in upstate New York that's supposed to be a leading edge program. If your mother was closer, perhaps it wouldn't be so difficult for her. You could visit her more often."

Her throat locked. The visits to see her mother in rehab had been the worst. Angry, bitter Della Carmichael had not gone easy despite recognizing the help she was getting. To put herself through even more of that with regular visits? The coward in her shrank from the idea, but she was starting to realize running from her problems hadn't gotten her anywhere—not with her mother and not with her marriage.

"We could go see it," her husband offered. "Then you can decide."

She eyed him. Her husband wanted to solve her problem because it was just one more obstacle between him and what he wanted—a wife able to devote her full attention to him. And yet, when he had comforted her last night she could have sworn he truly cared. That she meant something to him.

Perhaps she needed to exhibit a show of faith in them if this was going to work—a tiny, baby step forward, with her head firmly on her shoulders, of course. Last night had proven the need for that.

"All right," she said. "Let's go see it."

Angie and Lorenzo flew to upstate New York the next morning and met with the staff of the treatment center. Nestled in the foothills of the Adirondacks, the setting was lovely. By the time they'd finished touring the facility and meeting with the staff and doctors, Angie had an immediate comfort level with it.

They flew her mother up there to see it later in the week. If Della approved of the choice, the center could take her immediately. Surprisingly, her mother liked it. Angie's emotions were torn to shreds by the time her mother cycled through the anger and sadness that was her pattern before agreeing to stay. But, somehow, with Lorenzo at her side, it wasn't as much of a nightmare as she'd expected. Her husband was endlessly patient with her mother, commanding when he needed to be, caring when Della required a softer touch. Where had this man been, she wondered, during their marriage?

By the time they'd boarded the jet, headed for home, she felt numb.

"You okay?" Lorenzo looked at her from the seat beside her, his laptop conspicuously absent on the console.

She nodded. "I hate leaving her there. Please let this be the last time we have to do this."

He closed his fingers over hers. "Hopefully it is. If it's

not, we'll keep doing it until she's better. You're strong, Angie. You can do this."

She looked down at his hand curved around hers. Warm and protective, as he'd been all day. Her confusion heightened until it was that thick gray cloud, blanketing her brain. "Thank you," she murmured huskily, "for being there for me this week. I swore I'd never do this again because it hurts too much. But I'm learning running doesn't solve anything."

"No, it doesn't," he agreed, eyes darkening. "But sometimes we need to do things in our own time. Allow ourselves the space to heal."

Lucia. He was talking about Lucia again. A tight knot formed in her stomach. She couldn't ignore it any longer—this ghost that had always lain between them. She knew it was at the heart of figuring them out.

She pulled her hand out from under his. "What you said the night before the party—that you had worked through some things. Was one of them Lucia?"

A guarded expression moved across his face. "Yes. When I met you, I thought I had moved on, gotten through the worst of the grieving process. But after you left, I realized I hadn't left that process behind as fully as I'd imagined. That perhaps I had carried some of that baggage into our marriage—baggage which did make me emotionally unavailable at times."

She frowned. "You told me it was *my* issue with Lucia that was the problem."

His mouth twisted. "Because you made me furious. Pointing fingers at the ghost of Lucia was your favorite card to play when you were angry with me, *cara.*"

Her eyelids lowered. She couldn't deny that. She'd lashed out in whatever way she could to get a response out of him. Something, *anything* to show he'd cared. She'd known it was wrong to use Lucia as a weapon against him, but their fights hadn't exactly been rational ones.

"Tell me about her," she said quietly. "Tell me about what happened. I need to understand, Lorenzo. Maybe if I had, things would have been different."

He sat back. Rubbed a palm against his temple. "Where to start? Lucia and I were childhood sweethearts. We spent the summers together in Lake Como. Eventually our childhood crush developed into an adult romance. Our families were all for it, it seemed...*predestined*, in a way."

Her stomach clenched. She had felt that way about him when they'd met, their connection had been so strong, so immediate. But Lorenzo's heart had belonged to someone else.

"We didn't marry right away," he continued. "I needed to sow my wild oats. I wasn't sure I could marry the first girl I fell in love with. But after a few years, I knew it was her. We married when I was twenty-six. I was in New York by then, she joined me here." His dark lashes arced over his cheeks. "She was like a fish out of water, missing her family, missing Italy. I did the best I could to make her happy. She kept saying once she had a baby, once we started a family, everything would change. We were trying for that when she..."

Died. Her chest seized tight. She curled her fingers over his. "It's okay. You don't have to talk about it."

"No—you're right. You need to know what happened. It's...a part of me." He palmed his jaw, dragging his fingers over dark stubble. "The incident at the town house happened when I was in Shanghai on business. We had an excellent security system there. Impenetrable—like the one we have now. But the men who broke in were professionals—*violent* professionals. They knew how to talk their way into someone's home, knew the stories to tell. Lucia was so innocent—she never stood a chance."

Her stomach curled in on itself. "She let them in."

He nodded. "They put her in my den. Told her to stay there while they went and cleaned out the place. They left her alone for a few moments and she called for help on her cell. One of them came back, saw what she was doing and hit her with the blunt end of the gun." His fingers flexed on his thigh, his knuckles gleaming white. "The blow to the head caused a severe bleed on her brain. She never regained consciousness."

Angie pressed her fingers to her mouth in horror. "How do you know all of this?" she whispered.

"Surveillance video."

Her stomach dropped, a sick feeling twisting her gut. "Please tell me you didn't watch it."

"I had to. I had to know what happened."

The raspy note in his voice, the raw emotion in his dark eyes, tore a piece of her heart loose. What would it do to a person to go through that? To lose someone you love like that? It would change you forever.

"I'm sorry," she said quietly, a sinking feeling settling through her for all the wrongs they'd done each other. "For being so insensitive. I knew what happened to Lucia was horrible. I knew I should make allowances for it. But every time you retreated, every time you turned off, I hurt so badly, I just wanted you to hurt like I was hurting. It became instinctual, *reflexive*. But it didn't make it right."

He shook his head. "We were *both* experts at slinging arrows. It became easier than dealing with what was in front of us."

She caught her lip between her teeth. Stared out the window at a sea of blue, her ragged emotions begging her to stop. But to do that would stall them where they stood, suspended in a state of perpetual animation. It would not *fix* them.

"I know Lucia will always be in your heart," she said

quietly when she turned back to him. "I wouldn't expect any less. The issue between us was the emotional distance it caused, the emotional distance you put between us. I need to know you are over her, Lorenzo."

His cheeks hollowed. "I have let her go. I have moved on. That's what this is all about, Angelina—moving forward. I'm asking you to do that with me."

Her chest went tight. She knew they needed to let go of the past if they were going to make this work. But could she do it? Could she trust her instincts where Lorenzo was concerned? Could she trust that he had changed? Or was she setting herself up for an even greater fall than she'd taken the first time?

"Maybe what we need," he said quietly, a contemplative look on his face, "is a fresh start. A blank slate. No ghosts, no animosity, just us."

Her heart contracted on a low, painful pull. It was so tempting to believe they could recapture the good they'd had. That she could claim that piece of his heart she'd always craved. Because when it had been good between them, it had been good in a way nothing else could touch. And when it had been bad, he had eviscerated her.

Blood pumped through her veins, her breath caught in her throat. Suddenly her baby steps seemed like a heart-pumpingly, scary big leap.

"All of you," Lorenzo said evenly, eyes on hers. "That's what I'm asking for. A real shot at this. Can you give me that?"

She swallowed past a paper-dry throat. Took the leap. "I can try."

Lorenzo put his emotionally exhausted wife to bed after a light dinner, then headed to his study to work. The logistics with Angelina's mother had taken a big bite out of his week. He was behind and his inability to connect with

Marc Bavaro, who had disappeared on a multiweek trip to South America, meant the acquisition was still in limbo.

Resisting the temptation to drown his frustration in a potent shot of something strong because it would also dull his brain with hours of work ahead of him, he fixed himself a cappuccino in Constanza's steel marvel of a kitchen, returned to his study and picked up a report he had to review before his morning meeting, but the numbers blurred before his eyes.

His thoughts were consumed, instead, by his wife's haunted face as he'd put her to bed. With the fact that he had clearly never known her. Far from being the spoiled young woman he'd thought he'd married who was incapable of compromise, she was instead a vulnerable, emotional woman he'd never looked deep enough to see. A woman who had gone through hell under the purview of parents who had, in reality, been nothing of the sort.

That his wife had been strong enough at fifteen to police her mother at parties, to keep up a facade for as long as she and Abigail had, to take her mother to rehab not once but *twice*, by the time she was twenty, little more than a girl herself, boggled his mind. It was courage on a scale he couldn't imagine. Made him feel as if he'd just taken a hard shot to the solar plexus.

He sat back in his chair and closed his eyes, guilt twisting his insides. Twice now he'd failed to react when the most important women in his life had cried out for help. Failed to recognize what they'd been trying to tell him. *Failed to protect them.*

It shamed him on the most visceral of levels, raked across the dark presence that seemed to lurk just beneath the surface of his skin, searching for a way to the top.

Angie had always believed Lucia had his heart, that he wasn't over her and that was what had caused him to hold back with her. Instead the truth was something far worse. If he'd listened to Lucia, if he'd been *present* for her as Angelina liked to cite as his greatest fault, then she would still be alive.

Agitation drove him to his feet and to the window, where he stood looking out at a floodlit view of Central Park. The darkness pressed against his edges—relentless, *hungry*. He would never forgive himself for what had happened to Lucia because he didn't deserve it. But he could do things differently with Angelina this time.

He pressed a palm against his temple. If there was guilt for not being able to give his wife the love she so clearly craved, *deserved*, the love she'd never been shown, he would have to appease himself with the promise he would give her everything else. He would *be there* for her this time.

Because to allow his marriage to descend into the emotionally addictive union it had once been? To allow himself to feel the things for Angelina he once had? To experience more loss? Not happening.

Emotion had destroyed them the first time around, rationality and practicality would save them. That and the combustible chemistry he had slammed the breaks on in the Hamptons.

The lush, heady, spellbindingly feminine taste of his wife as she'd begged him to take her filled his head. He wanted to dull the edge, kill the need that drove him whenever he was within five feet of her. With a clean slate ahead of them, an agreement from Angelina to leave their ghosts behind them, he intended to accomplish that goal in short order.

He *would* have his delectable wife back in his bed, in every sense of the word. Would make this marriage into what it always should have been.

CHAPTER SEVEN

"DAMN." ANGIE SCOOPED the bracelet off the bedroom floor and attempted to refasten it around her wrist. She had been late coming home from the studio, where she'd been putting the final touches on Faggini's collection, which would debut at Fashion Week next week, not an ideal night to be running behind with Lorenzo's parents coming for dinner.

The clasp slipped from her fingers *again*. She grimaced. Was she that unnerved by the thought of a visit from Octavia the Great or did it have more to do with the fact she'd agreed to give her marriage a real shot? She suspected it was a combination of both.

"Need help?" Lorenzo emerged from the dressing area, rolling up the sleeves of the crisp white shirt he'd put on.

"Yes." She handed him the bracelet. "Please."

He slid it around her wrist, making quick work of the clasp. His gaze met hers. "Are you stressing about tonight? You have to stop doing that. Everyone wants us to work, including my parents."

"I'm not stressed, I'm late."

"You're not late. They're not even here yet."

He slid an arm around her waist and tugged her close. Smoking hot in dark pants and the white shirt, he made her heart thud in her chest. "I appreciate the fact that they are late, however," he drawled, "since I have not had time to greet you properly."

Her stomach clenched, heat radiating through her insides. He had a distinctly predatory look in his eyes tonight, one that suggested their adjustment period was officially over.

"Your parents will be arriving any minute,"

"Plenty of time." He slid his fingers into her hair, cupped her scalp and kissed her. A long, slow shimmer of a connection, it was leisurely and easy, a magic dancing in the air between them that stole her breath. Her palms settled on his chest, grabbed handfuls of shirt as her knees melted beneath her.

"Lorenzo," she murmured when they came up for air, "you are ruining my hair, not to mention my lipstick."

"Mmm." He slid his mouth across her jaw, down to the hollow of her throat. Pressed his lips to her pulse. It was racing like a jackhammer, revealing every bit of the tumult raging inside of her. He flicked his tongue across the frantic beat, his palms clamping on her hips to draw her closer.

He was all hard, solid muscle beneath her hands. The most exciting man on earth to her—always had been. She swayed closer, molding herself to his hard contours. He returned his attention to her mouth, each nip countered by a soothing lave of his tongue over tender flesh.

Drowning. She was drowning.

The doorbell rang. Jolted out of her pheromone-induced haze, Angie stiffened and dragged herself out of his arms. Lorenzo watched her with a satisfied look as he straightened his shirt. "Now you look like a proper wife."

She ignored him, walked to the mirror to straighten her hair and reapply her lipstick. It took several deep pulls of air to get her breath back. Her equilibrium.

Hand at her back, he guided her out to the foyer, where Constanza was greeting his parents. Lorenzo shook his father's hand, kissed his mother's cheeks, then drew Angie forward. She opted for the less threatening target first, Lorenzo's father, Salvatore.

Graying at the temples, shorter than his son by a couple of inches and stockier in middle age, Salvatore Ricci had always been much more approachable than his wife despite his fearsome business reputation.

"Buonasera, Angelina," he murmured, bending to brush a kiss against both of her cheeks. *"È bello rivederti."*

It's good to see you again. She forced a smile to her lips. *"Altrettanto."*

She turned to Lorenzo's mother, perfectly turned out as usual in an eggplant silk wrap dress that came to the knee and sleek Italian heels on her dainty feet. With her short, silver hair and her son's dark, dark eyes, she was still a stunningly beautiful woman. *"Buonasera, Octavia."*

"Buonasera." Octavia brushed a kiss to both her cheeks. "Thank you for having us."

"It's so lovely you are in town." Angie summoned the perfect manners she'd been taught since birth as she ushered Lorenzo's parents into the salon and offered them a drink. She had bemoaned all those social niceties as a teenager, finding them false and disingenuous, but right now, in this moment, she was exceedingly glad to have them to fall back upon.

It seemed everyone was on their best behavior as they enjoyed a cocktail before dinner. Lorenzo kept a palm to her back, a protective gesture Angie welcomed. Octavia didn't miss it, her shrewd dark eyes moving between the two of them every so often as if to assess what the real truth of them was.

Angie told herself she wasn't that twenty-two-year-old girl who'd been hopelessly intimidated by her mother-in-law. She was a successful business owner, every bit a match for Octavia Ricci. The thought settled her nerves as she sat beside Lorenzo at the table on the terrace Constanza had set with an elegant candelabra blazing in the final, hazy light of day. Lorenzo's parents sat opposite them, the humidity-free night a perfect choice for dinner outside.

The wine flowed freely, as did the conversation. By the time their salad plates were cleared, Angie had begun to relax, if not enjoy herself.

Octavia set her gaze on her daughter-in-law. "Lorenzo tells me you're partnering with Alexander Faggini on his show. That's impressive."

"Providing the jewelry," Angie amended carefully. "Alexander is the star. But yes, thank you, it's very exciting. Would you like to come?"

Octavia frowned. "We have dinner plans." She turned to her husband. "We could move them, couldn't we?"

"I'm sure that won't be a problem. It would be fun for you."

"Bene." Octavia flashed one of her queen-like smiles. "I would love to, then. Is your mother coming?"

Her heart skipped a beat. "I'm afraid not. She's out of town."

"Oh, that's too bad." Her mother-in-law looked anything but sad. "Where is she?"

"The south of France with family." She gave the cover she and Abigail had agreed on.

Octavia wrinkled her nose. "Isn't it *hot* there this time of year? I can't wait to escape the heat in the summer."

"We have a house there. She loves the flowers in the summer."

"I see."

"You must come with Lorenzo the next time he's in Italy," Salvatore inserted. "It would be nice for you to reconnect with the family."

"That would be lovely." She had no intention, however, of putting herself in the midst of Lorenzo's big, gregarious family until she and her husband had proven they could make this work. "It may be next year, I'm afraid. As soon as Fashion Week is over I'll be ramping up for the Christmas season. Things will be crazy right through January."

"I expect," Octavia interjected smoothly, "you will have to scale back once you and Lorenzo are expecting. My son tells me the pace you've been working at. That can't be good for a pregnancy."

Angie stiffened. Shot a sideways look at her husband. "Lorenzo and I are taking our time with that. But I see no reason not to keep working. I think it's healthier for a woman to stick to her usual lifestyle."

"Yes," said Octavia, "but it's common knowledge women who work too much have more difficulty conceiving. They are more stressed and the process doesn't happen so easily."

The *process* hadn't even happened between her and Lorenzo yet… How dare Octavia interfere like this? Lips pursed, she picked up her wine and took a sip. Lorenzo set a palm on her thigh.

"Give us time, Mamma. Angie and I have just reconciled. There will be plenty of opportunities to make babies."

"Angie is approaching twenty-six," Octavia countered. "You may need time."

Blood rushed to her cheeks. They were discussing her like she was a broodmare. Completely disregarding the fact that she wasn't *ready* to get pregnant, as her career was at a critical juncture. Or that she had miscarried the last time she had carried Lorenzo's baby, a soul-clawing experience she never wanted to repeat again. Not to mention the fact that her husband had shut down emotionally afterward, the impetus to the end of their marriage.

Lorenzo set a hard stare on his mother. "We had no problems conceiving before. We're not in any rush."

His mother lifted an elegant shoulder. "Angie was

young then—at the prime of her fertility. I'm simply giving you my advice. Women think they can wait forever these days and it just doesn't happen that way."

Angie drew in a breath. Lorenzo's fingers tightened around her thigh. He gave his mother a look that said that was enough and changed the subject.

She tried to shake it off as the meal wore on, but couldn't. Of all the things she and Lorenzo were battling through right now, a baby was not a priority.

Unable to do justice to the delicious chicken dish Constanza had cooked because her stomach had coiled up into a tight little ball, she set down her fork. By the time the elder Riccis got up to make their departure just after ten, she was fuming. She managed a few more minutes of civility, discussing the current theater runs with Octavia while Salvatore pulled his son aside in the study.

"*Maledizione*, Lorenzo, who the hell leaked this deal?"

Lorenzo leaned against his desk and crossed his arms over his chest. He'd been hoping to avoid this discussion, had almost managed it, until his father had pulled him aside.

"I have no idea," he said flatly. "There's only been high-level people involved. But you know what it's like—when there's a juicy story waiting in the wings, someone is always willing to spill."

"And if we don't close it?" his father countered. "This is Ricci's reputation you are gambling with. It's one thing to pursue a company that wants to dance, another thing entirely to drag it kicking and screaming onto the floor."

"I will close it," Lorenzo growled. "We will dance the final waltz, Papà. But I am not a magician. I cannot summon Mark Bavaro back from South America with a snap of my fingers. You need to give me time."

"I have given you time. A year this has been dragging

on, *figliolo*. This needs to be done before the next board meeting. Before they start wondering if we know what we're doing in the corner office or not."

Lorenzo scowled. "They are a bunch of overreactors with too much time on their hands."

"Who can make our lives hell if they choose to." His father crossed his arms over his chest, mirroring his pose. "I am beginning to think your ambition has got the best of you on this one."

His back stiffened. Bavaro's disappearance was raising his blood pressure. He didn't need the added pressure of his father trying to control everything around him even though he was no longer in charge of Ricci. But going head-to-head with Salvatore, he reminded himself, was like two stags locked in a fight to the finish. It never ended well.

"I am CEO of this company," he said, eyeing his father. "I will get the deal done. Back off and let me do my job."

His father gave a haughty tilt of his head. "October, Lorenzo. This needs to be signed and sealed."

Too riled up to sleep, Angie put on a swimsuit and headed for the hot tub on the terrace while her husband returned a phone call. Maybe it would unwind the Octavia-induced knots in her shoulders.

Built into the deck, with a sensational view of the Manhattan skyline, it was her favorite way to relax after a long day. She dropped her towel on the deck, set her half-finished glass of wine beside the tub and stepped into the hot, bubbling water, immersing herself up to her shoulders.

A sigh left her. Closing her eyes, she let the jets unwind the knots, ease the band of tension encircling her skull.

"In a better mood?"

Her eyes fluttered open. Her husband stood on the deck in navy trunks, a perfect male specimen in the prime of his life. Her heart rate skyrocketed as he tossed a towel over the railing. He was leaner than he'd been before, muscle and sinew arranged in a spectacular grid pattern across his pecs and abdomen. The perfect symmetry of it made her stomach curl.

She swallowed past a suddenly dry mouth. "I thought you had to make a call."

"It was a quick one." He lowered himself into the water, taking the seat opposite her. Her heartbeat calmed. His slow inventory of her, however, sent it ratcheting back up again. The bikini she had on, a halter top and briefs, wasn't overly revealing by any means, but her husband's thorough perusal made her feel as if there wasn't enough material to it. Not nearly enough.

"What happened with your father?" she blurted out, needing to distract herself from that…*heat*.

His dark gaze slid up to hers. "He is anxious about the Belmont deal. He is used to swallowing up tiny fish to build his empire. He doesn't have the patience to stalk a bigger prey, one that might not be quite so willing."

"You still haven't been able to tie down Marc Bavaro?"

"No." He exhaled a long breath and laid his head back against the tub. "He is MIA."

She studied the intensity that came off him like smoke. "What?" he asked, brow raised.

"I'm just wondering where this all-consuming drive comes from? This never-ending need for more."

He lifted a shoulder. "I was born with it. It's in my blood. Franco's, too."

"Franco has a sense of balance. A safety valve. You don't."

His gaze narrowed. "I am not my brother."

"No," she agreed. "But you weren't always like this. Franco told me that before Lucia you knew your limits. You knew how to live."

The glint in his eyes took on a dangerous edge. "My brother likes to play amateur psychologist. My ambition is strictly my own sin, *cara*, recognized and owned."

"It's not a badge of honor," she countered. "You push yourself to unsustainable levels, Lorenzo. You are going to drive yourself into the ground someday if you don't watch it. Maybe you should take a page out of your brother's book and allow yourself to be human once in a while."

"And maybe you should tell me what happened tonight." He raised a brow. "You knew my mother was going to bring up babies. It was a foregone conclusion. Why the overreaction?"

Heat seared her belly, her concern for him dissipating on a wave of antagonism. "It was not a foregone conclusion your mother would hammer me to the wall about a subject you know I am sensitive about. Knowing that, *you* should have diverted her. *We* haven't even discussed it yet."

He inclined his head. "Perhaps I should have. But you know you and I having a baby is a reality with Franco unable to conceive."

She lifted her chin. "It's not going to happen if you keep putting this pressure on me. We've promised to try this again, Lorenzo, and I will put my heart and soul in it, as you are asking. But I need time to adjust to *us* before we think about a baby. Not to mention the fact that I need to take advantage of the career opportunities in front of me. *Now* is not a good time for a baby. You said so yourself, we have time."

"We do," he agreed. "I'm not sure I'd say we have *lots* of it because my mother is right, it could take us time to conceive. Also—" He stopped in midsentence, a wary look in his eyes.

Her stomach bottomed out. "Also *what*?"

"We miscarried last time. It could happen again. Which is why we need to give ourselves *time*."

Fear and anger balled up inside of her. "I am not ready to have this discussion."

"Because you're scared?" he countered softly. "I understand if you are, Angie. I am, too. But we have to talk about it. We can't push it away as if it doesn't exist."

She pinned her gaze on his. "I'm *saying I'm not ready.* That we need to work on *us* before we start talking babies."

"Bene." His eyes glittered in the moonlight. "I am in full agreement on that point. So why don't you come over here? You're much too far away."

Her heart slammed against her ribs. "I don't think so."

"Oh, I think so," he murmured. "The only question is if you are coming over here or I'm coming over there. You make the choice."

Her blood pulsed through her veins in a restless purr. That kiss earlier, his hands on her all evening, had stirred her senses. But she was angry, too—furious about that baby conversation and being treated like a...*vessel* for the Ricci family.

"Time's up." He pushed away from the side of the tub, snared an arm around her waist and pulled her onto his lap, wrapping her legs around his hips.

Her breath caught in her throat, heart slamming against her ribs. "What are you doing?"

"Getting to know each other again. Just like you suggested..." He shot her a look filled with sensual heat, his throaty tone arcing straight between her thighs. "Relax, *mia cara*. I intend only to kiss you. *A lot.*" He lifted a brow. "What do you Americans call it? *Making out? Necking?*"

"Lorenzo," she said faintly, overwhelmed by all that heat and muscle singeing her skin, "stop playing with me."

"I don't think so," he murmured, laughter dancing in his eyes. "Isn't kissing the universal language? Maybe it will work for us, too."

She opened her mouth to tell him she was still angry with him. He lowered his head and caught her lips with his before she could get the words out. She set her palms on his shoulders to reject him, to tell him *absolutely not*. But his soft, seductive kisses seduced, persuaded. He nipped her bottom lip, sucking gently on her top one, sliding under her defenses like warm, sweet honey.

Melting from the inside out, she dug her nails into his muscular, sinewy shoulders. *Hard.*

"What?"

"I'm still mad at you. *You* can't avoid the baby issue by kissing me. I need time, Lorenzo. You have to give me that."

"Okay." He brushed his thumb over the pulse pounding at the base of her neck. "I'll give you time."

She blinked. "You will?"

"Sì."

Not expecting such an easy capitulation, she was momentarily silenced. He tucked a wisp of her hair behind her ear, dark eyes on hers. "What else is going on in that beautiful head of yours? It's like smoke coming out of your ears."

She shook her head.

"Angelina." His low, sensual tone promised retribution if she didn't spill.

"I'm scared," she said finally. "Terrified."

"Of what?"

Of letting herself want him again, *need* him again. Of letting herself feel the things she hadn't let herself feel since she'd left him because she could get hurt, because he would *see* beneath her skin as he always had. Of letting him make her whole again, then shatter her apart, because this time she wasn't sure she'd be able to pick up the pieces.

She closed her eyes. Pulled in a breath. "We were so good together. Then it all fell apart. I'm afraid of letting myself go there again only to have you shut down."

He shook his head. "I am not perfect. I have my moods, you know that. But I promise you it will not be the same. We will talk through our stumbles, work through them together. This is not about what *was*, Angelina, it is about what we are *building* together."

She swallowed past the fear bubbling up inside of her. The trust they'd built over these last emotional weeks together made her think they might be able to do it.

He tilted her chin up with his fingers. "*We* decide where this goes. But you have to commit. You have to trust. You have to believe we can do this."

"I do," she said quietly. "But we need to take it slow."

That wicked gleam in his eyes reappeared. "What do you think I'm doing?"

She didn't protest when he slid his palm to the nape of her neck and brought her back to him, his beautiful mouth claiming hers. Delivered on the leisurely, sensual make-out session he'd promised until her toes curled with pleasure. Full of heat and oh, so much promise, sweetness and play devolved into a deeper, fiery need.

She opened to his demand, his tongue stroking and licking while his hands kept her in place for his delectation. She curled her fingers in his hair, sighed his name and pulled him closer still. It had been too long, far too long since he'd touched her like this. It was like returning to heaven—a most dangerous paradise, she knew, but she couldn't deny she wanted it…wanted to revel in it.

Her husband shifted beneath her, his highly aroused body brushing against her thighs. Shock waves coursed through her nerve endings, lighting her on fire.

He lifted his mouth from hers, a wry smile curving his mouth. "This would be where the make-out session ends and something else entirely begins. Unless," he drawled, "you've changed your mind?"

Heat claimed her cheeks. All it would take was one more kiss, one sign from her she was ready and she could have him. But unleashing that kind of intimacy with her husband would bring all her walls tumbling down—it always had. And she wasn't ready for that. Not yet.

"I can wait," he murmured, tracing a knuckle down her cheek. "But be prepared, Angelina. When this does happen, one tame roll in that bed in there will not be enough."

CHAPTER EIGHT

ANGIE SPENT THE following week immersed in a flurry of activity leading up to Alexander's show. Likely a good thing given the confusing mixture of anticipation and apprehension engulfing her at the evolution of her and Lorenzo's relationship.

Their sizzling encounter in the hot tub had proven she was still as susceptible as ever to his expertly executed seductions, but had done nothing to illustrate they could make their marriage work. *That* they were going to have to prove in the days ahead.

Her husband, true to his word, was giving her the time she'd asked for. Not that he hadn't kept up a slow and steady campaign to put his hands on her whenever he could find an excuse to do so. She'd been so distracted at yesterday's rehearsal thinking about it, Alexander had had to ask her a question three times.

Determined to keep her focus, she'd buried herself in a couple of last-minute fixes to tailor her pieces for a model being substituted into the original lineup, keeping her mind firmly off her husband. Before she knew it, it was 7:00 p.m. on the night of the show, the lights had dimmed in the high-ceilinged Skylight Modern space, one of the premium, architecturally perfect Fashion Week venues, and Alexander's first model had begun her walk down the spotlit runway.

Anticipation built as one model after the next, with

a few supermodels thrown in for good measure, strutted their stuff, showcasing the collection the critics said would catapult Alexander to the top of the design world this season. The buzz and applause was electric as her friend's brilliance shone, his pieces the perfect backdrop for her jewelry.

It seemed like only a few minutes had passed instead of an hour before the show was drawing to an end.

Her blood fizzled in her veins as Astrid Johansson, the world's current *it* girl, stood spotlighted at the end of the runway to wrap the show, Angie's ruby necklace glittering against her alabaster skin. A shiver chased up her spine. It was perfect, a marriage made in heaven the way the necklace framed the square neckline of the sleek, avant-garde dress.

Lorenzo leaned down from his position beside her in the front row, bringing his mouth to her ear. "The highest paid model in the world wearing your jewelry. How does it feel?"

"Amazing." And her husband looked equally stunning in a charcoal-gray Faggini suit, his swarthy coloring set off perfectly by the light blue shirt he wore beneath it. She'd seen more than one of the models eye him as they'd walked by, eating him up with their confident gazes.

Astrid made her final pass down the runway, returning hand in hand with Alexander as the music died away and the lights came up, her fellow models falling into place behind them. Cheers and applause greeted the designer, who took it all in with a big smile on his expressive face.

She was shocked when he beckoned to her, motioning for her to join him. Oh, no, she couldn't.

Lorenzo gave her a gentle shove. "*Go.* Have your moment."

She found herself moving forward on legs that felt like jelly. Taking Alexander's hand, she followed him into the spotlight. The designer turned to her, gave a little bow and clapped his hands. Her chest swelled with happiness, a hot warmth stinging the backs of her eyes as the audience applauded. Her jewelry had been her light in the darkness when everything else had been falling apart. She would never be able to express what it meant to her. She only knew in that moment, it felt as if a piece of her was sliding into place.

She gave Alexander a kiss on the cheek, stood back and returned the applause. The lights went down. Alexander pulled her backstage for interviews with the media while Lorenzo and his mother went to enjoy a cocktail. She had expected only a smattering of media would be interested in speaking to her in the shadow of Alexander's presence. She was shocked when a handful of them chose to interview her, too.

She did a couple of broadcast interviews for television, then something with a leading newspaper's style section. Surprisingly, the media's focus remained mostly on her jewelry rather than on her lineage, the critics giving her collection an enthusiastic thumbs-up.

She was pretty much floating on air by the time Alexander hooked an arm through hers, propelled her into the crowd at the after-party and introduced her to the designers, fashion editors, models and actors starring in his next spring ad campaign, forging so many valuable connections it made her head spin.

An impenetrable glow filled her. Her career was skyrocketing, her marriage on the mend. It felt as if anything was possible.

Lorenzo watched his wife shine, her bubbly, animated demeanor taking him back to that night in Nassau when she'd transfixed him like the brightest star in the sky. The haunting, mysterious Northern Lights had had nothing on his wife that night as she'd flashed those baby blues at him, silky long lashes brushing her cheeks in a coquettish look she hadn't quite mastered, and asked him if he was going to brood all night or dance with her instead.

But even then, he realized, underneath all that sultry confidence and gutsy bravado, there had been a vulnerability to the woman in his arms, a sadness he hadn't quite been able to put a finger on—a knowledge beyond her years.

He had connected to that, even if he hadn't known it at the time. They had both been looking to escape their pain that night, he from his memories, Angelina from the inexplicably complex relationships that had formed her world. What they had found had been so powerful that for a while they had.

She caught him staring. Smiled. It was a blindingly bright smile that did something crazy to his heart. He had denied her this, the chance to be this shining light. To prove she was more than the sum of her parts. It was a mistake he refused to let haunt him.

He saw her say something to Alexander, nod at the woman they were speaking to and slip away, her long strides eating up the distance between them.

"Did your mother leave?"

"Yes." He swiped two glasses of champagne off a tray and handed her one. "She said to say thank you. To tell you your collection was impressive. And, yes," he added, a wry smile twisting his mouth, "she meant it."

Angie blinked. "Well, that's...*nice*. Did she have a good time?"

"She was in her element. Who knows," he murmured, lifting a brow, "there might be hope for the two of you yet."

"Don't get too hopeful."

He brushed a thumb across the delicate line of her jaw. "Positivity, *cara*. That's what we need here."

Her lashes lowered. "We should circulate if you don't mind."

He nodded. Kept a possessive hand at the small of her back as they made a couple of passes of the room. By the time the lights came down and the apparently wildly popular band Lorenzo had never heard of took the stage, he could feel his wife's energy level fading, her reservoir of small talk emptied out.

Tugging her into one of the intimate lounge areas, he plucked the wineglass out of her hand and pulled her onto his lap.

"Lorenzo," she murmured, "we are in public."

"At a party in full gear where no one is paying any attention to us." Setting a palm on her thigh, he pulled her closer, absorbing the tantalizing feel of her lush curves plastered against him. She looked insanely beautiful in Alexander's black dress with no back to it. Had turned every male head in the room. The need to have his hands on her was like a fire in his blood.

Bending his head, he traced the shell of her ear with his lips in a feather-light caress. His wife shivered. He moved lower, capturing her lobe between his teeth, scoring it lightly. "You are lit up tonight, *mia cara*. This is the woman I *appreciate*. The woman I was looking for."

She pulled back, eyes on his. "I needed this. For you to understand how important my work is to me."

"I do now." His voice was sandpaper-rough. "I am listening now, Angelina. Better late than never."

Needing to protect, to possess her in a way he couldn't even begin to articulate, he cupped the back of her head and kissed her. Passionate, infinite, it was a connection between them on an entirely different level than before, as if they were finally beginning to understand each other.

She slid her palm to his nape and kissed him back, the kiss turning hot and fiery. *Needy.* He moved his hand higher on her thigh, fingers tightening around the sleek, satiny skin he discovered. A primal heat consumed him, his body pulsing to life beneath her bottom. She shifted against him, a low moan leaving her throat.

"I want inside you," he whispered. "Inside this sweet, hot body of yours. Until you feel nothing but me, *cara*."

Blood roared in Angie's head. Light exploded in her eyes. She blinked against the sudden onslaught. It took her several seconds to realize it was a photographer's flash.

Lorenzo brushed a knuckle against her cheek, a wry twist to his mouth. "That must be our cue to leave."

Her legs felt like spaghetti as he set her on her feet. He kept a firm hand on her waist as he guided her through the thick crowd, stopping to say good-night to Alexander before they exited into the cool night air.

Wrapped in a sensual haze, she curled her arms around herself as Lorenzo retrieved the car. The sports car was deposited purring at the sidewalk moments later. Lorenzo tucked her into the passenger seat, then took the wheel to drive them home.

Her pulse hummed, her blood fizzled amidst the cacophony of sirens and honking horns that was New York, all of it blanking in her head as her senses focused on the man beside her. His quiet intensity as he controlled the powerful car and the hand he kept on her bare thigh were all she could register.

When this does happen, one tame roll in that bed will not be enough.

Her pulse jolted faster, her cheeks heated with anticipation. Her head might be wary about them, but her body was not. It wanted to experience the hunger he had promised. To feel alive again in the way only Lorenzo could make her feel.

Finally they were home. Parking the car in the garage,

he helped her out, ushered her into the lift that arrived in a whir of expensive machinery. Up they went to the penthouse, where she threw her purse on a chair, legs shaking. Walking to the bank of windows that looked out on the roughly drawn skyline of Manhattan, she took a deep breath, attempted to center herself.

The soft thud of her husband's jacket hitting the chair reverberated through the room. The tread of his footsteps across the hardwood floor sent a quiver up her spine.

"You are so damn beautiful," he murmured, setting his hands on her hips. "You make my heart stop in my chest."

Her breath caught in her lungs. Frozen, paralyzed, she couldn't move, her fears, her anticipation, blanketing her in a cloud of emotion. But this wasn't about the past, she reminded herself, it was about the future. And right now, it felt like they had one. A bright, shining light she was terrified to touch.

She did it anyway. Twisting around in his arms, she took in the dark, sometimes brooding man who'd stolen her heart once and threatened to do it again. His eyes tracked her, hot and focused. Her stomach contracted. Lifting her hand, she traced the sexy stubble shadowing his jaw. It was too tempting not to touch. She pressed a kiss to the abrasive canvas, sliding over the hard line of his jaw, *knowing* him again.

He let her play, drink her fill. Then impatience won out as he slid his fingers into her hair, tilted her head back and closed his mouth over hers. Greedy, laced with sensual purpose, his carnal kiss telegraphed his intent to know all of *her* tonight. To erase the pain.

She curled her fingers into the thick muscles of his shoulders, opened to his stark demand. The slow, erotic strokes of his tongue against hers coiled the muscles in her abdomen tight, his dark, sensual taste filling her senses, seducing her with its rich male flavor.

Fingers digging into his shoulders, she hung on tight. Lorenzo slipped a hand lower to her bottom, shaping her against him. The hard thrust of his desire, a thick, pulsing heat beneath his trousers, pulled a low sound from the back of her throat. She pressed closer, drunk on the feel of him. He rocked against her, slid his steely heat against her most sensitive flesh, scoring her through the thin material of her dress. "Feel how much I want you," he murmured against her mouth. "You make me crazy, Angelina."

A shudder went through her, her knees nearly buckling beneath her. He backed her up against the windowsill, kneed her legs apart so he could stand between them. Supported by the wall, she welcomed the hot press of his flesh. Allowed him to tease her, play with her until she thought she might go up in flames.

Her hands moved to his belt, greedy, desperate for him. Yanking the leather free of the buckle, she undid it, unbuttoned his trousers and slid down the zipper. Pushing her hands inside his pants, she cupped the thick length of him in her palms.

Lorenzo cursed low and hard. Removed her hands from him. "*Mi bellissima.* You need warming up or I will hurt you."

"No," she said, trying to free her hands. "I need you inside me."

"*Sì.*" Hard, uncompromising. He captured her hands, placed them palms-down on the sill. "Keep them there."

Eyes on hers, he sank his fingers into the knot of his tie, pulled it loose and stripped it off. Tossing it on the floor, he reached for the top buttons of his shirt and pulled them free. Her heart thrummed the frantic beat of a bird trapped in a cage as he dropped to his knees in front of her.

Reaching for her foot, he worked the delicate clasp of her shoe open, slid her foot out and tossed the stiletto aside. He did the same with the other. Setting his hands on her ankles, he trailed them up her calves to her knees. Pushed them apart with a deliberate, firm motion that had her sucking in a breath. "Lorenzo," she breathed, feeling far too exposed.

He looked up at her, an implacable expression in his dark eyes. "Stay still."

Oh, dear Lord. A shudder went through her. He pressed a kiss to the inside of both her knees, worked his way up the sensitive flesh of her inner thighs, caressing her with his mouth, the scrape of his teeth. She bit her lip, willing him on.

She was aching, pulsing for him by the time he got to where she wanted him. Ready to beg. Mouth dry, she watched as he pushed up her dress and tucked it beneath her hip, baring her lacy, black panties. A wisp of nothing—meant to seduce.

Hand on her thigh, he considered her. *Bold. Focused.* "You wore these for me?"

"Yes."

A smile tugged at his mouth. "I thought you said you weren't going to wear lingerie for me."

"I said I wouldn't greet you at the door wearing it."

A play of laughter in those dark eyes. "Appreciate the distinction."

Shifting his attention back to the job at hand, he lowered his head and caressed her through the silk with one long stroke of his tongue. Her knees buckled. Sinking back on her palms, she braced herself against the wood. Closed her eyes as he stroked her again and again, desensitizing her, she knew, for the pleasure he would give her.

When she stopped bucking under his tongue, he pressed a kiss to her trembling abdomen, slid his fingers under the edges of the silk and stripped the panties from her. Moving back between her thighs, he spread her wide.

Ran his thumb through her cleft. Blood surged from her fingertips to her toes as he examined her flesh.

"Already wet for me, *cara*." He looked up, eyes blazing. "Maybe I should stop."

She reached for him. Received a reproachful look as he put her palms back on the wood. "Move them again and I will."

She closed her eyes. Felt the heat of his breath before his tongue found the hard nub at the center of her, nudging it with sensual precision. Back and forth, up and down. When her legs started to shake, her voice a low plea, he licked her slowly, deliberately, talking to her as he did it, telling her the taste of her made him hard. Hot.

Insane for him, at the very edge, she curled her fingers into the wood. He circled her with his finger. Delved inside of her. Her muscles clenched around him, drawing him in. Slowly, relentlessly, he moved his finger in and out of her, another kind of pleasure stirring to life that was deeper. More intense.

"Look at me." His husky command brought her eyes fluttering open. Seeing him between her spread legs, pleasuring her, sent her right to the edge. "You want it like this? Or with me inside your beautiful body?"

She swallowed past the need constricting her throat, the raging hunger he inspired in her. "With you," she rasped, keeping her hands on the wood. "I want it to be with you."

Lorenzo removed his hands from his wife, swung her up in his arms and carried her into the bedroom, working to blank his mind from the emotion pouring through it. But his wife had always cast a spell over him and tonight was no exception, despite his attempts to tell himself going there was unwise.

He set her down near the bed and moved behind her to lower the zipper of her dress. Pushing it off her shoulders, Alexander's creation hit the wood floor in a swish of feather-light material.

Hands on her shoulders, he turned her around. Drank in his wife's mouthwatering curves. Lushly feminine in all the right places, her breasts were more than a handful, perfectly shaped and high, her delectable hips flaring above long, fantastic legs he wanted wrapped around him so badly, it was all he could do to keep this the leisurely seduction he'd planned.

Stripping off his shirt and pants, his gaze never left her. Kicking his clothes aside, he snaked an arm around her waist, pulled her to him and plastered her curves against the length of his body. Fingers curving around her jaw, he dropped a lingering kiss on her mouth. Shared with her the essence of their mutual passion until the raw, unvarnished truth of their connection swelled him so hard he thought he might break in two.

This time when she reached for him, her touch like silk around his throbbing length, he arched into it, desperate for more.

"That's it." His breath was hot against her ear. "I've missed your hands on me, *mia cara*. I *crave* them."

His skin began to burn, *tremble*, her exploration of his body firing his blood. He closed his eyes, primal sounds leaving the back of his throat as she stroked him to the edge.

When he could take it no longer, he pushed her hands away, sank his palms into her hips and lifted her onto the bed. The moonlight spilling in the French doors edged across her face, illuminating the beautiful vulnerability he was starting to believe was the truth of her.

He slid his hands around her back, released the catch of her bra and threw it to the floor. Her full, swollen breasts were a temptation he couldn't resist. A shudder raked through her as he swept his thumbs across the tips.

"Like ripe, delectable fruit," he murmured, lowering his head to her. He took a nipple in his mouth and sucked hard. She gasped, threw back her head and pushed her flesh farther into his mouth. He devoured her, satisfied his hunger. Played her other nipple between his thumb and forefinger while he brought the hard bud to a swollen erectness with his lips and teeth.

She moaned as he lavished the same attention on her other breast, digging her fingers in his hair. *"Please."*

Her broken plea contracted his insides. He joined her on the bed, shackled his fingers around her ankles and bent them back so she was open to him. Moving between her thighs, he palmed his length, brought himself to her slick entrance and rocked against her so just the tip pushed inside.

"You want me, *cara*?"

She nodded, her big blue eyes glued to his.

"Tell me how much."

"All of you," she gasped. "I want all of you."

Bracing a palm on the bed, he tipped his hips forward and filled her with another inch. "Lorenzo," she breathed, arching up to meet him, "I need you."

A primal satisfaction claimed him. All of those nights since she'd left when no one else would do, when her memory had made a mockery of his libido, were vindicated as she lay begging beneath him, beautiful and oh, so vulnerable. Exactly as he'd wanted her. And yet, as he rocked forward again, her body clenching around him like a hot, silken glove, he would have been delusional to deny he was as affected as she was.

He leaned forward, slicking his tongue across her bottom lip in an erotic caress that made her clench tighter around him. "There is no going back," he rasped, "only forward. Tell me you understand that."

"Yes." She arched her hips, eyes glazed. *"More."*

He buried himself inside her with a smooth, powerful stroke. Her gaze met his in an electric, soul-destroying connection. "You feel like heaven, *cara*. Perfection."

Her slick, aroused body absorbed him, stretched to accommodate his length and girth. He gritted his teeth, forced himself to hang on. Fine tremors snaked through her body, her inner muscles rippling around him. He moved inside her then with hard, powerful drives designed to drive her to orgasm. He lacked his usual finesse, but was beyond caring. Her fingers clutched his hips as his big body rode hers, claimed her, found that spot deep inside her that made her moan with pleasure.

She arched into it, wanting everything he had to give. He braced himself on one arm, slipped the other hand between her legs and found the bundle of nerves at her center. "I can feel you clenching around me," he murmured, stroking his thumb teasingly over her clitoris. "Like that," he whispered when she jerked beneath his touch. "And that," he said as another shiver raked through her. "Come for me, *cara*."

His next firm caress set her off. Her husky groan, the way she gloved him in a tight squeeze, pushed him into a violent, body-shaking release. Relinquishing control, he tightened his fingers around her hips, drove into her and made her come apart a second time.

Lorenzo was awake long after his wife fell asleep in his arms. Soft and warm, her body curved against his, their fit together was so perfect it was as if she'd been made to fill in his missing spaces. To complete the parts of him that had been empty so long he'd had no idea they still existed.

A knot fisting his stomach, he disentangled himself from his wife and lay staring at the sky through the window overhead. He'd crossed a line tonight—allowing this thing between him and Angelina to become emotional when he'd promised himself he wouldn't. It had been that kind of a night, to be sure, but he knew if he wasn't careful, he'd start walking down a path he could never go and it would be Angelina who got hurt, not him.

He'd been falling in love with his wife when she'd left, his instincts warning him if he let himself, he would have fallen harder for Angelina than he had ever fallen for Lucia. His love for Lucia had been a pure, untainted first love that lacked the passion and emotion he and Angelina had shared. The depth of his feelings for Angelina, the betrayal those feelings had seemed to Lucia, the youth and unhappiness Angelina had displayed that had made her an unsure bet, had made him cauterize his feelings, refuse to acknowledge them.

And his instincts had been dead-on, he thought, staring up at the cloudy night sky. Angelina had walked out as soon as the going had gotten tough, had made a mockery of the vows they'd made. And that was why certain lines could never be crossed.

If he was smart, he would follow his original plan. Burn out the attraction between him and his wife until it no longer held any power over him.

Now that he had her back in his bed, he intended to do exactly that.

CHAPTER NINE

"How about you come to Mallorca in a couple of weeks? I have to be at our flagship property for a few days. You can meet with the management team and we can go through the last few points face-to-face."

Lorenzo blew out a breath. He'd spent two weeks anticipating Marc Bavaro's return from South America and now he wanted him to gallivant off to *Spain*, Belmont's global headquarters, to make this deal happen? He ran a global corporation, for God's sake, three times the size of Bavaro's. How the hell did he have time for that?

"As much as I'd love to," he said in an even tone, "my schedule is insane. We can't do it before then?"

"I'm headed to London as we speak. I'm not back to New York until mid-October."

Too late, with the board meeting looming. "I'll see what I can do," Lorenzo conceded. "How long are you thinking?"

"Come for a couple of days. We can have dinner with my brother, Diego, the night you arrive, then we'll do the management meeting the next morning. Oh—" the CEO's voice dropped to an intimate purr "—and bring your beautiful wife…she can keep Penny company."

He wasn't sure Bavaro lusting after Angelina was going to go over so well in his current mood. "Angie is in her busy period. I'll have to check her schedule."

"Let me know." The roar of a jet engine fired in the background. "I should go."

He cut off the call. Turned the air blue. Gillian popped her head in his office and asked if he needed help. He told her to clear his schedule for the time in Mallorca, then turned his thoughts to his wife. How to get her to agree to go to Spain was the challenge. She was so busy with commissions after Faggini's show she'd even hired a couple of part-time designers to help with the rush. She would balk at a trip, no doubt about it.

He sat back in his chair and contemplated a solution. Things had been better than good between them. They were learning to compromise, to manage their expectations of each other. They were communicating both in bed and out of it. His marriage was *working*. The last thing he needed was to rock the boat.

But this, he thought, tapping his fingers on the desk, was necessary.

A plan came to him. It was a good one. Satisfied, he picked up the phone.

"I have a proposal for you."

Angelina cradled her mobile against her ear as she put down her pliers, the intimate, seductive edge to her husband's voice unleashing a wave of heat beneath her skin. The huskiness, she knew, came from the inhuman working hours he was keeping.

"If it involves sleep for you, I'm all for it," she said lightly. "What time were you up this morning?"

"Five. And, yes, it involves sleep for both of us," he replied in a throaty tone that sent goose bumps to her heated skin. "Well," he amended, "it involves a bed and *us*. Sleep not so much."

Her heart beat a jagged rhythm. They hadn't been able to get enough of each other since Alexander's party, thus contributing to *her* sleeping deficit. Not that she was complaining. She was so happy she was afraid to blink, because history had taught her something *would* implode in her face if she did.

But she wasn't *thinking* that way, she reminded herself. "What are you proposing?"

"The only way I can pin Marc Bavaro down is to hook up with him at his property in Mallorca in a couple of weeks' time. Penny's going. He wants you to come, too."

She pressed a palm to her temple. "Lorenzo… I have so much work to do before Christmas."

"That's part of my proposal. You come with me to Spain and I will absolve you of any social obligations until the hotel opening in October."

"What are you going to do? Go to them alone?"

"*Sì.*"

She didn't like the idea of her gorgeous husband attending all those events alone the way women fell all over him. Leaving the country for a week was also an unwise idea given the work in front of her.

But how could she say no after everything Lorenzo had done for her? He had been her rock as she'd navigated her emotional visits with her mother, pushed her to hire a couple of assistants to keep her sanity with all the work pouring in. And when she was exhausted from managing them, he deposited her bodily into bed when she no longer recognized her limits. She wasn't sure what she would have done without him.

"I will take you to Portofino for a couple of days afterward." Her husband's voice lowered to a sexy rasp. "We can do walks through the village. I'll take you to that seafood restaurant you love…"

Her heart turned over. By far her most magical memories with Lorenzo were from that heavenly week they'd spent together in the tiny fishing village on the Italian Riviera on their honeymoon, the view from the Riccis' villa perched in the hills spectacularly romantic. It had been impossibly perfect with their strolls through the cobble-stone streets, leisurely, seaside dinners and long, unin-hibited nights of lovemaking in which her husband had taught her wicked things, *delicious* things her innocent mind could only have dreamed of.

Going back would be like walking into a piece of the past she wasn't sure she was ready for, but perhaps that was exactly what she needed to do.

"Well?" her husband prompted. "Say yes. It will be good for us, *cara.*"

She blew out a breath. "Okay. But I can't be gone longer than a week. And I'm holding you to your promise."

"Bene." Satisfaction laced his tone. "I'll get Gillian to work with you on the details. *Grazie mille, bella.* I should go."

She hung up. Stared at all the pieces on her desk that needed to be finished. Thought of the massive influx of orders to be filled. She was a tiny operation—she wasn't built for this.

Panic clawed at her insides. She couldn't afford to mess up this chance she'd been given. The interest in her work following Alexander's show was a once-in-a-lifetime op-portunity to make her name. But neither was she prepared to mess up her marriage.

She could do this. She just needed to lean on the de-signers she'd hired and make a plan.

Angie worked like a demon over the next two weeks, mak-ing a good dent in the list of commissions. Reserving the trickier pieces for when she got back, she handed the rest of the work over to her assistants and stepped on the jet for the trip to Mallorca with Lorenzo.

Shocked at how exhausted she was, she put the reclin-ing seat back as soon as dinner had been served and slept while her machine of a husband worked.

When she woke, it was to the darkest of ebony eyes and a very seductive kiss from her husband. "Wake up, sleeping beauty. We're about to land."

She blinked. "We *aren't*."

"We are. A half hour tops. Go freshen up so you can have some breakfast before we land."

She slid out of her seat and headed for the bedroom, where she changed her top, so she wouldn't look so wrinkled when they met the driver, and freshened her hair and makeup. Breakfast, however, wasn't to be. Her stomach still felt like it was 2:00 a.m. Coffee and orange juice would have to suffice.

The driver took them up into the lush green mountains of Mallorca's peaceful northwest coast to the Belmont Mallorca, considered to be one of the world's finest hotels. Nestled into a valley surrounded by soaring peaks, its two stone manor houses offered a spectacular view of a medieval village.

Still inordinately tired, she took a nap in the afternoon in their beautiful airy suite to arm her for a late dinner while Lorenzo spent the afternoon with Marc. But even after she woke and pulled herself out of the white-silk-draped canopy bed and showered, her limbs still felt as if they were weighted with lead.

She hadn't felt this inexplicably tired since the first trimester of her pregnancy, she mused as she stood at the wardrobe selecting a dress to wear for dinner. Ice slid through her veins... *No. There was no way.* She couldn't be. She was on the pill. She had been so careful.

Rationality, however, did not stop her from flying into the bedroom to find her purse, where she retrieved her birth control pills and found they were all accounted for. Slackening with relief, she saw the antibiotics she'd been taking following a dental procedure. Remembering she hadn't taken one today, she popped one into her mouth, swallowed it with a gulp of water, then padded back to the wardrobe to choose her dress.

A cream-colored jersey sheath called to her. She pulled it off the hanger, then froze, her stomach bottoming out. *Antibiotics and birth control pills...* Hadn't she heard somewhere...

Lorenzo watched Angelina in the mirror as he did up his shirt. Stunning in a knee-length ivory dress with a floral scarf draped around her neck, she was amazing to look at as always, but it was the preoccupied air about her that held his attention. He hadn't seen it in weeks.

"You okay?"

She nodded. "Just tired. Sorry, I'm quiet I know."

He did up the last button of his shirt and tucked it into his pants. "You don't ever have to be sorry about being quiet. I just want to make sure you're okay."

"I'm fine." She turned back to the mirror and spritzed some perfume behind her ears.

"Is it work?"

She shook her head. "It's fine. I'll catch up when I get back."

"Then what is it?"

She spun around, a frown creasing her brow. "You don't have to treat me with kid gloves, Lorenzo. I'm *fine*."

He lifted a brow. She expelled a breath. "I am a little stressed about work. And the time change kills me."

He crossed over to her. "Try and put it out of your head and enjoy the week," he murmured, tracing a thumb over her cheek. "It's only a few days. You deserve a break."

She nodded.

"There is no goal tonight, *amore mio*. Unless you count paying attention to me," he added huskily, thumb sweeping over the lush fullness of her lips. "That is most definitely on the agenda."

Color stained her cheeks. He lowered his head and pressed his lips to her temple, breathing in the sexy, Oriental fragrance of her, her perfume the perfect match for his strong, sensual wife. They were intoxicating, both the scent and her.

For a moment, he just held her, drank her in. Knew, in that moment, he felt more for her than he would ever admit. More than he should.

Her head dropped against his chest. "We should go," she said quietly, but she didn't move.

His mouth curved. Sliding his fingers through hers, he moved his lips to her ear. "Hold that thought."

Dinner with the Bavaro brothers took place in the Belmont's famed terrace restaurant, with its spectacular view of the mountains, the live piano music lending a distinctly sophisticated atmosphere to the setting. Marc's brother, Diego, the Belmont's other controlling shareholder, joined them for dinner along with his wife, Ariana. With Penny to round out the table of six, it was an entertaining and lively dinner.

Diego, who had been a bit of a dark horse during the negotiations, content to let Marc take the lead, could have been a double for his brother with his swarthy, dark Mediterranean looks and lean build. But that was where the similarities ended. Whereas Marc was cagey, careful in what he revealed, Diego was an extrovert who liked to hear the sound of his own voice.

If Lorenzo got the younger Bavaro brother talking, he might make some progress. He waited until the fine Spanish wine had had a chance to mellow all of them, and an amiable, content atmosphere settled over the table. Sitting back in his chair, wineglass balanced on his thigh, he eyed Diego.

"I'm sensing some hesitation on your part. If the regulatory issues aren't going to be a problem in most jurisdictions, perhaps you can tell me where the pause is coming from?"

Diego took a sip of his wine and set down the glass. "My father is concerned the Belmont legacy will cease to exist with the sale. That you will absorb what you desire of our marquee locations to fill the empty dots on the map, then dispose of the rest."

A warning pulse rocketed through him. That was exactly what he intended to do—certainly the Bavaros had been smart enough to figure that out?

"We'll have to see what our assessment says," he said coolly. "But since I am offering to pay you a fortune for this chain, more than half again what it's worth, I would think it would keep you from lying awake at night worrying about it."

"It's not always about money," Diego responded. "It's about family pride. National pride. Spaniards look up to Belmont as a symbol of international success. It is bad enough to have it eaten up by a foreign entity, but to have its name extinguished along with it? It negates a hundred-year-old legend."

"It's always about the money," Lorenzo rejected. "Nothing lasts forever. You wait a few more years and you'll get half what I'm offering."

"Perhaps." Diego lifted a shoulder. "You want to make my father happy? Put a clause in the deal that you will keep the name."

Heat surged through him. He kept the fury off his face. *Just.* "What sense would that make?" he countered. "This deal will make Ricci the number one luxury hotel chain in the world. To split the brands would be counterproductive."

Silence fell over the table. Lorenzo eyed the younger

Bavaro brother. "May I ask why this is coming up at the eleventh hour?"

"My father's feelings have grown stronger on the issue." Diego pursed his lips. "I'm not saying it's a deal breaker. I'm saying it's a major twist in the road."

Lorenzo's brain buzzed. His own father would do the same, he knew—would refuse to see his legacy destroyed. He couldn't necessarily blame the Bavaros. What infuriated him was that this hadn't come up earlier. It changed the entire landscape of the deal.

"This acquisition needs to happen," Lorenzo said evenly. "If this is the issue, you need to get your father onside. There will be no postsale conditions attached to it. It is what it is."

Diego's eyes flashed. "It was never our intention to sell, as you know."

That was when Lorenzo knew he had a big, big problem on his hands.

Angie paced the suite while she waited for her husband, who was having an after-dinner cognac with the Bavaro brothers. After the tension-filled end to the meal, she was glad to have escaped, but now she had a much bigger issue on her hands than her combustible spouse.

Penny had driven her to the local pharmacy on the pretext of finding some allergy pills. She'd shoved two pregnancy tests on the counter instead, two *positive* pregnancy tests that now lay in the bathroom garbage can, irrefutable evidence that fate had once again taken a hold of her life in the most indelible way.

How could this possibly have happened? What were the odds? What was she going to do?

Unable to breathe, she crossed to the windows and stood looking out at the dark mass of the mountains. She knew this baby was a gift. Even as sure as she'd been at twenty-two she hadn't been ready to have a child, as terrified as she'd been she wouldn't be a good mother given her own history, she'd developed a bond with her unborn child, a wonder at the life she and Lorenzo had created together.

She felt the same way now. But she was also scared. *Terrified.* The timing was all wrong. There was no way she could run her business, be a mother and juggle her and Lorenzo's busy social schedule all at the same time. And then there was the thought of losing another baby that sent panic skittering through her bones.

It was too soon. *Too much.*

Anxiety clawed at her throat, wanting, needing to escape. The click of the suite door brought her spinning around. The look on her husband's face kept all the anxiety buried inside.

"What happened?"

He walked to the bar, threw ice in a glass and poured himself a drink. "Preserving the Belmont name is going to be an issue."

"You don't think they'll give on it?"

He took a long gulp of the Scotch. Leaned back against the bar. "I don't know."

"Maybe you need to talk to the father? He seems to be the roadblock."

"I'd have to go over Marc and Diego's heads. It would be a last resort."

She frowned. "They didn't mention *any* of this before? Surely they knew it might be an issue?"

"I'm fairly sure I would remember if they had."

The biting sarcasm in his voice straightened her spine. She absorbed the incendiary glow in his eyes, the flammable edge to him she remembered so well from the past. *This* was the old Lorenzo—the one who could transform into a remote stranger in the blink of an eye, focused only on the end goal and to hell with anyone in his path.

Tension knotted her insides, the need to know this wasn't devolving into the old them burning a hole in her insides. Not now, not with the news she was holding inside.

She wrapped her arms around herself, fingernails digging into the soft flesh of her upper arms. "It was a rhetorical question," she said quietly. "I know this deal is important to you, Lorenzo, but it either works or it doesn't. You need to be able to find a way to walk away from these things and not let them get to you like this. *Consume* you."

He gave her a scathing look. "It's a fifteen-billion-dollar deal, Angelina. Ricci's reputation rides on it."

"And yours," she said quietly. "Isn't that the real issue here? You losing face? You becoming anything less than the unbeatable Lorenzo Ricci, king of the blockbuster deal?"

"This is not about me," he growled, voice sharp as a blade. "It's about my family's reputation. Rumors about the deal are running rampant…investors are getting antsy. It is my responsibility to close this acquisition."

"And if you don't?" She shook her head. "One of these days you *will* lose. You are only human. Then what? Would it be the end of the world? You have fifty of these deals you *have* landed, Lorenzo. Isn't that enough to command the confidence of your investors?"

His jaw turned to stone. "You have no idea what you're talking about."

"Maybe not," she agreed. "But I do know how I feel. You like this—I've seen it before. *This* always marks the beginning of one of your binges—it scares me where it will end."

"I'm good," he said harshly. "*We* are good. Stop trying to make problems where there aren't any."

Was she? The jet lag was killing her, her head too achy and full, her emotions all over the place. But now was not the time to tell Lorenzo about their baby. To make him understand why getting this right was so important to her.

"You wanted us to be an open book," she said, lifting her gaze to his. "Here I am, telling you how I feel."

He prowled over to her and pressed a hard kiss to her lips. "And I'm telling you, you don't need to worry. We are fine. I just need a few minutes to take the edge off."

She sank her teeth into her lower lip. Nodded. He ran a finger down her cheek, his eyes softening. "You're exhausted. You need rest. Go to bed. I'll join you in a few minutes."

"You should come, too. You didn't sleep at all last night."

He nodded, but it was an absentminded nod that told her he wouldn't be coming for a while. She went to bed, but it was hard to sleep, empty in the beautiful bed without him, the intimacy that had wrapped itself around them the past few weeks missing, leaving her chilled and scared to the bone about what lay ahead.

Lorenzo went to bed at two. Extinguishing the lights, he slid into bed with his sleeping wife, no closer to a solution to his problem than he had been two hours before. The urge to wake his wife, to bury his agitation in her beautiful, irresistible body, was a powerful force. But she was so peaceful, so deeply asleep, he couldn't do it.

He thought about how quiet she'd been earlier, his instincts telling him something was still off. He was so scared of missing something again, of not *seeing* what he should see.

Inhaling her scent, he slipped an arm around her waist and pulled her against him, her back nestled to his chest. She murmured something in her sleep and cuddled closer.

A smile on his lips, he pressed his mouth to the sweet curve of her neck. To the silky soft skin of her cheek. The salt that flavored his lips caught him off guard. Levering himself up on his elbow, he studied her beautiful face in the moonlight. She had been crying.

His fingers curled, the urge to shake her awake and make her tell him what was wrong a furious current that sizzled his blood. They had promised to be open books with each other and still she was keeping things from him.

He forced himself to resist waking her, drawing her back against his side. Tomorrow in Portofino would be soon enough to discover what was eating his wife.

CHAPTER TEN

PORTOFINO WAS AS lovely and picturesque as Angie remembered, with its narrow, cobblestone streets, pastel-hued houses dotting the Italian Riviera and bustling shops, restaurants and luxury hotels lining its half-moon-shaped harbor.

Lorenzo had taken her to their favorite seaside restaurant following his meetings in Mallorca and their short plane ride over from Spain. He had come down from his volatile mood of the night before, his attention focused solely on her. Too much so, she thought nervously, fidgeting with her water glass as he slid her another of those long looks he'd been giving her. The secret she carried was burning a hole inside of her.

She had been waiting for the right time to tell him her news, but it just hadn't seemed to come. Lorenzo had been working the entire plane ride and something about "Could you pass me the tartar sauce, and, oh, by the way, I'm pregnant" wasn't working for her.

Her stomach did a slow curl. So here she was, making every attempt to look like she was enjoying herself and hoping her husband bought the performance.

Lorenzo snapped the spirit menu closed and handed it to the hovering waiter. "I think we'll take the check," he said in Italian.

Angie's heart skipped a beat. "I thought you said you wanted a brandy."

"I'll make an espresso at home."

The deliberate look on his face made her heart beat faster. She had the feeling he hadn't bought her act for a minute. Blood throbbed at her temples as he settled the bill, wrapped his fingers firmly around hers and they walked up the hill toward the villa.

Embraced by fuchsia-and-coral-colored bougainvillea that climbed its whitewashed walls, Octavia's retreat from her busy city life was paradise personified. Although, Angelina allowed, as Lorenzo slid the key in the door and ushered her in, her mother-in-law's description of it as her "simple abode" hardly seemed apt. The dark-wood, sleek little villa with its cheery, colorful accents that matched its vibrant surroundings, was hardly *simple*.

She walked out onto the terrace while her husband made an espresso. Hands resting on the railing, she drank in the spectacular view as a breeze lifted her hair in a gentle caress. *Paradise.* If only she could just get the damn words out.

Lorenzo returned, settled himself into one of the comfortable chairs arranged for an optimum view of the sea and deposited the coffee cup in his hand on the table. Her heart lurched in her chest at the stare he leveled at her. "You going to tell me what's wrong?"

His neutral tone did nothing to lessen the intensity of his expression. Heat stained her cheeks.

"Lorenzo—"

"*Dannazione*, Angelina." His fury broke through his icy control. "How many times do we have to have this discussion? I can't help you, *we* can't do this, unless you talk to me. I have spent the entire dinner waiting for you to tell me whatever it is that's eating you. Do you think I can't read you well enough to know that something is?"

Her tongue cleaved to the roof of her mouth. "You

weren't in the right state of mind last night and it wasn't a discussion for a restaurant."

"How about before dinner in the very *private* suite at the Belmont?" Fire flared in his eyes. "I asked you if something was wrong. You said no. Then I come to bed only to discover you've been crying."

She blinked. "How do you know?"

"I checked on you when I came to bed. You had tearstains on your face."

Oh. She wrapped her arms around herself. Took a deep breath. "I couldn't understand why I was so tired yesterday. Jet lag always gets me, yes, but I hadn't felt like that since my pregnancy. I went to check I'd taken my pills after my nap and found the antibiotics I've been on in my purse. It made me put two and two together."

His face went utterly still. "To equal what?"

"Antibiotics can interfere with birth control," she said quietly. "I'm pregnant, Lorenzo."

A behavioral psychologist could have scoured his face and found nothing it was so blank. It was in his eyes that she saw his reaction—deep, dark, raw emotion that made the knots inside her tie themselves tighter.

"How do you know?"

"Penny drove me to the pharmacy."

He was silent for so long she couldn't stand it. "What are you thinking?"

"I'm trying to absorb it," he said huskily. "In my mind, we were waiting."

Not so much.

"You're scared?"

She nodded. Her chin wobbled, the emotion welling up inside of her threatening to bubble over. "I know I should recognize this as a wonderful thing and I do, but all I can feel is the fear right now. I *hate* that I feel that way, but I do."

His gaze softened. "Come here."

She moved to him on unsteady legs. He pulled her onto his lap, wrapping his arms around her. "You're allowed to be scared," he murmured against her hair. "We lost our baby. It was scary, it was unexpected. It wasn't supposed to happen."

She closed her eyes and burrowed into his warmth. Waking up to those severe abdominal cramps, the spotting, *knowing* something was wrong had been so scary. The loss of something so special like losing a piece of herself. But it was the fear she had somehow precipitated it that haunted her the most. Her mixed emotions, her worry she wasn't ready to be a mother, that she wouldn't be a *good* mother. It was a fear she'd never shared with Lorenzo because she had been too ashamed to even think it, let alone *admit* it to him.

She curled her fingers around a handful of his T-shirt, tugged at the soft material. "I worry about what this is going to do to *us*. We're in a good place right now. What's going to happen when the stress of this kicks in?"

"We're going to manage it," he said quietly. "Just like we've managed everything else. Life isn't going to stop throwing curveballs at us, Angelina. That's the way it works."

"I know." She bit her lip. "But what about my career? I have worked so hard for what I've achieved. I can barely keep up with the demand as it is. How am I going to handle it with a child?"

"Keep your assistants on a full-time basis. Do what you need to do. We're lucky money is no object for us."

"And if I want to get a nanny?"

His face stilled. "We can talk about it."

She read his reluctant expression. "You want me home raising our child just like your mother was."

"I know I need to make concessions," he conceded

stiffly. "I'm just not sure I want a nanny bringing up our child." He lifted his hand in a typically Italian gesture. "A child needs its mother. You, of all people, should know that."

She wasn't sure what sparked the violent reaction that rose up inside of her—fire licking her spine, heat flaming her cheeks. Whether it was because this was Lorenzo and his perfect family he was using as a benchmark, or whether he saw her as a deficient product of her mother's lack of maternal ability and wanted to make sure his child had better.

She pushed a hand against his chest, rolled to her feet in a jerky movement and stood facing him, hands planted on her hips.

"Angelina—"

"No, you're right." Fury crackled beneath every syllable. "I do know what it's like. I also know what it's like to feel as if my life is utterly out of control—to navigate those curveballs you talked about on a daily basis, to not know what's going to blow up in my face next. I am an *expert* at navigating the perils of childhood, Lorenzo. So trust me when I say, I will never neglect our child."

His jaw hardened. "I didn't say that."

"Yes, you did." She lifted her chin. "A part-time nanny would not be detrimental to our child's development."

"You didn't say part-time, you said 'a nanny.'"

"Well, I'm saying it now. I *will* be in control of this, too, Lorenzo. You will not decide how this works and negate all my decisions or I will take the Ricci heir and walk so fast you won't know what hit you."

His gaze narrowed, an icy black flame burning to life. "You need to settle down and not say things you'll regret, *cara*. You are overreacting."

"Overreacting? You are the one who *blackmailed* me back into this marriage."

"Sì." A flash of white teeth in his arrogant face. "A marriage you promised to make work. And just to point out—*you* have sprung this on me just this minute. *I* have not had the time to process the fact that I am going to be a father. You might give me some time to do that."

Guilt lanced through her. She thought she *might* be overreacting as she stood there, chest heaving with God knew what emotions, but it was all just too...*much.*

Lorenzo snagged an arm around her waist and pulled her back down on his lap.

"We," he said, visibly pulling himself back under control, "are going to figure this out. *You* are not going to create one of your dramas to throw us off track. There will be no decrees from me, Angelina, but we *will* talk this out in whatever way we need to to reach common ground."

She stared at him for a long moment. Took a deep breath and nodded.

"That said," he continued, "what was it about what I just said that set you off?"

She was silent for a moment. "Part of it is Octavia. How you build her up to be this mythical creature who can do no wrong—the earth mother who created the perfect family. The other part of it is about me, I think. I worry about being a good mother. I worry I don't have the skills to do it—that it isn't in my DNA."

His gaze softened. "You have a deep, loving relationship with your sister. You have mothered your own mother since you were fifteen. How is that not a sign you will be a caring mother?"

The adrenaline surging through her veins eased, her breath escaping in a slow exhale. She'd never thought of it that way. She'd thought she'd had no choice but to take care of her mother because that's what family did. But in reality, she could have done the opposite as James had—

as her father had—and pretended the problem didn't exist, that the disease ravaging her mother wasn't tearing her apart. But *that* hadn't been in her DNA.

Her tendency to sabotage the good before it disappeared was suddenly cast in a bright, blinking light. "I'm sorry," she said quietly. "It's my instinct to reach for anger, to lash out when I don't know how I feel…when my emotions confuse me."

"I know you now." His stare was level, unwavering. "I'm not going to let you drive wedges between us because of your fears. This baby is our second chance to do this right, Angelina. But you have to fight for us like I'm fighting for us. Fight for what we are building here."

She nodded. Rested her forehead against his. "I know. I'm sorry. Old habits die hard."

He lifted a hand to cup her jaw. Brought his mouth to hers. She met his kiss hungrily, wanting, *needing* him to wipe away her fears. Because she knew in her heart they could do this—that what they were building was more powerful, more *real* than what they'd been before. She just needed to get past the fear.

He slid a hand into her hair, held her more securely while he consumed her, *feasted* on her. She kissed him back, giving of herself without reservation. Hotter, brighter, the flame between them burned until it was an all-consuming force that engulfed them both.

Undoing the buttons that ran up the front of her dress, he exposed her body to his gaze. She shivered as he took the weight of her in his palms and teased her nipples into hard, aching points with his tongue, his teeth, nipping then laving her with soothing caresses. Moaned when he drew her deeper into the heat of his mouth, his hot, urgent caress turning her core liquid.

His eyes were hungry when he broke the contact, devouring her face with an intensity she felt to her toes. "My child will suckle at your breast," he rasped. "Do you know what that does to me? How much that makes me want you? How can this not be right, Angelina?"

Her heart slammed hard against her breastbone, stealing her breath. Her gaze locked with his for a long, suspended moment before he lowered his head and covered her mouth with his. Sliding his hand up the inside of her thigh, he found the strip of silk that covered her most intimate flesh.

She spread her thighs wider, giving him better access. Sweeping aside the silk, he dipped inside her heat, stroking her with a touch that made her arch her back, mewl a low sound of pleasure at the back of her throat.

Nothing, no feeling on this earth compared to being in Lorenzo's arms. He had become her addiction again as surely as she'd known he would. And yet it was more, so much more this time.

He sank two fingers inside of her. She gasped, her body absorbing the intrusion. He worked them in and out, his urgent, insistent rhythm sweeping her along with it until she was clenching around him. Begging him to let her come.

He pressed a kiss to her temple. "We should go inside."

"Here," she insisted, desperate to have him.

She slid off him, moved her hands under her dress and shimmied her lacy underwear off. Straddling him, she left enough room between them to find the button of his trousers and release it. He gritted his teeth as she slid the zipper past his throbbing flesh, closed her hands around him.

"Angie," he groaned, eyes blazing. "The neighbors could see us."

She ignored him, stroking her hands over him, luxuriating in the velvet-over-steel texture of him. He was made to give pleasure to a woman and she wanted him to lose control as surely as she did each and every time he drove her to it.

Her husband closed his eyes. Let go. Told her how much he loved it, how good it felt, how much it turned him on to have her hands on him. Her blood burned hotter, so hot she thought she might incinerate.

He let her have her fill, then he took control, snagging an arm around her waist and pulling her forward. Lifting her with one hand anchored around her hips, he palmed himself, brought his flesh to her center and dipped into her slick, wet heat.

His penetration was controlled and so slow it almost killed her. She shuddered, clenching her fingers around his nape. The look of pleasure written across his beautiful face, the naked play of emotion he couldn't hide were all she needed to fall tumbling into him. And this time she did it with all of her.

She caught his mouth with hers. "More."

He gripped her hips tighter and impaled her in one impatient movement that made her gasp. Clutching his shoulders, she absorbed the power of him. How he filled her in ways she'd never been filled before. How what they were becoming accessed even deeper pieces of her than she'd even knew existed.

She knew in that moment she'd never stopped loving him. Wondered how she ever could have denied it. The admission sent a frisson of wild, unadulterated fear up her spine.

Eyes on his, she rode it out, anchored herself to him with the contact, trusted him with all of her. Circling her hips, she took him deep. He was hard as a rock and thick enough to stretch her muscles to the very edge of her pleasure. She sucked in a breath as the power of him caressed her with every hard stroke, pushing her toward a release she knew would be intense and earth-shattering.

The glazed look in his eyes told her he was just as far gone as she was. Banding his arm tighter around her hips, he drove deeper, harder.

"Lorenzo—" His name was a sharp cry on her lips.

He shifted his hand to the small of her back, urging her to lean forward, to grind against him, to take her pleasure. She moaned low in her throat as his body set her on fire. He drove up into her shaking body until he hit that place that gave her the sweetest pleasure. Nudged it again and again until she splintered apart in a white-hot burst of sensation that knocked her senseless.

Her husband joined her on a low, husky groan, his big body shaking with the force of his release. It was erotic and soul-searing in a way that sucked the breath from her lungs.

She wasn't sure how long they stayed like that, joined with each other, before Lorenzo picked her up and carried her to bed. The dusky shadows of the room enveloped her as sleep carried her off to unconsciousness, her limbs entangled with his.

He had to move faster.

Lorenzo pressed his finger against the biometric scanner, heart pounding in his chest. The lights of the sports car, still running in the street, illuminated the number 29 on the red door.

The system flashed green. Jamming his hand on the handle, he swung open the door and strode inside, scanning the dimly lit main floor. Nothing.

Lucia had called from his study.

Running for the stairs, he climbed to the second level. Deep voices echoed above. The intruders were still there...

Back against the wall, he scaled the length of the narrow hallway until he reached the pool of light sprawl-

ing from his study. Silence, black silence, pumped ice through his veins.

He pushed the half-ajar door open. Levering himself away from the wall, he slipped inside. Stopped in his tracks. Blood—red, sharp, metallic, everywhere. His heart came to a shuddering halt. He followed the trail that dripped slowly to the mahogany floor up to the woman at the center of it all, slumped over his desk.

The world began to spin. Snapping out of the trance he was in, he started toward her—to help her, save her. A flash of movement—fingers banded around his arm. He lifted his other arm to strike. The glimmer of the officer's gold badge froze his hand in midair.

He was too late. He was always too late...

Lorenzo sat bolt upright in bed, sweat whipping from his face. His heart, gripped by terror and grief, stalled in his chest. It took him a full two or three seconds to realize the woman beside him was not Lucia, it was Angelina.

He was in bed with Angelina in Portofino.

She stirred now, putting out a hand to touch him. He set a palm to her back and told her to go to sleep. Making a sound in the back of her throat, she curled an arm around her pillow and went back to sleep.

He sucked in deep breaths, attempted to regulate his breathing. Soaked with sweat, he slid out of bed and put himself under a cool shower in the guest bedroom so he wouldn't wake his wife.

Water coursing over him, he stood, head bent, palms pressed against the tile as the brisk temperature of the water cooled his skin. When the hard spray had banished the worst of the fog, he stepped out of the shower and dried off.

Wrapping a towel around his waist, he walked out onto

the terrace, the lingering fragments of his dream evaporating as the pink fingers of dawn crawled across the sky. They had used to come nightly, his nightmares. He couldn't remember the last time he'd had one.

He watched the sun rise over the hills, a fiery yellow ball that crept into the hazy gray sky. *I'm going to be a father.* It had been the goal, of course, but he hadn't expected it to happen so quickly, not when they hadn't even been trying. His brain, his emotions, needed time to catch up, because they were mixed just as his wife's were.

There was joy, undoubtedly, at something he'd at one point decided might never be his. Bittersweet regret his brother would never have that opportunity. And fear. Fear that what happened before might happen again. The fear of more *loss.*

Losing his unborn child on the heels of Lucia had pushed him into a red zone where any more emotional deficits were too much. Where any more losses could push him over the line. So he'd shut down—refused to feel, and avoided any chance of that happening. In doing so, he had pushed Angelina away when she'd needed him the most—when *she* had been at her most vulnerable. No wonder she was so terrified to do this again.

His jaw locked, a slow ache pulsing beneath his ribs. This time would be different. This time he'd made sure he and Angelina's relationship was built on a solid, realistic foundation of what they were both capable of. He would make sure he kept them on track—he would be the steady, protective force she needed as they went through this pregnancy together.

If he worried his emotions for his wife were wandering into dangerous territory—into that red zone he avoided— that his efforts to exorcise her power over him weren't having any effect at all, he would just have to make sure he was extravigilant he never crossed that all-important line.

* * *

Angelina awoke to the sensually delicious smell of coffee and spicy, hedonistic male. "Breakfast," her husband intoned in her ear, his sexy, raspy tone sending a shiver up her spine, "is served."

She wasn't sure which she wanted to inhale more—him or the coffee. She opened her eyes to find him dressed and clean-shaven. The kiss he pressed to her lips was long, leisurely, the kind that squeezed her heart. Curling her fingers around his nape, she hung on to the magic for as long as possible.

He finally released her, sprawling on the bed. "I bought pastries in the village," he said, gesturing to the tray he'd tucked beside her.

"Is that a chocolate croissant?"

"What do you think?"

Yum. Her husband knew all of her weaknesses. She picked up her espresso and took a sip. Eyed him. Not as bright-eyed and bushy-tailed as she'd first imagined with those dark shadows under his eyes. "Were you up last night? I thought I heard you."

"I woke early." He plucked a croissant off the plate. "An annoying habit I can't seem to get rid of."

She watched him over the rim of her coffee cup as he inhaled the croissant. "I had a thought on the walk back," he said.

She lifted a brow.

"We're going to have to renovate the Belmont locations before we fold them into the Ricci chain. Your clientele is a perfect match. Why not open Carmichael Creations boutiques in them?"

"You haven't even landed them yet. Aren't you getting a little ahead of yourself?"

"It will happen. It's a perfect marriage of brands, don't you think?"

He was serious about this. Her heart contracted. Once she would have given anything to hear him say that. To know he believed in her work that much. But their child needed to take precedence now.

"That's a big compliment," she said carefully, "but I have more business than I can handle at the moment and I want to remain hands-on. Plus, with the baby, I think we'll have our hands full."

"True." His brow creased. "I suggested the hotel boutiques because you've always said you wanted a partnership between us. But the point is for you to be happy, Angelina. That's what I want for you."

A glow inside her sparked, grew to almost scary proportions. She'd never imagined they could be this good. This *amazing* together.

She didn't want to be afraid of loving him anymore. She wanted to trust that this was going to work out, that they were meant to be together, just like he'd said that night in the Hamptons. Taking that last step, however, making herself completely vulnerable, was painfully hard.

His eyes darkened with a sensual heat that made her pulse leap. He nodded toward the half-eaten croissant in her hand. "You going to eat that?"

She shook her head. Put it down. He reached for her, covered her mouth with his in a kiss that was pure heat. Pure possession. She relaxed her grip on the sheets as he stripped them off her, working his way down her body, tasting, idolizing every inch of her.

It was the most leisurely, spine-tinglingly good buildup he'd ever lavished on her. The most perfect thing she'd ever experienced. By the time he joined their bodies, she was so far gone she was never coming back.

Mouth at her ear, his hand closing possessively over her breast, he started to move, seducing her with words

as well as with his body. Heart stretching with the force
of what she felt for him, she refused to consider the possibility her husband would never love her. She was through
sabotaging her happiness.

CHAPTER ELEVEN

THE WEEKS FOLLOWING her trip to Italy were as busy as Angie had expected as she caught up on the backlog of commissions that had come in. She ploughed through the work with the help of her fellow designers, knowing it was a *good* problem to have—growing pains for a business that seemed to have come into its own.

Burying herself in her work allowed her to achieve her other goal of putting her pregnancy into a manageable box and not let the fears eating away at the fringes of her psyche take control. The doctor had confirmed her pregnancy upon their return home, giving her a clean bill of health. She wasn't going to fret about it. Or at least she was *telling* herself that.

Her husband, however, had clearly elected to take the opposite strategy. Although he was giving her the time to work he'd promised her, he had been monitoring her eating and sleeping habits like a hawk, enforcing periods of rest. When he happened to be around, that was. Ever since they'd come home, he had been working day and night to close the Belmont deal. Add to that another acquisition Franco was negotiating that required her husband's counsel and Lorenzo wasn't doing any eating or sleeping himself.

She knew it was an inordinately busy time, but the feeling that their life was sliding into its former self was growing stronger with every day. Their bond was too new, too nascent, not to allow the warning signals to affect her.

Another long day at the studio behind her, she walked into the penthouse just after eight, kicked off her shoes and made herself a cup of tea. Carrying it into the living room, she sat reading a book while she waited for her husband. But the book failed to keep her attention.

Weeks like this were the worst when Lorenzo was gone for nights on end. Old fears crept around her unsuspecting edges, insecurity set in. Given their dinners together at home had vaporized with her husband's insane schedule and he refused to wake her up when he came to bed so late, she didn't even have the comfort his passionate lovemaking offered, that seemed to make any obstacle seem surmountable.

The minutes ticked by, her agitation rising. Perhaps now that Lorenzo had had his fill of her, now that he'd gotten everything he wanted, he would lose interest again. Perhaps whatever client he was out wining and dining tonight was a convenient excuse to stay away. Perhaps the emotional distance she'd sensed in him since Portofino was a reality.

The clock struck ten. Discarding the book, she decided to take matters into her own hands. To be proactive rather than reactive. To take control of her relationship, something she hadn't done the last time.

In her bedroom, she dug out the lingerie she'd bought earlier that week and slipped it on. The sexy cream-and-black baby doll that just covered her pertinent assets was fairly indecent. She stared at herself in the mirror, rosy color stinging her cheeks. The cream lace bodice did nothing to hide the bold thrust of her nipples, the silk encasing her curves a seductive caress that was pure temptation.

She pulled the elastic from her hair and let it fall around

her shoulders the way her husband liked it. A slow smile curved her mouth. *If this didn't bring him running, nothing would.*

Lorenzo arrived back at the table at the trendy restaurant in the meatpacking district, where he and his CMO were entertaining his Japanese business partners to find his phone sitting on his chair.

An amused smile curved his CMO's mouth. "Figured you might not want the whole table seeing that," he said, nodding toward the phone. He leaned closer. "PS—I'd go home if I were you."

Lorenzo glanced at the screen. Almost choked on the sip of beer he'd taken. His wife dressed in a piece of lingerie he'd never seen before—an outrageously sexy piece, by any male's standards, occupied the entire screen. Hair loose around her shoulders, the lingerie doing little to hide the dark shadow of her nipples beneath the transparent lace, she was the twenty-first-century version of a pinup poster. *Times ten.*

He glanced at the message.

Are you coming home?

Heat claimed his cheeks. It took very little of his creative ability to imagine peeling that silk off of her. How she would taste under his mouth. He'd thought his crazy social schedule might prove an ideal cooling-off period for the two of them given the depth of the emotion they'd shared in Portofino. But this, *this* was too much to resist.

"You didn't see that," he muttered to his CMO.

"What?" Gerald said innocently. "I'll cover for you if you want to make an exit."

Lorenzo tucked his phone into his pocket. Put his exit strategy into motion. Except his Japanese colleagues were intent on taking in the entertainment the club provided. It would be rude for him to cut the night short.

He texted his wife back.

Hold that thought.

It was close to midnight, however, by the time he walked into the penthouse. Devoid of light, it was cast in shadows. He let out a low oath that turned the silent space blue and threw his jacket on a chair.

Body pulsing with frustration, every ounce of his blood so far south it was never coming back, he reached up and loosened his tie. A flash of movement near the windows caught his eye.

He took in his wife, silhouetted against the New York skyline, the sexy negligee plastered to every centimeter of her voluptuous body.

Her breasts were bigger with the advance of her pregnancy, their lush, creamy expanse drawing his eye. That tantalizing glimpse of nipple beneath sheer, gauzy fabric made his mouth go dry.

"You waited up." His voice was husky, laced with a need he couldn't hide.

"I was on my way to bed."

Chilly. Distinctly chilly. He gathered his wits as he moved toward her. "I tried to get away, but my business colleagues were in from Japan. It would have looked rude to leave."

"It's fine." She crossed her arms over her chest, amplifying the view of the bare flesh he ached to touch.

He reached for her. She stepped back. "I don't think so."

"There was nothing I could have done, Angelina."

"I'm tired. I'm going to bed."

He caught her hand and pulled her to him, content to

work his way back into her good graces. Her perfume drifted into his nostrils, a tantalizing tease that stroked the heat in him higher. "Clearly you're angry," he murmured. "Let me make it up to you. I'm so hot for you, *cara mia*. I will make it so good."

She lifted her vibrant blue gaze to his. "No."

He blinked. "What do you mean 'no'? You sent me a photo of you in lingerie."

"That offer expired an hour ago."

"You are my wife," he barked. "Offers don't expire."

A mutinous set of her lips. "This one just did. Maybe next time I'll be a compelling enough attraction that you will be home before midnight. Maybe next time you won't blow off those dinners *you* insisted on. Maybe when I remember what my husband *looks like*, the offer will be available for redemption."

He scowled. "You are being completely unfair."

She shook her head. "This *is* history repeating itself, Lorenzo. I don't like it, and I'm not imagining it this time."

He drew his brows together. "It's nothing like the past. We have been great together. We're talking, we're communicating. Just because you have hurt feelings that I didn't jump when you sent me that photo doesn't mean I'm ignoring you. It means I was *busy*."

Her eyes darkened to a stormy, gray blue. "Just because you've had a few drinks and you're hot for a booty call doesn't mean you get to act like a child when it doesn't go your way. Learn your lesson and maybe next time it will work out for you."

Dio, but she was beautiful when she was angry. He loved this strong, sexy version of his wife—it turned him hard as a rock. The problem was, he needed her to give so he could get his hands on her.

"Bene." He lifted his palms in a conciliatory gesture. "I've learned my lesson. Mission accomplished. You've

made your point." He trained his gaze on hers, hot, deliberate. "What would you like me to do? Get down on my knees and beg?"

Her confident swagger faltered, a blaze of uncertainty staining her beautiful eyes. He took a step closer. "Just say yes," he murmured, raking her from head to toe. "While I'm there, I'd be happy to indulge you. Mouth, hands, name your pleasure."

A blaze of sensual heat fired her eyes before the ice made a swift reappearance. "I am not a possession to be used and discarded according to your whims."

"You've said that before," he murmured, his good mood rapidly dissipating. "I find it as objectionable as I did the first time. That is *not* what this is, Angelina. These are extraordinary circumstances trying to land this Belmont deal."

"There will always be another deal…another pot of gold at the end of the rainbow. It never stops, Lorenzo. It never will."

"It will. Once we land Belmont, I will be able to breathe again."

She shook her head. "I've watched my mother go through this a thousand times, wondering when my father will deign to pay attention to her again, always putting her second, *third*, if he happened to be having an affair at the time. I've lived through it with you. I won't repeat these hot and cold patterns again—that roller-coaster ride we do so well."

"I am *not* your father." Irritation edged his voice. "And I've put you first every time since we've been back together in case you hadn't noticed."

"Yes," she agreed, "you have. Which is why I'm speaking up. Because we've built such a great thing together… because I refuse to see things go back to the way they were."

He shook his head. "You're being too sensitive."

"No, I'm not."

He crossed his arms over his chest, too tired, too frustrated to know how to respond. He was giving her all he had and still she wanted more.

Her lashes lowered. "I need sleep. I have a long day tomorrow."

He let her go, refusing to run after her, tongue wagging, like some desperate fool, despite the way he burned for her. Pouring himself a glass of water, he collapsed into a chair, too wired to sleep even though he couldn't remember the last time he had enjoyed that particular human luxury.

Things *would* get better after he landed Belmont. His wife was completely overreacting—a guilt trip he didn't need when making sure she was okay, that she and their baby were healthy, had been his primary obsession amidst the insanity of his life.

He sat back in the chair. Downed a long swallow of water. His wife's indignation, quite honestly, was the least of his problems. Losing the Belmont deal was a real possibility. It was becoming more and more clear the branding issue might be a deal breaker. The business pages were ripe with speculation on the potential megamerger, Ricci stock was on a roller-coaster ride, the board meeting was looming and he needed to get Erasmo Bavaro, the Bavaro scion, onside. But the Bavaro brothers weren't offering access to their father. He had to play the situation very, very carefully and it was driving him mad.

Oh, the world wouldn't end if the deal fell apart, he conceded, but Ricci's stock and reputation would take a serious hit. Confidence would be shaken. And it would be his fault.

I am beginning to think your ambition has got the best of you on this one.

A nerve throbbed at his temple, his fingers tightening around the glass. Had his father been right? Had he finally overstepped himself? Gotten too confident? Cocky?

He rested his head against the back of the chair and closed his eyes. His culpability was a moot point at this stage. All that mattered was getting the deal done. Pulling it out of the ashes.

As for his wife? He'd never promised her perfection—had warned her this was who he was. He'd vowed to be there for her and he would. But perhaps she was right. Perhaps he'd dropped the ball on his promise to be present of late, had let their dinners together slide.

He could rectify that—take her out for dinner tomorrow night. Calm the waters at home.

CHAPTER TWELVE

IT WAS GOING to be a late night.

Angie set the almost completed, black-and-white diamond bracelet on her workbench, sat back in her chair and rubbed her eyes. *Almost there* wasn't good enough when the bracelet was due to one of Manhattan's most noted philanthropists tomorrow, a woman who could make or break her reputation. And since she had already pushed the delivery date back because of her trip to Europe, then had to wait for some stones to be delivered, it needed to get done tonight.

She headed for the coffee machine, thinking maybe java might perk her up. But she suspected what was really bothering her was the fact that although her husband had made an effort to reinstate their dinners at home whenever his schedule permitted, although he was making an effort to be *physically* present, he had become even more emotionally distant over the last couple of weeks.

Keeping the faith, believing in them, was growing increasingly difficult when not knowing if he'd ever love her was burning a hole in her soul. She wanted him to say those three words so badly, it was almost painful. But she knew if he ever did, and it wasn't a given he would, it would take time.

"Do you want me to stay and work with you tonight?" Serina threw her a glance as she put on her coat.

Angie poured herself a cup of coffee. "You have a

date." She gave the diminutive blonde an amused look. "That exciting is he?"

Serina made a face. "Friends set us up."

"Then you should definitely go. That's how all the good matches are made."

She wasn't so sure how love at first sight was going to work out for her.

Picking up her coffee, she nursed the steaming cup between her hands. "I have to finish Juliette Baudelaire's bracelet. The clasp I'd envisioned isn't working."

She and Serina conferred on the issue, the other designer agreeing her current design wouldn't work. They tossed around a couple of alternatives, then Serina headed out for her date.

No sooner had Angie settled into her work than her cell phone rang—it was her husband's name on the caller ID.

"Yes," she purred, craving a taste of his raspy, delicious voice to ease her jagged emotions. "I thought you had to work late."

"Marc Bavaro's invited us to the opera tonight. I need you to come."

No hello. No preamble. No sexy rasp. Cool, rapid-fire words thrown at her with that hint of edge he'd been wearing all week.

She bit her lip. "I can't. I'm sorry. I have a bracelet due to an important client in the morning."

"It's a bracelet. Not life or death. Finish it tomorrow."

She stiffened. "It's *due* tomorrow. I've already put her off once because of Marc Bavaro."

"A few hours isn't going to make a difference. Stop being so contrary and get ready. I'll be there in fifteen minutes to pick you up."

The line went dead. She stared at the phone. Had he just called her *contrary*? *Dismissed* her like that?

She put down the phone. Took a couple of deep breaths.

Seriously considered calling him back and telling him what he could do with his opera invitation. Except Marc Bavaro was driving him crazy. She could see it on his face when he walked in the door at night…in the dark circles under his eyes he was wearing like a badge. He was under immense pressure to close this deal and the strain was showing.

She exhaled a long breath. Even though her own work would suffer, she would *not* be the one to sabotage their relationship this time.

Juliette's nearly done bracelet glittered on her desk. She supposed she could send her an email and let her know it would be done in the morning, afternoon at the latest. Surely that would be fine?

Decision made, she sent the email and gathered up her things, her animosity growing by the minute. By the time Lorenzo pulled up at the sidewalk in front of her studio, her blood was boiling.

"Ciao." He leaned toward her to give her a kiss when she got into the car. She gave him her cheek instead. His ebony gaze narrowed. "What?"

"If you don't know what, you don't deserve an answer."

He eyed her. "Is it because I called you contrary?"

She didn't deign to respond to that.

A muttered oath. "It's one night, Angelina."

She turned a furious gaze on him. "I have a commission due tomorrow. How would you feel if I insisted you attend a party with me when you had a security filing the next day? I can just see you now—'Pff, it's just a security filing…the lawyers have this. Be right with you, honey.'"

"Now you're being ridiculous."

She turned to look out the window.

He gave up after that, getting them home in record time. She changed into a cap-sleeved, navy classic sheath dress, adding elegant gold sandals and jewelry to spice it up. Lorenzo looked devastatingly handsome in a dark suit, white shirt and an ice-blue tie he had clearly put on to match her dress, but she was in no mood to acknowledge it.

They met up with Marc and Penny outside the stunningly beautiful Metropolitan Opera House, with its white travertine stone facade and five massive, graceful arches that, lit up at night, made it a sight to see. It had always been one of Angie's favorite places to go for its sheer magnificence. Her first trip there, to see a ballet as a little girl, had been full of wide-eyed wonder. But tonight she was too annoyed to register much other than the fact that she was itching to shrug off the hand her husband held at her back, but couldn't.

They shared a cocktail with the other couple in one of the bars. Sparkling water, sadly, for Angie, when a glass of wine might have mellowed her out. She focused all her attention on the Belmont CEO and his girlfriend, ignoring her husband completely, to the point where Penny jokingly asked her if Lorenzo was in the doghouse as they settled into their seats in the Belmont box to watch Puccini's *La Bohème*.

She denied it, of course. Made a joking comment that Penny would see what it was like when the honeymoon phase was over. Lorenzo must have heard it with that laser-sharp hearing of his because his face turned dark. A mistake, she recognized, as the whisper of a chill rose up her spine. She had insulted his male pride.

She focused on the performance. He had earned that one.

La Bohème was one of her favorites, but tonight it couldn't have been a worse choice. The story of Mimi and Rodolfo, the fiery, star-crossed lovers, sung to perfection by the visiting Italian soprano and her American tenor—had always moved her. But tonight, given her rocky emotions, her insecurities about her and Lorenzo, it affected her in a way she couldn't hide. By the time the two lovers decided to stay together in the face of Mimi's heartbreaking illness at the end of the third act, her imminent death on the horizon, tears were running down her face.

Lorenzo put a hand on her thigh. She ignored him, kept her eyes focused on the stage. When the act came to a close, she rooted around desperately in her bag for a tissue, a necessity at the opera, and *dammit*, how could she have forgotten them?

Lorenzo shoved the handkerchief from his front pocket into her hand. "Excuse us, will you?"

"What are you doing?" she whispered as he grabbed her arm and propelled her out of the box.

A tight, intense look back. "We are going somewhere to talk."

"I don't want to talk."

"Well, that's too bad, *amore mio*, you don't get to choose."

Into the multistoried lobby they went, past the two glorious murals Marc Chagall had painted. Somewhere along the way, Lorenzo dropped the general manager's name. The next thing she knew, he was directing her down a hallway and into an empty dressing room marked Visiting Performers.

Lorenzo twisted the lock on the door and turned to face his wife. What the hell was wrong with her? Watching her cry like that had made him want to crawl out of his skin, because he didn't think all of it had to do with the admittedly heartbreaking opera.

Angie swept her hand around the room, dominated by the sofa that sat along one wall and a dressing table and mirror on the other. "We can't be in here."

"I was just told we could." He crossed his arms over

his chest. "Explain to me why you are so angry, *cara*. I asked you to do me a favor. You know how important this deal is to me. What's the problem?"

She jammed her hands on her hips, eyes flashing. "You *ordered* me to come. You know how important my career is to me and yet you completely discounted my work. The bracelet I'm creating is for Juliette Baudelaire—a huge commission, particularly if she spreads the word to her friends. It's not just a bracelet, it's a *stepping stone* in my career. And yet here I am, not delivering on time— *twice*—because of you and your needs."

His irritation came to a sudden, sliding halt. "I had no idea it was for her."

"*How could you?* You hung up on me before I had a chance to tell you."

He muttered an oath. Pushed a palm over his brow. "*Mi dispiace.* I'm sorry. I wasn't thinking when I called you. I was behind, annoyed because I had prior commitments I, too, had to cancel."

She hugged her arms around herself. Glared at him. He scowled back. "You," he said, waving a hand at her, "are so emotional tonight. What's going on? Is it the pregnancy effect?"

The daggers in her eyes would have sliced him to shreds if they'd been real. "*You*, Lorenzo Ricci, are so oblivious, so *emotionally unaware* sometimes it blows my mind."

He didn't think that was fair. He thought he was *very* emotionally aware at times and had been with her *a lot* lately. They were talking. *Communicating.* Being honest with each other. The last couple of weeks had just been particularly brutal.

The thought vaporized from his head as his wife headed for the door. Moving with a swiftness born of his superior height and muscle, he made it there at the same time she did. Jamming his palm against the wood, he looked down at his very beautiful, very angry wife.

"We aren't done talking."

"Oh, yes, we are."

"No," he said deliberately, "we aren't."

She crossed her arms over her chest. "What else would you like to say?"

"I'd like to say I'm sorry again. I sincerely feel badly that I did not check to see what it was you were working on. If I'd known, I would have come by myself."

Her stormy blue gaze softened.

"I would also like to know how I am being *emotionally unaware*."

She pursed her lips. "You're kidding, right?"

"No." He frowned. "I thought we had the pregnancy thing out in the open. We're dealing with it."

"It's not that." She shook her head. "Women cannot *stand* when a man plays the hormone card, Lorenzo. It's like waving a red flag in front of a bull."

"Oh. *Certo*," he said, nodding. "I will remember that for the future. I had no idea. I thought pregnancy hormones were a documented thing."

"Lorenzo." She glared at him. "I'd stop while you're ahead."

"Bene." He snagged an arm around her waist and pulled her close. "Is there anything else you would like to tell me? Why you are so upset?"

Her gaze dropped away from his. "You haven't been emotionally present the last few weeks. I don't know where your head is. I don't know where *we* are. I miss you."

Guilt tied a knot in his chest. In trying to pull back, to not lead them down a path he couldn't go, he'd hurt her.

"I'm sorry." He bent his head and buried his mouth in the curve of her neck. Drank in her irresistible scent. "Things have been crazy. I will do better."

"It's… I—" She sighed. "We should go. Find Marc and Penny."

"Not until you say you're not angry with me anymore." He slid his hands down over her bottom and pulled her closer. "I hate it when you're angry with me."

Tracing the line of her neck with his lips, he sank his teeth into the cord of her throat where it throbbed against her skin. Her breath hitched. "Fine. I'm not angry at you anymore."

"I'm not convinced." He dragged his mouth up to hers. Pushed his fingers into her hair and kissed her. Dominant, persuasive, he sought to fix whatever was going on with her. To fix *them* in the only way he knew how.

She melted beneath his hands. "Okay," she whispered against his lips. "You're forgiven."

But he was too far gone now, his body pulsing with the need to restore the natural balance of things. Denying himself Angelina was carving a hole inside of him he didn't know how to fill.

He backed her into the wall, pushed his thigh between hers, imprinting her with the throbbing evidence of his need. She gasped. *"Lorenzo."*

"What?"

"We can't do this here."

"Why not?" He slicked his tongue over her lush bottom lip, tasting her. "You liked it in Portofino. The element of risk…"

"Yes, but—"

He delved inside the sweetness of her mouth. Made love to her with his tongue like he wanted to do to her body. Her bag clattered to the floor, a low moan leaving her throat. Lust coursing through him, he nudged her legs farther apart and swept her dress up her thighs. She was damp when he cupped her between her legs, as turned on as he was.

He ran his palm over the hot, wet silk that covered her. Moved it aside to find her slick and ready for him.

"I need to have you," he rasped.

Her stormy blue gaze locked with his. *"Yes."*

He stroked her. Readied her. She made more of those sexy sounds at the back of her throat, arching into his hand. Shallow strokes of his fingers inside her tight channel to tease, insistent circles against the tight bundle of nerves at the heart of her with his thumb. Throwing her head back, she said his name in a broken voice that ripped right through him.

Urging one of her legs around his waist, he released himself from his pants, pushed aside the wet silk and entered her with a hard, urgent thrust. She gasped, the sensation of her tight, velvet warmth gripping his swollen flesh indescribable. It had never been so good.

"Okay?" he murmured.

"Yes."

Bending his knees, he drove up inside of her with an urgent desire that annihilated anything but the need to have her. His erection pounded in time with his heartbeat, his control shredding. He captured her hand in his and brought her fingers to the hard nub that gave her pleasure.

"Touch yourself," he whispered. "Come with me, Angelina."

She closed her eyes. Rotated her fingers against her flesh. He kept his hand over hers, absorbing the tiny quakes that went through her. Held on to the very threads of his control while she pleasured herself. When she was close, when the deeper shudders came, moving from her through him, he gripped her hip tighter and stroked deeper, setting a hard, wild rhythm that blew his brain apart.

His body tightened, swelled, his breathing hoarse in the silence of the room. In perfect sync, they came together in a soul-shaking release like none he'd ever experienced before.

Mouth buried in her neck, he held her as her legs gave out. He wasn't sure how long they stayed like that, wrapped around each other, before he recovered enough to straighten and push back.

Bracing a palm against the wall, he leaned in to kiss her, to acknowledge what that had just been. His heart stopped in his chest at the tears streaming down her cheeks.

"Angelina?" He cupped her face with his hands. "What is it?"

She shook her head. Pushed away as she straightened her clothes. "It's nothing. I'm emotional from the performance."

The bell sounded to end the intermission. He ignored it, focusing on his wife's tear-streaked face as he zipped himself up. "It's a hell of a lot more than that."

She swiped the tears from her face with the backs of her hands.

"Angelina," he roared. "Out with it."

She bent and scooped her purse off the floor. Straightening, she rested her blue gaze on his. "I'm in love with you, Lorenzo. Silly me, I forgot the rules."

CHAPTER THIRTEEN

LORENZO'S JAW DROPPED. "Angie—"

The bell rang again. His wife turned, unlocked the door and walked out. Blood pounding at his temples, he straightened his shirt and followed her out.

How he sat through the last act, he wasn't sure. It was like someone was driving nails into his head in some kind of ancient torture. When it was finally, mercifully over, they bid Marc and Penny a good night and acquired the car from the valet. Neither of them spoke in the loaded silence of the car.

The penthouse was in shadows as they entered, Manhattan spread out before them in all its glory. He threw his jacket on a chair and headed straight for the bar and a stiff shot of whiskey.

Angelina kicked off her shoes. When she headed for the bedroom, he pointed to the sofa. *"Sit."*

She lifted her chin. "What's the point? I know you can't tell me what I want to hear. You would have said it to me in that dressing room if you could."

It was a truth he couldn't deny. He wanted to—he wanted to tell her everything she wanted to hear if it would wipe the hurt from her eyes, but he'd promised her honesty and they'd come too far to give each other anything but.

He set down the whiskey. Pushed a hand through his hair. "To lose someone you love like I loved Lucia changes a person. You *know* too much. Things you should never have to know…things that make you question everything you once took for granted—the *natural order* of things. It isn't a faith I'll ever have again. Loving someone like that isn't something I'm *capable* of doing. But it doesn't mean I don't care for you. You know I do."

Her eyes grew suspiciously bright. "Not capable," she asked quietly, "or simply unwilling to try?"

He lifted a shoulder. "It is who I am."

The brightness in her eyes dissolved on a blaze of fire. "You know what I think, Lorenzo? I think it's a cop-out, this 'I am who I am' line of yours. Saying you can't love again is easier than making yourself vulnerable…easier than exposing yourself to the potential for pain, so you choose not to go there. You choose to believe you are incapable of love."

He shook his head. "I won't tell you lies. We promised each other that. But what we have, Angelina—is something *more* than love. What we have is based on rationality, on that great partnership you've always wanted, on the affection we have for each other. It is *real*. It's what's going to make this marriage work. *Last*."

She wrapped her arms around herself. Turned to look out the window. He closed the distance between them, curled his fingers around her shoulder and turned her to him. "We have a good thing," he said softly, "an electric connection—a special connection. The kind that rarely, if ever, comes along. We will be great parents to our child because we know the gift it is. What more could you ask for?"

"The love of a lifetime," she said quietly. "You had yours. Maybe I want mine. Maybe *this* isn't enough."

His stomach contracted, her words sucking the breath from him. He inhaled, dragged in a breath. Searched for something, *anything* to say. But he knew what she was saying was true. She deserved to have that untainted love—everything he couldn't give her. But he'd thought he could make her happy by giving her everything else. He should have known it would never be enough.

Naked pain wrote itself across her beautiful face. "I have to go to bed. I need to deliver that bracelet to Juliette tomorrow and I still have to figure out the clasp."

He watched her leave the room, a heavy, hollow ache in his chest, because he wasn't sure he could fix this. It was the one thing he *couldn't* fix.

Bleary-eyed from a restless, sleepless night, Angie forced herself into the studio shortly after her husband left for the office, putting on coffee just as the birds were beginning to sing.

She sat down at her desk with a cup of the strong brew, numbly processing the events of the night before. She hadn't meant to confront Lorenzo. She'd meant to give him time. But somewhere along the way, her emotions so raw, it had just come tumbling out. Maybe it had been the way she'd been desperately begging for crumbs in that dressing room when they'd made love, terrified they were falling apart again—needing to know they were okay. How they were once again using sex to solve problems they couldn't fix.

Her heart throbbed. How could she have allowed herself to make the same mistake she'd made the first time around? To think, on some instinctual level, her husband might love her but not be able to admit it?

It was never going to happen even if he did. And she knew, even if she convinced herself that what they had was enough, even if she bought his whole line about them being *more* than love, she'd end up hating him for never offering her what she so desperately wanted. Because she wanted it—she did. The love she'd never had. The love she knew they could have together.

She deserved it. She had always deserved it. She was *worthy* of it. She knew that now. And what hurt the most was her husband was capable of it. He'd loved Lucia once. He just wasn't going to offer it to her.

The ache in her insides grew. She wanted to be the light in Lorenzo's life, his everything as he was becoming to her. As he'd always been to her. This wasn't her sabotaging them, it was *him* sabotaging them.

She took another sip of her coffee. Pulled herself together. Allowing her work to slide wasn't going to make this any easier.

A return email from Juliette Baudelaire sat in her inbox. A short, curt reply.

Not to worry. I found another piece to wear to the luncheon. Given that, I no longer require the bracelet.

Her heart sank. Thousands of dollars of diamonds had gone into that bracelet. But that wasn't even the point—she could resell it. The point was that Juliette knew everyone and loved to talk. Her reputation was going to take a bump for this, she knew it in her bones.

She sat back in her chair. Closed her eyes.

"You okay?" Serina breezed in and hung up her coat.

No, she decided, tears stinging her eyes. She was most definitely not okay. But she wasn't going to let that man take her apart again. Not this time.

"Do you want the good news or the bad?"

Lorenzo eyed his lawyer, his mood vile. "Why don't you start with the bad and work up to the good?"

"The Belmont lawyers called while you were in your

meeting. They want to meet tomorrow in Miami to discuss some final issues."

Lorenzo's fingers curled tight around the toy football he held. Marc Bavaro was going to be the one to finally make him snap. He could feel it.

"What's the good news?"

"The meeting will be at Erasmo Bavaro's place."

He sat forward. "That is good news." But *Miami*...tomorrow?

Cris eyed his scowl. "Please tell me we're saying yes."

"Bene." He blew out a breath. "Make it happen. We need to get this done. But I swear this is the swan song."

His lawyer left. Lorenzo sat back in his chair, his satisfaction at finally moving this game to a place he was comfortable with only slightly improving his foul mood. His volatility had as much to do with his wife's ultimatum as it did with Bavaro's antics. With the fact that she'd thrown that explosive three-word phrase at him, pushed him for things he couldn't give and destroyed the delicate, satisfactory stasis he'd had going on. Backed him into a corner with nowhere left to go.

Flying to Miami tomorrow seemed unwise given the current state of affairs. But what could he do? If he didn't get Erasmo Bavaro on board this deal was as good as dead.

Swinging his feet off his desk, he threw the things he'd need for Miami in his briefcase and headed home to solve his problem. His wife was making herself some hot milk in the kitchen when he walked in.

"How was your day?" he asked, setting his briefcase on the floor. *Reintroducing stasis.*

"Busy." She put down the cup and rubbed her palms against her temples.

"Did you get Juliette's bracelet done?"

She lifted her gaze to his, her face expressionless. "I

lost the commission. She went out and bought something else to wear."

Uh-oh. This did not bode well for the conversation they needed to have. "I'm sorry," he said quietly, "that was wrong of me. But we still need to talk. Work this out."

She shook her head. "*You* need to work this out. I know how I feel."

A twinge of unease spread through him. "What are you saying?"

"I'm saying I can't live without love. I can't stay in this marriage unless you can offer that to me." She shook her head, teeth sinking into her lip. "You have made me face up to my past, Lorenzo. You have made me see how I run from the things that scare me so I won't get hurt. Well, I'm not running now. I *deserve* to be happy. I deserve to have all of you. And if you can't offer that to me, it will break my heart, but I will walk away because you've also helped me realize how strong I am."

His chest clenched. "You're willing to throw everything we have away because I can't say three words?"

Her eyes darkened. "It's more than that and you know it. I've watched you struggle over the past few weeks. I know how hard this is for you. But I can't live with pieces of you. It would break my heart. We would end up hating each other. You know we would."

"No, I do not know that." His fists tightened at his sides. "This is not negotiable, Angelina. You are carrying my child. Our fate was sealed the day that happened."

"No, it wasn't." She shook her head. "You have your heir. We will work that out. But you can't have me. Not like this. I must have been insane to ever agree to that deal we made."

"You aren't walking out on me again." His voice was pure frost. "You know the conditions I attached to this."

"You won't do it." Her eyes were stark in a face gone

white. "The other thing I have learned is that under that armor you wear is the man I met. The man I would have given anything to have. *He* wouldn't let my family suffer. He would not hurt me."

Blood pounded in his ears, a red-hot skewer of rage lancing through him. "Try me, *cara*. Just try me. You think you can leave me and cozy up to *Byron* again with my child inside you? It will never happen. I will drag this divorce out for all eternity."

She stared at him as if she couldn't believe what she was hearing. He couldn't believe what he was saying. But the rage driving him didn't care who or what he hurt.

She didn't flinch. Held his gaze. "Byron and I were over when I realized I was still in love with you and you damn well know it."

He raked a hand through his hair. Struggled to see past his fury. "I have to go to Miami tomorrow. Erasmo Bavaro has agreed to meet with us. We will talk about this when I get back."

"I won't be here." The pain staining her blue eyes nearly tore him in two. "I know who I am, Lorenzo, and I know I can't do this."

She turned on her heel and walked toward the bedroom.

Corrosive anger roped his heart. "Goddammit, Angelina, get back here."

She kept going.

In the center of the red zone, well aware of where it could take him, he downed the rest of the whiskey. He could not afford to go there, not now with the most important deal of his life hanging in the balance. Not ever when his wife was asking more of him than he could ever give.

CHAPTER FOURTEEN

ERASMO BAVARO WAS as cagey as his son Marc and as animated as Diego, a fearsome combination in a silver-haired
fox who reminded Lorenzo of his father.

It would have been fascinating to see the two titans
face off in their heyday, but on a brilliantly sunny afternoon in Miami, with the Bavaro scion's palatial poolside
terrace the backdrop for the negotiations, his focus was
on pulling Erasmo into the twenty-first century.

Erasmo, for his part, looked content to stay right where
he was. Flanked by his lawyers at the long, olive wood
table, coolly dressed in a flamboyant short-sleeved shirt
and trousers, he swept a palm over his neatly trimmed,
salt-and-pepper goatee and eyed Lorenzo. "Let me tell
you a story," he said in a deeply accented voice. "Perhaps
it will help you to understand where I'm coming from.

"The night we opened the Belmont in South Beach in
1950, we had the most popular blues singer on the planet,
Natalie Constantine, lined up to play. Near the end of her
set, Arturo Martinez walked onto the stage and joined
her for the last two songs."

Arturo Martinez. The Spanish megastar who had sold
more albums in those days than any singer alive.

"They closed out the night in the piano bar. Two leg-
ends. Such was the mystique of the Belmont legacy. You
could not have paid to be there that night."

"They were great days," Lorenzo acknowledged. "I

wish I had been there that night. But that time has come and gone, Erasmo. It's time for the mantle to be passed on. All good things must come to an end."

"Speaks the man who puts money above meaning." The Bavaro patriarch lifted a brow. "Can I share something with you, Ricci? Money will not give your life meaning when you are my age. Money will not keep you warm at night. Money won't nourish your soul when you've spent fifty years in this business and every boardroom table looks like the rest. *Meaning* will. Your legacy will."

"Speaks a man perhaps lost in his own sentimentality..."

Erasmo dipped his head. "Perhaps. But I would prefer to be remembered as a man who built things rather than tore down the work of others."

The rebuke stung his skin. Lorenzo lifted the glass of potent, exotic rum his host had unearthed from his cellar to his lips and took a sip. It burned a slow path through his insides, but it didn't take the sting out of the old man's words. Nor did the fact that his wife, who'd walked out on him *again*, felt the same way.

Angelina thought he'd sold his soul for his success. Bartered it for an escape from the guilt he refused to acknowledge—the feelings he refused to address. The ironic thing was, in that moment, as the cast of lawyers digressed into legalese he couldn't be bothered to follow, he couldn't remember why this deal had ever been so important to him. Why he was sitting here haggling over a name when the most important thing in his life was back in New York. *Refusing to take his calls.*

And why would she? Regret sat like a stone in his stomach. He'd threatened to withdraw his funding of Carmichael Company if she left...to drag their divorce out for all eternity. Had he really thought that would make her stay?

His insides coiled tight. What the hell was wrong with him? He had no idea what he was doing anymore. Hadn't since Angelina had laid all his truths out for him and challenged him to do the same. Since a phone call in the middle of a meeting in Shanghai had obliterated the life he'd known and had him planning a funeral rather than the family he and Lucia had envisioned.

He rubbed a palm across his forehead, a low throb sitting just below his skin. He'd told Angelina he wasn't capable of loving again. Had meant it. But watching her walk out on him a second time, watching her lay her heart on the line about how she felt about him had done something to him. If his wife, who'd been hurt so many times it was a scar on her soul, could be that courageous, what did that make him? A *coward*?

The tightness in his chest deepened. He'd allowed her to walk away, continued to pretend he didn't feel the things he did for her because then he wouldn't have to face the truth. That he loved her. Had loved her from the first moment he'd laid eyes on her. That he was so afraid of losing someone else, so afraid of losing *her*, so angry at her still for leaving him, he didn't have the guts to put himself out there. To tell her how he felt.

His heart punched through his chest. *Blaming yourself for Lucia's death is easier than making yourself vulnerable again.*

He curled his fingers into his thighs, waiting for the shame, the guilt, to dig its claws into him, to claim him as it always did when he allowed himself to think of that night. But it didn't come. His fear was greater—his fear of losing his wife, the woman who made him whole.

He closed his eyes. What would she think if she knew the true story? That his inability to be present for his wife, to listen to her, the same failings he had brought to his marriage with Angelina, had led to Lucia's death? That *he* was responsible for it?

He finished his drink in a long swig. Set the glass

down. What was clear was that he hadn't fulfilled his end of his bargain with his wife. He'd insisted Angelina be an open book, but he hadn't been with her. He owed her the truth, because if he continued to use his guilt as a crutch, to hide from his emotions, he would lose her anyway. And losing his wife, he realized, wasn't an option.

The lawyers droned on. The sun beat down on his head. Perhaps knowing, *accepting* he should have done things differently and forgiving himself for Lucia's death were two separate things. Maybe he needed to forgive himself for being human in the decisions he'd made…maybe that was something he could live with.

He leaned forward, palms on the table. "We will co-brand the hotels," he interjected, cutting through the din. "'The Ricci South Beach, *formerly a Belmont hotel.*' That's as far as I'm willing to take it."

Cristopher gaped at his about-face. Lorenzo stood up. "You have twenty-four hours to give us a response—after that, the deal is dead."

Marc eyed him. "You're walking out?"

"I'm taking a page out of your father's book. I'm finally getting my priorities straight. You've had a year to do that, Bavaro, I'm giving you another twenty-four hours' grace."

Whether he had that with Angelina after the things he'd said to her remained to be seen.

"Why don't you just take his calls if you're this miserable?"

Angie looked up from her bowl of pasta to find her sister's watchful gaze on her. "Because we both need space. And," she said, dropping the fork in the bowl and pushing it away, "I'm angry at him."

Furious. Lonely. Miserable. But she wasn't about to add fuel to the fire by dragging her sister into this. They were supposed to be having a nice night out at their favorite restaurant, something she desperately needed.

"You know," Abigail said quietly, "Lorenzo called James this afternoon."

She sat up straighter. "*James?* Why?"

"Father is stepping down and making James CEO. Lorenzo's going to come in and work side by side with him to right-side Carmichael Company."

Her jaw dropped. "And I don't know about this why?"

"Apparently it's been in the works for a while, but Father just made the decision this week. According to James, Lorenzo gave Father an ultimatum a few weeks back— step down or he will withdraw his financial support."

"He's good at that," Angie muttered. "Throwing his weight around." She frowned, playing with the straw in her iced tea. "The question is why? He can barely manage his own schedule. How is he going to accommodate this?"

"I don't know," Abigail said softly, her attention on something behind Angie, "but you could ask him. I think your *space* just ran out."

She whipped her head around. Felt the blood drain from her face. Lorenzo, in a silver-gray suit, navy tie and white shirt, stood talking to the hostess. All magnetic, bespoke elegance, the pretty blonde was clearly dazzled by him, her megawatt smile as she pointed to their table blinding.

Angie turned back to her sister, butterflies swarming her stomach. "How did he know I was here?" Her gaze narrowed. "*You* told him."

Abigail sat back in her chair, wineglass in hand. "You just said you're in love with him. Not that that's a news flash. You two need to work things out."

"Traitor," Angie growled. But then her husband was standing beside their table and everything inside her seemed to vibrate with the need to hold him, to have him, she'd missed him so much.

She pressed her lips together. Looked up at him. "What are you doing here?"

He eyed her, his dark stare making her heart thud in her chest. "I've come to get my wife."

Her stomach lurched. "You can't order me around, Lorenzo. I'm done with that."

"It wasn't an order. I'm asking you to come home with me and talk this out."

She sank her teeth into her lip. "Lorenzo—"

"Please." The husky edge to his voice raked her skin. Deepened the ache inside of her to unbearable levels.

She took a deep breath. "I'm not sure it's a good idea."

"You think I don't love you?" he rasped, his gaze holding hers. "What do you think this has all been about, Angelina? Me running after you like a lunatic? Me not being able to forget you? Me acting like a complete jackass? I've been in love with you since the first moment I laid eyes on you. If my behavior hasn't made that clear, I don't know what will."

"He has a point," Abigail said dryly. "As much as I'm enjoying this spectacular grovel, however, there are at least two tabloid reporters in the house tonight. Perhaps you should hear the man out."

Angie barely heard her, she was so utterly gobsmacked by what her husband had just said. At the truth glimmering in his black eyes. Never had she expected to hear him say those three words. Certainly not in a restaurant full of people now staring at them.

She glanced at her sister. Abigail waved her off with an amused lift of her hand. "I'll have the fudge cake while I imagine being a fly on the wall. *Go*."

Lorenzo captured her fingers in his and dragged her to her feet. Through the crowded restaurant they went, her half running to keep up with his long strides.

The car sat waiting with the valet. Lorenzo tucked her

into the passenger seat, got in and drove home. Angie watched him, head spinning. "What happened in Miami? Did you sign the deal?"

"No. I told Erasmo Bavaro I would cobrand the hotels, that was my final offer, and gave them twenty-four hours to take it or leave it."

"Oh." She frowned. "You said you'd never do that."

"Things change."

"The Bavaros got to you, didn't they?"

"Perhaps. My wife also made it clear she disapproves of my slash-and-burn approach to business."

She eyed him. "Why are you helping James?"

"Because I think Carmichael can be great again, but it needs your brother at the helm. A modern leadership. And," he added, flicking her a glance, "I like the idea of building something again."

"You have no capacity. What if you land Belmont?"

"I will hand it off to the VP I hired last week. It's all part of the plan."

"What plan?"

"To keep you." Quiet words, full of meaning. *Promise.* "It was always about keeping you, Angelina. I just didn't go about it the right way."

Oh. Her heart melted. It was hard to stay angry when he said things like that.

Traffic unusually light, they made it home in minutes. Lorenzo flicked on the lights in the living room, poured them glasses of sparkling water, handed one to Angie and lowered himself into a chair. She curled up in the one opposite him.

"I need to tell you about Lucia," he said quietly. "All of it."

Her heart beat a jagged rhythm. "Lorenzo—"

He held up a hand. "I need to do it."

She sat back, heart in her mouth.

"My trip to Shanghai, the week Lucia died, was an intense trip for me. Three days in and out—nonstop meetings. Lucia wanted to come. I told her no, I wouldn't have any time for her. She was…nervous living in New York. She was from a small village in Italy, she didn't feel safe here. I thought by not taking her with me on that trip, not dragging her through those time zones when we were trying to conceive, she would be better off." His mouth flattened. "I also thought it would help toughen her up. Show her she could do it on her own."

Oh, no. She pressed her fingers to her mouth. The guilt he must feel.

"When the robbers left her alone," he continued, cheekbones standing out like blades, "she called me instead of 911. The call went to my voice mail. I was in a meeting. When I listened to the message, I lost my mind."

Her throat constricted. "No," she whispered. "Lorenzo, no." Tears welled up in her eyes. She got up, closed the distance between them and slid onto his lap. "It wasn't your fault," she murmured, pressing her lips to his cheek. "Tell me you don't think it was your fault."

The soul-deep wounds in his eyes said otherwise. "I should have respected her fears and taken her with me."

She shook her head. "You were trying to make her *stronger.* You were protecting her in your own way. I know that because you've done it with me. You've pushed me when I needed to be pushed, forced me to face my fears. It's how you care."

His dark lashes swept across his cheeks. "I'm not telling you this to inspire your pity, I'm telling you so you understand me. *Us.* It was never about me still loving Lucia, Angelina. It was about me being consumed by guilt. Me not being able to forgive myself for what I'd done. Me never wanting to feel that pain again."

Hot tears ran down her cheeks. She brushed them away,

salt staining her mouth. Finally she understood what drove her husband. Finally she understood *him*. He'd lost the most important thing in his life to a senseless act that could not be explained so he had blamed it on himself instead because, in his mind, he could have prevented it.

She cupped his jaw in her hands. "You have to forgive yourself. You have to accept what happened was beyond your control or you—*we*—will never be whole."

He nodded. "I know that. Watching you walk away from me this week was a wake-up call. I thought I could outrun the past—the guilt. But having to face it or lose you, I realized that wishing I'd made different decisions, acknowledging I've made mistakes, is something apart from forgiveness. That maybe I need to forgive myself for being human. I think it might help me let go."

Her heart stretched with the force of what she felt for him. For the peace she hoped he would find now.

"And then there was you," he said quietly. "Admitting how I felt about you. How angry I still was with you. When you walked away from me the first time, I was just learning to trust, to love again. I *was* in love with you. But I wouldn't admit it—wouldn't allow myself to love you—because I didn't think you were a sure bet. When you left, you proved me right."

Her heart squeezed. "I should never have left. I should have worked through things with you."

He shook his head. "I think it needed to happen. You needed to grow up—to become who you've become. *I* needed to realize who that woman is—to appreciate her. Our timing was off."

Maybe he was right. Maybe it hadn't been their time. Maybe now was.

"Forgive me," he said, pressing his mouth to her temple. "I was a fool to let you walk away a second time… to say those things I didn't mean. If I don't have you, *mi amore*, I am nothing. I am a shell of a man, because you take a part of me with you every time you leave."

Her heart climbed into her throat. "Promise me you will always tell me when you're hurting. Promise me you will always be that open book you talked about and I will."

"Sì," he agreed, lowering his mouth to hers. "No more holding back."

He kissed her then. Passionate and never-ending, it was full of such bone-deep need, such *truth*, it reached inside her and wound its way around her heart, melting the last of the ice. She curled her fingers around the lapels of his jacket and hung on as every bit of the misery of the past week unraveled in the kiss and was swept away.

A sharp nip of her bottom lip brought her back to reality. "That," her husband remarked, "was for ignoring my phone calls this week."

"You deserved it."

"Yes," he agreed throatily, standing and sweeping her up in his arms, "I did. Allow me to demonstrate how very sorry I am."

He carried her through the shadowy penthouse to their bedroom. Dispensing with her dress, he set her on the bed. She watched as he stripped off his clothes, his body showcased to delicious advantage in the close-fitting black hipster briefs he favored.

His eyes turned a smoky black as he stripped them off and joined her on the bed. "You like what you see? Take it, *cara*, I'm all yours."

She straddled his beautiful, muscular body, emotion clogging her throat. "I've missed you," she murmured, leaning over to kiss him. "Nothing is right when I'm not with you. You are my heart, Lorenzo Ricci."

His kiss said the words back. Passionate, perfect, it was everything she knew they were going to be. Because now that they were an open book, now that they had exorcised their last ghost, anything was possible.

Breaking the kiss, she took him inside her slick heat. Gasped when he tilted his hips and filled her with his thick, hard length in a single thrust that stole her breath.

"You can't do it, can you? Let me take control?"

His dark eyes glittered. "You wouldn't have it any other way."

No…she wouldn't. Not in this particular arena.

She let herself drown in his black eyes as he made love to her slowly, languidly, telling her how much he loved her until their breath grew rough and they were both poised on the edge of a release that promised to be spectacular.

"Say it again," she murmured.

"What?"

"That you love me."

His mouth curved. *"Ti amo, angelo mio."*

I love you, my angel.

Her heart wove itself back together. "I love you, too, Lorenzo," she whispered back before he closed his hands around her hips and took her to heaven.

Her first love. Her only love. *Her forever love.*

EPILOGUE

Nassau, Bahamas,
El Paraíso de Mar—the Carmichael Estate

"Papa!"

A squeal of delight from one of her girls was Angie's first hint that her husband had arrived home in time for the Carmichaels' annual winter party, just as he'd promised, after a week's trip to Italy.

Ready for a shower before the party, she slipped on a robe, tied it around her waist and walked to stand in the doorway of the adjoining bedroom. Her husband stood in jeans and a T-shirt, his bag abandoned, a giggling, excited daughter under each arm as their nanny looked on.

Abelie Lucia and Liliana Ines, their four-year-old identical twins, were playing their usual game.

"Lili," said Abelie, pressing a hand to her chest.

Lorenzo gave her a kiss and set her down. *"E, Abelie,"* he said, giving his other daughter a kiss.

The girls collapsed into gales of laughter. *"Mia Abelie,"* her oldest reproved, wrinkling her nose at her father.

"Ah, sì," Lorenzo said, keeping a straight face. "Silly me."

Her heart swelled, too big, it seemed, for her chest. The arrival of their daughters, the love the four of them shared, had changed her husband. The darkness was gone, replaced by a man who embraced the moment. There were still times when she could tell he was remembering, a sadness would come over him that would perhaps never leave him completely, but those times were few and far between.

"Festa?" Liliana said hopefully, turning her big blue eyes on her father.

"No. This party is for big people. But perhaps you can take your gift to bed with you."

Liliana spotted the brightly colored packages Lorenzo had left on the table. *"Regali,"* she crowed.

Lorenzo handed a package to each of them. Her chubby hands moving as fast as she could maneuver them, Liliana ripped open her gift to find a beautiful, dark-haired doll inside that looked exactly like her. Abelie did the same in a more sedate fashion, as was her personality, discovering an identical doll. A deliberate choice, Angie knew, to avoid the inevitable meltdown if one choice was more popular than another.

The girls oohed and aahed over their dolls. Angie observed her eldest's quieter admiration. It had been Angie's suggestion to name Abelie after Lucia. She'd wanted to honor her memory, to honor her husband's memories, to make it clear Lucia would never be forgotten. Lorenzo, in a very emotional acceptance, had agreed.

Abelie, sharp as a tack, noticed a third present on the table, wrapped in a different paper. *"Mamma?"* she asked.

"Sì."

"Can I open it now?"

Her husband turned to face her, a warm glint filling his dark eyes, the one he reserved exclusively for her. He picked up the gift, prowled toward her and bent and kissed her soundly. The girls devolved into another fit of giggles.

Lorenzo's mouth curved as he set her away from him. "Off to the bath," he commanded the girls. "I will come in and give you a kiss good-night when you're done."

"E bambole?" Abelie said.

"And your dolls," he agreed. "You," he said, handing the package to Angie, "put this on and meet me downstairs when you're ready. I need to find your brother before the guests arrive."

He was still giving orders, she noted. But tonight she didn't mind. She was too excited to have him home.

She showered while the girls had their bath, applied a light dusting of makeup in her dressing room and slipped on some naughty lingerie as a "welcome home" present for her husband. Opening his gift, she found a sparkly, beaded dress lying in the tissue, an Italian designer label attached.

Her heart contracted. She slid the dress over her head. The material settled over her curves in a whisper of silk, falling to just above her knee, its fit perfect. Exquisitely crafted, it hugged her body like a second skin, a plunging neckline offering a tantalizing glimpse of cleavage. *A very sexy dress.*

She left her hair loose as it had been that magical night she'd met her husband, slipped on high-heeled sandals and spritzed herself with perfume. After kissing the girls good-night, she made her way down the circular stairway to the main floor, the house ablaze with light and the chatter of hundreds of guests.

The Carmichael winter party, never an occasion to be missed, attracted friends and acquaintants from every corner of the globe. Tonight was no exception. Even the Bavaros were here, the two families having formed a close friendship.

Where before there would have been dread in her veins as she stepped out onto the terrace, a rejection of everything this represented, tonight there was only an all-encompassing glow. Her mother was stable and happy. Four years sober, Angie was cautiously optimistic this time her mother would stay healthy. But she'd accepted it was beyond her control. She had her own family now and they were her priority.

She sought out her husband in the thick crowd. It didn't take long because he was exactly where she'd figured he would be—leaning against the bar at the far end of the pool where the band was playing.

Just that little bit aloof, more than a bit untouchable, he looked dazzling in a black tux, his hair slicked back from his face. Her breath caught in her chest. Would she always react to him this way? As if her world had turned on its axis?

She took the last few steps toward him, his dark gaze tracking her. Coming to a stop in front of him, she rested a hand on the bar and looked up into his arresting face. "That's an awfully serious look for a party."

The forbidding line of his mouth softened. "Maybe I'm a serious man."

"Maybe you should stop brooding," she suggested huskily, "and ask me to dance. Unless, of course, you intend on holding up that bar all night."

A sensual glitter entered his gaze. "I think that's an offer I can't refuse, Mrs. Ricci."

Reaching behind him, he produced two glasses of champagne. Glasses in their hands, they took to the dance floor, soaking up a perfect Bahamian night, the scent of a dozen tropical blooms in the air.

Eventually they drifted off into the gardens, majestic palm trees swaying overhead. "I do believe you have dishonorable intentions," she teased when her husband drew back and set her empty glass on the stone wall beside his.

"Certo," he agreed, a heated promise in his eyes. "But first I have something for you."

He slid his hand in his pocket and pulled out a ring. A platinum eternity band set with blazing canary yellow diamonds, it was jaw-droppingly beautiful.

She lifted her gaze to his, heart thumping in her chest. "A circle of fire," her husband murmured, eyes trained on hers. "What we are, Angelina. What you've always been to me. The woman who gave me my life back...the woman who has given me two beautiful daughters who remind me every day what love is."

Her stomach plunged. *Their anniversary!* She opened her mouth to apologize for forgetting, to tell him how crazy it had been with him away, but her husband shook his head, pressed his fingers to her lips.

"I know how you feel. I've always known how you feel. I want *you* to know what you are to me so there can be no doubt as to how I feel." He pressed her palm to his chest. "This is where you are, *mi amore*. Always here."

A lump in her throat grew until it was too big to get any words around it. She stood on tiptoe and kissed him instead. Passionate, reverential, it spoke of a million forevers.

They danced under the stars then, the party forgotten, a brilliant blanket of light their only witness.

Sometimes you caught the elusive corporate raider.
Sometimes you even captured his heart.

* * * * *

If you enjoyed this book, don't miss
Jennifer Hayward's contribution to
THE BILLIONAIRE'S LEGACY *in*
A DEAL FOR THE DI SIONE RING

Also available now is the fabulous
KINGDOMS & CROWNS *trilogy!*

CARRYING THE KING'S PRIDE
CLAIMING THE ROYAL INNOCENT
MARRYING HER ROYAL ENEMY

'Get in the bath or I'll put you in it myself,' Tomas said softly.

That order melted the last frozen part within Zara.

'Really?' She couldn't help smiling at him. 'How d'you think you're going to do that?'

He looked up at her for just a moment longer, his focus dipping to her mouth. Then suddenly, in one smooth movement, he caught both her wrists in one of his hands and to her astonishment swiftly lifted his jumper and pressed her cold, cold fingers to his bare skin.

She gasped at the shock—and the sensation. She looked up into his face and saw how intently he was gazing at her.

'Tomas…' she whispered. Pleading. She couldn't help it.

He didn't reply. He just stepped that last inch closer and kissed her.

She moaned in instant delight, despite the fact his kiss was furious. He subjected her to the full force of his anger—and his passion—and both only brought forth the desire she'd tried to hold within herself for so long.

She moaned again, her legs weakening, but he abruptly broke the kiss.

Never had a man made her feel like this. Made her *want* like this.

He stared down at her silently, his breathing quick, his expression burning. But he didn't smile back at her.

'Go and get into the bath,' he breathed, releasing her completely. 'Go. *Now.*'

'Y-yes,' she stammered. Then turned and fled.

Natalie Anderson adores a happy ending. So you can be sure you've got a happy ending in your hands right now—because she promises nothing less. Along with happy endings she loves peppermint-filled dark chocolate, pineapple juice and extremely long showers. Not to mention spending hours teasing her imaginary friends with dating dilemmas. She tends to torment them before eventually relenting and offering— you guessed it—a happy ending. She lives in Christchurch, New Zealand, with her gorgeous husband and four fabulous children. If, like her, you love a happy ending, be sure to come and say hi on Facebook—facebook.com/authornataliea—follow @authornataliea on Twitter, or visit her website/blog: natalie-anderson.com.

Books by Natalie Anderson

Mills & Boon Modern Romance

Tycoon's Terms of Engagement
Blame It on the Bikini

The Throne of San Felipe

The Mistress that Tamed De Santis
The Secret That Shocked De Santis

Mills & Boon Modern Tempted

Whose Bed Is It Anyway?
The Right Mr Wrong
Waking Up in the Wrong Bed
First Time Lucky?

Visit the Author Profile page
at millsandboon.co.uk for more titles.

THE FORGOTTEN GALLO BRIDE

BY
NATALIE ANDERSON

MILLS
BOON

All rights reserved including the right of reproduction in whole
or in part in any form. This edition is published by arrangement with
Harlequin Books S.A.

This is a work of fiction. Names, characters, places, locations and
incidents are purely fictional and bear no relationship to any real
life individuals, living or dead, or to any actual places, business
establishments, locations, events or incidents. Any resemblance is
entirely coincidental.

This book is sold subject to the condition that it shall not, by way of
trade or otherwise, be lent, resold, hired out or otherwise circulated
without the prior consent of the publisher in any form of binding or
cover other than that in which it is published and without a similar
condition including this condition being imposed on the subsequent
purchaser.

® and TM are trademarks owned and used by the trademark owner
and/or its licensee. Trademarks marked with ® are registered with the
United Kingdom Patent Office and/or the Office for Harmonisation in
the Internal Market and in other countries.

First Published in Great Britain 2017
By Mills & Boon, an imprint of HarperCollins*Publishers*
1 London Bridge Street, London, SE1 9GF

© 2017 Natalie Anderson

ISBN: 978-0-263-92514-2

Our policy is to use papers that are natural, renewable and recyclable
products and made from wood grown in sustainable forests. The logging
and manufacturing processes conform to the legal environmental
regulations of the country of origin.

Printed and bound in Spain
by CPI, Barcelona

THE FORGOTTEN
GALLO BRIDE

For Toni—thank you.

CHAPTER ONE

'Type the security code quickly and get through the gates before he sees you, or he'll override the system and won't let you in. Don't get there after dark or you haven't a hope...'

ZARA FALCONER SQUINTED through the relentless rain, mentally reciting the long code while struggling to hold her freezing fingers steady enough to tap it into the keypad. Because of the storm clouds the sky had darkened early and Jasper's warning rang loudly in her ears.

Nervously she entered the last number he'd given her and held her breath, but the heavy wrought-iron gates remained as tight-locked as ever. She glanced back at the keypad, wondering if she should try again. A sudden loud clang told her she didn't need to.

The gates creaked more as they slowly opened, complaining they were unused to the movement. Zara didn't trust them to remain open for long. The *DO NOT ENTER* and *TRESPASSERS WILL BE PROSECUTED* signs pretty much gave it away. She hurried back to her car, slithering on the wet path in her haste. She inhaled deeply and tried to move more calmly. She'd only just driven through the gap when the iron gates began to close again behind her, groaning as they locked back into their defensive position.

She switched her windscreen wipers onto a faster setting and put her headlights on full to try to see more clearly where she was going. Her breathing quickened as the wet gravel crunched beneath her tyres. Big, barren branches from the large trees overhead obscured the bruised, weeping sky. She inched her battered old car down the long driveway, taking the corner at the end. That was when she had her first glimpse of the large Georgian manor that was his home. With its two stories of imposing bricks and empty windows, it was a vast, gloomy obstruction at the end of the drive. The whole building was in darkness save a feeble light gleaming in only one low window.

Her heart pounded as she pulled up right in front of the mammoth front door. She'd been driving all day and couldn't quite believe she was finally here. She'd tried to imagine this moment every day for the past year, envisaging all kinds of possible scenarios—maybe she'd bump into him on the street, or maybe they'd be at an event together and see each other across a room, or maybe he'd come to find *her*...

She'd really had no idea how it was going to happen or indeed if it ever actually would. But then Jasper had found her and basically got on his knees and begged her to visit the man to whom they both owed so much. Jasper's tired appearance and desperation had surprised her. He didn't know she needed no real encouragement to see the man who'd changed her life so drastically. She wanted to. Secretly she'd been aching to for months.

So now here she was with her shoes and jeans wet, her hair a straggly mess, and she was late...but she was *here*.

She grabbed her bag and got out of the car but, despite running to the door, only got more drenched. She no longer cared. She was too busy wondering how he'd react to seeing her again. Would he smile and laugh? Would he look concerned and caring? What would he say?

Unable to suppress the scared-but-excited shivers running up and down her spine, Zara rang the doorbell. She bit her lower lip but she couldn't stop the shy smile from slipping across her face. They'd had such a short encounter, but it had changed everything in her life. She'd relived those precious moments every day since. And every day she'd longed for just a few more.

She didn't hear any footsteps over the thumping of her own pulse. It seemed that the door just silently swung open without any warning. And then he was standing in the doorway frowning down at her.

Tomas Gallo.

All she could do was stare.

He was taller than she remembered, and leaner-looking in his faded black jeans and thin black sweater. His hair wasn't now cut in that perfect, almost preppy, businessman's style, instead it was longer, a jet-black unruly mess with a hint of curl that ended just above his collar. Despite his olive skin, he was pale. There was no Caribbean holiday tan on him now. Not that devilish smile either. He hadn't shaved in a couple of days and the stubble emphasised the sharp edges and planes of his jaw. He looked harder, unhappier. But his eyes were the same—still that beautiful dark brown. The soulful kind of eyes that you could look into for ever, but still never understand the secrets they held. And there were definitely secrets. Even more of them.

He was so striking and so unforgettable. In that one second he stole her breath—and her heart—all over again.

'What?' he snapped as she stood there speechlessly staring at him.

Her shy offer of a smile froze.

'How did you get in here?' He glared down at her, clearly expecting an immediate answer.

She wasn't able to give him one. She wasn't able to speak at all. She watched him closely for a hint of recognition in his eyes, but there was only mistrust—and building anger.

'I don't know how you got inside the gates,' he added roughly, 'but the gardens haven't been open to the public in almost a year.'

'I'm not here to see the gardens,' she finally managed to answer.

'Then what are you doing here?' He continued to glare at her. There was no recognition, no softness, no humanity.

The smile faded from her lips altogether. Awkwardly she stared back up at him. Jasper had said it was better to arrive unannounced. That he wouldn't tell Tomas she was coming. But did he *really* not remember her?

She knew she'd changed, but it was only clothes, a new hairstyle…she didn't think such superficial things would have made that much difference.

'I don't want whatever it is you're selling.' He began to shut the door.

That galvanised her into action. She'd not driven all day in such horrendous conditions to be given the brush-off in the first two seconds. In that way, she *had* changed.

'I'm not here to sell you anything,' she said, boldly stepping forward and blocking the doorway. 'I'm here to help you.'

For a beat he looked stunned before snapping back, 'I don't need help.'

Defiantly she stood exactly where she was, uncaring that she was getting wet; she was not walking away from this just yet.

'Yes, you do,' she argued, taking another step forward right into the doorway. 'Jasper sent me to you.'

Jasper had told her Tomas was still recovering from the accident. That he needed more help than he liked to admit. And while Tomas might not want her assistance, she owed him for more than he'd ever know and she wanted to pay him back for that.

He looked her over again, more slowly that time. There was still not the recognition in his expression that she'd expected, but as she watched something else emerged— something raw.

'I don't need or want your help,' he said slowly, cynicism harsh in his eyes.

She tried not to be insulted, but she failed. 'You don't even know what I can do for you.'

'I'm not interested in anything that you think you can do for me, sweetheart.' A bitter smile curved his lips as he glanced over her again. He looked so thoroughly and slowly it was as if the rains had stripped her naked and he could see every tiny intimate detail of her body.

Embarrassed heat stormed through her as his gaze lingered on her breasts. She fought hard to control her reaction to his perusal but sensual awareness circled around her, fogging everything.

'Excuse me?' she choked, stunned at her own horrendous reaction.

'What is it you're offering?' he asked. 'A massage?'

'You think I'm here to give you a massage?' she asked, utterly astonished.

'And other…services as required.' Now he was looking at her mouth with a dark gleam in his eye.

She could feel herself blushing, she could almost see into his mind and knew exactly where he thought she might use her mouth on him…and the dreadful thing was, the truly dreadful thing was, she'd once dreamt about that. But she'd rather die before she admitted that—even to herself.

'Does Jasper usually send women to provide these "services" for you?' she asked huskily.

'No.' He frowned suddenly, that gleam vanishing, as if he too rejected the idea outright. 'This is…unexpected, even for him.'

She drew herself up, gaining less than an inch in height and she was still far from being able to look him straight in the eye, but it was better than shrinking in front of him. She wasn't that naive girl any more. She wasn't afraid to stand up for herself now. She wasn't going to run away and hide. 'I'm not here to provide you with intimate entertainment.'

His gaze clashed with her own fierce one. Something changed within his expression. Then he too straightened.

'What did Jasper say to you?' he asked harshly, even angrier now.

'That you were going to be alone this weekend.'

'And he thinks that's a problem?' he asked bitterly. 'Does he think I can't handle being alone?'

'You'd have to ask him that,' she answered crossly. 'I'm just doing what he asked me to.'

'Well, Jasper was mistaken in asking you to do anything for me. I apologise for my crass assumption. You may leave.'

It couldn't have sounded less like an apology. The sky was darkening more and she could see less of his face but she could sense his anger and his resistance to her presence. Her own anger bubbled. That he could be so rude? Had he truly forgotten her? She didn't care if he couldn't cope on his own or not, he didn't look remotely incapacitated to her. As far as she was concerned, Jasper was worrying about nothing and she couldn't wait to get out of the place. But she couldn't get past him not recognising her. 'Don't you know who—?'

But it was then that the heavens truly opened, turning from torrential rain to ice. Marble-sized hailstones pelted down, bouncing on the gravel and her car and creating such a din she could no longer hear herself think let alone catch a word of what he was now saying. She saw him mutter something else—most likely impolite—then he stepped back and held his arm out towards her.

Was he inviting her in now?

Furious, she didn't move. He sent her such a speaking look and then reached for her. His grip on her upper arm was hard and her feet were moving before she'd thought better of it. The door slammed behind her, shutting out the worst of the icy racket. But it was colder indoors than it had been out there. Her heart pounded. He'd stepped back only enough to drag her inside and suddenly they were face to face and only a couple of inches apart, his grip on her wasn't any less ferocious and she could feel his breath on her frozen face.

Her gaze clashed with his. In the dim light she could see little of his expression, only that it was harsh. Her breathing—and her pulse—quickened at his nearness. Her body remembered his touch and she shivered.

Abruptly he released her. As he turned away his hand brushed hers and she quivered again as that electricity arced into her.

Yes. For her, he'd always packed a punch.

'You may wait in here, until the hail has stopped,' he said stiffly, taking another step back from her, frowning down at his hand before turning to switch on the light.

She blinked as the sudden brightness hurt her eyes—as did his silence. Shaken by her intense reaction to his proximity, she decided it was better to stay silent herself.

He didn't invite her into a warm room and offer her a seat or a drink or anything more comfortable, only shelter from the storm that should hopefully pass quickly overhead.

It was clear he didn't want to wait with her, yet he didn't want to leave her alone in his large, inhospitable house either. She suppressed a vicious smile at his quandary, still smarting from his lack of recognition of her.

A year ago she'd seen him smile and heard him laugh as he'd joked with Jasper. From her hidden corner she'd been so drawn to him. He'd been arrogant then too, confident and assured, but it was different now—cold disapproval radiated from every inch of his body. He didn't want the intrusion. He didn't want her.

Well, he'd *never* wanted her. And that was just fine, wasn't it?

Except there'd been one moment all those months ago. One moment when he'd teased her, smiled at her, reassured her. And then come close to her. Her cheeks burned at the memory of just how close he'd gotten to her then. He'd taken her by surprise—and her own reaction?

'Miss—?'

He interrupted her thoughts, dragging her back to the cold, miserable presence.

He was staring, his eyebrows raised slightly as if he was wondering what she was thinking. Embarrassed, she glanced around the vast interior. It was freezing and so unwelcoming.

'Falconer.' She told him her new name. 'Zara Falconer.'

She looked back at him as she spoke but there was no reaction at all in his expression.

And there was no outward sign of injury either. He seemed perfectly capable of taking care of himself. Yet Jasper had been adamant that Tomas needed her. He'd been agitated about it. And curiosity had been too much for her.

Tomas was undeniably the same lethally attractive man, but the shadows in his face were deeper and darker. He didn't look like the carefree, rapier-sharp devil she'd met that day.

'Jasper asked me to housekeep for you for a few days,' she finally, formally explained her mission.

'You're too young.' He dismissed the idea in an instant.

She bristled, a bitter smile twisting her lips. How many times had she heard that in her life? Yes, she did look younger than she was, but she wasn't stupid and she could work as hard as anyone. In fact, she could work harder. She had for years. 'I'm not as young as I look.'

* * *

Tomas stared down at the bedraggled woman standing in front of him. She might think otherwise but he knew what Jasper's intentions had been in sending her to him. The old schemer had been insisting for months that what Tomas really needed was some fun times with a beautiful woman. That if he relaxed, it would all come right, but his old friend was completely wrong. And the minute he got rid of her, he'd be phoning Jasper to tell him so. Again.

But it surprised him that Jasper had sent someone so unlike the usual high-maintenance-model bombshell that the old man himself preferred. This girl was too sweet. She looked so damned young in those thin sneakers, wet jeans and the light jacket that didn't offer sufficient protection from the rain and annoyed the hell out of him. But as he looked closer he saw she was right. She wasn't quite as young as her appearance first suggested.

When Tomas had opened that door she'd had a shy smile on her glowing face. The rain had been like dew on her radiant skin. Her loosely tied back rich brown hair had been starting to tumble, so wet tendrils curled softly at her temples. Her sweetheart-shaped face was dominated by those large sea-green shining eyes and full rosebud lips. Hell, she'd even had a dimple when she smiled. She'd looked the very picture of innocence and *joie de vivre*.

Everything he wasn't. Everything he'd never had.

Right now she looked the picture of indignation. It was no less attractive and he was finding it very hard to wrench his eyes off her.

His thoughts were appallingly sexual in nature. He'd taken one look at her and been hit by the almost irresistible urge to draw her close and kiss her—and made a fool of himself in thinking that was why she'd come here. But her mouth looked full and soft and perfect for kissing and she was just the right size to fit in his arms and press against his hard body. He ached for that even now.

He couldn't remember when he'd last kissed a woman. Or last wanted to. But then, he couldn't remember anything.

Angered, he stepped towards her, not stopping even as her eyes widened in wary surprise. He didn't want to know why she was here making a small puddle on the hall floor as the water streamed from her stupidly light jacket. He didn't want to be bothered by how frozen her fingers had felt when the back of his hand had brushed against them. He didn't want to see those still-shining eyes casting their innocent, cautious appeal at him.

He didn't want to want her.

What he wanted was for her to be gone.

'How do you know Jasper?' His voice still sounded rusty. No real surprise given he hadn't spoken to anyone in two days, not even a quick phone call.

She looked uncomfortable and didn't answer. His eyes narrowed. What didn't she want to tell him? Was she *Jasper's* latest little affair? His anger flared irrationally. He forced himself to breathe evenly and assess the facts. She wasn't Jasper's type. And given the way she'd blushed before at his out of order assumption, she wasn't the type at all.

'He helped me out with something a while back,' she eventually answered evasively. 'Have you eaten dinner?'

'That's not your concern.' But even as he answered his stomach growled. He wondered if *she'd* eaten. She looked as if she could do with something hot and filling. Where the hell had she driven from anyway? And why? And he did not want to be wondering about her like this.

She walked the length of the hall, not bothering to hide her curiosity behind a veil of politeness. 'The house is dark and cold.'

Her tone wasn't judgmental but he felt argumentative. 'Maybe I like it that way.'

'You like to make it as unwelcoming as possible?' She flashed that impish smile as she turned back to face him. 'Are you that afraid of people?'

The edgy question was softened not so much by that smile as the shining candour in her eyes but it didn't defuse his simmering anger.

'I work hard and I don't like interruptions,' he corrected, refusing to be melted by her radiance, refusing to be drawn nearer to her. But the pull was powerful. He glared, infuriated by his primary, base response to her. 'And I don't need a baby-faced babysitter. It really is time for you to leave.'

Except he couldn't help wondering where she would go.

Her smile faded and a confused look entered her eyes, dulling the sea-green brilliance. Stupidly he felt he'd disappointed her in some way. He didn't like it.

'I'm not as young as you seem to think,' she suddenly declared with a lift to her chin, as if she'd made up her mind about something and was determined to see it through. 'I was married once.'

He huffed out a breath, stunned that her words wounded him in a niggling way. 'But you're not now?' he replied softly. The silence hung with significance.

Her eyelids dropped and she looked down, as if it hurt to hold his gaze. 'I guess it wasn't meant to be.'

'I'm sorry,' Tomas said stiffly. Not so innocent then; she'd been bruised. The thought of her being hurt grated on his already strained nerves.

He cursed Jasper for sending her to him.

He walked back to the front door, but when he opened it he saw that, while the hail had stopped, the rain had returned. It was almost completely dark now and it would be impossible for her to see three feet in front of her while driving. No way could he let her leave in this weather. Inwardly he cursed more.

'It isn't safe for you to leave tonight,' he said gruffly. 'You'll have to stay here.'

He looked at her again and something stirred in the back of his mind. Had he said those words to her before?

He scowled at the *déjà vu*—the trick of a feeble mind.

He loathed it when it happened. Hated thinking there might be a memory just out of reach and that there was nothing he could do to draw it closer or clearer. The most random, inconsequential things sparked it. He paused, waiting, hoping the fragment would float to the forefront of his mind.

It didn't. It never did.

Frustration flamed his anger to fury. He stepped towards her, his gaze narrowing. The shine in her eyes had gone. So had her smile.

'Do I know you?' He rapped the question, like machine-gun fire, hating that he was compelled to ask. Hated giving his weakness away.

'No,' Zara answered baldly, her throat aching from holding back her disappointment. She'd tried to prompt him just then, but it seemed that what had happened a year ago had been so minor that he'd forgotten it. He'd forgotten her.

She knew it was stupid to feel it, but the reality of her insignificance crushed her. Yet what had she expected? This wasn't a fairy tale. It never had been and never would be. It had been one afternoon, one night, one morning. It had been nothing to him, not even worth remembering.

And she hadn't just lied. He *didn't* know her. He never truly had.

But that hadn't stopped him from marrying her.

CHAPTER TWO

'I want your niece.'

IT HAD BEEN for less than two days and it had been total madness. But it had been real. They'd married.

She should try again to remind him outright, but she was too mortified. That year's worth of imaginings, of meeting him again and hoping to change his first impression of her? That she could show she was no longer that weak woman who'd needed rescuing—that she was strong and capable and going places—that kernel of hope that he might see her in a different light?

She'd been so stupid.

She had to get away from him—from here—immediately.

She stepped towards the still-open doorway, but before she got there he closed it and faced her, blocking the exit.

'You'll stay here for the night and travel on in the morning when the weather has eased,' he said.

His dictatorial tone checked her momentarily, but she held her ground. 'And if it hasn't eased?'

'You'll at least be able to see in the light.'

'My car has good headlights, I think it's better if I leave now.' The last thing she wanted was to stay here.

'No.' His tone brooked no argument.

She remembered that implacable decisiveness and the air of authority so very well. Once he'd made his mind up that was it. Done. He couldn't be crossed or fought. She'd seen that when he'd dispatched the argument of her uncle with an icy blade. And there was that weak part of her that still wanted his recognition to come.

'If you'd care to show me the kitchen,' she said coldly. 'The least I can do is make some supper for us both.'

And she'd be on the phone to Jasper as soon as she was alone.

'I don't need anything, but please help yourself to anything you may like,' he replied equally coolly.

He refrained from indulging in a smile of satisfaction, but that obvious restraint made her all the more annoyed. He was too used to getting his own way.

'You must be hungry after your journey,' he added formally.

He was determined to reject her assistance in any way, yet was insistent she accept his help. It was an arrogantly unfair power play. He'd ensured she was reliant on him, yet he refused any assistance or even kindness from her.

One day she'd make him accept it somehow, some time. Just for once she didn't want to be the weak one.

She followed him down the long cold corridor. In the light she now noticed a very slight limp as he walked.

'My office is on the second floor, but the kitchen is this way,' he explained briefly. 'Where have you driven from today, Zara?'

'Up north,' she answered carefully.

She was hyper aware of the latent strength in his lean physique as she followed him. He seemed more ruthless, he smiled a whole lot less, but he was still breathtaking. She'd forgotten just how much he fascinated her. Fortunately he didn't appear to realise the effect he had on her. Thank goodness. He'd never noticed how he made her feel.

Her heart thudded at the strangeness of this arrangement. She shouldn't have agreed to come. He didn't need her help at all—what had Jasper been worrying about?

'I'm sorry if I've inconvenienced you,' she said politely,

still trying to get over the smarting hurt that he'd not re-membered her.

'I will ensure there is a room ready for you,' he replied and left her.

She watched as he left. Not big on small talk, was he?

The kitchen was beautiful and scrupulously clean and she realised she needed food. She'd think better if she warmed up. She'd prepare something and then speak to Jasper.

She checked the cupboards. There were barely the sta-ples in the pantry. She opened the freezer and found a stack of containers—single-serve portions—labelled with the dish and the date it had been made, but also the date for him to eat. Someone had prepared enough for him to last the next few days. Who had done that, when Jasper had in-sisted that Tomas's housekeeper had walked out suddenly, leaving him in the lurch?

Someone had organised this for him. She frowned. So why had Jasper been so insistent she come then, if he'd al-ready been taken care of?

Her frown deepened as she looked in the fridge. There was milk and another—uneaten—prepared whole meal, but no raw ingredients.

But the meal he was supposed to have eaten last night was still in there. So was the container labelled as his lunch. She glanced at the counter and the sink again; there wasn't even a drop of water from the tap in the bottom of the sink. If he'd prepared anything for himself, he'd not left a sin-gle sign of it.

She shrugged, telling herself not to care. But she would make herself—and him—something to warm up.

She took off her jacket and scrabbled round in the bot-tom of her shoulder bag and found the bar of plain choco-late she had there. Thank goodness she'd not eaten it on the drive down. She found a copper pan and gently warmed the milk on the stovetop and grated the chocolate in. As she stirred it to melt the slivers she couldn't stop the memories from tormenting her. She'd made him coffee that morning, served it with her special lemon-slice cake—that first recipe she'd ever tweaked.

'He's here to invest in the casino—don't screw it up. Stay out of sight as much as possible.'

By then she'd got good at staying out of sight. Her uncle's temper had been worsening by the day and she was the easiest person for him to vent it on. So she knew when to avoid him, but that day he'd needed her skills.

She'd been the only child of doting parents who'd died when she was just twelve. Her only living relative had flown in to console her. Uncle Charles had said he lived on a luxury yacht in Antigua and ran a casino. He'd sold her parents' home and told her she'd love it on his boat, with his glamorous second wife.

But that wife had walked out ten months later, fed up with the chauvinistic abuse he served up twenty-four-seven. She'd left teenaged Zara there alone to witness the drinking and womanising and gambling and sleaze.

Her uncle had blamed her for his wife's departure. In the end everything was her fault. That flashy 'home' had offered no relief from isolation and grief—it only exacerbated it, because she didn't fit the mould.

She'd been nothing but a disappointment to her uncle and he'd let her know it. She'd been so scared and lonely she'd let him stomp all over her—had shut herself away like some sad Cinderella. She'd been so stupidly quiet and shy.

She'd never been able to live up to the expectations he had of her. He'd told her time and time again she was useless. He refused to send her to school and begrudged the correspondence-school paperwork she requested.

She'd retreated below deck. Len, the Scottish chef he employed, became her one true friend and mentor. Over the next few years he'd taught her everything he knew. But then Charles sacked Len and told Zara to take over the food prep full time. At the time she'd thought it had been to spite her, but in hindsight she realised it was one of several signs of the financial failure he was verging on.

By then she'd long since lost contact with her school friends. She was isolated, lonely and trapped; her uncle held her passport and was the sole trustee of her finances—and the money her parents had left her?

All gone. Didn't she know how much it had cost her uncle to house her? Wasn't she grateful for that?

Her uncle Charles had been embarrassed that *she'd* had to wait on his unexpected, important guests. She wasn't decorative enough—not thin enough, not perfect enough. Not for investment guru, Tomas Gallo, and his lawyer, Jasper Danforth. She was the useless, mousy niece he'd inherited and had never wanted.

But for that business meeting she'd had to be the hostess as well as prepare the coffee and cakes. When she'd caught sight of Tomas Gallo as she'd carried the tea tray into the room, she'd nearly dropped everything.

He'd not appeared to notice when she spilt some of the coffee, but he'd eaten some of the lemon slice. Two pieces in fact.

She'd sat in the corner, mute, suffering silently as her uncle had made joke after joke at her expense. She'd been bowled over by Tomas's appearance and the bottomless depths of his eyes. He was the most striking man she'd ever seen but he and Jasper had appeared amused, as if they'd agreed with every one of her uncle's words. And she'd died that bit inside to see that someone so gorgeous could be so cruel.

Almost an hour had passed when Tomas had dropped the bombshell.

'Sorry, Charles, I don't think the casino is the right fit for us at this time.'

Her uncle had been beyond furious at losing the investment. He'd been unable to contain his rage, venting it on her down in the galley while the two guests upstairs were readying to leave. She'd stared at the floor as he'd berated her in a bitter hoarse whisper.

'You're worse than useless. If you were attractive you could have seduced him. But as if any man would ever want you. You're a millstone, you ungrateful, lazy little cow. You can't even pour a coffee properly.'

The blow had come sudden and hard. It had stung so much.

She'd run from the galley only to collide in the corridor with Tomas Gallo. She'd gasped, appalled that he was down there—that he might have heard...

Firm hands held her upper arms and she flinched when she looked into his thunderous face. He quickly stepped back into the side room, lifting her with him and swiftly closing the door behind them.

'Don't be afraid,' he muttered harshly.

But the lethal anger in his eyes told her he was so very much more dangerous than her uncle. He visibly made himself relax and force a small smile. That was when she realised his fury was not for her.

'He hit you.' He tilted her chin and inspected the red of her upper cheek.

'It doesn't matter.' She wanted him to leave before her uncle found out he was down here and made everything worse.

'It always matters,' he replied curtly.

Her heart was his in that second.

Tomas released her and she dashed the tears away with

the back of her hand, willing him to go back up to the deck and leave with his lawyer. But he didn't.

'You've lived here how long?' he abruptly asked. 'How long?' he prompted when she didn't answer.

'Almost ten years,' she whispered.

'You have money?'

She shook her head.

'Passport?'

'My uncle...' She trailed off hopelessly.

'I see.'

Yes, she'd known he saw more than she'd ever wanted anyone to see—not only had he seen through her uncle's 'joking' façade to the emotional abuse that it was symptomatic of, he'd witnessed the occasional physical violence her uncle subjected her to. She'd hated that she hadn't the strength or resources to leave, she'd loathed the depth of her dependence on her uncle. Flushing with mortification, she'd made to push past Tomas but he'd grabbed her arm again. She'd been forced to meet his gaze. There she'd read the steel and the concern, the sympathy and—to her shock—empathy.

It was as if he'd understood, because he'd been there himself.

But that had to have been her own projection. She'd wanted out for so long, but she'd become so trapped by imposed gratitude, felt so beholden and been so downtrodden, she hadn't known which way to turn or how to get herself out of it. She'd had no money, no chance to study, or to work. She'd been made to feel as if she owed Uncle Charles everything.

'Do you want out?' Tomas asked bluntly.

'Out?' She blinked uncomprehendingly. 'You mean do I want to leave?'

'Yes. Do you want me to help you?'

His question was brusque and unexpected. She instinctively knew he wasn't going to wait for her to um and ah. He wasn't going to cajole or try to convince her. This was a single offer and she had a single second to decide.

She nodded.

'Follow my lead.' He let her go and turned towards the stairs. 'No matter what.'

Back up on deck Jasper was standing with his briefcase in hand. Her uncle was attempting to hide his anger and disappointment by talking incessantly about the tourism boom. Zara stood terrified at a distance, knowing her uncle would be even angrier that she'd returned to the deck.

'Sit back down, Jasper,' Tomas said with deceptive softness. 'I've had some time to think about things some more while freshening up.'

'You have?' The glow of bitterness in her uncle's eyes morphed to avaricious excitement. 'Go fetch more drinks, Zara. Now.'

'No, I want her to stay,' Tomas overruled him firmly. 'She's a crucial detail to this possible deal.'

Cold sweat slid down Zara's spine. Surely he wouldn't call her uncle out for hitting her? She sent Tomas a desperate look, but he wasn't looking at her at all.

'I want your niece,' Tomas said bluntly. 'I'll invest in your casino operations, but only if I have Zara.'

Zara's heart stopped. She couldn't have heard right.

'You want Zara?' Her uncle narrowed his eyes. 'You can't want—'

'Those are my terms.' Tomas didn't let her uncle continue. 'Without Zara there will be no investment.'

'You want...' Her uncle just stared at him in shock. 'How do I know you're serious?'

'I'll marry her,' Tomas answered bluntly. 'How soon can we arrange that, Jasper?'

It took five seconds for Charles to collect himself and shut his dropped jaw.

Terrified, she stared from Tomas to Charles to Jasper. The lawyer's face was utterly impassive while he checked data on his tablet, as if his boss made outrageous queries every day. He'd said to follow his lead, but this was almost barbaric.

'It seems...er...that you can marry today if you really want to,' Jasper said, sending his boss a covert look. 'There's no notice or stand-down period required. Just the fee, two witnesses and passports.'

'Good,' Tomas said, ignoring that warning plea in the tone from his lawyer. 'So we can leave now.'

Zara stared at her uncle, trying to read his reaction. Surely he'd say no to such a preposterous suggestion? Surely he'd have some compunction?

But a greedy light entered his eye. 'You'll be my nephew-in-law.'

'That's right.' Tomas nodded. 'We'll be family.'

A prickle ran down Zara's spine at something in Tomas's tone. There was something so very cold when he said that word.

Uncle Charles smiled. 'She can cook.' He nodded, as if suddenly approving of her skills. 'She's a virgin too, you know.' His proud smile made her skin crawl. 'She's been very sheltered.'

She closed her eyes, engulfed in scalding shame and mortification. He was talking about her as if she were a thing to be traded. And as if her sexual experience were anything that mattered?

'Then it's decided. Zara, go pack your bag.' Tomas issued the order without even looking at her.

Sickened to her soul, she knew she had no choice. If she stayed she'd be her uncle's skivvy and, increasingly, his punchbag, for the foreseeable future. His temper would *only worsen the more his business failed. And now she knew how he really saw her. How he'd trade her for some stupid business deal.*

'Wait.' A suspicious twist tightened her uncle's mouth. 'I'll come with you to the register office.'

'Of course,' Tomas said unblinkingly, staring her uncle down. 'You'll want to witness the wedding. Go and pack now, Zara.'

Her uncle hadn't even bothered to ask her how she felt about it. He was acting as if he owned her. But then, that was how he'd always acted. She meant absolutely nothing to him. She'd been a source of money—and when that had gone, she'd become little more than another of his staff. Only he hadn't had to pay her.

She left the room without a word. And then she ran.

Zara poured steaming-hot chocolate into two mugs and blinked back the tears at the recollection of how little her uncle had cared for her. But she was away from him now—and so much stronger.

She sprinkled a hint of cinnamon on the top of each. She found a half-empty packet of biscuits at the back of the cupboard and added a few to a small plate and loaded the wooden tray she found in a cupboard.

It had all happened so quickly it was almost a blur. Yet those moments were seared in her mind. There she'd stood in the council offices shivering in a cheap sundress and make-up covering the mark from where her uncle had hit her.

The ceremony had been ridiculously brief. Uncle Charles had witnessed it. Jasper had been the other signatory and given Tomas a ring to slide onto her frozen finger. Heaven knew where he'd found it so quickly.

She could have said no. She could have tried to tell the

officials that it was all a farce and that her uncle was insisting she marry a stranger. But she didn't. She'd just said yes.

There'd been no photos. No glasses of champagne. No
speeches. And no kiss. Tomas had given her a cool peck on
her cheek when the official had given the corny 'you may
kiss the bride' permission. She'd pushed away that fleeting
feeling of disappointment, reminding herself it wasn't real.

Her uncle had stood practically rubbing his hands in
glee as she married the wealthiest man either of them had
ever met. But Tomas Gallo had flipped the tables on Uncle
Charles completely. He'd waited until they returned her
uncle to the marina before dropping the bomb. He'd told
her to remain in the car, but she'd opened her door already
and could hear every word between the two men now eye-
balling each other.

*'I've changed my mind about the deal,' Tomas said coolly.
'I'm not going to buy into your company.'*

'But you just—'

*'We signed nothing and there was no formal agreement,'
Tomas continued, ignoring the interruption. 'Jasper, Zara
and I are leaving now and you won't see us again.'*

'You...you...'

*For the first time she saw her uncle lost for words. Sud-
denly he spun towards her, his face contorted with rage.*

*'You manipulative little...' He lunged for her through
the open car door but Tomas stepped in front of her like
an avenging angel.*

*'She's my wife.' Tomas bit the words out. 'And you'll
leave her alone.'*

'Your wife? She's worse than useless. She won't be—'

*'I neither want nor expect anything from her,' Tomas
interrupted, still ice-cold. 'She's not a commodity to me.'*

He jerked his head at Jasper and the lawyer closed

the car door, sealing her away from the ugliness and the threats. But she could still hear their conversation.

'Try to contact her again and I will destroy the little you have left of a life.'

She shivered at the ruthless promise.

Her uncle fell back a step. 'You can't destroy me. I'll go to the media—'

'And tell them you sold your niece to a total stranger? The same girl who bears the bruises from your fist?' Tomas coolly goaded. 'You're a gambling man. You know it's time to cut your losses and leave.'

Tomas got back into the car and drove them away. The last time she saw her uncle he was red-faced, sweaty and defeated.

Tomas's mouth was held firm and she didn't dare speak a word as he drove them away from her uncle and towards the hotel he was staying in. She could feel the cold rage rolling off him. Jasper, sitting in the back seat, was utterly mute.

Tomas glanced at her and suddenly broke the silence. 'Don't be frightened. He won't bother you again.'

She was still afraid. She had no idea what she was going to do.

'You'll fly to London in the morning,' Tomas continued, turning his attention back to the road. 'I have your passport from your uncle as we needed it for the wedding. Jasper will ensure the marriage is annulled in the next few days. I will gift you a one-off payment. You never have to return here and you never have to see him again. Or me, for that matter. You're free to do as you wish.'

Her fears melted away. She bit her lip. She didn't know how to thank this man. She couldn't even look him in the eyes; he was so gorgeous, and now he'd done this?

'Your uncle is a greedy gambler and poor businessman. He thought our marriage would mean I'd committed to his

company. He didn't bother asking me to draw up any bind-
ing documents in regards to any investment. He thought
he'd won the lottery and showed just what he was capable
of.' He shook his head regretfully. 'He thought he could sell
you.' He pulled up outside the hotel and sent her a small
smile. 'But we got him, didn't we?'

He was so handsome and, in that moment, almost mis-
chievous...

On a whim she'd probably never fully understand, he'd offered her an escape and she'd sold herself to him that very
afternoon.

But he'd never actually wanted *her*. He was too much the
maverick for that. It was his distaste for her uncle that had
forced him to act. In less than forty-eight hours Tomas had
gotten her out of there and then disappeared from her life.

She lifted the tray and made herself lift her chin. She did
owe him. And now it seemed she was going to owe him for
yet more—a night's accommodation to wait out the storm.

As she walked back along the corridor and headed up
the wide staircase, she realised his wing of the house was
warm. The luxurious thick carpet was plush and intricate.
It truly was a stately home with its antique furniture and
polished wood. On the first floor she glanced at the walls,
expecting gilt-edged frames of the family portrait gallery.

That was when she paused in amazement. There were
pictures, but they weren't in frames. Slowly she progressed
along the gallery towards the lit room at the end that she
assumed was his office. But she was unable to look away
from the pages and pages pinned to the wall. Pictures of
people with notes written underneath all of them—dates,
times, messages about meetings, details about the individuals pictured.

Her heart pounded. It was like the case room in some

FBI movie. Was she in a house with a total psychopath or was he some kind of overachieving stalker?

Of course he wasn't. She knew that about him. She knew he was ruthless, yes. But he was also kind. And he was ferociously good at his job.

She looked again and saw there was a rough timeline to the wall. It covered almost a decade. There were pictures of Tomas as well and hand-scrawled notes in pencil beneath. Press clippings about himself as if he were a total narcissist? It just didn't make sense.

A horrible feeling sank into her bones. All these people pictured were people connected to him, mostly through business. They were people he knew.

Or *had* known.

She replayed that conversation they'd had only minutes ago on his doorstep—remembering his abruptness, his defensiveness. And when he'd asked that question—*'Do I know you?'*

He hadn't looked angered as much as guarded. He hadn't wanted to ask her that question. What had he been wary of? Her answering *yes*?

Why would that have been a problem? Because he hadn't remembered her?

If he'd asked 'have we met?' she wouldn't have lied. But she'd hidden behind semantics. Now she registered that there was more than an arrogant aloofness to him, there was a barrier. He was locked away. She remembered Jasper's agitation and insistence that Tomas was still suffering since that accident. Her own hurt pride had blinded her to the obvious.

She knew Tomas had carried Jasper to safety seconds before the car had exploded—that had been well documented in the press. It had been reported that Tomas had been thrown to the ground with his leg shredded. And his head?

He didn't welcome guests, didn't want intrusion. Why? Because he didn't want to talk about anyone, or himself?

She feared there was a very good reason for that and she was furious with Jasper for not telling her the truth. What else hadn't he told her?

'What are you doing in here?'

She jumped at the furious demand and almost dropped the tray she was carrying. Turning, she saw Tomas had come up behind her. The iciness in his eyes was impenetrable. He was *livid*.

Her blood quickened. 'Looking for you.'

But the plush carpet had masked his footfall.

'You do not come up here. *Ever,*' he snapped.

Zara's anger flared—a mixture of guilt and outrage. He was rude and arrogant and she didn't care how much of a hard time he'd had, there was no need to be so vile to someone. She'd been spoken to like that too many times in her life and she no longer stood for it. *Ever.* 'No wonder you can't keep staff when you speak to them like that.'

He visibly recoiled and then blinked. 'The Kilpatricks have been loyal to me all this last year. They're only away this weekend to attend a family celebration.'

She gaped at him for a second. 'That wasn't what I was told.'

'And what were you told exactly?' He stepped forward and grasped her shoulders. 'And by whom?'

'I told you. Jasper. He said you'd been left without any staff. That you needed someone for a week or so.'

'How do you know him?'

'I told you that already too. He helped me out a while back.'

'Helped you out?'

She threw him a look as she heard the insinuation in his tone. 'He's old enough to be my father.'

'That doesn't stop many women. He's very wealthy—'

'You just can't stop insulting me, can you?' She glared at him. 'I'm here to help you, because your friend asked me to come. If you have an issue with it, take it up with him.'

'I intend to.'

Biting her lip, she glanced at the wall again. She couldn't help it. And the thing was, she had taken *Tomas's* money.

But that was partly why she was here. To make amends and show her gratitude. Only now did she realise just how impossible that might be.

'Don't ask,' he said shortly as he followed the line of her sight to the picture-strewn walls.

'I wasn't going to.'

Because now she thought she understood. Her anger melted as her heart broke for him. She was so very sorry. 'This part of the house is cosy.'

'I've put the heating on in your room.' His expression became remote and he released her to step away. 'And in the kitchen. It should be better in a few more minutes. The whole house temperature is controlled to protect the art and furnishings that are in storage. I'm not into wasting resources.'

Tomas watched as Zara nodded and placed the tray she was carrying onto a nearby low table. She lifted up one of the mugs. He refused to be tempted but he could smell the chocolate. He hadn't had chocolate in a long, long time.

But when she turned back, Tomas read pity in her eyes and it infuriated him. 'Still think I can't cope alone?' he asked bitterly.

'I don't think that,' she said briefly. 'Jasper was the one worrying. He said you're likely to work so hard you'd forget to eat. That you won't bother taking the time to cook yourself something decent. And it's not like you can get a pizza delivery tonight.'

For some reason the thought of Jasper talking about him with her got right under his skin. His right-hand man had always had affairs with beautiful women. Young and old. But with Zara? It didn't gel. And it hadn't happened. She didn't need to tell him again.

Now her small smile returned and it mollified him.

'So here you are,' he muttered. Like a temptress.

'Would you like some hot chocolate?' She held out the mug to him. 'That's why I came up here.'

Slowly he shook his head. 'I don't eat sugar.'

'You're diabetic?' She frowned and clasped the mug back close to her with her other hand. 'Any other dietary requirement I should know about?'

'I'm not diabetic. I simply prefer not to eat too much sugar.' He wanted to get back to peak physical health.

'Maybe you should, it might sweeten you up,' she mumbled as she turned away about to return downstairs.

'What was that?' Her attitude took him by surprise. She was like a little spitting kitten with not very sharp claws but she wasn't afraid to give him a swipe.

'No sugar. Got it.' She turned back and smiled brightly at him. That dimple appeared.

Her small show of fearlessness amused him. He almost smiled back.

'It's not good for my recovery,' he explained reluctantly, because he didn't want her to walk away just yet. That smile was bewitching.

A small frown pleated her brow as she looked him over—but her checking for his recovery took a twist. Her expression changed and a dazed look entered her eyes, colour ran up under her cheeks. Tomas tensed at her undeniable sensual awareness of him and he couldn't resist another assessment of his own.

She'd taken off that almost useless rain jacket, revealing she wore only a thin T-shirt underneath. The curves in those jeans were not girlish in any way; frankly they were generous. The sneakers didn't help her in the height department at all and when he'd held her from him just before he'd felt the slenderness of her shoulders. The sheer femininity of her made him catch his breath. It had taken every ounce of will to refrain from sliding his hand to her narrow waist and pulling her flush against him. He ached to feel those soft curves against him.

Hell, he'd turned into a pervert in two minutes flat.

She gulped at the hot chocolate as if she needed to do something with herself. He watched as she swallowed it back. The scent of the warm liquid assailed his senses. It was the first time in ages he'd regarded food as anything other than fuel. He looked at the speck of creamy milk left on her lip and his mouth watered.

'Are you sure you don't want some?' Her eyes were wide and her voice a mere whisper.

Any other woman and he'd have thought it was a come-on, but the candour in those eyes spoke volumes.

He ought to tell her that she'd left a bit of chocolate milky foam on her lip, but he wasn't going to. Too much of a cliché. He would not notice. He was well practised at eliminating extraneous thoughts from his mind. All that mattered was his work and rebuilding his company into something better than before the accident that had almost destroyed him.

No one would ever know how bad his injuries had been or the degree to which he'd suffered. The public perception of him—the belief in his knowledge and skill—needed to be unshakeable. Because he was his company.

No one could ever know the truth. He could never allow himself to be that exposed.

As he silently regarded her, her pupils grew and that sweet colour deepened in her cheeks as she realised the *double entendre* she'd inadvertently uttered. She caught her lip with her teeth. And then—to his surprise—she smiled again.

Grimly he stared at her, unable to speak. He wanted to kiss her—taste that smile and the sweetness deep inside her.

'Tomas?' Her voice was the thinnest of whispers now and uncertainty had stolen into her expression as she looked into his face.

No, she wasn't one of Jasper's ladies of pleasure. She was too confused by this undeniable electricity that arced whenever they so much as glanced at each other. But she couldn't help the way she looked at him or hide the hazy desire evident in her eyes and in the way her breathing quickened the nearer he got to her.

She was as thrown as he. Only Tomas was a master of hiding everything now.

But the temptation was almost too great.

'I'll get your bag from the car,' he said abruptly.

'I'll go tidy the kitchen.' She turned and all but ran from him.

He watched her go.

No, he wasn't doing anything about this sexual attraction no matter how intense. He didn't have the time or the desire to fool around. And he couldn't risk exposure.

Except all he could think about were her curves. And her mouth. And the irrepressible sparkles in her eyes. She was like a sensual pixie specially sent to torment him.

Damn Jasper.

CHAPTER THREE

'You can't sleep?'

ZARA WAS STILL trembling when she made her way to the kitchen. She'd been so overwhelmed by the desire to kiss him, she'd almost leaned into him. But she'd mistaken that look in his eyes, because he'd then looked so forbidding. She'd almost humiliated herself all over again.

She fished her phone out of her bag, frowning at the low number of battery bars. She needed to charge it soon. Before anything, though, she needed to talk to Jasper.

She hit him with it the second he answered. 'Why didn't you tell me the truth?'

'Zara?'

At his sharp reply her bravado faded. 'Why didn't you tell me about Tomas?'

There was a pause. 'What did he say when he saw you?'

'He has no idea who I am.'

'He didn't recognise you?' Jasper's disappointment was more than audible; she felt it echoing over the ether.

'Why did you tell me his staff had walked out on him?' she asked plaintively. 'You lied to me. You set me up.'

'I thought it might work,' he answered a touch belligerently. 'It was my last—'

'What might work?'

'That he'd see you again and...'

She waited. Then she guessed anyway. 'You hoped he'd remember me.'

'Zara.'

'That's what you meant, isn't it? When you said he had injuries, you meant his memory. Because there isn't anything else. He's very…fit.' She drew in a shuddering breath and leaned against the kitchen counter. 'I'm right, aren't I? He's lost his memory.' She waited for his reply. 'Jasper?'

'I can't tell you. I promised him.'

'I'm different.' She wasn't just anyone. She'd been the man's wife.

'No. Not even you,' Jasper muttered, sounding older than his years. 'He saved my life too, you know.'

'Jasper—'

'He needs help.' Jasper suddenly interrupted her. 'He's not left that house all year. All he does is work—'

'He doesn't need *my* help. He needs professional help.' She wasn't a professional *anything*. She blinked back the tears as she whispered, 'I'm not the right person. He deserves better than this.' He deserved better than her.

Jasper had been wrong in setting them both up like this. He'd lied to Tomas and made her an accessory. She hated that.

The phone cut out a couple of times and she guessed someone else was trying to phone Jasper, but he ignored it.

She thought of that lonely gallery up there with Tomas's life in pictures and articles on the wall. The notes he had and what must be a desperate attempt to make sense of it all. 'Can he remember anything?'

'I can't talk about it, Zara. I promised him I wouldn't. But he's lost so much. You can see how isolated he is. I thought if he just saw you…'

But she'd been nothing in Tomas's life—only a moment, a whimsy. She hadn't truly touched him or made any lasting impression on him. He'd turned her world upside down, then walked away without so much as a backwards glance. All done in a little over a day.

She'd meant nothing to him.

'I can't stay here,' she said. Jasper had trapped her in

a situation she'd never have agreed to had she known the truth.

'You must,' Jasper said firmly. 'It will take a couple of days until I get there. Work as his housekeeper. I can get him to agree to that.'

'No—'

'You can't leave, Zara.' He overrode her.

'Why not?'

There was a hesitation, then a sigh. 'Because you're still married to him.'

'What?' Every muscle in her body weakened and she almost dropped the phone. *'What?'*

'You're still married. The annulment was never processed. I'm sorry.'

She was still married to Tomas? Goosebumps skittled over her skin. She drew in a breath so jagged it seemed to slice her lungs. 'How is that possible?' she whispered.

'After the accident, I was so distracted it slipped my mind.'

'But the paperwork… I signed—' She broke off, too stunned to speak.

'It burned in the car. We were in hospital for weeks. Tomas was there for months. Then I was concerned about him—protecting him.'

She'd read in the newspaper about the car accident in France less than a week after their crazy wedding. She'd felt sick at the time as she'd learned how Tomas had fought to get Jasper free of the wreckage before the car had exploded. But they'd both survived the accident and the blast and, according to the reports, both were going to be fine. There'd been little about the man in his bio on his business website. Other online searches had been business related and largely fruitless.

Not long after that that she'd forced herself to stop searching for information on him. She couldn't turn into some sad obsessive. She'd had to forget him to move forward with her life. But her repayment plan had always burned in the background. In the long term she'd aimed to track him down, successful, a whole new woman. With the money plus interest to return to him. She'd wanted to impress him with her transformation and her success.

She'd never do that now.

'No one knows?' She turned and stared at the dark window but she could see nothing but her own pale face in the glass.

'No one knows anything about you. Only his medical team know about...'

She felt the ground had been cut out from under her. All this time they'd been married? And all these months he'd been so *hurt*?

'You're coming here now, aren't you? Please,' she begged. She couldn't handle this alone. 'He has to know,' she said, her old anxiety rushing to the fore. She should go in there right now and tell him, but she couldn't do it. More than that, he wouldn't believe her. She had no proof. He'd think she was crazy. And she wouldn't blame him. 'Please, you have to tell him...'

She didn't want to do more harm than good. She didn't want to make anything worse for him. And she didn't want him to know how weak she'd been.

Truth?

She was still weak. And she was still half in love with him.

She heard the series of interruptions signalling Jasper was getting another call, but again he ignored it.

'We both owe him, Zara.'

She closed her eyes against the emotional manipulation. So many times that had been used against her. But this time was different. Because this time she *did* owe.

Tomas. *Everything.*

'I know,' she said softly.

'Stay until I get there.'

'Yes,' she agreed. Defeated.

'Is that Jasper you're talking to?'

She jumped at the question that cracked across the room like a bullwhip. Tomas stood in the kitchen doorway, looking furious, his own mobile phone in his hand. How long had he been standing there? What had he heard?

Then it hit her. She was staring at her *husband*.

'Zara?'

She didn't answer Jasper's sharp query because in two steps Tomas was across the room and had snatched the phone from her limp fingers.

'*Never* ignore my calls,' he said furiously into her phone to Jasper, not taking his eyes off her.

She heard Jasper's immediate reply. She hadn't got that apologetic deferential tone from him. The grim look on Tomas's face deepened as Jasper muttered something else she couldn't hear because now her mind whirled at the implication of Jasper's words.

She was still married to Tomas. She was his *wife*. She quivered as a frisson of intimacy that she had no right to feel skittered down her spine.

She'd always been too aware of him, too attracted, too ready to say yes.

Now she was here in this huge house alone with him and while he might have no clue about the truth, that didn't mean he wasn't totally, utterly in control.

And she wasn't. Not of herself. Not of those stupid yearnings she'd felt when he—and only he—was near. She'd been too isolated. Too inexperienced. Too insecure.

She licked her lips nervously as she watched his anger flare at Jasper.

At totally the wrong moment that one precious memory slipped its leash to torment her.

* * *

'You can't sleep?'

She shook her head, feeling her colour mount because he'd found her awake and alone at two in the morning, pacing the corridor outside her hotel room like an undead wraith unable to rest. She stopped outside her door, her bare toes curling into the carpet, and half hoped he'd just pass by and leave her to her own agony.

She had the most massive crush on him. How could she not? He was gorgeous and kind and mesmerising. And he'd helped her.

She knew the crush was mostly gratitude—she was confusing desire with appreciation. Their wedding that afternoon wasn't real in any way. He'd said it would be annulled in a couple of days once she was safely back in England. So this awareness of him could just die a death.

'And you're a bit scared?' Tomas asked with a gentle smile. 'I remember when I left Italy with nothing but the clothes I was wearing, I was scared, but it was an adventure.'

Her surprise grew; he'd become this successful from absolutely nothing? 'How did you make it?'

'Hard work. Determination.' He shrugged as he stepped closer until he was right in front of her. 'You have skills, you have more resources than you know. You're going to be fine.' He tilted her chin and looked into her eyes with a small smile. 'And your uncle was wrong, you know. You're very attractive.'

His lips brushed hers in the lightest gesture of support—and finality.

She screwed her eyes shut, her humiliation total. Her first ever kiss had come from her first lethal crush, and it had been born of compassion.

'Please don't pity me,' she muttered, then forced herself to look at him. 'I am going to be fine.' She echoed his words, drawing strength from them. Determined to believe they would be the truth.

His eyes were only millimetres from hers, bottomless, unreadable, so beautiful and for a timeless moment all she could do was drown in them.

'I know,' he answered, his voice suddenly roughened.

And to her surprise, he quickly bent and brushed his lips over hers ever so lightly again. Without volition she parted her lips, lifting her chin so the sweet contact lingered just for a fraction longer. She closed her eyes to hold onto the magic. And then everything changed.

He was back, his mouth moving over hers more firmly. Then more so again. She quivered, stifling a gasp when his tongue slid between her teeth, searching out her secrets. It felt foreign, but it felt so good as he stroked her that she simply leaned into him.

She heard a low growl in the back of his throat as his arms came around her. He kissed her again. She opened more for him; she couldn't not. And she sought the same knowledge, darting her tongue to tangle with his, to push past and explore him. A wave of emotion rose in her, tearing apart the veneer of fear and releasing an intense desire that had never before been roused. It was so raw and new she had no hope of either containing or controlling it. Instinctively she knew that her response inflamed him too—the kiss grew more passionate. She wound her arms around his neck, curling her fingers in the hair at the back of his neck. Her action bringing her body into full contact with his—her breasts pressed against his hard chest. Spasms of awareness shot from her taut nipples to the depths of her most private parts. It was shocking and delightful all at once and she simply didn't know what to do other than press closer and closer still.

This wasn't gratitude. This wasn't anything as easy as that. This was a desperate meeting of two spirits that had *suddenly curled together and couldn't be forced apart. She moaned as that fire inside built to an unbearable temperature. She needed something more...*

But all of a sudden he wrenched his lips from hers. She gasped in disappointment, but then clamped her mouth shut as embarrassment crashed down on her.

There was an unreadable expression in his eyes as he pulled her arms from where she'd wound them round his neck. She had to lean back against the wall for support as he put three feet of distance between them.

Oh, Lord, she'd been clinging to him. She closed her eyes tightly to hide from him. She wanted to apologise but she couldn't. She was trembling too much to summon coherent speech.

She heard the sound of her hotel-room door opening and she opened her eyes in a flash. But he'd stepped back from it and wasn't looking at her as he crisply ordered her to bed.

'You'd better try to sleep now, you have a long journey tomorrow.'

Alone.

As if she could ever sleep after that. Her husband had kissed her—meaning nothing but a little comfort—but she'd succumbed so totally, tumbling into a heady fantasy of fate.

That fantasy had been hers alone. He'd almost wordlessly walked away, unable to even look at her. And her humiliation was complete all over again.

She closed her eyes briefly now to force the burning memory back into its padlocked box. And she bit down on her lip to stop that pulse of desire tormenting her.

Not now. Not ever.

He'd never been hers in that way. And now he never could be.

* * *

Tomas gripped Zara's phone, his annoyance burning brighter as he looked at how pale she now was. What had Jasper been saying to her?

There was an almost beseeching look in her sea-green eyes, as if she was wordlessly asking for something. Asking for—

He didn't want to know what it was. He could never give her it anyway.

He had nothing to give anyone.

But now he had a woman before him looking so damnably beautiful. And alone. Looking as if she needed comfort. And contact. And—

He turned on his heel and stalked out of the kitchen.

'Leave your playgirls in London,' he growled in a low voice. 'I have too much to do for this distraction.'

'You always have too much to do and not all distractions are bad,' Jasper tried to joke.

But Tomas wasn't in the mood. 'Why did you send her to me?' he barked as he braved the rain to get her bag from the car. The car was cheap and not in the best condition and he was surprised it had got her here safely. Her bag wasn't heavy; she obviously hadn't planned to stay long.

'Because you shouldn't be alone for weeks at a time.'

Tomas snorted. Being alone was exactly how he liked it. As it was he hadn't been going to be alone for long enough. 'The Kilpatricks will be back next week.'

'You don't exactly let them into your life.'

Tomas paused. How did Jasper know that? Did he get them to report to him? He was livid at the intrusion— well-intentioned or not. 'Don't interfere, Jasper. Work is all that matters.'

'Haven't you proved that already?' Jasper argued quietly. 'The company is more successful now than it ever has been. No one can believe the way you've pushed it on this last year…isn't it time you had a break and took care of other aspects of your life?'

'There are no other aspects,' Tomas snapped. 'And there never have been. You know it as well as I.' That was how he liked it and wanted it. 'I pay you for your legal advice and nothing more. If you want me to *keep* paying you, then I suggest you stick to the books.'

There was silence as Jasper digested that threat. 'I'm sorry. I shouldn't have…' He cleared his throat. 'But Zara is a good worker, please give her a chance for these few days. She needs it.'

Tomas closed his eyes at the plea in the older man's voice and blocked the memory of the anxiety in Zara's eyes. He'd known there was more to her story than what she'd told him.

And he knew Jasper had a habit of helping out stray dogs.

'She's been through all the checks?' He needed to know she could be discreet.

She suspected already; he'd seen it in her eyes as she'd looked at his gallery. It was exactly why he didn't want strangers in the house. And he sure as hell did not want her pity.

Anger coursed through his blood again.

'Of course.' Jasper sounded distracted.

'Where did you find her?' Tomas asked, not entirely believing him.

'The usual agency.'

'I don't need her.' Cait Kilpatrick had left enough meals to last him six months. Though, to be honest, he didn't like them.

Jasper's sigh came heavily down the phone. 'It's just for three or four days. She needs the money.'

'Then have her come and work for you,' Tomas said irritably. He hated being coerced. It was only because the old guy was so loyal that he'd let him. Because Jasper once helped him in a very similar way all those years ago. It was one of the last things Tomas could remember before it all went blank.

'Tom—'

'She can have the money and just leave,' Tomas said. She didn't need to stay and disrupt his solitude. He didn't want her here, making him think. Or wonder. Or want.

He only wanted to focus on his work.

'But she has pride,' Jasper said quietly. 'Not unlike you.'

Tomas gritted his teeth.

'The experience would be good for her,' Jasper added in a wheedling tone.

'You're saying she's inexperienced?' Tomas looked to the heavens in frustration. 'How do you know what would be so good for her if she was just from the agency—she's worked for you?' There was more to Jasper's story than he was letting on. What was it about Zara that was so important?

'For a short time, yes,' Jasper muttered.

Tomas knew Jasper was lying but he didn't know why. 'You really think I can't handle a few days all by myself?' he jeered.

'I think you can handle almost anything,' Jasper replied. 'You might even cope with her for a few days if you try hard enough.'

Tomas managed a laugh. But he wasn't so sure. He was staying out of her way.

That smile? Those brightly shining eyes? She was like a damn puppy, so eager to please and cheerful and, he suspected, in need of affection and attention.

He didn't have any of that to give.

'I'll come see you in a few days and make sure she hasn't poisoned you. I wouldn't blame her if she does if you're this grouchy with her.'

Was he grouchy? Probably. But then he had reason to be, didn't he? 'Come soon and take her away. I don't need her.'

And he refused to want her.

He walked back down to the kitchen. She stood staring out of the dark window but when she caught sight of his reflection over her shoulder she whirled to face him.

'What did he say to you?' he said as he held her phone out to her. His eyes narrowed as he saw how pale she still looked. How warily she ensured her fingers did not brush his again as she took her phone from him.

'He apologised.'

He almost smiled, surprised with her honesty. 'He did the same to me. You'll stay a few days and be my housekeeper.'

Her stiffness eased. 'Until he gets here.' She nodded, her lips twisting wryly. 'I'm sorry he foisted me on you.'

He couldn't help the small smile at that mental image. Did she really think it was Jasper who'd made the final call? 'I guess I'll get over it,' he muttered ironically.

Did she even have anywhere else to go?

But her dimple popped back as she returned his smile with that small one of her own. He was glad. But he was still damn uncomfortable.

'I'll be in my office most of the time,' he explained roughly. 'Working.'

'I promise I'll stay out of your way and only come to find you at mealtimes,' she said, a little too meekly.

He shot her a look. 'I will come to the kitchen.'

'Will you remember to?' A spark of mischief lit her eyes.

'Of course I will.'

Her brows flickered at his snap and her smile widened. 'Thank you.' Ultra-meek that time.

He drew in a steadying breath. She *was* an undaunted kitten. 'I'll show you to your room.'

Silently she walked alongside him as he led her back

up to his wing. It was the only one with the furnishings uncovered and ready for use. She had to stay too close for comfort.

He was too aware of how close she was now. How warm she looked with that flush back in her cheeks and the shine back in her eyes. She looked soft and the desire to pull her close was too intense.

Inwardly he cursed Jasper again.

'You'll sleep here.' He stopped by the open door and tried not to look at her. He failed. 'Don't be afraid to turn up the heater if it still isn't warm enough for you.'

He remembered too well how cold her fingers had been when she'd first arrived.

'Thank you,' she said, subdued. The light, sparring moment had passed and whatever thoughts she'd had before were troubling her anew. She avoided looking him in the eyes as she waited, clearly tense again.

He frowned, another wisp of *déjà vu* distracting him.

'I'm just along the corridor should you need anything.' He walked away abruptly, wondering how on earth he was ever going to sleep tonight.

CHAPTER FOUR

'*He can afford this, you know, it doesn't mean
anything to him.*'

ZARA STEPPED INTO the vast room. Beautiful wood panelling
lent warmth to it, as did the intricately patterned rug thrown
over the thick carpet. Antique furniture gleamed in the soft
light from the table lamp—a pair of plump armchairs sat
at angles in front of the small fire, a polished free-standing
mirror reflected the grandeur of the room, while dominat-
ing the lot was the large four-poster bed with its beautiful
moss-green and gold brocade coverings. Heavy-looking
curtains were drawn over the windows, blocking out the
wild weather and adding to the air of luxurious sanctuary.
She felt as if she'd walked onto the set of a sumptuous period drama and the effect was spellbinding.

She toed off her cold shoes and stepped towards the
gently flickering flames in the decoratively tiled fireplace.
But the fire was more for ambience than heat, for there
was hidden modernisation—a discreet switch that allowed
her to control the temperature with the touch of a button.
Through an open doorway she saw an en suite bathroom
with gleaming porcelain and fluffy white towels.

Her bag was on the low wooden luggage rack and she
opened it, hunting for the winter pyjamas she'd thrown in
there. Then she showered, her body slowly warming at last
under the strong stream of steaming water.

She still couldn't believe any of it—that she was here,
that he'd lost so much.

That he was still her *husband*.

She stepped out of the shower, wrapping herself in the

thick towel as she shivered again, unwilling to let herself
think too closely about that. He wasn't *really* her husband.
There wasn't any intimacy at all between them.

No matter what that rogue part of her might want.

Dressed in her nightwear, she walked towards the large
bed, hyper aware of the tiny, muted sounds coming from
somewhere in the house. The last time they'd slept under
the same roof they'd been in that hotel on Antigua before
she'd returned to England for the first time in ten years.

'Ready to go, Zara?'

*Tomas's quick glance was keen as he met her in the hotel
restaurant to take her directly to the airport, but then he
looked at his watch as if he was impatient for them to go.
For her to leave.*

'Yes, thank you.' She knew she looked pale.

But he looked a touch paler to her eyes too.

'You have all you need?'

*'Thank you for everything,' she offered quietly once he'd
escorted her to the departure gate.*

Words weren't enough. Nothing would ever be enough.

*'Thanks are not necessary.' For just a second he hesi-
tated. Her heart fluttered with the hope he might say for
her to go with him instead. Or that he'd say he'd meet up
with her in England. Or that he might kiss her again.*

*But he did none of those things. He stepped back. 'Go
well.'*

*As she got to the corner of the air bridge she glanced
back, but he'd already turned and was walking back
through the busy airport.*

It was over.

She'd spent the entire flight to London terrified she'd get
turned back at Customs or something. But she hadn't been.
She'd made her way north—choosing to go away from

where her parents had lived because she never wanted her uncle to find her. She'd changed her surname for that reason too. She'd found a cheap bedsit near the centre of the town. That dream of studying *patisserie* in Paris had faded to the realistic aim of working in a café while studying at the local technical institute. Alone and with the resources to become fully independent.

Finally. And only thanks to Tomas.

But she'd wanted to use as little as necessary of his money because since that kiss, and their too-brief conversations, he'd become something more to her than just a source of escape.

Pushing away the painful memories, she curled up in the vast bed with its rich coverlets and luxury sheets. She didn't think she'd ever fall asleep, she was too wired. But sleep came—shockingly sudden and deep.

She had no idea of the time when she woke. She quickly got out of bed and pulled back the curtains to see how light it was and what the day was like.

The rain had stopped but the sky was covered in purplish, snow-heavy clouds. The world seemed eerily still as if on pause, waiting for the weather bomb. The clouds threatened that the worst was yet to come.

As she looked from the sky to the ground, the magnificence of her bedroom paled as she took in the marvel that was outlaid before her. Now she understood what Tomas had meant when he'd said the gardens had been closed to the public, for even in the heart of winter these were show gardens.

With a high brick wall around the perimeter, immaculate rows of precise hedges divided the garden into four separate formal 'rooms'—each decorated with fountains and immaculately patterned beds that even in this desolate weather were verdant and beautiful. And in the centre of the four sections stood the masterpiece—a perfectly maintained Victorian glasshouse. A third of the size of the manor itself, it was constructed of pristine white-painted ironwork and a myriad of gleaming windows through which she could see deep green exotic foliage. The whole vista was a beautiful, bountiful secret that only those in the manor— or those invited—would see.

It was a shame they were no longer open for people to enjoy because they were incredible. And someone maintained them to this perfection.

As she gazed in awe Tomas stepped out of the glasshouse into the centre of garden.

Zara froze, unable to stop herself staring. He wore shorts and a thin T-shirt and running trainers. Even from this distance she could see the jagged marks on his thigh. It had to have been a horrendous injury to have left such scarring, yet he had a barely noticeable limp. That was down to his sheer determination, she was sure. He'd clearly been working out—and by the look of him, he did that every day.

What other injuries had he worked hard to overcome? And what of his memory? Was his amnesia complete or did he have some memories still? Would those he'd lost ever return?

'Why did you do this?'

She'd finally got the courage to ask Tomas when Jasper had got out of the car to arrange the hotel room just after they'd left her uncle at the marina.

He'd helped her. He didn't have to. He could have just walked away leaving her uncle to fester in his own failure, leaving her there to cope with whatever onslaught and repercussions the man dealt. People turned a blind eye all the time. But Tomas had chosen to take action. He'd married her.

He sighed and turned in his seat to look at her directly.

'I dislike bullies.'

He gazed intently at her.

'You do understand there's nothing I want from you? I know what it's like to feel trapped.'

Silently she stared back at him.

'And I know what it's like not to be wanted.'

Tears burned her eyes but she couldn't blink. She couldn't tear her gaze from him...not even for a tenth of a second.

For that endless moment she'd looked just as intently back at him and she swore she'd glimpsed a once lonely youth beneath that confident, driven exterior.

Everyone had a past, everyone had hurts and suddenly she'd known that he'd done what he had because he'd been there himself. Abandoned. Afraid. Alone. The flash of insight hurt.

'We should get inside.'

He'd turned away from her. The moment had been broken.

She stared—here he was now, back from broken. But still wounded? He'd clearly fought so hard.

Her mouth dried as she got sidetracked by the visual of just how strong he was. There wasn't an ounce of fat on him, only a sheen of sweat over his skin, emphasising the defined muscled beneath. She'd never seen him so exposed and he was more gorgeous than she'd ever imagined. Unthinking, she inched closer to the window.

He looked up. For a second her gaze clashed with his— even from this distance she felt the burn in his eyes. Embarrassed, she stepped back, her skin all but blistering from being caught—*ogling* like some immature fangirl.

When she finally made it down to the kitchen twenty minutes later, he was already there. He'd showered and dressed in jeans and T-shirt and looked outrageously handsome with his hair still damp and his jaw unshaven.

That hot accusation in his eyes was still there too.

She tried to dodge it—hoping she could breeze through her embarrassment and that he hadn't read the raw attraction in her own eyes—by adopting a smile and avoiding meeting his gaze. 'What can I make you for breakfast?' she asked.

'I've already eaten,' he answered brusquely, turning his back to her.

Her smile became fixed. Of course he had. 'A drink, then—tea? Coffee?'

He shook his head.

'Then what would you like for lunch?' she asked, determined not to let his mood destroy her own.

He shrugged.

'You have no preference?' she persisted. 'None at all?'

'No.'

She rolled her eyes. 'Tomas, help me out a little. I'm only trying to do my job.'

'Cook whatever you want and I'll eat it. I have more important things to think about.'

'Good,' she snapped back. 'Go get on with that, then.' Suddenly she couldn't wait to get rid of him.

A startled expression flashed across his face but she could be tetchy too, if that was how he wanted it. And if he didn't want her cooking much for him that was fine too. She'd make what she enjoyed and he could eat it or not. The rest of the time she could test her recipes. She didn't exist purely to serve him, she had her own plans to be getting on with and his *you're here under my sufferance* attitude meant she now had some time to be getting on with them. And she wasn't going to feel guilty about it.

Even so, the first thing she did once he'd left was defrost one of the meals his housekeeper had left for him. She wrinkled her nose as she sampled it. While it was okay, she could see why he wasn't that enthused—nutritious but bland, it could do with some pep.

She surveyed the pantry again. There was no way she was going to be able to make anything decent without a trip to the shops. She was going to have to go to the nearest town and stock up.

Tomas sat at his desk and stared sightlessly at the screen. He couldn't muster any attention to read the reports that had landed in his inbox first thing. He'd been rude and he regretted it. Which annoyed him even more because she—and what she thought of him—shouldn't matter at all. But she'd worked her way under his skin already—and the way she looked at him?

It was exactly the way he tried *not* to look at her—with raw interest. That sensual awareness that was simply impossible. He had no need, time or desire for any kind of relationship. Not even the temporary, physical satisfaction kind.

He'd learned early on relationships weren't worth the risk—not if you wanted to survive and succeed. The only way to operate was alone. The only guarantee he had was his own.

He pulled out the thick leather-bound book that he always kept on his desk. The specialist had suggested he keep a daily journal but Tomas wasn't about to write about his 'feelings'. Rather he kept a record of each day's activities—his exercise regime, his reading, his work decisions and reasons.

If he lost more of his memory, he'd have that record as his reminder.

He'd had to retrain so much—had to read and concentrate round the clock to regain the confidence and knowledge he needed to lead his company again. He couldn't let anyone decimate his focus now. Especially not a young woman in a thin T-shirt and skinny jeans and an oversized apron. But last night was the first journal entry he'd missed in months. He didn't quite know how to classify Zara.

All he wanted to know was what she was doing right now.

It seemed his legendary focus was shot. Grimacing at his weakness, he pushed back his seat and quietly walked down to the kitchen.

She had her back to him as she leaned over the bench. He angled his head and saw she was rifling through a recipe book, but he was distracted from reading the title by her circling jeans-clad hips. He froze for a second, his tongue cleaved to the roof of his mouth as he watched the rhythmic undulations of those sweet curves. It took him a second to realise she had earbuds in and that she was partly dancing as she read. He zoned into the melodic strains leaking from the buds. It was familiar but he didn't recognise it. Of course he didn't.

'Zara?'

She didn't stop with the hip-circling.

'Zara.'

She jumped, gasping as she caught sight of him behind her.

'I didn't mean to startle you,' he said gruffly.

'I'm so sorry.' She hurriedly switched off the music on her phone.

'You don't need to apologise.' He frowned at how thrown she was by his appearance.

She coloured and her speech rushed. 'I didn't want to disturb you—you seem to like to work in silence.'

Only because he hadn't thought to put any music on. Maybe it would help. At the very least it would be something to break the silence and his wonderings about what *she* was doing.

'It's not good for your ears to wear earbuds all day,' he said. 'I don't mind if you play music using the sound system.' He gestured to the cupboard where the heating and media systems controls were.

'Really? You're sure?'

He frowned again, this time at how surprised and pleased she looked. Had he been that much of an ogre?

But now she'd recovered herself and that irrepressible smile appeared and he found he couldn't resist a reluctant tease.

'Of course.' He shot her a look. 'Just not too loud.'

He didn't miss the flash of her truly brilliant smile as he turned away. Feeling more at ease, he walked back up to his office, ready to restart his day.

Zara did a full reconnaissance of the garden and found a herb garden and vegetable plot hidden from the main vista. The produce was abundant but she needed other supplies. Clearly the housekeeper wasn't expecting Tomas to want to cook at all for himself given she'd left the pantry all but bare apart from the basics.

Deciding to brave his wrath, she walked up to his office, studiously not looking at the line-up of photographs and accompanying notes. The door was open so she knocked on the doorframe and tried not to stare too hard.

His office was a massive library—complete with roaring fire and bookcases lined with leather-bound classics, but there the period-drama set ended. Because he was seated at a desk in the centre of the room frowning at a screen full of numbers. A row of other computer screens were on the desk and switched on and showing markets information. A television was on mute but she saw it was switched to a twenty-four-hour news channel. Two phones were on the table beside him.

She knocked a second time.

'Yes?' He glanced at her.

This time she managed to bite back the automatic apology that sprang to her lips. She'd spent a decade doing nothing much but apologise—to her uncle for everything and anything. She'd never been able to do a thing right, a decade of not being or doing what he wanted.

She'd gone to him aged twelve—right in the middle of that rough phase of puberty with pimples and puppy fat and no confidence and grieving unbearably and his disappointment and disapproval only made it all worse.

But she'd done enough apologising in all that time. She'd learned to stop it now.

Well, almost.

But it was okay to interrupt Tomas. She was *helping* him. 'I'm going into the village to pick up some supplies. Is there anything in particular I can get you?'

'No.' He blinked at her. 'Thank you,' he added as an afterthought.

'What shops are there?' She risked a smile. 'Is there a good greengrocer?'

'I wouldn't know.' He turned back to the screen.

'You've not shopped there?'

'I don't go into the village.'

'You prefer London?' She waited, but got no answer. 'You don't go out much since your accident?'

Her first mention of the crash didn't impress him. 'It really is no concern of yours.'

Wasn't it? Wasn't it every concern of hers?

But he didn't know that yet. And she managed again not to apologise. Just.

'You'll need money.' He opened a drawer in the desk.

'I don't need that much,' she protested as she saw the roll of notes in his hand as he stood.

'Take it just in case.' He strolled over to give her the money.

'I'll go and investigate the shops, then.' She couldn't resist teasing a little. 'I might be a while.'

'Fine.' He headed back to his desk.

She shot him a look at his deliberately bland response.

'You won't change the security code at the gate while I'm gone?'

'So you're actually planning to come back?' he asked dryly.

'I promised Jasper I'd stay.' She tossed her head, pleased as his eyes narrowed in annoyance. 'I'm not afraid of a challenge. As long as you're not afraid to be honest.'

His eyebrows shot up and he took a step back towards her. 'What makes you think I wouldn't be honest?'

'Your desire to argue with me is too strong. Are you man enough to actually admit it if you like what I make for you?'

'Zara,' he said softly, a small smile playing about his lips. 'I've never been afraid to admit what I like.'

The innuendo was blatant—as was the look he directed from her top to toe, lingering in the middle.

Heat scorched her cheeks and his softly jeering laughter chased her from the room.

Her heart pounded and she touched her cold fingers to her hot lips. She knew he didn't mean it. He was just teasing; for a moment he'd been the Tomas she'd met that day—arrogant and decisive and with flashes of fun.

'Take care out there,' he suddenly called after her. 'The forecast isn't good.'

He was right about the weather. She'd barely got down the long driveway before light snow flurries began to fall. She wasn't worried—it wasn't too far to the village and she shouldn't be more than a couple of hours.

She walked the length of the picturesque main street, interested in the cafés and shops. She spent some time in each, looking at the artisan products they had on offer. There was a well-stocked general store and she browsed the aisles, stopping to read the notice board. A poster advertised the local farmers' market in the town square on the weekends.

'Can I help you?' a uniformed young assistant asked her.

'Is the market good?' Zara asked, gesturing to the poster.

The young woman nodded. 'It's in the town square, all year round. It's really good.' She smiled in a friendly way. 'Are you staying nearby?'

'Yes, at Raxworthy.' She mentioned the manor just to see the girl's reaction—if any.

It was instant. Her eyes widened in curiosity.

'At Raxworthy?' She was agog. 'With Tomas Gallo?' She looked eager for more information. 'You're working there?'

'For a few days,' Zara admitted briefly, now unable to avoid answering the question. Was it so obvious she wasn't there as a social guest? Of course it was.

She wasn't glamorous enough or well-dressed enough or anywhere near perfect enough to be anything other than the hired help.

No one would ever believe she was actually his wife.

That old unworthy feeling arose in her. She'd never been the confident social butterfly and her uncle's attempts to berate her into his ideal mould had failed.

Zara's only confidence had grown in the kitchen.

But while she was never going to be a society hostess type, that didn't mean she didn't have ambition. She knew what she wanted—her own business.

'So what's he like?' The young woman leaned forward, inviting confidence. 'We never see him. Is it true he's scarred?' Her voice dropped to a whisper. 'I've seen his picture on the Internet and he was so gorgeous. And so *wealthy*...'

'I really...couldn't say,' Zara answered weakly, regretting having said anything at all. She was aware the older woman standing nearby was listening intently.

Tomas was very private and Zara now understood why. She didn't blame him for keeping his distance from the village.

She paid for the groceries and put the bags into her car. The snow was falling heavily now and the visibility had reduced. But it was only a short drive.

Except five minutes into it her car made an appalling groaning sound, jerked and shuddered to a stop.

She pushed the accelerator to the floor but nothing happened. She tried the ignition a few more times—but still nothing happened. The fuel gauge showed there was quarter of a tank of petrol in it, which meant it was some kind of engine trouble.

Not something she had either the time or the money to deal with.

Worriedly, she got out of the car and looked up and down the quiet country lane. She couldn't leave her car in the middle of the road like this. She put it in gear and then tried to push it to the side of the road. She slipped and whacked her knee the first time. The second she got precisely nowhere. The third time the car began to inch forward. Pleased, she got a bout of energy and pushed harder, except the car then got away from her and slowly and gently crashed into the low wall at the edge of the road. The metal crunched.

Great. Just great.

Sighing, she fished her phone out of her bag only to stare at it in horror. It was totally out of charge. She'd forgotten to plug it in. She shook her head at her own uselessness. It didn't matter that she'd been so distracted last night, she should have remembered something so simple.

Now she had no choice but to walk. Fortunately she only had a few bags to carry and it wouldn't take more than another half-hour. No doubt Tomas would be appreciating the peace and quiet of having his big house to himself again.

She hoisted the bags in her hands, but then put them down again to double-check she had all the change to give back to him safely in her pocket. And she would give it all back to him.

* * *

'Why don't you want to take it all?'

Jasper looked stunned the morning after their wedding when she told him she didn't want to accept all the money Tomas had offered her the night before.

'He's done enough. I don't need all that amount. I only need enough to get started, and even then I'll pay that back. I want to pay him back as soon as I can.'

'He can afford this, you know,' Jasper said bluntly. 'It doesn't mean anything to him.'

'But it means something to me.'

Her heart ached as she remembered that kiss last night.

'Please,' she said quickly when she caught sight of the tall figure walking across the restaurant towards them. 'But I don't want him to know. Not yet.'

'Why not?' Jasper's smile was curious.

'He'll make me keep it.'

'Yes, he will.'

Jasper chuckled, but sobered just before Tomas came within earshot.

'Okay, but you must let me know your address once you're settled. You must let me know if you need anything more.'

She hadn't needed anything more. She'd *wanted*, but not needed.

Now she loaded up the shopping bags again and walked along the edge of the road, hoping any traffic would be able to see her. It was slow going as her sneakers had little tread and it was slippery on the fresh fallen snow. Her feet were wet already and her cheeks stinging from the cold and her hands sore from the heavy plastic bags.

Served her right for being so forgetful.

There was no traffic, almost no noise as the snow fell. All the sensible people would be safe indoors. Zara suddenly smiled to herself. So what? She was out in the snow and it might be cold but it was very beautiful and when she got back she could make hot chocolate and sit by the fire and try not to think about him—

'Zara! Zara!'

She stopped where she was on the side of the road, unwilling to believe either her ears or her eyes. But she recognised that tall figure materialising out of the white glare ahead of her. And she certainly recognised the abrupt tone of his voice as he furiously called out to her again as he saw her.

'Where the hell have you been?'

'To the village.' She swallowed. 'Remember?'

'What took you so long?' Tomas walked to within an inch of her personal space, looking slightly wild with his hair askew and fire in his eyes.

'I was getting what I needed.' Her voice went embarrassingly feeble.

Because he was staring at her, making the world shrink to those few inches between them. In this whitened world there was nothing but him any more.

'And what are you doing now?' he asked.

His implicit criticism galled her—firing her own anger. She didn't need him to judge. 'What do you think?'

'Why aren't you driving?'

She gritted her teeth and sent him a foul look.

'Where's your car?' he demanded.

'I'm not sure. It broke down back that way.'

Impossible as it ought to have been, he looked even more furious. 'Why didn't you phone me?'

'Because my phone ran out of battery.'

At that he just stared at her, his mouth ajar.

'I was distracted last night, okay?'

'No, it is *not*—'

'Is everything all right? I noticed the car broken down a mile or so ago…'

Zara jumped at the stranger's voice. She turned and saw that a man in a green four-wheel-drive had pulled up alongside them. She'd been too focused on Tomas—and too angry—to even notice the car thrumming behind her.

'Can I offer you a ride?' the man asked with polite concern.

'No,' Tomas answered in customary surly fashion, still glaring at Zara. 'Thank you,' he added shortly after she'd turned back and pointedly frowned at him.

'Tomas Gallo?' The man's face brightened. 'It is Tomas, isn't it? I've been hoping I might see you about.'

Only now did Tomas turn and actually look at the man.

'I'm sorry, I can't stop to talk,' he said curtly. 'I need to get Zara home—she's been out in the cold too long.'

'Oh, right. Of course. If you're sure I can't help…'

'Thank you but no. I can handle it from here.' Tomas reached for the bags Zara was carrying.

'Maybe I'll stop by the house some time…' The man trailed off when Tomas turned and looked at him again.

'Things are very busy for me at the moment,' Tomas said curtly.

It was a total brush-off.

'Er…okay, then.'

The man didn't offer them a ride again and Zara didn't blame him.

Zara didn't trust herself to speak until the car's lights had disappeared into the white. But as soon as they had she tightened her numb fingers around the plastic handles and pulled them away from Tomas's reach as she glared at him. 'I don't need you to "handle it from here".'

'No?'

'No. I don't need you to rescue me.' He'd done that once and it wasn't ever happening again. 'I am not incompetent.'

She was not the pathetic excuse for a human she'd once been. She'd studied. She'd got a job. She was making her own way. She was damn well happy for the first time in years. And she wasn't allowing him to make her feel inferior.

'No? You've been out walking in a snowstorm for hours wearing nothing but jeans and thin sneakers and a totally useless jacket. You're two minutes from hypothermia.'

'It hasn't been hours.'

'It's been three in total.'

Had it? Surely not. But she refused to try to look at her watch while he was staring so huffily at her. And frankly she was amazed he'd noticed what she was wearing or that he knew exactly how long she'd been gone for.

But come to think of it, she couldn't feel her feet or her fingers any more.

'Put this on.' He undid his coat.

'I am not wearing your jacket,' she spat.

'You'll wear it and like it.'

She tried to step around him to keep walking.

'Don't,' he warned her through gritted teeth. 'I am not in the mood.' He dropped the jacket around her shoulders.

'You're the one recuperating,' she argued.

'I'm ten times fitter than you are.'

That was probably true.

'And I am dressed for this weather,' he added pointedly. 'I have several layers on.'

Oh, he was just so perfect, wasn't he? In his leather boots and layers of wool and far too gorgeously broad shoulders.

'Give me the blasted groceries,' he bellowed when she resisted him taking them again. 'Stop trying to stop me from helping you. It isn't a crime.'

He confiscated the grocery bags, shouldered them and scowled at her. 'Are you sure you can keep walking? I have the car a little further back but decided to walk from there in case...' He trailed off, his frown returning.

'I'm *fine*.' She stomped her feet, hoping to thud some feeling back into them as she walked a step behind his punishing pace.

And she really was fine.

She was also furious.

Tomas could barely contain his anger. What the hell did she think she was doing walking out in this weather? How had her car broken down? As for her phone? Incompetent wasn't the word.

He'd been anxious about her for over an hour already. He'd had to phone Jasper to get her number and her phone had constantly switched straight to answer phone. That was when he'd really started to worry.

He hated worrying. He'd had to go out and find her.

And find her he had, smiling and basically singing to herself through a snowstorm. It was irresponsible and impossible and all he wanted to do was—

He stopped those thoughts in their tracks. They only made him all the more mad.

His anger continued to build as he got to his Jeep and threw her shopping onto the back seat. As he drove the final five minutes to home he noticed that she was suppressing her shivers. But his anger became incandescent when she shrugged off his jacket and determinedly set about putting the groceries away in the kitchen. As if all that were remotely important compared to her health?

'What do you think you're doing?' He glared at her.

'My job.'

He grabbed her hand to stop her, his grip tightening when he felt just how cold her fingers were. He swore beneath his breath then tugged her towards him. 'You're going to get changed, now.'

'What?'

He didn't bother answering, he just switched his grip

to her upper arm, wrapped his other arm around her waist and marched her from the kitchen.

'Tomas—'

'You're going to have a shower and get into some warm clothes,' he informed her as he half carried her up the stairs.

'This is ridic—'

'Your fingers are freezing. You should wear gloves.' He'd hunt some out for her tomorrow.

'I'm fine.'

'Maybe you will be. After you're warm and dry.' He walked her into her bedroom and released her.

But she didn't move, she just gazed up at him. 'Tomas…'

He couldn't bear to look into her radiant face—she was too pretty with those huge, expressive eyes and that sweetly curving mouth.

So he looked down at her wet jeans and refused to register the feminine shape of her legs. But he did notice and he didn't want to. He looked lower still. Her shoes were even wetter with their tangled, filthy laces. No way was she going to be able to undo those laces when her hands were that cold.

So he dropped to his knees and worked on the knots himself.

Zara stared, her heart arresting as Tomas knelt at her feet, intently working to undo her laces. She couldn't move. Couldn't think. He was so furious. So handsome. And so fantastically kind underneath all that gruff exterior. He finished undoing the laces and made her lift each leg to slide each shoe and sock off. Then he sat back on his heels and looked up at her.

Her heart turned over in her chest as she gazed into his beautifully dark and sombre eyes. She'd never known anyone like him. She'd never wanted anyone the way she wanted him either. And she couldn't hide it any more.

'Get in the bath or I'll put you in it myself,' he said softly. That order melted the last frozen part within her.

'Really?' She couldn't help smiling at him. 'How d'you think you're going to do that?'

He looked up at her for just a moment longer—his focus dipping to her mouth. Then suddenly in one smooth movement he stood. Before she could step back he caught both her wrists in one of his hands and to her astonishment swiftly lifted his jumper and pressed her cold, cold fingers to his bare skin.

She gasped at the shock—and the sensation. She looked up into his face and saw how intently he was gazing at her. Her brain shorted out at the intensity in his eyes—and at the steady beat of his heart beneath her hand. His chest was rock solid and hot and her suddenly super-sensitive fingertips traced through the faint covering of hair.

'Tomas,' she whispered. Pleading. She couldn't help it.

He didn't reply. He just stepped that last inch closer and kissed her.

She moaned in instant delight, despite the fact his kiss was furious. He subjected her to the full force of his anger—and his passion—and both only brought forth the desire she'd tried to hold within herself for so long. But it was impossible to hold back under his onslaught. He overwhelmed every one of her senses. As she moaned again he pulled her closer, his hands roving down her spine to her waist and lower still, to pull her hips against his. She leaned against him, spreading her hands to explore more of his chest, loving the sensation of his hot, bare skin. She couldn't get close enough. He was so deliciously hard and she just wanted more. She could feel her toes now, curling them into the plush carpet as he kissed life and heat back into her.

The kiss deepened and, inexperienced as she was, she strained to get closer, knowing she had to get closer still. But he teased—his tongue wickedly curling around hers, then stroking within her mouth. So intimate and so in control. And so totally destroying her inhibitions. He broke away to press tiny, teasing kisses across her jaw and then down her neck. She arched, letting him caress that vulnerable, sensitive skin with his lips—and then with a gentle nip of his teeth. She gasped, shivering at the contrary sensation and he returned his attention to her hungry mouth. Her blood hummed as he ignited the most basic and undeniable of needs within her so easily. So desperately.

Closer. She ached to get closer.

She rubbed her fingers harder against his rigid torso, aching to feel more. She spread her hands that little bit wider, and rubbed the tips of her fingers against his tight, flat nipples. His arms tightened about her and his kiss became nothing short of ruthless. She bent back in his embrace, letting him plunder—wanting him to take more. Taste more. Wanting him to claim every part of her exactly like this. Completely.

She moaned again, her legs weakening, but he abruptly broke the kiss. He pulled back to look into her face and she couldn't stop smiling up at him, almost blind with sheer sensual joy.

Never had a man made her feel like this. Made her want like this.

He stared down at her silently, his breathing quick, his expression burning. But he didn't smile back at her.

Her smile faltered as she felt his tension growing—and it wasn't in a good way. Coldness stole back into her body as the tide turned. He straightened and so did she.

'Go and get into the bath,' he breathed, releasing her completely. 'Go. *Now.*'

'Y-yes,' she stammered. Then turned and fled.

CHAPTER FIVE

It won't happen again.

ZARA WASN'T AT all cold any more but she scrubbed her body all over—shocked and frustrated and *aching*. It was more than her body—her heart hurt too. Which was stupid because she knew he didn't feel the same way at all. He hadn't kissed her because he'd been thinking about nothing else for the last twenty-four hours. His action had been fuelled by anger, not lust. He'd only exploded because she'd defied him and he wasn't used to it. He'd been exerting his will…it wasn't that he felt *want* for her. It was just pent-up aggression.

But her feelings for him? Pure desire. She wanted so very much more.

And he knew it. Which was horrendously embarrassing.

Finally she made herself get out of the shower and dress. She refused to hide in her bedroom all evening, or, worse, leave. She wasn't running away from a difficult situation. She was staying to finish what she'd said she'd do. She'd promised and she was stronger now.

And that was thanks to Tomas. Not that he knew it.

He was in the kitchen when she went down to prepare dinner. He too had changed from his damp clothes, into a crisp black shirt and pressed trousers and loafers. He might have been aiming for businesslike but he just looked ruthlessly sexy to her. She glanced at the table to avoid staring at him like some lovestruck teen. The bags containing the groceries had gone. He must have put them away.

'I would like to apologise about what happened before,'

he said with grim deliberation, watching her from where he stood leaning back against the bench.

She flushed from head to foot but cleared her throat, determined not to sound as weak as she felt. 'I was as much at fault.'

After all, she'd encouraged him. She'd moaned. She'd clung and touched and—

'It won't happen again,' he continued as if she'd not spoken.

She nodded, annoyed as she felt her blush deepening. Because she *wanted* it to happen again. But he didn't want anything more. He couldn't look as if he wanted her less—his expression was so chilling. No doubt her over-the-top, sex-starved reaction had embarrassed him and he was trying to extricate himself from her neediness as quickly and firmly as possible.

Mortified, she couldn't bear to look him in the eyes any longer. 'I'll get on with dinner now.'

He nodded and walked out of the room.

She breathed out, both relieved and sorry at his departure. The only way she was going to get through the next day or two was to keep herself as busy as possible. But as she prepared the steak she'd bought in the village and chopped herbs and vegetables, her mind raced. She should tell him the truth about their past. That she knew so much more than what she'd admitted to him.

But he'd be angry and she didn't want to face that conflict alone—she wasn't as brave as she kidded herself. And she didn't want to hurt him. So she had to wait it out until Jasper arrived. But in the meantime she could get over her own weak desires and stay out of his way.

She already knew there was nothing worse than not being wanted.

Tomas walked back up the stairs to his den, distractedly gazing at the pictures in the gallery as he passed them. All faces he knew but didn't know. Faces he couldn't remember but that he'd since learned.

She'd smelt like sunshine after her shower. So contrary to the silent wintry storm settling in outside. He'd wanted her to come nearer instead of staying as far away as possible with the table between them. But what had happened *couldn't* happen again—even if she'd looked as if she'd wanted it to.

So he'd had to apologise and redraw the boundaries with her. He'd had to put distance between them again.

He had no idea how long it had been since he'd last had sex—and he certainly hadn't enjoyed any sexual relations over the last twelve months. Apparently he'd dated, but according to his research he'd never had any long-term relationships. That resonated as truth within him. Relationships—and family—weren't things he believed in. He had not had them, he would not have them. He knew too well that the only person he could rely on was himself. His own 'family' had taught him that well.

But he'd definitely forgotten how good it felt to hold a soft, willing woman in his arms. He stifled a groan; he was rock hard at the mere recollection of it.

He wanted sex. With her. Now.

He wanted it so badly he could barely think.

But he didn't want anything more than sex—no relationship, no opening up and emoting. No sharing of anything other than body and touch. Not with her or any woman. But he couldn't demand Zara's physical surrender and offer her nothing else. She didn't come across as a woman ready and willing for nothing more than a quick fling. Her eyes held too many secrets and sorrows. And with the painful truth about his mother, he could never have sex with a woman on his payroll.

But that didn't stop him wanting her.

He stared at the screens, forcing his concentration, slaving over the reports until he was up to date. He then opened up a new file. Then another. He sent screeds of emails to his staff working at the office in London under Jasper's eye—instructing him and them on what he wanted him and them to do. There was always more to do. More work to win. More opportunities to generate.

He just had to keep working. That was what he could control. And what he did best.

But then he heard the approach of soft footsteps and his concentration blew.

She didn't look at him; she was too busy watching that she didn't spill whatever it was she had on the wooden tray. He should stand to help and take it from her, but he found he couldn't move. Her cheeks were lightly flushed and her skin glowed and he couldn't look away from how beautiful she was with her hair half falling out of its ponytail and a smear of sauce on her white T-shirt.

'Here you go.' She set the tray down on his table. 'I won't be offended if you don't like it.'

She wouldn't even meet his eyes. Annoyance surged inside him again. He hated that apologetic tone from her. He wanted her smile back, together with that imp of defiance and the strength he knew she had when pushed. He liked it when she was true and not hiding.

'I promise I'll be honest in my assessment,' he muttered dryly, hoping to provoke a bite.

She glanced at him—a quick, sharp look—but said nothing.

Disappointment drilled deeper as he watched her leave the room. She'd basically run away from him and he didn't blame her.

He never should have touched her. He never should have let her stay.

He never should have hauled her close and kissed her like a dying man given his last, most desired wish.

He looked at the tray she'd put on the end of his desk. He wasn't hungry in the least but he didn't want to make her feel even more uncomfortable.

At the first taste he closed his eyes. The soup was full of rich flavour and hearty. The steak was tender and juicy. And the potatoes? It was comfort food and there was no mistaking it. God, it was delicious.

His mouth watered. For the first time in months he was ravenous.

It seemed she'd wakened two appetites within him. He could sate only one. But with each mouthful—as she filled one need in him, the other began to bite harder.

He wanted to carry the tray down to the kitchen and dine with her. Food this good ought to be shared—eaten at a table framed by laughing, talking people. But he couldn't. There was too much tension between them, too much need in him. And bitterly he suspected she knew more about him than he'd told her.

She knew something wasn't right.

So he savoured the dishes she'd prepared and brought his unruly body to heel with the determination that had made him recover so much of his physical strength. But he couldn't beat his own weakness. Not truly.

Sighing, he put the knife and fork down, unable to finish the last of it. But he had to be honest with her—at least in this.

She sat at the table, with her back to him, reading recipe books again. Her feet were bare and her slim-fit jeans and T-shirt emphasised her delectable body. It didn't need emphasising.

He tensed as his body swiftly reacted to her—that other hunger building to epic proportions. He gritted his teeth in annoyance at his base reaction. Being out of control like this was foreign to him, but at the same time all he wanted to do was indulge.

'Where should I leave the tray?' he asked roughly as he stopped in the doorway. He didn't trust himself to step a foot closer.

Startled, she turned, her eyes meeting his for the first time since they'd kissed. For a moment that passion hung between them.

She didn't speak. She didn't have to. Her eyes said it all. Shadowed and uncertain but with that flicker of desire that he knew he could bring to an inferno with little more than a kiss. What if he did more than that? How would she react then?

'It was delicious,' he said stiffly, determined to control himself. 'Thank you.'

'No problem,' she answered quietly. She stood and took the tray from him and then swiftly walked around to the other side of the table. Putting distance—a literal barrier—between them.

He leaned against the doorjamb, folding his arms across his chest, and glanced about the scrupulously clean kitchen. 'Did you eat already?'

She placed the dishes by the sink. 'I wasn't that hungry.'

He frowned. 'You should—'

'I ate as I cooked.' She turned and forestalled his lecture with a defiant tilt of her chin. 'The soup.'

At that he nodded, but he couldn't bring himself to leave her just yet. 'That man who offered us a lift earlier,' he said roughly, hating that he had to ask, but knowing he needed to for his own peace of mind. 'Had you met him before?'

She shook her head, her gaze now not leaving his. 'Had you?'

For the tiniest moment he felt like telling her. She looked so earnestly at him, her eyes soulful and her voice soft. But he didn't want to admit the truth and see her expression change. All he wanted in this moment was to forget it all.

The irony of *that* made him smile bitterly.

'You're a very good cook,' he muttered instead. 'That was the best meal I've eaten in a long time.'

'I'm glad you enjoyed it.'

It couldn't be more stilted. Allowing himself one last second to look at her, he straightened and headed back to his office.

Zara didn't feel the pleasure she'd expected from his concession she was good at her job. She wanted something else from him now and she couldn't get it.

She cleaned up the kitchen. Filling the late hours in the evening by scrubbing an already clean bench and floor and then wading through the next few books in the amazing cookbook collection she'd found on the shelf in the large pantry.

He didn't come down to the kitchen again and she didn't go to the office. She already knew he wouldn't want a hot chocolate or anything before he went to bed. She didn't bother with one for herself. She was still too hot.

When she finally made herself go to bed she found she couldn't sleep. She flicked the light back on and opened up yet another of the cookbooks. But her attention kept wandering—to those faint noises she could hear within the house.

Then the silence.

He would be asleep now. But still she couldn't find rest. Her brain had that kiss on replay. Her skin burned as the memory tormented her. Her muscles twitched as frustrated energy fired along her nerves. It had escalated so quickly. Total, raw lust.

She was so hot and flustered she couldn't bear to stay in bed a second longer. She sprang out of it and pulled on her jeans and a fresh T-shirt, not bothering to stop for underwear. In the dark she stole down the stairs to the kitchen because there was only one thing she could do. She'd work it out—physically and mentally and distract herself completely. She pulled out ingredients, piling them on one end of the table. She'd start with bread—make something that needed beating down over and over again. Just like this intense, unwanted lust he'd roused in her.

And she didn't care if he didn't like sugar, she did. She'd make biscuits. And cake. And pastry. And pies. Anything and everything to occupy her mind, body and soul until the sun came up and this impossible passion waned.

She flicked on both ovens. She'd try those recipes she'd been reading. She'd be so busy following instructions she wouldn't have the brain space to think about other things.

She measured. She chopped. She melted, smeared and mixed. She heated, stirred, glazed and—

'What are you doing?'

Almost dying of fright.

'Sorry.' He held up his hands as her scream's echo reverberated between them. He actually smiled. 'You do realise it's two in the morning.'

Really? She glanced at the clock on the wall and saw he was right.

Of course he was right.

She wiped her forehead with the back of her sticky dough-covered hand. 'Sorry if I woke you.'

'You didn't. I couldn't sleep.'

He too was in jeans and a T-shirt and no shoes, and with that stubble on his jaw and that burning look in his eyes all that effort in distracting herself was a total waste. She tipped the dough onto the bench and determinedly pressed it out. 'Why couldn't you sleep?' she said, just to fill the silence.

'My brain won't shut down.'

Her heart pounded harder and she squashed the dough into the wood. 'Work?'

'No.'

She met his gaze briefly, catching just a glimpse of scalding agony in his eyes. She looked back down at the mess she was making of the biscuit dough and knew she couldn't stay silent any longer.

'Would it help if I said I was sorry?' The words scratched.

'I don't want you to feel sorry for me.'

She looked up and met his eyes again but found she couldn't hold his gaze. It was impossible to be as honest as she ought to be. 'I don't—'

'I know you know,' he interrupted her harshly. 'I might not be able to remember many things, but I'm not an idiot.'

She put both hands on the table for balance. His memory. Amnesia.

He watched her relentlessly.

'Can you remember anything from before the accident?' she asked.

'I've lost about a decade.' His hands had curled to fists at his sides as he stood soldier-like on the other side of the table from her. 'Almost the entire time since I came to England from Italy.'

And how could she not feel sorry for him?

She cleared her throat. 'Do they think you'll get it back?'

'It's been a year since the accident. The longer it goes on, it seems the less likely full recovery is. But in truth, they just don't really know.'

'And you can't remember anything from that time?' she queried, her chest aching now. 'What about your work?'

'I read every damn textbook again.'

In the last year? She frowned. 'That's amazing.'

He shook his head. 'I have a natural aptitude for numbers, patterns. I haven't lost that.'

'But you remember everything—'

'Since I woke from the medically induced coma I was in, yes.'

She gave up on the biscuit dough altogether and moved to the sink to wash her hands. 'Your gallery upstairs…'

'Everyone I've met or had dealings with in the last ten years. Jasper has helped.'

'So no one knows?'

'Only my medical team. Jasper. My staff here. And now you.'

And no one else had the chance to find out because he'd locked himself away in this remote estate and refused to socialise with anyone.

She dried her hands on the small towel and turned to face him. 'Do you trust me not to say anything?'

'Do I have any choice?'

'I won't tell anyone.'

'Why won't you?' he asked. But his soft tone seemed dangerous. 'Why won't you sell your story?'

'Because… I just wouldn't do that.'

'Why not?'

Because she liked him and she felt loyal to him. Because he was her husband and he'd helped her more than he could ever know.

'Because that's just the way I am,' she said lamely.

'You don't want to hurt anyone.' An odd look crossed his face.

'I'm not a saint.' She grimaced. She didn't deserve his admiration at all.

'No?' There was a note in his voice that made her look up. A gleam warmed his dark eyes. 'You're telling me you've been naughty?'

That made her blush. His brows lifted higher but then the amused light left his eyes leaving them shadowed, the secrets hidden once more.

A harsh regular beeping interrupted. She turned, grateful for the respite. She grabbed the oven mitts and retrieved the tray from the oven.

'How hungry do you think we're going to get?' he asked dryly as she placed the chocolate brownie on the cooling rack. The bread rolls were already cool. As were the individual savoury tartlets. She figured the lemon shortbread mix might have to be ditched.

'Why couldn't you sleep?'

She could ignore that question, but she couldn't ignore what he'd admitted. She turned off the oven and then looked at him. 'It must have been very isolating for you.'

He walked to her side of the kitchen.

'Is all this pity?' He waved a hand at all her baking but she knew he meant her sleeplessness, her curiosity, her concern. 'Because that's not what I want from you.'

She couldn't move. 'What do you want from me?'

He was silent as he regarded her. 'Nothing,' he said almost inaudibly. 'I want nothing.' But he reached out and tucked a wisp of her hair back behind her ear. 'Except the truth.' His focus sharpened. 'Why did you come here?'

Yeah, he wasn't an idiot, he knew there was more to her story. Of course there was. But she couldn't bring herself to tell him. She didn't want to burst this bubble of intimacy and peace. 'Because Jasper asked me to.'

And that *was* the truth.

'Because you owe him?' Tomas persisted.

She nodded.

'He helped you once?'

She nodded again, her throat thick with unshed tears.

'He helped me too, once.'

'But you helped him. You got him out of that car...' She knew they'd crashed. That Jasper had been trapped and Tomas had got him free in an insane show of strength and determination. And yes, she was utterly in his thrall.

'Anyone would have done that,' he argued.

Not anyone. And not just anyone would have offered to

marry someone the day they met them to help them escape from an oppressive environment.

'Did he tell you about me?' he asked.

Her heart ached as she shook her head. 'He didn't mention it at all. Tomas…' She trailed off. The expression in his eyes was warm now and even though she didn't really believe in what she thought she was seeing, she didn't want to drive it away.

'What?' he prompted.

She couldn't tell him the truth, not now. But she couldn't ask him what she really wanted to either. She was still a coward.

'What do you want from me?' he repeated her earlier question.

It didn't matter. It wasn't right. And she was used to disappointment. But he moved that inch closer, his expression intense, his gaze focused.

'Zara.' He brushed the backs of his fingers along her jaw. 'Your skin is so soft.'

His focus shifted to her lips. She could almost feel the warmth emanating from him as he gazed at her. And she willed him to do what she was certain he was thinking about.

His lashes lifted and he looked directly into her eyes. Time hung suspended in the scented, steamed room. 'You're too much temptation.'

Before she could reply he brushed her lips with his. Too gently. Too briefly.

She drew in a small gasp of pleasure. Of disappointment.

But then he was back. She moaned as he claimed her mouth properly. He growled in recognition of her desire. He leaned her back, overpowering her completely until she caught his shoulders and all but collapsed against him.

Yes. This. *Contact.*

This was what she wanted. Him wanting her. Touching

her. Making her feel vibrantly alive. And in that instant she'd give him anything, as long as he kept touching her like this. He had one arm tight around her waist to support her, one hand holding her face to his. And his kiss? Pure passion.

He devoured her, there was no other word for it. And she was equally frantic—desperately meeting him slide for slide, lick for lick.

'You smell delicious,' he finally breathed as he broke from her lips to kiss across her jaw.

'It's the vanilla and sugar…'

'Not entirely.'

She smiled. 'You don't like sweet.'

'I was wrong about that,' he muttered, then returning to kiss her full on the lips again even as he straightened her so she could stand.

She whimpered as she felt him pulling back. She didn't think she could ever get enough of his kisses. But he smiled at her and grasped the hem of her top.

She froze but she didn't try to stop him when he tugged her T-shirt up and then over her head. In fact she helped, getting her arms free of the shirt. But she lowered her face, feeling the burn in her cheeks as he stood suddenly still and silent as he stared at her bare breasts.

Self-conscious, she glanced down. Her nipples were tight and tilting up towards him, inviting his touch. His tongue.

She shivered.

Her thoughts were so shameless they shocked her. But before she could turn to hide he grasped her waist with both hands.

'Zara…' He swept his hands up to cup her breasts. 'You're beautiful.'

She masked her inward grimace. She wasn't anything special but it was nice of him to say it.

'You are,' he insisted, gently swiping his thumbs across those taut nipples, making her quiver. 'I'll make you believe it.'

But he didn't kiss her again. Instead he stepped back and quickly yanked off his own shirt. She looked at him, her self-conscious awkwardness obliterated by sensory overload. Desire pulsed heat between her legs.

Now *here* was beautiful.

'Your muscles.' She gaped. They were so defined. So tight. She reached out without thinking, to trace another scar she'd not seen from the distance of her bedroom window when he was outside. His skin was warm and she stepped closer so she could feel more, pressing her palm flat against him. She wanted to feel *all* of him.

He clasped her close and kissed her again. Electrifying sensations ran untrammelled through her as his bare torso slammed against hers. She heard him mutter something but she clutched him that bit tighter because she didn't want him to pull away again.

He didn't. Instead he kissed her again but at the same time pushed her, backing her until her thighs hit the large kitchen table, and then he lifted her to sit on it. The pressure he applied wasn't harsh, but it was firm. Without breaking the kiss, he had her on her back and was leaning over her, his leg between hers—right where that ache was, where she needed him to press. She moaned as she felt his weight on her for the first time and she couldn't hold back from arching to grind herself closer against him.

A deep unbearable yearning opened within her. Instinctively she wanted more than all his weight; she wanted him to *pin* her. To hold her there, safe—yet so exposed—in his embrace. Everything was contrary. She wanted the same but more, slow but fast. She moaned, unable to voice her needs, and his mouth returned to hers. His tongue delved, filling one of the voids within her. She reached around him to run the tips of her fingers across his broad, strong back. He was so hot, his muscle so solid, she just craved *more*.

Her eyes drifted shut and she felt each of his touches more acutely. He threaded his fingers through her hair, holding her face to his, while with his other hand he caressed her breasts, shaping them, teasing them. Making her feel admired, treasured. Beautiful. He traced his fingertips, his palm over her body and all the while he didn't stop kissing her mouth as if it were all he'd ever wanted to do in life. Every moment of kissing sent her further along a path from which she wanted no return. She wanted to go further, never to stop.

His hand was now firmly down the front of her jeans, curving deep into her most intimate area at the apex of her thighs. Her eyes flashed open and she clamped her legs tightly together—half wanting to trap him, half wanting to stop him. She'd never been as intimate with a man before and she was suddenly embarrassed.

He lifted his head and met her tormented gaze. He didn't say anything. He just smiled with pure sensual intent. It was her complete undoing.

This was what she wanted. Him, warm and close and touching her and loving it. That need so deep within her spiked. His hand moved ever so slightly as he felt her heated reaction. His fingers stoked.

Her mouth parted but she couldn't form a coherent thought let alone actual words. His fingers stroked that bit faster.

He kissed her again. She had no resistance to his kiss. All she wanted was more.

Her embarrassment faded with every tiny, deliberate touch. All she wanted was to race along this path that seemed so imperative now. Urgency drove her own caresses. Tracing his broad shoulders and feeling the strong muscles rippling beneath his hot skin, she arched for more, rocking her hips against his clever, clever fingers that were still rubbing in that fantastic way. Tension built within her as he kissed her towards oblivion.

'Come for me,' he growled. 'I want to feel you.'

She writhed, embarrassment long forgotten in the heat of the passion he stirred within her.

'Tomas,' she begged, suddenly realising it was right upon her. 'Oh, no.'

She'd wanted to please him too—but it was too late.

'Oh, yes,' he muttered, lifting his head to watch her as he flicked his fingers relentlessly.

She ground hard against his tormenting touch, unable to control the writhing of her body, the shaking of her muscles, the moans tearing from her throat.

'Enjoy it.'

She shivered, instinctively twisting with unbearable delight. She screamed as pleasure pulsed, drowning her in tumbling, powerful waves. It was too intense. Too much. She shuddered, clutching at his shoulder to keep him close, to anchor her.

'Like that. Yes.' He kept her close, his satisfaction at her reaction evident.

Breathing hard, she gazed into his eyes for an age—he was so close, but still so unfathomable. She licked her lips, finally drawing an easier breath only to realise she was still hot. Still hungry.

That was when he kissed her anew.

She relished the invasion of his tongue. Desire flowed—renewed, strengthened. She curled her tongue around his, and then pushed past so she could explore his mouth. She wanted to give him what he'd given her. She wanted to see his satisfaction.

He let her play for a moment before asserting his dominance again, deepening his possession of her. He pressed harder against her as she lay spread before him. She couldn't help rocking against him as orgasmic aftershocks rippled through her.

'You want more,' he said bluntly.

Without bothering to wait for an answer, he unsnapped the fastening of her jeans and lifted her so he could slide them down her legs. 'No panties?' He flashed a sudden smile. 'Why, Zara—'

Stark reality hit, making her quickly sit up, drawing her feet up to the table and her knees high in a defensive pose. She'd never before been naked in front of a man.

He cupped her face, tilting it so he could see right into her eyes.

'The only thing I'm going to do,' he promised gruffly, 'is make you feel good. That's all I want.'

Her breathing quickened and she fought down her suddenly emotional response. No one had wanted to see to her needs, wanted to take the time to treasure *her* feelings. Not in years.

She wanted to say something, but her throat was too tight. Her eyes burning.

He kissed her. Light and gentle and questioning. She moaned, leaning forward to deepen it. So quickly and easily he led her into that firestorm of desire.

He put his hands on her knees and gently pressed them apart.

'Don't hide from me,' he muttered against her mouth. 'And don't hold back.'

She couldn't if she tried. Not when he kissed her like that. She let him pull her to the very edge of the table and then he stepped close again, right between her legs, so her most intimate part was pushed hard against his pelvis.

He was still in his jeans and she growled with frustration. She wanted to feel him this hard against her, but bared.

But he distracted her, kissing her breasts. Cupping them. Ever so gently kneading the full flesh, then nuzzling her puckered nipples, drawing one, then the other into his mouth to tease them.

She stared dazedly down at his dark head, watching his ministrations, the way he was almost worshipping her body, treating her with lavish care and attention. He moved lower, licking his way down her stomach, pressing her so she lay back down on the table. She gasped as he moved lower still, until he was right there, licking where she was most private. Most hot. Most wet.

She couldn't breathe. Couldn't move. 'Tomas…'

She didn't know if she was asking him to stop, or keep going.

His hands were firm on her thighs, keeping them spread so he could explore her the way he wanted to. The way she now wanted him to. Because what he was doing felt so unspeakably good.

His hand lifted, teasing her further apart, rubbing right where she was most sensitive. And then he was there, kissing her intimately, his tongue darted and circled, then he sucked her most sensitive spot. She gasped at how personal it was, how good.

He didn't stop despite her obvious surprise. And she didn't want him to. Not now. She rocked instinctively, her movements increasing the more he caressed her, until he was kissing her sex the way he'd kissed her mouth. Claiming full possession—deep and lush and unrelenting and she thrashed beneath him, desperately aching for the release he was pushing her towards.

'Please,' she begged, unable to hold anything back. 'Please, please.'

She thrust her hands into his hair, holding his head to her. But it wasn't necessary—he wasn't going anywhere. And he wasn't showing any mercy. He kept kissing, rubbing, sucking. He reached up with his hand to torment her tight nipple. She arched, her body locking on the brink.

She was going to die. She was almost in tears. She groaned
again and again, her breathing ragged and desperate as she
held fast on the edge as he licked her hot and fast. But she
wanted more. So much more. She wanted him to feel as
good as she did right now. She wanted *all* of him. In her.
Coming with her. Feeling everything with her.

'Tomas,' she implored him rawly. 'Please take me.'

But he drew her nub into his mouth again and pulled,
tossing her into that delicious abyss alone to scream loud
and harsh as ecstasy overwhelmed her.

She didn't know how long it was until she opened her eyes
again, but when she did it was to find him leaning over her
and watching her close, one arm either side of her bared
body. She couldn't move if she tried. But as he gazed down
at her she slowly became aware of how she must look. A
wanton woman, pleasured to within an inch of her life,
spreadeagled before him. Not even in a bed, but on his
kitchen table—as if she were the late-night dessert for him
to feast on. And he had.

But now that sombre expression was back in his eyes.

'You should get to bed,' he said as he straightened away
from her.

Oh, no, he couldn't do that to her *again*. His expression
remote, he took her hands in his and tugged her into a sitting position.

He stepped back, almost angry.

Her courage crumbled. 'I'm not wearing anything,' she
mumbled.

She wanted to get her clothes. Wanted to cover up and
hide and run away to privacy to process what on earth had
just happened. Most of all how he seemed to have rebuilt
those barriers so horribly quickly. Unless they'd not really
come down at all?

'Leave them.'

It was a harshly given order.

She was about to argue, determined to, but he didn't give her a chance. He gripped her hand in his and marched, not bothering to turn off the lights as he left the kitchen.

He held her hand as she walked alongside him up the stairs, unable to speak for fighting the disappointment crashing over her in waves. Those moments in the kitchen had been the best of her life. These were now not far from the worst. She was naked—utterly naked. And he was not.

She shivered as cold set in, covering her skin in goosebumps. Inwardly she tried to process what had happened, but all she could think was that *he* wasn't satisfied. It was over and it had been so unfair. And she was so selfish all she wanted was more.

But he didn't. She could feel him pulling away with every step they climbed.

That disappointment morphed into anger. What had that been about? Had he wanted to secure her silence by seducing her?

Her heart turned to cinders as mortification burned her inside out. She was both hot and cold and so horribly uncomfortable, all she wanted to do was get away so she could hide how wounded she felt.

But he stopped by her door. For a moment he stood stock-still, not looking at her, as if he was picking his words with care.

'I shouldn't have—' He broke off as he turned and finally met her gaze.

He huffed out a breath. 'Don't look at me like that,' he muttered angrily, his hand tightening on hers.

'Like what?'

'Like—' He broke off again, his expression tense.

'Like what? Like I'm confused? Like I feel used?' She squared her shoulders, damning the embarrassment to hell. She was naked and he'd tasted every inch of her body and made her more sensually aroused than she'd ever been in her life. And all of a sudden she was so cross with him because he hadn't let her do the same for him. 'Like I'm furious with you?'

CHAPTER SIX

'Please.'

'YOU FEEL USED?' he snapped.

She didn't get the chance to stalk off and slam the door in his face. Because he slammed into her—his kiss an explosion of passion and rage and need. He walked her backwards so quickly she stumbled and in the end he simply picked her up and dumped her in the centre of her huge bed. He instantly followed, his weight gloriously heavy and pressing her deep into the mattress.

'I want to make you feel good too,' she snapped her explanation when she finally got the chance to speak. 'I want you to—'

Her words were crushed again in his kiss. She held him to her as she had on the kitchen table. But she was over those jeans. As sexy as he'd looked wearing nothing but them, she knew he'd look better utterly naked.

'Let me...' she whispered, her mouth tender when he finally lifted his head long enough for her to speak again. 'I want to touch you. Turn you on. Make you—'

She broke off, finally realising the bluntness of her words. Words she'd never have dreamt of snapping to anyone ever. But they'd spilled out in her anger.

'You think I don't want you?' He shifted off her to lie on his side facing her. His anger was as apparent in the rigidity of his muscles. 'Touch me and find out for yourself.'

For a split second she just stared at him. But then she reached out.

She didn't really know what she was doing. She simply traced her fingers over his muscled chest and then she tracked lower, intently focused on what she wanted so much she shook with need. She struggled to undo the zipper, desperate to have him as naked as she was. Impatience made her fingers clumsy.

She heard his half-laugh and he moved, leaving the bed to stand and kick off his jeans. Her breath caught in her throat as she registered the magnificence of his physique. And the extent of that scar.

She scooted to the end of the mattress and reached out to touch him again before she thought better of it. Before he'd had the chance to get back on the bed. Before nerves made her shy. But instinct was riding her hard now—all she could do was touch him. Kiss him. Take him as deep as possible into her—wherever, however she could.

His breath hissed between his gritted teeth as she firmly palmed down his chest and curled her fingers around his rigid length. She glanced up at him, knew he was about to speak, but she held him fast and licked his tip just before he could.

His mouth parted, but no words came out. He stood, utterly rigid, his hot eyes staring at her.

She smiled—had she actually silenced him for a moment? Good. She kept her gaze on him as she lowered her head. Then she licked him again. She felt him jerk in her hand, so she tightened her grip then released to stroke upwards.

His breath hissed out again. She closed her eyes, and bent forward to totally take him into her mouth.

'Zara…'

She was still a little unsure of what she was doing, but quickly discovered that trying to give him pleasure like this only increased her own arousal. She panted as she rocked her hips in time to her rhythmic sucking. Oh, hell, she was so hot, and she couldn't get close enough again. Couldn't touch him enough.

She heard him swearing in a guttural tone. Then he stiffened under her hands.

'Zara,' he whispered. 'I… You…'

His hips jerked uncontrollably. She liked it and sucked him harder, deeper. That was the only answer she gave him.

He released a harsh sigh and combed his fingers through her hair, holding her head in place as he gave over to the urge biting him. She felt him trying not to thrust too hard but she wanted him to let go of his restraint altogether. Operating on blind instinct, she leaned closer and worked her hand that bit faster, rapidly tonguing his tip as she sucked as hard as she could.

His fingers were tight on her scalp as he tried not to push too deep into her. But she didn't care. She was too pleased.

When he released her with a shuddering sigh, she drew back to look up at him and smile. Now she felt better. Now they were almost even. But he didn't smile at her. His expression was fierce. He shoved her shoulders so she fell backwards onto the mattress.

'Spread your legs for me, Zara,' he ordered harshly. 'I need to taste you again.'

This time she didn't hesitate. Nor did he. He was there—kissing, sucking and rubbing right where she was wet and hot and almost hurting with hunger.

Relief swamped her for only a second before his sensuality sent her soaring. She wanted everything with him this time. Just this once.

'Please, please, please.' She couldn't contain her moans. She gripped the bedclothes beneath her as she arched up, offering herself to him completely. But he didn't let her have her release.

Not this time.

'I need to get something…' he growled as he pulled away with sharp, leashed movements. 'Just a second.'

That was when the reality hit her. He was going to give her *exactly* what she wanted.

'There can't be any consequences,' he said as he emerged from her bathroom carrying an unopened box of condoms.

Not physical ones. But she already knew there'd be implications for her. And she didn't care.

The dying firelight flickered, emphasising the angles and planes of his sculpted body with the warm glow. Her mouth smiled at the pure athleticism of him as he gritted his teeth and concentrated on the task of protecting them both. She wasn't surprised by his preparedness—there was everything a guest could ever need in that bathroom. She was pleased. Aroused. And slightly terrified.

He glanced up and caught her watching heavy eyed, her lips parted in admiration and anticipation. A muscle flinched in his jaw.

Maybe it was just that he'd been alone so long and she was here. That was okay. She'd take it. She wanted to give him pleasure, and relief, even for just a little while.

'Don't look so worried,' he muttered. 'I might not remember many things, but I don't think I've forgotten how this goes.' He knelt on the bed and leaned over her.

It wasn't as if she had the experience to help him. She should tell him. She knew she should tell him. But instinctively she knew that if she did, he'd stop and that was the last thing she wanted. He probably wouldn't even notice. If she just went with it. He'd made everything else happen so easily. So beautifully.

She wanted this. She wanted this more than she'd ever wanted anything. With a fierceness she'd not known she had within her she wrapped her arms around him and hugged him close.

He kissed her again. It was more familiar now, yet she'd never get used to how intensely and quickly his kisses could rouse the total wanton within her.

'You make it impossible for me,' he growled as he braced over her and nudged her legs apart with his knee. 'I cannot resist.'

'Then don't try,' she whispered. 'Please.'

She didn't care that she was begging. She just wanted him right there with her. In her. Fighting to reach that peak with her. And finding it.

She would give him anything. But she couldn't hold back the small cry as he pierced her physical purity.

He growled harshly and froze, his expression shocked.

She breathed out quickly, shifting beneath him just that little bit to ease the intense pressure she felt between her legs.

'Zara.'

She licked her lips and swallowed.

'I thought you said you'd been married,' he demanded her answer.

'I was…' She closed her eyes for a moment before making herself look at him. Making herself speak the truth. 'But he…he didn't want me that way.'

'He *what*?' Tomas stared at her, aghast. 'Did he have rocks in his head?'

She smiled ruefully. She could never answer that, not now. It was circumstances that were different.

But she saw the moment Tomas truly understood the implications of her words—of what her body had already told him.

'We should stop. This should stop.' He gazed at her with tormented eyes, but he didn't move. He didn't withdraw from her body.

'I don't want to stop,' she whispered. 'Please.'

He drew in a shuddering breath and she felt how much strain he was under to keep himself in check.

'Can't we just have tonight?' She wanted this one memory to treasure. She already knew no other man would ever make her feel this way. Never *want* in this way.

There might be regrets in the morning. But she'd never truly regret this. She wanted him more than she'd ever wanted anything. And she didn't care about the cost.

'You're a virgin.' He was still shocked.

Not any more. Not when he was there, inside her right now. And it was feeling so much better already. 'It feels *good*.' And it did.

He shook his head. 'I've hurt you.' But he was the one who looked pained. 'I didn't want to hurt you.'

'No.' She arched clumsily, trying to draw him closer still and tease those highly sensitive nerve endings again. 'The only thing that hurts is the thought of stopping.'

He was shaking with the effort of holding still. Beneath her back his hands had curled into fists.

'Unless you don't really want…' She trailed off.

Oh, heavens, that was it. He'd not wanted her before, why would now be any different? He'd been happy to fool around a bit but he hadn't really wanted her all that much.

'Zara.' His lips twisted as he smiled at her. 'Don't be an idiot.'

She tried to laugh but her heart squeezed.

'You know this won't be anything more,' he said. 'Just tonight. Just now.'

'Yes.' That was all it could ever be.

He kissed her. It was such a tender kiss that she thought he was apologising. That he was going to stop.

She held her breath as he braced on his arms and shifted, ever so gently pulling back. But then he probed deeper.

She moaned softly as a ripple of pleasure was sent from her core to every cell within her body.

'I'll make it better,' he muttered. It was a vow.

She fell a little deeper in love with him in that instant. He might have tried to distance himself from the world but he couldn't help but be kind when it counted. And he always put his own needs behind those of another. That was how he'd got so badly injured in the first place.

'It can't get any better,' she answered softly.

She felt him draw a sharp breath before he bore down on her again, watching her intently as he possessed her to his hilt. 'Yes, it can. And it will.'

She was like putty in his hands when he kissed her. She'd let him do anything and everything he wanted, as long as he kept kissing her like that.

Somehow she felt herself growing closer to him with every thrust. With every movement, every caress, he drew her further under his spell. She felt both protected and provoked—into opening up more to him, giving more. Taking more.

She grew greedy, raking her hands down his back to clutch and hold him closer to her. She arched, crying out in delight as he took her to the brink again.

'Please,' she begged, knowing she was so very close.

'You first,' he insisted, his teeth gritted.

'No,' she moaned. She wanted him *with* her.

'Yes.' He looked almost scarily determined as he bore down on her.

She trembled, her orgasm racking through her body. She'd never felt as exposed to anyone. Never so close. And never so good.

But as she sighed out the last of her release, she caught a pained look crossing his face and he thrust deep into her and held fast.

She cupped his jaw, forcing him to meet her eyes. 'Have I hurt you?'

A wry smile curved his mouth, despite the strain he was obviously under. 'It's my damn leg. I just need to...' He sighed, then held her super close and rolled, taking her with him, switching their position so he was beneath her and she sprawled over the top. All the while they'd stayed connected. And now that connection seemed stronger still.

More than physical.

Zara lay still for a moment resting on him, processing the shift—in both position and vulnerability. Ruefully he swept back her hair from her face.

'Sorry,' he muttered.

'No.' The sensation was something different again. 'Oh-h-h…' she breathed as she bent her legs and pushed her hands on his chest to lever herself into a sitting position. 'Is this better for you?'

He looked up at her and cupped her breasts, his small smile returned. 'I think I can live with it. Can you?'

Like this, he could reach down and stroke her just where they were joined. Just where she was so incredibly sensitive.

'Oh,' she moaned as he gently caressed her. 'I think so.'

He held her hips and slowly rocked her, showing her how to move on him. She bit down on her lip, testing pace, and then depth, watching his reaction as she did so. His eyes were almost black, and so focused on her. She felt so close to him and when she smiled at him, he smiled back.

She trailed her hand down his thigh, letting her fingers skim the scar. 'Better?' she asked softly.

He nodded. She was touched he'd not hidden that pain from her. And that he, like she, had not wanted to stop.

Sweat glistened, and his muscles rippled as he moved to complement her lead.

Being together like this felt so good. She leaned forward, pressing her hands on his shoulders as she settled into a rhythm.

'You keep making me come and you haven't,' she groaned, her head falling back as she began to crest the wave. 'Oh, Tomas.' She rocked harder, her instinct suddenly urging her to ride him fast. She threw her head back as her orgasm hit and she screamed her need for him. *'Come.'*

'Yes.' Hoarsely he gave in to her demand, thrusting up hard to meet her. 'Oh, hell, *yes*.'

This time she was the one leaning over and watching him. She smiled as he opened his eyes and looked at her. She was unable to think of a thing to say. There was nothing to say. She could only *be*—her body fizzing with warmth and satiation. But she smiled at him.

'You're still not tired, are you?' he teased, but there was a note of amused wonder in his voice.

'No.' If she'd thought her body was wired before, she was absolutely humming now. How could she ever sleep when she'd just experienced *that*? There was so much to process—she still couldn't believe it was possible to feel so good. For one person to make another feel this amazing. 'I don't think I'll ever be able to sleep again.'

He ran his hand up and down her thigh as he studied her. 'Then perhaps we'd better do something to fill in the time till morning.'

She shivered at the sensual promise in his low murmur.

'You're not sore?' he asked as he shifted under her.

'Not enough to care,' she said recklessly. 'You?'

'It's worth any amount of pain.'

She beamed at him. 'Then kiss me,' she asked shyly as she leaned down to him.

'Here?' He avoided her mouth to kiss her neck. 'Or here?' He scooted lower to catch the tip of her breast.

'Everywhere.'

She lost all track of time as he proceeded to do exactly as she'd asked. Lost track of the number of times she begged him. Lost track of where she started and he began. Lost track of almost everything but how good she felt.

And then she lost the ability to move altogether. She was so relaxed she was limp. She couldn't even roll to her side to face him.

'Sleep now,' he said quietly.

He kissed her. The softest touch to her temple. His passion had faded.

Her heart ached with the knowledge that it was over.

She kept her eyes closed because she didn't want to see the finality in his expression. She just wanted to curl against him and pretend a little longer except she hadn't the energy to move closer.

But then she heard the door snick. She snapped her eyes open and realised she was alone.

CHAPTER SEVEN

'The good feeling doesn't last.'

THE KITCHEN LOOKED as if it had been struck by a tornado.

She was going to have to scrape the dried biscuit dough off the end of that table with a jackhammer. She couldn't bear to look at the other end where she'd lain like a sexual offering to the lord of the manor.

There was no sign of Tomas. Not for the entire time it took her to scrape and scrub the table clean and do all the dishes she'd left out from her midnight bakeathon.

But then the door leading to the garden opened.

'What would you like for breakfast?' she asked as he silently stalked in.

He looked wind-bitten and irritable and too many muscles were on show in those shorts and T-shirt and trainers.

'I've already eaten.' He didn't even look at her. He didn't need to. The glower on his face said it all.

He wanted to be beastly again? Fine.

'I'll prepare lunch and let you know when it is ready,' she replied *faux* sweetly. 'I won't bother you again before then.'

He hesitated at the door and then swung back to face her. 'What happened last night was a mistake. It won't happen again.'

'That's what you said about that kiss,' she pointed out. Did he really think it could just be forgotten about?

Maybe it could. And maybe he regretted it completely.

He didn't answer. Didn't apologise. Didn't stay another second.

For a moment she leaned against the bench, absorbing the stab in her heart. Then she pulled herself together. She wasn't going to pine for his attention. Instead she point-lessly rubbed the silverware she'd found in the room to the left of the kitchen. It was so highly polished already she was making no difference, but she needed to do something.

Her anxiety was building, threatening to tear her apart.

She should tell him the truth. She *had* to tell him the truth. Especially now. But she couldn't bring herself to do it. Not without Jasper there to confirm it.

Tomas glared at the date and the name he'd written on the blank page in front of him, forcing himself to resist the almost overpowering urge to race back downstairs and apologise and pull her into his arms and do everything all over again. He couldn't believe his idiocy. How could basic instinct and lust dominate his reason so quickly or so completely?

It was because of the proximity, right? The weather out-side made everything inside seem more intimate. He'd been there and she'd been there and they'd been alone and she'd been willing. So very willing.

He frowned.

Why had she let him do that—why had she said yes to him so quickly, when she'd let no other man before? He hadn't earned the gift of her virginity. She barely *knew* him.

It didn't make sense.

His suspicions sharpened, arrowing in a direction he re-ally didn't like. She knew about his memory loss and then she'd let him do anything he wanted to.

Jasper's words lingered with him—that recommenda-tion to have some fun and 'come back to life'…but Zara wasn't one of Jasper's 'good time girls'. She was as sweet as she looked. And vulnerable.

Jasper had told him that too. He ripped the page from his journal and screwed it into a ball and tossed it into the fire.

He'd made a hash of everything. He didn't want to lead

her on. Didn't want her thinking there could be anything more. Because there couldn't be.

He was furious with himself. How could he have been that out of control? Was he that starved of sex? He'd barely thought about it these last few months. He'd been too busy working on his physical health, on his business, on reclaiming control of his life. Yet at the first opportunity he'd got—with the first woman who'd crossed his path in months—he'd pounced. He'd stripped her on the kitchen table and ravished her, barely giving her a chance to catch breath before beginning again. She'd come here as a temporary employee and he'd taken advantage of her in every way possible.

It had been horrendous behaviour.

And what would she be expecting from him now?

He didn't have anything to offer her or any woman. He'd kept his distance deliberately to protect his reputation, his business. The truth about his injury could never become public knowledge. But it seemed he needed to protect a woman from himself too—from his new rabid, uncontrollable lustiness.

He'd failed Zara as her employer. He wouldn't make that mistake again. He'd take control of his sex drive and leave her alone. It was only a few days and she'd be gone.

He ignored the raging tension in his body at the thought of denial. He wasn't letting lust overrule him—not when he'd overcome so much else.

He clamped his teeth together to stop himself from speaking to her when she brought up a tray with his lunch. His jaw ached with the effort.

A shadow entered her beautiful blue-green eyes as she placed the tray before him.

He ignored it—her, the tray, his own desires. He had to. He had to re-establish distance—coolness—between them.

She got to the doorway before she turned.

'You know, I get that last night was a one-time-only thing and that you don't want any more than that,' she said softly, only the faintest shake to her voice. 'So you don't need to be this rude to me. I'm not hanging around for more. You're not going to break my heart or anything. But you could still be polite.'

He stared at her, stunned at her annoyance. Annoyed at himself because she was right. He had treated her exactly as he'd once vowed never to treat any woman. He'd acted as if he'd *used* her. No woman deserved that. 'I apologise,' he said formally. 'I didn't intend to be rude.'

He glared after her as she stalked away, her back ramrod straight and her chin held high.

He had been a jerk. He wouldn't blame her if she didn't want anything more from him—except he didn't think that was quite true. Those sea-green eyes couldn't hide much—certainly not the way they deepened in colour when she looked at him.

He sighed. He'd been horrible. She had been a virgin, and he hadn't even bothered to stay and cuddle her to sleep after he'd finally been spent.

He was appalled with himself. Most of all because he still wanted more. He just didn't understand how he'd lost control of his desires in this way.

Zara pressed a hand to her chest as she ran lightly down the stairs, her legs wobbly from literally standing up to him. When really, she had nothing to stand on when she'd been the one keeping information from him.

But it was meaningless information really. What was one day? It hadn't meant anything to him. Nor had last night. And that was okay.

She bent over her work again. A long while later she heard him stomping down the stairs. She concentrated extra hard on the piece she was polishing.

'What are you doing?' he growled at her.

'My job, what do you think?'

'You barely got any sleep last night—'

'So? That's not stopping you from working.'

'That's different.'

Oh, that got her riled. 'How so?'

'Mine isn't physical work,' he said gruffly.

'This isn't exactly that hard.'

'But—'

'Don't try to stop me. What happened last night hasn't changed anything,' she argued. 'It's just a job. I'm being paid to do this job. If I don't do the job then what am I being paid for?'

He paused. An almost stricken look entered his eyes.

'Exactly.' She smiled sharply up at him in victory. 'I'm doing the cooking and the cleaning, Tomas, and you're not stopping me.'

'Fine.' A muscle jumped in his jaw. 'Just don't overdo it.'

'I pride myself on doing the best I can, just as you do.' She shook her head. 'Please don't patronise me.'

He huffed out a frustrated breath. 'Please don't be so damn prickly.'

Her jaw dropped. 'Look who's talking,' she bit back sharply.

He stared at her for a second. And then his smile flashed. Reluctantly at first and then it became broad and wide.

He shook his head. 'You don't make this easy.'

'You don't think?'

Too late she realised the implication of her words. Hadn't she been totally easy?

He threw her a stunned look and burst into laughter at her mortification. 'You're blushing.'

'Don't comment on it, you make it worse.' She glanced at him, then started to get mad at him all over again. 'Don't do that.'

'Do what?' He grinned.

Look gorgeous. Look human and hot and fun. She turned it on him. 'Are you really going to spend all day ignoring me and then decide to be nice just because you're bored again?'

'I'm not bored,' he answered ruefully. 'I could never be bored with you in the house.' His brows pleated. 'Last night didn't happen because I was bored.'

Flattery wasn't going to work. She refused to let it.

'You're not bored either,' he added thoughtfully. 'Are you?'

'How can I be, when I don't know if you're going to bite my head off or try to—' She paused in her retort.

'Or what?' He dared to grin at her.

'Do something…unspeakable,' she finished.

Something gleamed in his eyes but he straightened and pressed his knuckles against the table. 'Why did you do it?'

She paused. Knowing what he meant but not wanting to answer. How could she explain it to him?

'You were a virgin.' He crossed his arms and glared at her.

'Does it matter all that much?' she asked, more bravado now than honest. Because, yes, to her it did matter. But she didn't regret it. She'd *never* regret it. And she wasn't going to let him taint the memory of how perfect those moments in his arms had been.

'You met me less than forty-eight hours ago.'

She swallowed. How could she tell him now that she'd fantasised about him for a *year*?

'And you let me do all that and more. More than once.' He shook his head. 'Why?'

She didn't know how to answer him.

'Did Jasper send you here to seduce me?' he asked. 'Did he pay you to…entertain me?'

'Are you honestly asking me that? *Again?*' Angrily she

tore back at him. 'You think I'd really do that?' She rose from the table and stomped towards the door. Unfortunately that meant she had to stomp past him. 'No money would be enough for me to do that. I can't and won't ever be bought.'

He grabbed her as she made to get past.

'Then it's because you feel sorry for me. Because of my injury.'

His hands were firm on her waist and it took every ounce of willpower to suppress her trembling. But to her surprise he was pale—as if he really questioned why she'd slept with him.

'You think I held onto my virginity all this time only to give it up out of pity?' She shook her head because he was crazy. 'If I felt sorry for you I might make you a cup of tea and cook you your favourite dinner…but I wouldn't let you *inside* me.' She was so emotional she couldn't hide her shaking now. 'I wouldn't ever be that *intimate* with a man just because…'

His eyes narrowed as he ruthlessly watched her. Making her admit it all.

'So if it wasn't because of those reasons, then why?'

But saying it was so much harder than showing him. 'It's much simpler than that. I let you have me, because I wanted you. I wanted you so much I ached. I couldn't stop and I didn't want to.'

'So it was just lust?' He looked disbelieving.

'Why did you sleep with me, then?' She turned the tables crossly. 'Why did you…do all that to me over and over and over when you'd only just met me too? Even when you realised how inexperienced I was…'

'No, I didn't want to stop. You're gorgeous.'

'So I can't lust after a guy for his looks, but it's okay for you to lust after a woman?'

'But I wasn't a virgin, Zara.'

'Like that matters all that much?'

'Doesn't it?' he dared her. 'You said it yourself, why would you have held onto it all this time? If it didn't matter all that much, why were you still a virgin at this age?'

How could she tell him she'd been unable to look at any other man in that way since she'd first met him?

'You're saying I'm old?'

He laughed and gave her a gentle shake. 'No and don't try to change the subject. I refuse to believe this was the first chance you'd had to have your wicked way with a man. If you'd wanted to, and if it didn't matter to you all that much, you would have lost your virginity years ago.'

Silenced, she looked at him.

'So why me?' he pressed her. 'Why now?'

She swallowed. 'You have a very beautiful body.' She faltered. 'And very beautiful eyes. You're…fascinating.' She was simply absorbed by him. 'And you're very good at kissing me,' she whispered.

'Kissing turns you on?'

She touched her tongue to her lip very quickly, but he saw. He saw and he knew.

'Has no one else ever kissed you?' he asked softly.

'Not the way you do.'

'How do I kiss you?'

She gazed up into his eyes and one secret thought spilled out. 'Like you can't get enough of me.' As if he were pouring every ounce of himself into her—and it made her so warm, so beyond herself.

'Well, that's true,' he answered almost inaudibly. 'I can't.' He cradled her face in his hands. 'You like to feel wanted? Is that what it is?' he asked. 'Because, sweetheart, you have no idea how much I want you. How many times I want you. But I can't do anything more than want you just for now. Do you understand?'

'What I understand is that in a couple of days I'll leave here and most likely will never come back. I'll get on with my business and you'll get on with yours,' she answered. 'I don't want anything more from you. I won't take anything from you. Other than…'

'Sex.'

She nodded, wincing a little at the blunt admittance.

'You'd better mean it, Zara. Because if you agree to this, then, I have to warn you, it's not going to be a restful couple of days.'

Her breathing quickened. She was aroused at what he was implying. 'You mean—'

'I mean if you say yes now, I'm likely to want you every damn moment from now until you walk out that door and drive away. But when you do drive away, you mustn't look back. You mustn't come back. Not ever. You promise me you can do that? You promise me you won't want more. Because I haven't any more to give.'

She didn't care how needy she was, how accepting of what little he had to give. Because the truth was she had no more either. This was all she wanted from him because it was all she could have. Once he knew the truth he'd be so mad with her, but she was too selfish—and too hungry—to deny herself just this little time.

Because what Tomas didn't know was that this would end the second Jasper arrived and the truth came out. There was only this night before the lawyer was due. Tomorrow it would all be over.

'You won't come back,' he pressed her.

'I won't.' But only because he truly wouldn't want her to.

He pulled her close to him. 'Promise me.'

'I promise.'

He kissed her, instantly sending her back into that cauldron of desire. She flung her arms around his neck and kissed him back. She was so mad with him. But as she rubbed against him she felt just how aroused he was. He walked her backwards until her back hit the wall.

Not the table this time? She tore her lips from his so she could look into his eyes and read his intent. To see if he was as wild as she.

In answer he reached into his pocket.

'You have a condom with you?' She glared at him accusingly. 'When you were so *rude*?'

'I'm sorry,' he muttered, quickly kissing his way to her forgiveness. 'I'm very, very sorry.'

And suddenly she was even more turned on. And even more angry.

'Then maybe you'd better use it.' She fumbled, but somehow yanked his trousers open.

For a second he glared back at her. Then he fought to get the condom on fast enough. As he worked she undid her jeans and shimmied them and her panties down. Finally sheathed, he pushed her so her back was right against the wall in support.

But then he hesitated. 'Zara—'

'Take me,' she said, daring him. Daring *herself*.

'You're not ready.' He shook his head. 'You can't be ready.'

'I've been ready all day,' she said scornfully.

His pupils dilated. Without breaking that searing eye contact, he slid a firm hand up her inner thigh, not hesitating to go higher, to stroke her and find she was right.

His word was short, pithy and to the point. And he'd stepped up before he'd finished saying it.

She screamed raw victory as he bucked hard and filled her right where she needed him. *Physical*. That was what this was. For the first time in her life she was in thrall to unrefined, hot lust. And it was the best thing ever.

Tomas watched the savage emotions flicker across her face as she first softened, then tightened about him. She couldn't hide it from him—the need, the rapture she felt as he took her. Saucy little moans spilled from her mouth as he thrust again. Hot desire flooded him, blinding him in a flash to everything but the need to feel her even more. *Now.* He thrust harder, his need overtaking him sooner than he'd ever intended.

'Zara,' he warned her hoarsely as he felt his control slip. But she was too slippery, too hot, too welcoming and his body's demands drove him on. He needed to get deeper inside her. Deeper, harder, faster. He grabbed her, lifting her a fraction so he could.

'Yes,' she cried as he uncontrollably rammed into her over and over. 'Yes. Yes. Yes.'

'Oh, Zara.' His world splintered as satisfaction gushed through him, out of him, and into her. Too soon. Too damn soon.

'Tomas!'

His relief was multiplied tenfold as he felt her come hard at the exact moment he locked into her in his one last, fierce thrust to orgasm. They clenched together for a long moment. Both shaking, revelling in the wild pulses of pleasure.

Then he pressed his head against her shoulder, breathing hard in recovery. He half laughed. That had been too fast to count.

But for the first time in months he felt wholly strong again. He wanted to prove it, to revel in it and take every pleasure with her. Sex with Zara made him feel invincible. Not even his leg seemed to bother him as much today. Maybe this was the exact kind of workout it had needed.

He kissed her deeply, then led her back to her bedroom to reposition her on her bed, determined to take it slower this time. Wanting to show her every way he could think to pleasure her. Her eyes widened but she welcomed him with that hot, sweet enthusiasm of hers. He wanted to hear her scream his name again and again. He wanted to feel the dynamism in her body, and then feel her fall soft and relaxed and curl into him. Sated and sweet and sexy.

But her lids grew heavy again as she drank in his body when he pulled away after the second time, to fetch them both a drink of water.

Insatiable minx.

'So you didn't give me your virginity because you were in love with me?' he teased as he lifted the glass to her lips as she lay sprawled in a tangle of sexiness on the bed.

She spluttered as she sipped and took the glass from him with a baleful look.

'Were you in love with the woman you lost your virginity to?' she asked him with a frown. Then her eyes widened in horror. 'That's if you... Oh, I'm sorry.'

Her blush was beautiful.

'Actually, yes, I do remember it, because I wasn't as old as you when I lost it.' He half laughed at her concern.

His sexual awakening had been during the torment of his mid-teen years when he'd been on the streets and hustling cards to survive.

She was silent a second. 'Were you in love with her?'

He shook his head. He was never in love with anyone. And wouldn't be. He didn't really know what love was. But he sure as hell knew what it wasn't.

'I was tired and alone and she made me welcome.' He set the water down on the table beside the bed. 'She did things that made me feel good and showed me how to make her feel good too.'

She'd shown him that sex didn't have to be anything other than a physical pleasure between two willing partners. That was all it had to be. Nothing tacky or a sleazy transaction, but nothing meaningful either. Just release. And for him, that was all it would ever be. Except he'd forgotten just how good it could feel.

But hedonism took you only so far.

'But?' she prompted, sensing his hesitation.

'The good feeling doesn't last,' he admitted, needing to warn her. 'Other things get in the way.'

'What other things?' She looked wary.

'Other wants.'

'She wanted what you couldn't give?'

'I wanted different things from her,' he clarified. 'Don't be mistaken, there was no love between us. No heartbreak. We were together only a handful of times before it ended.'

But he remembered too well the fine line it was between mutual pleasure and the need for more. What people would do when they were desperate. He'd vowed not to take advantage of the vulnerable in the way that people had tried to take advantage of him as a youth. Of the way people had taken advantage of his mother. And he knew how vulnerability led to temptation. Selling out might seem like an easier option, but it had only led his mother to destitution and despair.

He'd fought a different battle, leaving Italy to further his prospects in England—knowing he needed education and opportunity. He'd worked to gain both. He'd worked hard.

Zara had quietened as she watched him remembering.

He frowned, knowing if he thought too much further there'd be too much he couldn't remember. The darkness would settle.

He moved so he could tease her most sensitive parts as gently as he could.

'How is it possible it can feel even better than before?' she muttered dreamily as she arched into his embrace.

His arms tightened about her. She had a point there.

CHAPTER EIGHT

'Would it be so awful if the world knew?'

'THE SNOW IS too severe for Jasper to drive,' Tomas announced as he walked into the kitchen in the late morning.

The knife clattered on the bench as Zara quickly put the bowl she was holding down. She licked her lips, pretending to focus intently on the cake she'd been icing. 'So he's not getting here today?'

Her heart had been racing all morning—her whole system in a state of high anxiety, knowing the axe was about to fall. Knowing she should have said something sooner.

'He thinks tomorrow or the day after should be fine.'

Another day. She breathed out. She had been granted one more day. She still couldn't bring herself to say it. Not when she could have a few more hours of bliss.

'Can you do something for me?' she asked, her voice catching.

He angled his head. 'Depends what it is.'

Yeah, there was no automatic reply of 'anything'—he was still wary. And she didn't blame him.

'Try these and tell me which you prefer.'

He looked at the two slices she'd plated up and pushed towards him. 'They look the same.'

'Can you just try?'

'You know you don't have to go to all this trouble just for me.' He smiled wolfishly. 'Though I do appreciate it.'

'It's not for your benefit.' She rolled her eyes, muttering caustically, 'I'm testing recipes.'

'Oh, now I see.' He smiled as he bit into the first piece. 'So I'm just your guinea pig.'

'Lab rat, yes.' She smiled, relaxing as she teased him.

It was fun teasing him.

'Recipes, huh?' He pulled her notebook around so he could read it. 'May I?'

'You already have.' She pushed a piece of the second slice towards him.

His brows lifted as he flicked through the pages. 'You have a lot of notes.' He glanced up and levelled her with a piercing gaze. 'Does the world really need another baking blog?'

'Does the world really need another rich recluse?' she countered pleasantly.

He laughed. 'Touché.'

Impatient, she watched as he bit into the second piece. 'So which do you prefer?'

He took his time, watching her as he savoured the slice. 'They're both delicious,' he pronounced, picking up her recipe book to rifle through it in greater depth.

'That's not helpful. I actually need a decision.'

'Can't do it.' He glanced over the page and shrugged at her. 'They're both so good.' He put the book to the side and picked up another small piece of cake. 'What else have you got?'

'A lot, as it happens.' She stepped to the pantry and came back with the container of samples she'd been working on.

'What are you going to do with all of them? If not a baking blog.' He watched as she selected a couple of biscuits and added them to his plate.

She smiled but shook her head. She wasn't about to tell him. Not when he made his fortune predicting the success or otherwise of companies. Especially when he did that with incredible accuracy. She didn't need to be shot down quite so soon.

'I won't steal your idea.'

She laughed at the thought of Tomas up to his elbows in

flour and white icing. 'I don't want to give away the recipes, I want to sell the product myself.'

'Go into manufacturing?'

'On an artisan scale, not mass produced.'

'For farmers' markets and the like?'

Of course he'd grasp it right away. She nodded. 'I've been selling some of my products at my local one for a while and a couple of the nearby cafés have asked me to supply them.'

'You're a baker more than a housekeeper, then?'

'Yes, but I need to work while I get established.'

'Of course.' He picked up another biscuit but studied it rather than eating it. 'You've had training?'

'I learned a lot from my uncle's chef and I took a course this past year.'

'Full time?'

She nodded. 'I need to do more but at the same time—'

'You don't want to wait to get your business under way.'

'Yes.' She felt self-conscious about sharing her ambition with him. No one had ever believed in her, least of all her. 'I know it probably won't work—'

'Why wouldn't it?' he argued matter-of-factly. 'According to the newspapers I built up my business while studying.'

She put down her container and sent him a look. 'You're not like most people.'

'I'm not?'

'You work harder than any normal person can. You have more focus and drive than anyone I've ever met.'

'Maybe it comes down to motivation, then. How badly do you want to succeed?'

'You must want to succeed very badly.'

'When your life depends on it, I guess that gives you focus.'

Why had his life depended on it? Where was his family? She was so curious and he couldn't really help her. She wished she could help him. But the only thing it seemed she could really do was 'entertain' him.

Which, frankly, she loved.

'Speaking of work, I have to go do some now.' But for the first time in ages, Tomas didn't really want to. He wanted to stay near and talk to her.

'So when you said we'd be at it every moment, that was an empty promise?'

He nearly choked on the cake. Was that a sultry taunt from his blushing lover? 'I'll be back downstairs later and you will pay for that.'

'Will I?' She looked all innocence.

Now there was a challenge from her. Eyes narrowing, he walked closer to her, smiling as the colour ran up under her cheeks.

It took little to arouse her. A fact he relished given he permanently ached for her. For her touch.

So touch her he did. Until she was soft and hot and whispering those pleas in that broken voice. And then he stopped, leaned against the bench as he half growled. 'How badly do you want to work now?' he challenged her.

'That's mean,' she breathed balefully. 'That's so mean.'

'You do the same to me.'

She distracted him. Tormented him. Made him want to cast everything else aside and only be with her.

'Then go away so we can both concentrate, please,' she begged.

She was right. He needed to leave before this escalated further. As it was he'd been late starting because he'd gone back into her room to wake her.

He backed out of the kitchen, his gaze trained on her the whole time.

'Stop it,' she mouthed.

He was rock hard and aching but he forced himself to

leave the room. He was still in control of this situation and himself.

But less than an hour later he was pacing in his large office. This distraction had to stop. Thing was, he knew it was going to. She'd leave soon enough. His housekeeper would return. There was only today. He'd been disciplined for so long, what would one afternoon cost?

He went down to the kitchen but found it empty; only her music and the lingering scents of lemon and vanilla were there to remind him of her. His mouth watered. He paused in the hallway, listening for sounds. Then headed back up the stairs.

She'd not gone to the left wing—where he worked and their bedrooms were—but the right. She was in the drawing room, peeking under the drop cloths at the furniture that had been covered for storage. She'd opened up the shutters so the light was let in and she was really being nosy.

He leaned against the wall and watched her move around the room looking at each object in fascination.

'What are you doing?' he asked when he realised she still hadn't noticed him.

She whirled in surprise but then that dimple popped and her eyes were glowing.

'Snooping,' she confessed as she failed to bite back her smile. 'Do you have any idea how amazing this stuff is?'

He lifted away from the wall and walked towards her. 'I've seen it.'

'It seems such a shame to hide it all away.'

'There's no need for me to have every room ready. I can't be in all of them at once.' He knew the house was too big for him. But he'd wanted space.

'It's like a museum.' She walked across the room. 'You bought it furnished?'

He nodded. He hadn't bothered to look too closely at all

the treasures. He'd just turned a small part of the place into what he needed as quickly as possible.

'But you then covered everything up?'

'Are you judging?'

'No. I'm exploring. It's fun.'

She lifted a small clock from a nearby cabinet and brought it to him. 'This should not be hidden away.' She gave him a stern look. 'This should be enjoyed.'

'I don't know that it even works.'

'So what?' She held it to the light. 'Shouldn't we just enjoy the decoration of it? The beauty?' She placed it back on the cabinet. 'Small things,' she muttered. 'All the small things.'

He watched as she uncovered more treasures. He refused to feel guilty about them; some time they'd be on show again. But her appreciation of them all got under his skin. He couldn't help smiling at her animation. She was a conundrum: the way she handled the objects led him to think she'd been around valuable things before, but at the same time she showed an almost naive enjoyment of them.

'I suppose I'd better get back downstairs.' She suddenly sent him a guilty look.

'Yes or I'll start cracking the whip,' he said dryly.

She laughed even as that gorgeous blush swept under her skin. 'I was taking my duty as housekeeper very seriously and checking on the condition of the rooms.'

'Of course you were.' He walked with her down the corridor towards the stairs, thinking he'd sidestep with her into her bedroom. All he wanted to do was kiss her.

He noticed her looking at the pictures on the wall as they passed by. He grimaced. He knew it was weird, but it was a system that had worked for him.

She suddenly stumbled.

'Are you okay?' he asked.

When she straightened he noticed she'd paled.

'Are you hurt?'

'No.' She kept walking, her pace quicker.

He didn't believe her. Something had bothered her. He glanced back along the row of photos they'd passed.

'Which ones are your ex-girlfriends?' she suddenly said, switching on a bright smile. 'Don't they get their own corridor?'

He hesitated, still certain something had upset her. And it wasn't going to be any ex-girlfriend.

'I'm picking this one.' She pointed to a picture of a willowy blonde.

'She's the wife of one of my main clients and never, ever would I consider it,' he answered dryly.

'Because she's the wife of one of your clients?'

'No.' He rolled his eyes. 'Because she doesn't attract me in that way.'

The colour had returned to her cheeks and she took a step closer to him. 'You prefer brunettes?'

His lips twitched.

She sent him a swift look from under artfully lowered lashes. 'And shorter rather than tall? Perhaps with blue-green eyes?'

'You wouldn't be fishing for compliments, would you?'

'If I were, I'm not getting any bites.' She sighed mournfully.

'I can bite if you really want me to.' His voice dropped as his blood stirred. 'It's just a question of how hard.'

Quite the apprentice minx now, she was getting good at the art of distraction. And for now he'd go with it. He liked seeing her sensual confidence blossom. 'For the record, none of these women were long-term lovers. Apparently I worked more than played.'

'And that's still true.' She actually pouted.

'I think it's true for you too.' He walked with her past

more rooms in which the furniture was covered up and hidden from the light.

'You know, I didn't think you'd care so much what people think.'

'I don't.'

'Oh?' She turned away, innocently. 'Then why do you go to such lengths to hide from them?'

He shot her a look. 'Don't try to change things for me, Zara.'

'You're not just a bit lonely?'

'No.'

'Yet…' She trailed off.

He turned to glare at her. 'This fling we're having isn't because you're the first woman who's been to stay here with me.'

She smiled weakly.

'I'm not that much of an animal and you're more of a treasure than you believe.' He frowned. 'You need to value yourself more.'

Zara snapped her spine straight at his zinger but she ignored his point because she knew what he didn't. She knew the truth. Before his accident he'd met her. And he *hadn't* wanted her.

She wasn't a treasure—not then or now. What was happening between them now *was* because of circumstance. Because of his loneliness and a basic instinct that needed fulfilling. The fact that he'd denied it showed he'd thought about that himself.

And that was okay.

'If you're not hiding, then it wouldn't be a problem to have other people to stay,' she pointed out.

'It's not possible,' he said gruffly, that finality in his reply. 'And it's not what I want.'

Her heart thudded as she saw just a glimpse of emotion in his eyes. But she had to press just a little more. He was locked away in this beautiful home, not even enjoying all of it. It seemed such a waste to her—most especially of his life and what he had to offer.

'Would it be so awful if the world knew?' she asked.

He straightened his shoulders. 'My clients would lose faith in my investment choices.'

She shook her head. 'But your company has done better in this last year than any other previously. Wouldn't that cancel out any criticism?'

'Doubt would begin to creep in,' he replied, all authoritative businessman now. 'There is no room for any doubt. There must be unshakeable belief.'

'But people know you're human. You're not an oracle. Certainly not made of stone.' Though he looked it now.

'I never would have remained in place at my company if I hadn't been sure of my ability to do my job,' he said sternly. 'I've lost many memories, but some things are still there. Just as I know how to brush my teeth, I can still see the patterns and understand the numbers... But I employ a number of people and I need to be mindful of their position too. That is why Jasper is currently the public face of the company and he's doing a good job. Eventually I will return.'

'Will you? When?'

'When I am ready.'

'Really? You really see yourself breaking out of here and going back to London?'

'Don't you think I can?'

'I think you can do anything you set your mind to. It's whether you really *want* to that's the question.'

He gritted his teeth. 'I'm happy here.'

'You're *safe* here. That's a different thing.'

'Is it? Doesn't being safe make me happy?'

'Maybe there would be other things to be happy about.

And are you truly safe or are you constantly worried you're going to get found out?'

Wasn't that why he'd been so reluctant to even open the door to her? Wasn't that why he never went into the village? He was *trapped* here. And he shouldn't have to be.

He didn't answer.

She ventured closer. 'Have you forgotten anything else since the accident?'

'No,' he answered tightly. 'But that's not to say it might not happen. I work hard to keep my memories.'

'What do you do?'

'I write a daily journal. Archive articles and so on.'

'You hoard newspapers?' she teased gently.

'Online. Sure. I keep a record of every conversation. Every interaction. Every decision.'

'Do you have a record on me?'

'Yes.'

'Do I get to see it?'

'No.' He almost smiled then.

'How detailed is the record?' She suddenly couldn't meet his gaze as she realised the implication of what could be in his journal.

'Not that detailed.' She heard the smile in his voice. 'I've found it difficult to know what to write. Although...' he paused wickedly '...maybe I should detail it all. Looks to me like you'd be curious to read it.'

She shook her head.

'What can you remember before the accident?'

'You want to know what my childhood was like?' He walked ahead of her and then turned to block her path. 'You want to analyse me?'

'Is there something to analyse?' she countered, knowing she was too curious. But she wanted to help him somehow.

'Maybe. As much in me as there is in you.'

'I'm not afraid of telling you my story,' she said quietly.

'I had a happy childhood here in England until I was twelve and then my parents died and I went to live with my only living relative—an uncle in the Caribbean.'

An uncle whose photo was upstairs in his gallery. A small, single photo. A sparse single sentence detailing an invitation. No mention of his ex-wives. Or of her. She'd nearly fainted when she'd spotted it.

He looked startled.

'I know.' She shrugged ruefully and tried to make light of it. 'I don't look like I ever lived there. I have no tan. Never could get a tan.'

'It wasn't a happy time?'

She shook her head. 'I hadn't known him. Neither he nor his wife knew me before they flew in to rescue me. But I wasn't what they were expecting.' Or wanted. 'The first day with them in their home isn't something I can ever forget.'

'What did he do?'

'Owned a casino, not a very successful one.'

'No,' he said slowly. 'What did he do to *you*?'

She hesitated.

'He hit you?'

'Only a few times.' She'd learned what not to say and when to keep out of the way. But sometimes there had been no avoiding him at all.

'Once is one time too many.' Tomas frowned. 'Being hit hurts.'

She interlaced her fingers to stop herself reaching out to him, knowing that if she made a fuss he'd stop talking. 'Someone hit you?'

He met her gaze with a wry twist to his lips. 'Lots of someones. Lots of times.'

Goosebumps riddled her skin and she felt as if a chasm had opened up at her feet. One false move and she'd fall. She didn't want to fall, she wanted to understand. She wanted to care.

'Why?' she could only whisper.

That wryness faded as steeliness replaced it. 'My mother was a whore.'

She flinched but managed to hold in her gasp. He'd chosen that word to shock her; he was watching too closely for her reaction.

But her next reaction was unstoppable. A deep, painful pity rose—his poor mother. And poor Tomas. 'She must have faced some very tough times.' Zara picked her words carefully, but knew they were useless platitudes.

He hesitated a second, then it seemed the words spilled out, even though she sensed he didn't want them to.

'She became pregnant with me when she was fifteen. Her parents were not supportive. She ran away to the city and once there…ruin. Unfortunately I was left to grow up in a small village in rural Italy where such mistakes of morality were unforgivable.'

'She gave you up?' The poor woman had been little more than a child herself. 'You lived with your father?'

'Who knows who he was?' He dismissed the idea bitterly. 'A village boy, most likely. One who did not step up to his responsibilities when my mother's pregnancy was revealed. No, I was brought up by my mother's father.'

'Didn't he protect you?' Zara's heart lurched painfully. Or had he been the one to hurt Tomas—making the child pay the price for the mother's mistake? And what had happened to his mother? There was such deep hurt there. Years of hurt.

'He was the one who refused to allow my mother to stay. She came to him when I was four, desperate to return home. He allowed her to leave me, but not stay herself. He hit but only to discipline. It was the other kids who hit—cowards who attack only when they're certain of winning. In groups, against the smaller or weaker. Bullies.'

'So you were shunned.'

'Of course.'

Had there been no one to love him? And now he chose isolation. Because not even his family had offered the protection a child should have by right.

'Do you forgive her?'

He stared at the door, his face an expressionless mask. 'What is there to forgive her for? Desperate times force people into desperate acts. She did what she had to, to try to survive. The world's oldest profession.'

'No,' she said softly. 'For leaving you.'

Because even though she knew it was possible to understand on a rational level, it still hurt emotionally. She still hurt that her parents had died, she still hurt that her uncle hadn't cared for her at all.

'She made her choice,' he answered almost robotically. 'She had no choice.'

'Have you ever seen her again?'

His lack of reply told her it all. And now her eyes watered at the image of a small boy left alone to face the judgment of a closed community. And for a desperate mother who'd done what she'd thought was for the best.

'Don't cry for me, Zara. It is so long in the past. They can't hurt me any more.'

Couldn't they? Couldn't those memories hurt? Couldn't scars stop skin from stretching properly again?

'So what did you do?'

'I ran away,' he said simply. 'I was fifteen and I'd had enough.'

'Where did you go?'

'Milan initially. Then I travelled across Europe to London.'

'You weren't scared?'

'All the time.' He grimaced. 'The thing I remember most is the hunger. That fear of not knowing where your next meal is coming from. Of not knowing where I was going to sleep that night. I remember making the decision and feeling that drive to get me there.'

'You still feel that drive?'

'Like it was yesterday. So if you want to analyse, you could say it's the need for security that drives me.'

'Financial security?'

'What other kind is there?' He shook his head and smiled as if she were totally naive. It wasn't a nice smile. 'Love doesn't last when you're starving and have nowhere to sleep. It doesn't feed you or shelter you or even keep you warm. Not for long. You need money to survive.'

'And that's all you need? Just money?'

'Some would say money can buy you everything else you need,' he said. 'It can't for everyone. But it can buy all *I* need.'

She disagreed. She'd had shelter and warmth and food. But she'd had *no* love. And as a result, she'd had no life. Sure, she'd not been starved physically, but emotionally?

That hurt. In a different way for sure. But it still hurt. It still damaged.

She figured they both deserved more.

'A fortress with a big wall,' she said sardonically. Hiding away from the rest of the world wasn't what anyone needed. Not for ever. He was as human as she. And humans needed companionship. They needed love.

She needed love—to give it and be given it.

'Privacy. Space. Time.'

She almost laughed but it was too sad. 'You don't have any time. All you do is work.'

'Work will always be my focus, I'm not going to apologise for that.'

She didn't expect him to. She understood how important a fulfilling career could be. She just didn't believe that he was as hundred per cent happy as he claimed. And of course he wasn't with the injury he'd suffered.

'No balance, then, huh?'

'It's what I like. It's what gets me up in the morning. I like the challenge of it.'

'There are other things you like,' she argued. 'You shouldn't isolate yourself.'

'And you're the expert?'

'I am, actually. I was isolated when I went to live with my uncle. I let that happen. I didn't stay in touch with friends and people who could have helped me sooner. And I became so unhappy it was hard to help myself.' She admitted her weakness. 'I lost all my confidence. But now I'm getting it back and I won't lose it again.'

'Is that right?' His voice lowered.

A frisson of danger rippled down her spine as he faced her.

'What happened to make you lose that confidence? *Who* happened?' He walked closer. 'Was it your husband?'

'Sorry?' Zara asked, hoping she'd misheard him.

'There's no need to apologise,' he muttered as he intently watched her. 'Just tell me about your husband.'

Her scalp prickled. She supposed she'd asked for it, what with chiming in with her opinions on how he was living his life. But she really couldn't answer his question.

'Why did you marry him if he didn't want you in "that way"?' he prompted when she remained silent.

'It was a convenience thing,' she finally answered.

'Convenience?' Tomas looked mystified. 'Was he gay and had a disapproving family or something?'

Did he think that because her husband didn't want to have sex with her? She smiled wanly. 'No, it was more complicated than that.'

His eyebrows shot up. 'More complicated how?'

She should tell him, confess it all this second. But she couldn't. How did she tell him how weak she'd been?

'He helped me out of a situation…' she began but fal-

tered. She tried to walk past him but he reached out and
snagged her hand.

'You don't want to talk about it?' His thumb swept over
the back of her hand. 'Yet you ask me personal questions.'

'I was curious. I'm sorry.'

'No apologies,' he reminded her with a low mutter. 'I
want to know more about you. You're the most interesting
woman I've met in a long time.'

'We both know I'm the *only* woman you've met in a
long time.'

'And we both know *that's* irrelevant.' He drew her that
little bit closer, but he didn't pull her all the way into his
arms. 'Tell me.'

'There's not that much to tell.' She tugged her hand
gently but he didn't release her. 'It was never intended to
be anything more than a temporary thing.'

His eyes narrowed on her. 'But you cared for him.'

All the air left her lungs. He was too astute. And suddenly she was too scared.

'More than he cared for me.' She shook her head at
Tomas's frown. 'That was okay. He was a nice person. He
was honourable.'

'Was?' He looked concerned. 'He died?'

Almost.

She bit her lip. 'No, but he's no longer in my life.'

Not for real. These few days didn't count.

He let go of her hand. 'I'm sorry.'

'Why?'

'Because that saddens you.'

It did.

'I think I've left the oven on,' she invented, wildly flustered and too near to tears. 'I'd better check it.'

CHAPTER NINE

'She made her choices. Now you make yours.'

TOMAS LET HER RUN. It was obvious she was distressed and he didn't want to upset her more. He walked into his office and closed the door, determined to shut her out and himself in. A low ache throbbed in his temples. He needed his peace, solitude and space back. But tumbling thoughts hounded him. He should not have pried. Why did he feel this nagging need to know everything about her? Let her keep her secrets. Heaven knew he had his. But God only knew why he'd blurted half of them to her just then. Telling her about his mother? About the stupid bullying he'd suffered as a kid? Why had he done that?

He'd been a child. It was over. He was over it all.

Yet for some reason he'd wanted to see her reaction. He'd wanted to shock her, to see if it would drive her away.

But she'd crept that bit closer, her big eyes holding such tender concern and inviting confession. Looking at her, he'd lost control of his own emotion. The scalding hurt that nowadays seemed to lurk so close to the surface had broken free and he'd spilled too many of his little secrets.

What a fool.

But she had her hurts too and that angered him more. The shadows in her eyes had darkened with wariness when his questions had got too direct.

That shouldn't bother him, but it did. And the fact that he was bothered at all bothered him all the more. Because this fling with her meant *nothing*. It had to. He'd not got as far as he had, as quickly as he had, twice over, by getting distracted or invested in other people.

'She made her choices. Now you make yours.'

Nonno Gio had been blunt to the point of cruelty, informing him that his mother hadn't cared enough to want to keep him. That he was on his own. For years he'd not known that his mother had begged Gio to let her stay too. That it had been Gio who'd refused. Tomas had been led to believe she'd just dumped him and run.

'It'll be better here, Tomasso. You'll be happy here.'

He remembered her voice. Remembered her crushing embrace. He'd been so angry because she'd lied. He hadn't been happy. And so yes, for a long time he hadn't forgiven her.

Because from the age of four he'd been tested again and again, through isolation and intimidation, unsupported through the trials with his classmates, even his cousins. Nothing he'd achieved had been good enough—not even when he'd topped his class in every subject, every damn year.

Nothing he did could pass as penance for his mother's indiscretions. Gio just waited for him to slip up and if he ever did, he came down hard. And then, in the heat of another argument with the old bastard, Tomas had learned the truth. That his grandfather had forced his mother to choose between a certain home for Tomas without her, or a life with her on the streets. It had been no choice for her.

And no choice for him either. He'd run, hoping to find her. He never had.

He'd learned early on, more than once, that the only person he could truly rely on was himself.

Yet he'd not even been able to do that much in this last year. His amnesia had weakened him in a way he simply couldn't tolerate. The only way for him to fight it and move forward was to focus on his company. To make it secure. To *succeed*. On his own.

Hours passed by incredibly slowly as he reined in his

wayward concentration. A semblance of peace returned to him as he studied reports and checked on the market fluctuations. This was what he knew. This was what he did best.

But in the late afternoon he heard the music coming faintly from the kitchen. No doubt she was in there baking up a tsunami of sweetness. They were going to be buried in biscuits at the rate she was going. His stomach rumbled. Maybe a little sugar wasn't such a bad thing.

He glanced out of the window at the view across the garden to the wall and the snow-covered fields beyond. The church spire in the centre of the small village was only just visible through the lightening clouds. The locals would be pleased the bad weather was lifting, the farmers' market was on early in the weekend and attracted many people to town. Jasper would be able to arrive and she would leave with him. That was good.

But an idea occurred to him. One he couldn't resist. It would be easy to arrange and amusing to watch. He wanted to see her dimple peep when she smiled one last time. He picked up his phone and put his rusty voice into action.

Then he made himself work some more. He had to pay before their final moment of lightness and pleasure. But in the end the temptation grew too strong.

He silently prowled down to the kitchen. Sure enough, she was there, meeting his stare with pink skin tinged with sugar and eyes filled with cautious reserve.

He stopped just inside the door, forcing his muscles to stillness, but his body was a riot of want. He blatantly stared, trying to read her thoughts—her desire. Because he didn't want to ask, didn't want to talk. This couldn't be about talking or sharing. This could only be about the physical pleasure and release they found with each other.

'Come upstairs with me,' he asked. His voice sounded husky and alien to his own ears.

She didn't speak, but she moved. Slowly she walked

towards him. His muscles tightened with every step she took, at the acceptance and anticipation in her gaze. His desperation burned through his reserve. Finally she was near enough for him to touch. A feral growl escaped him. He didn't give a damn about the twinge in his leg as he lifted her up. He just had to hold her. Had to have her. And it had to be now.

Zara rose super early again the next morning. She'd been unable to sleep once he'd gone from her bed. And he'd left her only moments after tearing her soul apart with pleasure.

It had only been the once and that devastated her. Was he trying to pull away? Did he want this to be over? Had that conversation yesterday been too intense for him?

Intuition told her the truth.

This wasn't what he'd wanted. He lived here in isolation because he liked it that way and he wasn't planning on changing any time soon. That awareness made her heart ache.

'You're baking at stupid o'clock again?' His dry question interrupted her ruminating.

Startled, she looked up and forced a smile at him. 'It's not that stupid.' It was only a little after six in the morning now. 'There wasn't much other work to do. I didn't think you'd mind.'

'I don't mind.' He reached over the kitchen bench and snaffled one of the warm cupcakes. 'But I think you have far too much food here for us to eat. It's just going to waste.'

'That doesn't matter. I was only trialling some recipes.' She hadn't made complete batches, she'd been switching up different ingredient amounts and additions to test new flavour combinations for the fragrant shortbreads. So far she had lavender, violet, pineapple, sage and primrose.

'It's not good to waste food, Zara. There's a ton of hungry people out in the world,' he chided gently.

She smiled for real as she transferred biscuits one by one from the tray onto the cooling rack. His mood had lightened; that was good. 'What do you want to do with it?'

'I've booked a stall at the farmers' market today.'

'You've what?' She nearly dropped the tray and all the biscuits on it.

He grabbed the end of the tray, rescuing their load. 'Let's see how well they sell.' He grinned at her.

'Oh, no.' She put the tray carefully on a board and wiped her hands on her cloth. 'They're not good enough. I'm not ready. Don't they need to be inspected by the food police or something?'

'Stop panicking and relax. It's fine. I checked with the manager of the market. He's going to bring some supplies so you can bag and tag the goods before we start. Your baking is delicious and we're not throwing it in the compost. Give it all away as free samples if you like and ask people what they think of it. You can think of it as product-testing research.' He leaned against the table, a curious smile hovering at his mouth.

She breathed in and straightened up as she began to think about it properly. In all, it wasn't that bad an idea.

'I've put a fold-up table by my car already,' he added helpfully.

That was when other implications of his offer hit her.

'You're going to take me into the village?' she clarified.

He was going to leave his lair to help her out on this crazy whim?

'Sure, I'll drop you in there.' He straightened and turned away.

Did that mean he wasn't going to stay with her? Because she really wasn't sure she wanted to do this on her own. Not in a new village. At least up north she'd had one of her fellow students with her to keep her company when she'd started in the market round there. And she did want *him* to stay with her. She wanted him to get out and have some *fun* outside his cave. Even on a frosty cold morning.

'I thought you could go through the cupboards to choose some plates or something to display them on,' he said, distracting her completely. 'You need to be quick though—the market opens in ninety minutes and you need to get set up.'

She didn't even have any signs made up. Or prices. Or a cash float...

But maybe she could wing it. Giggling to herself, suddenly giddy with excitement, she spent twenty minutes poring over the fine china. There were so many beautiful treasures she was scared of breaking them. 'Are you absolutely sure about this?' she asked as she handed a box of her selections to him. 'Some of these are worth a lot—'

'They're just sitting in storage.' He shrugged. 'It's good for them to be used.

Tomas loaded the boxes and the table into his big four-wheel-drive.

'Stop looking so scared,' he teased. 'It'll be fine.'

It wasn't so much the market that she was scared of. It was him leaving her right away to go back into hermit-man mode.

The market was larger than she'd expected and quite the beautiful affair with charming displays and beautiful hand-crafted goods and foods.

'I'm not dressed well enough,' she despaired as she checked out the 'posh country' attired women.

'You look good enough to eat,' he murmured, a lewd look in his eye.

'But I don't have bunting. Or fairy lights. I can't compete.' She half laughed, but felt more like crying as nerves threatened to get the better of her.

'You have antique crockery, sweetheart.' Tomas waved one of the priceless plates at her before carefully placing her decadently iced violet cake on it. 'You don't need to compete.'

But once he'd helped her set up the small table and bag the bulk of biscuits and cake slices, she clutched the sleeve of his thick coat. 'Please don't leave me alone to do this.' She hoped it wasn't bad to call upon that chivalrous instinct she knew he had.

'Zara, I can't stay—'

'Of course you can. You don't have to give your name. No one will recognise you behind the sunglasses. And with the woollen hat you look like a tourist or something. Truly. Please,' she begged him. 'Please, please, please. Please stay with me.'

All of a sudden that plea had a whole other meaning to her, and too late she realised she'd sounded *too* heartfelt.

He gazed at her, an arrested expression in his eyes as he wavered. Then he blinked and expelled a sharp breath. 'Ten minutes to get you started, then you're on your own.'

She was so happy she beamed at him, swiftly reaching up and pressing a quick kiss to his lips before she'd thought better of it. 'Thank you.'

Ten minutes into it there was no way he could leave; there were too many people crowding the stall. Forty minutes into it they were in danger of running out of stock.

'I'll go get the rest from the car, you stay here,' Zara said while he was dealing with a customer, quickly leaving before he had time to turn and argue with her.

But she slowed as she carried the last two boxes back to the stall. He was in full flight, smiling and talking to the group of customers who were basically breathing in the biscuits and exclaiming about their delicacy. But they all had eyes on Tomas. It wasn't just his looks, it was that smile and that charming way he looked and talked to them, as if they held his undivided attention. And she knew holding his attention felt like the best thing in the world.

Clearly she wasn't alone in having that reaction to him. He had that rare ability to draw people near—old, young, female and male—they were all there now. He'd made her small stall the most popular at the market. It was that undeniable, undefinable X-factor.

'Zara is the baker.' He called her over as he spotted her hanging that short distance away. 'She's the one who made them.'

She had to walk forward then and unload the last supplies.

'I should go back to the car,' he said when a brief quiet moment finally happened.

'No, you have to stay. You're my customer magnet.'

'Your *what*?'

'You heard me.' She giggled, then sobered when she saw his look. 'It's not that any of these people have any idea who you are,' she assured him saucily, her success loosening her tongue and her inhibitions. 'And it's not that you're super-rich and successful because they don't know that. It's because you're big and tall and handsome and you have this sexy accent and a gorgeous smile and you look at people like…' She shrugged, unable to express it. 'You're a charmer.'

For a half-second he just stared at her. But then he laughed and, heaven help her, became more attractive than ever.

She shook her head in mock distress. 'The thing is, I'm not really joking. It's all truth.'

Tomas picked up the last piece of cake and munched on it to save himself answering her. But he didn't leave. He couldn't. Not when she was so radiant and smiling at him. Not when he was having this much fun.

They didn't make it to the end of the market—they'd sold

out too quickly. But they took the time to walk around and
check out the other stalls. He loved watching her touch the
soft wool scarves on display, and seeing her sample some
of the rich cheese. He gave in to her demands and tasted
some too, and had to concede that it was divine. *She* was
the magnet—her vitality intoxicating.

He was almost sorry when it was time to leave. She
helped him pack everything back into the car and jumped
up into the passenger seat. Once he'd started along the narrow road back to his home she turned to him, her joy obvious and overflowing. 'That was just amazing.'

Tomas grinned as he listened to her non-stop recap of
the morning's trading. She was aglow with her success.

'They loved the primrose snaps, did you notice that?
They just disappeared so quickly. And *you*...' She turned
that brilliant smile on him once more. He could almost feel
the warmth hitting him. 'They just loved you.'

'No, they didn't.'

'Oh, yes, they did.' She nodded, a small frown pulling
her brows. 'Especially that woman with the reddish hair.
She kept coming over to sample stuff just so she could smile
and talk to you some more. Like *all* the time.'

He couldn't help a small chuckle at that small truth. He
wasn't sure if she'd have noticed that, given she'd been so
busy herself. But despite the obvious play that woman had
made for him, he'd enjoyed the market more than he'd ever
imagined he would. It hadn't mattered who he was or what
he'd forgotten. He'd just stood alongside Zara, laughing and
talking to people about nothing in particular, feeling more
free than he had in aeons.

'It was just so cool,' Zara said again. 'Thank you so
much.'

He smiled, pleased she was happy and enjoying her endless chatter as he navigated his way home.

'It's such a beautiful house,' she enthused as he drove

down the snow-lined driveway and the manor came into view. 'Do you know what you should do? Open it up to weddings—and other functions. The kitchen is big enough to be upgraded to a full commercial size. I could serve cream teas. With that garden and the greenhouse, it's just such a gorgeous destination and so suits my kind of traditional baking with a twist. Don't you think?'

She was in raptures, and, while he still smiled at her enthusiasm, his core was growing colder by the second.

She had good business instincts and rationally he could see these were all good ideas that could work well. But the thought of her remaining here? Working here as chatelaine of his estate?

He tightened his grip on the steering wheel as all pleasure was decimated. His gut reaction to her plan wasn't favourable—but for all the wrong reasons. He didn't want her baking all hours in that kitchen for everyone else. If she was baking in that kitchen, he wanted it to be for *him* and him alone, not the rest of the world. He didn't want to share either his house—or *her*—with anyone else. When she'd asked him to stay with her? He'd been unable to resist.

But the idea of her staying here with him long term?

It was impossible.

His heart raced as bitterness surged. He was no better than that fabled dog in the manger. He couldn't have her but didn't want anyone else to have her either. The realisation appalled him. He couldn't be *jealous*. He couldn't want more than these few days he'd already had with her. He couldn't have that. He'd *never* have that. He knew what was best—and for him, it was best to be alone. Utterly independent.

This morning had been a mistake. He'd known after their talk yesterday that it was time to pull away from her, but he'd failed. He had to do it properly now. Get back to work and distance himself from the warmth of her.

Having anything else with her—or any other kind of life—was an unsustainable fantasy. He might have got away with a couple of hours in public one morning without anyone figuring him out, but he couldn't risk more than that.

'I need to catch up on my work,' he said briskly as he parked the car. He walked straight to the door, unable to even look at her in his haste to get away. 'Do not bother with dinner for me tonight. I'll have something at my desk later.'

Zara bit her lip, fighting her blush. But he walked away without a second glance so what did it matter that she was probably as red and bruised as a crushed tomato?

He'd dismissed her. It was as if the sun had gone behind a monstrous storm cloud, leaving the once warm world cold and dark.

But she'd been the one to summon the cloud. She'd been so stupid, totally overstepping the mark blurting all that fantasy. What had she been thinking? Of course he wouldn't want all that. He didn't want *her*—not for anything more than a short-lived fling.

It had been obvious enough yesterday that he was uncomfortable with how much he'd told her. He'd clammed up and in a way she'd been glad because she hadn't wanted him to keep asking *her* questions. She hadn't wanted to admit the truth to him yet.

But the real truth was that she didn't belong here and she never would.

His coldness had shattered the happiness she'd felt from the morning at the market. He was so very controlled, locking his emotions tightly back behind that fierce guard. And wasn't that fair enough? Didn't he have enough on his plate already without her being emotionally needy and placing demands on him that he had no desire to meet?

She needed to grow up. To protect herself the same way he did. To lock her heart away in that layer of protection.

So she wouldn't let him see her insecurity now. She could get through this last day without awkwardness. She'd stay in control and keep it light. And then maybe, when the truth did come out, when Jasper explained everything, maybe everything could *stay* okay. Maybe they could even become friends once it was all revealed.

Her heart squeezed, knowing the futility of that hope.

But she had to get through this. She'd lift her chin and let him know he wasn't going to hurt her—because she understood that was a big part of his motivation for pulling away. He'd never wanted to hurt her. She didn't want to hurt him either. So she could handle this and respect the boundaries he needed.

'I know you only wanted a small snack, but I've made it for you anyway.' She placed the small tray on the edge of his desk in the early evening, almost six hours since she'd seen him last.

'Thank you.' His smile was small and set and he looked straight back to the papers in front of him.

Despite her best efforts, she was still too soft. Disappointment slithered down her spine as she walked away from him. She'd made a mistake in taking her talk too far, in encroaching on him. But she had to make this end easier for them both. She had to be like him. She had to be brave.

CHAPTER TEN

'You're a bad influence.'

TOMAS PUSHED AWAY the food she'd brought. He didn't want to be tempted by her at all—not her food, not her body, certainly not her smile.

He'd go for a workout and burn off the excess energy making his blood race. He'd missed his usual session this morning because he'd taken her to the market instead. It had been a mistake. Discipline and routine were too important to toss aside so recklessly. He always worked out in the morning because mornings were the worst for him. At night he could go to bed with that little hope that he'd wake up in the morning and his memories would be restored and the nightmare would be over.

It never was.

Damn it. He pushed back his chair. He needed to go burn out the self-pity.

Thing was, that usual agony hadn't lasted this morning. Once he'd risen he'd been too busy anticipating her reaction to his farmers' market plan. And then she'd made him stay with her. And it had been fun.

Too much fun.

He sighed as he set the treadmill to a faster pace and harder angle than usual.

An hour later he walked in through the kitchen all hot and sweaty but feeling better. Yet feeling bad too. He'd been rude to her again and she didn't deserve it. He could be civil until she left, couldn't he? Didn't she deserve that little at least?

She glanced up from where she was stirring a pot on the

hob. The room smelt delicious. It was insane the way she could cook. Her gaze raked over him, that wariness in her eyes that he hated seeing. He'd been the one to put it there.

But to his surprise that dimple suddenly appeared and those sea-green eyes turned impish.

'You've not gone and turned that beautiful glasshouse into a home gym?' She arched her brows at him.

He was so pleased she was smiling, but still felt vaguely ashamed.

'You *haven't*.' She began to laugh at his expression, lightening the intensity of the atmosphere completely. 'It's so beautiful.'

'There might be a treadmill in there,' he conceded reluctantly, rubbing his hand through his hair, his chest aching—and not from the exercise.

She looked at him. 'And?'

'And a rowing machine.' A smile tugged at the corners of his mouth because she was too astute. 'And maybe a stationary bike.'

'Maybe?'

Her tease was too cute. And was just asking for retribution of the best kind.

'Maybe you should come and have a look at it,' he invited, fresh energy firing him. 'You shouldn't leave without seeing it.'

There was a moment of stillness as they both absorbed what he'd said and what it meant.

But then she lifted her head and her shoulders straightened. She looked him right in the eye. 'Then I'd love to see it.'

He held out his hand and she took it. Bittersweet peace settled within him as he walked with her along the snowy path through to the centre of the garden. The sun was setting, sending the last of its golden light through the masses of window panes.

'You're not cold?' She glanced at his shorts and tee.

'No.' Never around her. He stood back to let her go into the glasshouse first, then moved alongside so he could see her reaction.

'Oh. My.' Her jaw dropped.

He grinned, appreciating her incredulity. Pleasure rippled along his muscles, priming them for more.

'You've put a pool in.' She walked forward, gazing at it in frank admiration. *'Tomas...'*

He *really* liked the way she breathed his name like that. 'There was a pond, but we excavated it further. You like it?'

'I've never seen anything so beautiful.'

'So it's not an awful, boring home gym?'

She sent him a look. 'You know it isn't.'

'This is the only part of the estate I made significant changes to. I'm sure everyone will disapprove once they see it.'

'No, they won't,' she protested loudly. 'There are still all the beautiful plantings.' She stepped deeper into the verdant room. 'And the pool design is so sympathetic to the style of the building.' The Grecian-style marble looked as if it had been there for centuries. 'It really is just the perfect place for a party.' She sent him another look.

'You're not going to give up on trying to socialise me, are you?'

She giggled.

'I hate the thought of cocktail parties and polite chat,' he said bluntly.

'Are they too boring and shallow for a deep-thinking loner like you?'

He smiled at her sass and found himself being utterly honest.

'It's more the awkwardness of people knowing things that I don't. Things about myself. Things I've said and done that I have no recollection of. I hate them having that over me.' It made him feel weak, unable to hold his own and fight back. He loathed that feeling. He never wanted to feel that way again.

'So what?' She lifted a shoulder and let it drop in an expressive shrug. 'There's so much in general that I don't know about. I'm sure I always seem a fool. It's just too bad.'

He chuckled. 'I don't think so. You're inquisitive.'

'Yeah, well, we all know what happens to the curious cat.' She smiled wryly, but then sobered. 'I think if people knew about you, it would be awkward at first, but then…' She trailed off hopefully. 'They'd forget about it after a while. You're so smart and so up to date, you could converse on any subject better than most people ever could anyway.'

It was nice of her to say so, but it didn't change the incontrovertible. 'It's not possible, Zara.'

'Maybe in a while?'

She just wouldn't give up hope, would she?

She looked away from him back to the green foliage. 'I don't really like parties either,' she said softly.

'You're always in the kitchen?' He offered a weak joke.

'Pretty much.'

He didn't want this to get serious again. He wanted to escape with her for a little while longer. 'I guess we could have a pool party of our own.'

Her smile came back—sinful and sweet at the same time. 'I don't have my swimsuit with me.'

'No?' He reached out and wound his arm around her waist. 'Gosh, nor do I.' He mulled the problem with a *faux* serious expression. 'Whatever will we do?'

'Oh.' She smiled again as she caught his eye. 'I think you're a little bit wicked, Tomas Gallo.'

'Only a little bit?' He tugged her closer, enjoying the way she blossomed with him. It satisfied him in a way nothing else had. 'I'm going to have to work on that.'

His playfulness entranced her, seducing her all over again. But her heart ached at the same time. This was so fragile. So close to finished.

She forced herself to shut her mind from that imminent future. She'd make the most of this moment. It was almost all she had left.

'Promise me it's heated?' she asked as he deftly undid the fastening of her jeans.

'Of course.' He laughed again. 'The lengths aren't long, but the distance adds up and the weightlessness feels nice. It was to help my recovery.'

She nodded.

'You go first,' he dared as he released her.

'You want to watch me?' Surprise flooded her, followed swiftly by anticipation. And pleasure.

'Yes,' he admitted unashamedly.

He wanted to look at her. He liked to.

Well, *she* liked the way she affected him. That he took pleasure in her body pleased her. Because she very much liked looking at him.

She pushed her jeans down her legs and stepped out of them with a little shimmy.

He stood stock-still, his attention utterly focused on her.

'I've never skinny-dipped before,' she admitted shyly as she flung off her T-shirt and then unfastened her bra.

'So you're a bad influence,' she teased, bending to peel her panties down.

'I wouldn't say…' he breathed in deep as he looked at her '…bad.'

She blew him a little kiss and stepped towards the water. She slowly stepped in—to her ankles, her knees, her upper thighs. Then she stood still, her legs slightly apart.

It was warm, but not too hot, still refreshing on her super-sensitive skin. She glanced over her shoulder and saw he'd moved right to the edge, his hands on his hips as he kept his hot gaze trained on her. She cupped the water with her hands and lifted them to sprinkle some over her tight, bared breasts and down her belly. A little rivulet ran down from her navel. She shivered despite the civilised temperature of the water. There was nothing civilised about the need coiling deep within her. She arched her back a little as she repeated the water sprinkling. As the water trickled over her hot skin, she couldn't help rocking her hips. Back and forth. Back and forth.

'Zara?'

'Yes,' she breathed.

'Are you turning yourself on?'

'No.' Licking her lips, she faced him. 'You're doing that just by watching me.'

'Holy hell,' he muttered. 'You know you're a natural born seductress.'

She'd laugh if she weren't so aroused. 'What do you want me to do?'

He closed his eyes for a moment, clearly pulling himself together. 'Come here.'

'That's not going to be a problem.' She smiled at him impishly.

'Come here *now*.'

She dived, feeling the water wash over her hot body, then swam over to him. He took her by the hand and pulled her—not gently—from the pool.

'It seems impossible to believe there's snow outside when it's this steamy in here.' She ran a finger down his torso.

'Dare you to go out in it for a minute.'

'Stark naked?' She shook her head. 'You were the one all irate about me getting hypothermia a couple of days ago and there's far more snow out there now.'

'But I like warming you up again.'

'Then why aren't you?'

He looked slightly sheepish. 'I ought to rinse under the shower for a second.'

'Don't go anywhere,' she muttered. 'I want to look at you too. And I don't mind it when you're sweaty.'

She couldn't take her eyes off his body as he shrugged out of his shorts and tee. After his workout he seemed more ripped than ever—every muscle acutely defined and that sheen over his skin just emphasised it all the more.

'You don't mind my being a little...'

'Animal?' She planted a palm on his chest, loving how broad he was.

'You want to ride me?' he dared, a glint in his eye.

Her mouth dried. What had he just said? 'Um—'

'How is it you can still blush?' he softly teased. 'You want to take charge?'

She was steaming up on the inside now. But she pressed her hand against his mouth. 'Don't tempt me.'

'I live to tempt you,' he breathed against her fingers. 'So say anything. Do anything. Whatever you want. If you want to have your wicked way with me here on the floor, then I'll happily submit.'

'Oh, really?' She tried to tease him back. 'Because it would be such a sacrifice for you?'

He sighed theatrically. 'It might be hard to restrain myself, but for you I will try.'

'You'll just lie there and let me?' She didn't believe him; even that first time when he'd pulled her astride him, he'd still really led their dance.

'I'll lie there for as long as I can.'

Her eyes narrowed as she recognised the caveat in his promise. 'In other words, you'll take over when you want to.'

His smile widened. 'Probably.'

She'd almost run out of time. There was only now. So

she was taking and making it hers. Making *him* hers. 'Then you'd better get down on that floor.'

'I think you're a little bit wicked too, Zara Falconer.'

'Not as wicked as you.' She shook her head. 'You can have me any time and you know it.'

'The same goes for you so I guess we're even.'

He was wrong about that. She was going to take full advantage because she knew this was going to be the last time. It had to be purely physical. Not emotional. Nothing more than a simple delight.

Except there was this humour they shared, this fun.

'If you're that wild,' he muttered, a gleam in his eye as she moved to kneel astride him, 'why don't you try riding a little higher? I could lick that trail of water from you.'

Heat washed over her body as she skimmed her fingertips up his chest. 'What?'

'You heard.' His hands gripped her waist, pulling her upwards, towards his chest. His face. His lips curved into the sexiest smile she'd ever seen. And his eyes gleamed like onyx.

'You're—'

'Tempting you.'

Oh, he was. So very much. Holding his gaze, she moved that bit further up his body. Sensing his victory, he wrapped his arms around her thighs, holding her wide.

Oh, it was scandalously intimate. It was also the most blatantly erotic moment of her life. She rocked her hips gently and he lifted his head a little to catch her with sweeps of his tongue. With kisses that grew hungrier and more powerful. She groaned, writhing as he thrilled her. But just before she came, she pulled away—teasing herself as much as him.

He growled in protest, but said nothing. A calculating gleam entered his eye as she kissed her way down his body.

'My shorts pocket,' he muttered.

'It's okay,' she said. 'I have one in my jeans.'

His little laugh pleased her. His muffled oath as she tried to sheath him pleased her too.

'Have mercy,' he muttered, pushing her hands out of the way in the end. 'Let me do it before I lose it too soon.'

She knew she probably wasn't going to last long once she started properly on him, so she paused to look up at the patterned glass ceiling high above her. 'This is truly beautiful.'

'Yes.'

She shot him a look. 'Flattery will get you everywhere.'

'It's not flattery.' He reached up and tweaked her nipple. 'Are you really looking at the scenery at this exact moment?'

She laughed as she looked down at the strain in his body as he waited for her to stake her claim. 'Am I taking too long?'

'You're killing me.'

'Well, we can't have that,' she teased.

But her laughter died as she slid down on him, finally taking him to the hilt.

'Hell, Zara.'

She looked into his eyes as they both paused to savour that moment. Suddenly it was nothing *but* emotional. He knew how amazing he could make her feel. How incredible she found making love with him. That was what this was for her—she was making love to him as freely as she could this final day.

She tried to ride him fast, but in the end all she felt was frantic. She abandoned the attempt altogether, reaching forward to kiss him. She needed to kiss him so badly. He gripped her shoulders, holding her to him and meeting her mouth with as much passion as she felt. The orgasm almost took her by surprise, hitting as she simply lay over him, on him, ground as close as she could get. No fierce thrusting, or playful fingers pressing the point above where they joined. Just kissing and straining connection. And she was there.

Home with him.

'It really is getting too cold out here, Sleeping Beauty.' Tomas bent low and scooped his sleepy lover into his arms.

Her eyes finally flashed open. 'You can't carry me all that way.'

'Don't think you can tell me what I can and can't do.' Tomas hoisted her higher in her arms just to prove the point.

'As if you don't try to do that to me.' She rubbed her cheek against his chest as he carried her across the snowy path and into the big house.

'I've discovered my latent desire to be a naturist,' he said as he set her down inside the warm kitchen. 'There's nothing better than walking around this house with you completely bare. I might have to hide all your clothes and you'll have to stay naked always.'

'Could be dangerous while cooking,' she answered tartly. 'I wouldn't want to get burned somewhere personal.'

'No.' He leaned close. 'We wouldn't want that.' He kissed her and found his lust resurging. 'The only marks on this body should be made by my mouth.'

She shivered as he bent to her breasts.

'Only from pleasure,' he added.

'You're insatiable.' But she moaned as she said it.

'I'm merely trying to keep up with you.' He laughed with arrogant satisfaction as she wriggled that little bit closer, wanting him to resume his teasing touch. 'So very demanding.'

But he was every bit as needy as she. He simply couldn't resist any more. He bent his head to kiss her again. The beast in him liked to make a mark on her. To brand her as his in a deeply personal, physical way, so the world would know that she was his. That only he had the right to touch her most privately.

He was in trouble and he knew it. But he was too far gone to stop now. One more night. Just one more. He couldn't bite back the growl of satisfaction as she arched towards him, angling her head so he could keep suckling the tender skin of her neck.

He knew she liked it too.

With a groan he bent his head and succumbed to his appetite, consigning that nagging concern to the back of his brain while his body—his soul—was sated. Despite that fear of impending disaster, he didn't think he was ever going to get enough.

CHAPTER ELEVEN

How sorry she was.

HER CONSCIENCE STABBED her awake, but it was centuries till dawn. She counted the slow minutes as she waited for a more reasonable hour to wake him. She ought to do it now. Wake him and tell him. Apologise over and over. But it was the first night he'd not left to go to his room and he was in such a restful sleep and she couldn't bear to just yet.

The room slowly lightened. He'd left a chink in the heavy curtains to let the starlight gleam in and eventually a beam of sunlight lit a bar across the bed.

Secretly, silently, she gazed at him, indulging for a last moment and telling herself she wasn't really a stalker. A year ago she'd thought she'd fallen in love with him—that man who'd walked into her life and tipped it upside down before walking out again just over twenty-four hours later. He'd been her shining knight. The man who'd helped her escape misery. But she'd been so naive. In these last few days she'd got to know him for real—his humour, his struggles, his truth. There was so much more to love than just that gorgeous, scarred exterior. He was so much more complicated, more human than that beautiful bone structure and roguish charm.

She froze as he stirred.

His eyes opened and he blinked sleepily. She braced, strengthening her aching heart, knowing she had to do it now. She saw the moment he completely wakened. Awareness sharpened his eyes and for a half-second that frown appeared. But then he smiled and a look entered those eyes that melted her heart. But not her resolve.

But before she could speak he lifted up onto his elbow and leaned over to kiss her. Heaven help her, she couldn't deny herself—or him—that kiss.

But that kiss led to another. Then another. And then he covered her. Wordless, worshipping, it was the gentlest of possessions. His arms were strong but tender bars as he held her. Oh, she couldn't resist this last moment of absolute joy. She wanted to give him everything.

It wasn't a frantic, passionate coupling but this was no less demanding. If anything, it was more so. She was wound unbearably tight, her body aching for more. Each slow, deep thrust was the most exquisite torment.

He looked into her eyes as he pressed closer, still too deliciously slow. She couldn't cope with the intensity. Her body taut as a bowstring, she strained to kiss him, to show him how sorry she was, how much she cared, how much she wanted. His pace finally quickened. His teeth nipped her lips as she neared the peak, sending her higher in a sudden rush. Her orgasm collided with his into that timeless moment of shared ecstasy. She clutched him closer still, yearning that it would last for ever. But it was a moment that, like all, slipped from her grasp.

And so did he.

She barely heard the words he whispered as she sank into the dark depths of exhaustion.

'I like waking up to you.'

When she woke the second time the sun was much higher in the sky. She sat bolt upright in the bed. She was alone and heartsick. But she heard noises from along the corridor. *Voices.*

She leapt from the bed. Cold sweat slicked her body and her pulse scurried. Quickly she tugged on jeans and a T-shirt as she remembered that sweetly whispered confession from such a carefully guarded soul.

'I like waking up to you.'

It was the nearest to a declaration of affection he'd probably ever give. And she'd made such a mistake by being such a coward.

So much for thinking that she'd developed as a person. For so long she'd been silent—willing to put up with misery because she was too scared to take any kind of risk. And she'd thought she'd moved on from that. She'd studied. She'd taken a small bedsit on her own. She was developing her business and had had some success with it already...but at her first real chance to prove her strength, she'd failed.

She'd taken the easy way out. By doing nothing. Saying nothing. Being silent and passive and pretending she was doing the right thing.

But it was *her* responsibility to be honest with Tomas. She was the one who'd entered into that marriage with him. She was the one who had benefited. But she'd hidden behind Jasper, not wanting to face up to the consequences herself.

Not face up to the truth.

If Tomas hadn't had the accident, the truth was she'd most likely never have seen him again in her whole life. Their marriage had been little more than a joke to him. A cavalier moment of chivalry that he'd probably not thought twice about since. It had been a way of giving her money and setting her free.

In anyone else it would have been an extreme action, but for Tomas Gallo—it had been a piece of calculated retaliation and risk with the reward for her. A transaction her uncle couldn't argue with and that soothed her pride at the same time.

She thought she understood a little more now why he'd done it. And that flash of maverick outrageousness was some of what she loved about him. Beneath the ruthless businessman, there was scarring and old, old wounds. But he'd not become embittered, there was kindness and generosity in him. He was a man who played the game his way.

Only his way.

But he would not be pleased to know she'd kept this from him. He might not be forgiving. His pride was part of his desire for isolation—he did not like to be made a fool of. But more importantly, more deep, was the distrust he had of people. Of relationships. Of 'family'. She was his family now.

And she had let him down terribly.

But she had no time to waste because if that was Jasper she had to get to Tomas before he said anything.

She swiftly ran to his office. She'd never felt as cold as she did in that moment. The two men were standing on the other side of Tomas's large desk. Jasper looked as dapper as ever in his grey three-piece suit, but it was Tomas, clad completely in black again, with his shirt sleeves rolled to just below the elbows, who commanded all her attention.

He glanced up the second she'd made it to the doorway. The look in his eyes was enough to render her immobile. There were papers spread on the desk. Official-looking forms.

Her heart stopped.

'Jasper,' she said breathlessly, but she couldn't tear her gaze from Tomas.

He knew.

'Zara,' Jasper said with too much joviality. 'You're looking well.'

She was looking as if she'd just gotten out of bed after a sleepless night of seduction. Which she had. But she was too afraid of Tomas's reaction to this news to blush. Sickened, she still couldn't move.

The awkward atmosphere grew.

'He's told you,' she whispered, forcing herself to break the silence.

'Told me what?' Tomas prompted in staccato tones.

'That…'

'What has Jasper come all this way to tell me, Zara?'

'Now, Tom—'

'Zara can tell me.' Tomas cut Jasper off without releasing her from his imprisoning gaze. 'Can't you, Zara?'

He was going to make her say it after all. And wasn't that fair enough?

Tears sprang to her eyes and a hard lump of emotion clogged her throat. Such regret. But she swallowed it back. She refused to look away and fail. Not now. Even when it was too late.

She drew in a harsh breath, determined to get her voice stronger than a weak whisper. 'That we've met before. That you once helped me.'

'I helped you,' he echoed, still in those staccato, undeniably angry tones. 'How did I do that, exactly?'

'You married me.'

She saw his eyes widen as she put the truth into words. He was furious; she could feel his anger coming at her in waves.

'You—'

'Tomas,' Jasper interrupted sharply.

Tomas whirled to face him. 'You. Leave. Now.'

'Tomas—'

'Go look at the goddamn garden.' He silenced the older man.

Jasper hesitated and looked searchingly at Zara.

'Don't worry, I'm not about to go crazy and attack her. She's in no danger from the damaged—'

'Jasper, it's okay,' Zara interrupted Tomas. She needed to speak to him alone.

Jasper walked past her, his eyes sharpening on her as he neared. It was a silent query that she met with something as near to a smile as she could muster.

Then she stood silent, waiting for Tomas to vent.

He waited until Jasper was well out of earshot. But it wasn't a shout, it was a very soft single question. He barely even moved his mouth, but she heard it as if he'd hollered it through a megaphone.

'Why?'

'Why what?' she asked, bravely walking towards him. 'Why did we marry? Why didn't I tell you?'

'Why are you here?'

She breathed out. That was the easiest of all the questions. 'Jasper thought it might help. That seeing me might spur your memory.'

'And sleeping with me would help too? Did you discuss that idea with him?'

'Of course not. That just…'

'Just what?'

'Just happened.'

He looked sceptical. 'Because you felt sorry for me? Did you sacrifice your virginity to say thank you?'

'I—' She broke off. It had been no sacrifice. Her anger began to build. 'As I told you before, I slept with you because I wanted you. And because I care about you.'

He laughed. A bitter, disbelieving mockery of a laugh that scalded her like acid. She'd told him the truth and he'd laughed at her.

He sat down behind his desk. She stood on the other side of it, feeling as if she'd been summoned to the boss's office for a bawling out.

Which was pretty much the case.

'Who are you really?'

'I'm exactly who I said I was. Zara Falconer.'

His expression didn't change.

'I've been studying at a cookery school up north. I sell my cakes and biscuits at a local market—that was how Jasper tracked me down.'

'Before that. Tell me everything that happened between us. From the beginning.'

She swallowed. 'There's not that much to tell. You and Jasper had been on a business trip to Antigua in the Caribbean. To look at my uncle's casino operation amongst other things. You had a business meeting on his yacht. That's where you met me.'

'And this was the uncle you lived with after your parents died?'

'I'd lived on that boat for almost a decade.' She nodded.

'How is it possible that you couldn't just leave of your own accord?'

She looked at the floor. She understood how it sounded. She was a grown woman. Why couldn't she just have given her uncle the finger, walked out of the door and not looked back? There were no chains holding her there...but then there were. Invisible chains that hurt in their own vindictive way.

'When someone tells you you're worthless, day in and out...several times a day. When you've been transplanted from your home, your country and you're isolated from your old friends...and the only people you have around you are the ones telling you to be grateful. So grateful because without them you'd have nothing. That you *are* nothing...'

She forced herself to try to explain. 'I had no money of my own. No job. No training. I had no idea how to get out of there. Most of the time I was literally stuck on a boat in the middle of the ocean. He had my passport and was the trustee of what little money my parents had left me...'

That had all gone. He'd said they'd needed it for her expenses.

'I was so shy. I tried, but I was so afraid of doing everything wrong.' And she had done lots wrong—worn the wrong thing, said the wrong thing. She'd retreated more and more, hiding below deck.

She'd processed it since, worked it through. But all those years of isolation had left their mark; the shadow lingered.

'My uncle was determined to impress you. He thought you were a prospective investor. He'd always had plans to expand his casino. He was so angry when I served you at your meeting. He made jokes at my expense. You smiled, seemed to go along with them…' But then she'd looked at him surreptitiously and had caught him looking at her. That moment that he'd held her gaze then? 'But you told him you weren't going to invest. He was very angry but hid it from you.' She drew in a shaky breath. 'He didn't hide it from me.'

She paused, hating having to relive this, hoping that Tomas could see she was speaking the truth. If only she'd told him sooner.

'You overheard him,' she muttered. 'You saw the mark on my cheek. And you asked if I wanted to get out.'

'So I bought you?'

'That's how my uncle saw it.' Because he'd viewed her as a chattel. 'And he didn't hesitate to let you. You framed it as part of the business deal. It was only afterwards that you told him you'd never ever invest in his company. And that he was never to come after me or ask me for money. That if he did you'd destroy his business and his reputation by telling the world he'd basically sold his niece. He's not contacted me since.'

'And that's what you wanted?'

'I changed my name the minute I could to prevent him from finding me.'

'That was why Jasper couldn't find you sooner?'

'Yes. He spotted a piece about me in my local papers. It was about my cakes at the market and there was a photo with it. I guess he thought it was worth a shot.'

'How much did I give you?'

'You offered me a million as our annulment settlement.

I took ten thousand. I have just less than half of it. I'm still saving to repay the amount in full. The money you gave me enabled my escape, but it was your ability to pull it off that just…' She couldn't explain it. Her confidence in him had given her confidence in herself. He had made such a difference to her. He'd never truly understand it.

And from the look on his face, he didn't even want to try.

'Your uncle's picture is upstairs in the gallery?' he asked sharply.

'Yes.'

'But not yours.'

'No.'

He breathed out.

'I don't think you ever had a picture. And there was no record…'

'Jasper had a record. *You* knew.'

'But I didn't know about your amnesia. I'd read about your accident, of course—' She broke off. 'But all the reports said you'd made a full recovery. And I thought the annulment had gone through.'

'So then you came here and after all I'd done, you lied to me.'

'I didn't lie.'

'You told me we hadn't met.'

'I said you didn't know me. And you didn't.'

'Semantics,' he spat. 'You omitted vitally important information. I don't care if you thought it was for the best, it was wrong. It was especially wrong to sleep with me while withholding that information.'

But if she'd told him, he wouldn't have slept with her. And yes, now she realised she'd been so desperate. She was still desperate.

'Back that day, I thought I was in love with you,' she said, her breath seizing. 'Love at first sight, even though you didn't really see me at all. I knew you weren't really interested in me. It was just because my uncle's behaviour annoyed you so much. But now I realise that, all this time, what I felt was just a huge crush. You came along when I was so trapped and you were like this flash of lightning. So bright. So mesmerising. And you got me out of there. How could I ever look at any other man?'

She swallowed.

'So, yes, when Jasper said to come and see you I couldn't resist.' She moved towards the window, trying to summon the courage to keep speaking as honestly. 'When you didn't recognise me at first I thought it was just because... I hadn't been anything important to you. Then I worked it out.'

'So you're over your crush now?' he asked so dryly her heart almost shrivelled.

'Yes,' she answered softly. She held her hands tightly together, her fingers twisting into each other. 'I'm out of the crush and fully in love with you.'

'You think you're in love with me?' he scoffed bitterly. 'You've fallen for a fantasy. The Prince Charming who rescued you that one day. It's not real. It'll never be real. I'm not that guy and I never will be.'

'No, I know you now.' She fought back the tears. She'd never been so exposed.

'What do you think you know? *I* don't know who I am, so how the hell can you know anything?'

'I know the man you are, the things you do. The way you treat people—me. I know you're strong and determined and loyal. You're arrogant as hell but kind with it. *How* you are is *who* you are. And you're so much more than the man who rescued me.'

And she was more than the wraith of a person who'd needed that in the first place.

He stared at her for a long moment. 'There is nothing between us,' he said matter-of-factly. 'This was a fun few days. It's been a while since I've had a woman in my bed. You were here. It was convenient. But we're finished.'

Anger bubbled deep in her belly. Was he really going to play this that way—after everything she'd told him? Everything she'd tried to show him?

She walked towards him. 'So that's it—I made a mistake and you're saying it's all over?'

'It was always going to be over,' he said bluntly. 'When the Kilpatricks come back you'd leave and we'd be done. You knew that was the deal. Now I just have to hope that you won't sell your story.'

'I haven't yet,' she threw back at him angrily.

'But we both know you'll sell anything you have to when you need money.'

She gasped. 'You *offered*,' she said in a fierce voice. 'I took less than you offered. And I was always going to pay you back.' She'd started a savings account for that purpose already. And one of the reasons she'd come here in the first place was to pay him back.

'Consider your virginity as full and final payment.'

Oh, that was cruel. 'People make mistakes every single day, Tomas. And other people forgive them.'

'Some things are unforgivable.'

'Was wanting you so very awful of me?' She flared up at him. 'Was it so terrible to care? To want not to hurt you? Was being attracted to you such a terrible sin?'

'You're confusing gratitude with desire.'

'Give me some credit.'

'Why should I?'

'You know what?' she asked as she lost control of her emotions. 'You didn't die in that accident, but you're barely living now.' Her anger spilled over. 'I don't understand it. Don't you of all people know how fleeting and precious life can be? But you've trapped yourself here and you're so bitter—'

'Don't I have a right to be?' he snapped back at her.

'Of course. To a point. But not for ever. You're letting pride get in the way of having a full life—'

'I don't want this from you. I don't want you for anything more than what I've had. I didn't then and I don't now.' He strode towards her, his fury frothing as the words tumbled from his mouth. 'All this was was sex. When you were offering everything why wouldn't I take it? But it means nothing. I don't need you or anyone to make my life complete.'

'Fine,' she said. 'Lock yourself away here for ever. Lie to yourself and think you're happy making your pots of money so you can be safe and hide away for ever. Be lonely and grumpy and isolated and miserable.'

'I *am* happy here. How can I not be?' He swept his arms wide.

'With everything covered in dust cloths and left unused?' she cried at him. 'You could have so much more. You *deserve* so much more.'

He halted a few paces away from her. The anger in his eyes suddenly died, but the expression that replaced it was even worse. It was a deadening of all emotion, until he was simply a blank.

'You realise I can't trust a word you say,' he said quietly, his words striking like mortal blows. 'And I will never be able to.'

CHAPTER TWELVE

'I don't want to leave.'

JASPER WAS MAKING a muddy track as he paced back and forth on the wet lawn. Tomas bit back his anger as he stalked up to him. He'd had to get away from Zara. He needed to get away from them both.

'Don't be angry with her,' Jasper said as soon as he saw Tomas walking towards him. 'It was my idea. She didn't know any of it.'

'Didn't know she was my wife?'

As if he could believe that.

'Not until the day she got here, no.' Jasper puffed out a breath. 'She thought the annulment had gone through a year ago. I didn't tell her about the amnesia when I met her again. I'd hoped your seeing her might jolt your memory.'

'Why would that happen when I'd spent only a day in her presence?' It was preposterous.

Jasper ran his hand through his hair and coughed. 'Because…'

'Because what?'

'You married her, for God's sake,' he muttered. 'You, who never dated anyone for more than a month or so, took one look at this little mouse and married her. I was gob-smacked.'

'Apparently it was to help her.'

'It was.' Jasper nodded. 'And she needed it. But there was more to it than that.'

'What?'

'I saw the way you kissed her.'

Tomas's eyes narrowed. He hadn't kissed Zara since Jasper had arrived this morning. 'When did you see that?' He straightened. 'When I was allowed to "kiss the bride"?' It would have been for show.'

Jasper shook his head. 'You didn't kiss at the ceremony. It was afterwards. When you went to say goodbye to her. I was along the hallway and you...'

'What?'

'It was...' Jasper cleared his throat awkwardly. 'That's why when I found her I sent her to you. She's the only person you've ever reacted to in that way. You kissed her. Hell, you kissed her like—'

'You forget yourself,' Tomas snapped. 'You're my lawyer, not my friend. Stay out of my personal life, Jasper. Never, ever interfere like this again. Be very grateful you've not been sacked this second.'

'You asked me to hold off on filing the annulment papers,' Jasper said quickly. 'I don't know why, but you did. We went to Paris for your next series of meetings and then the accident happened.' Jasper lifted his hands in a helpless gesture.

And it was helpless; he was hopeless. He could never know the truth for certain. He could never trust her.

Tomas went back indoors and took the stairs two at a time. He needed them both gone from his home.

Now.

There was a wildness in his eyes but every movement was so controlled, he was like burning ice. Zara rubbed her arms as she watched him coolly sign the annulment papers.

He didn't speak, he didn't look at her. Just through her.

Destroyed inside, she followed his lead and signed, then dated the papers. She needed to talk to him again, to try to make him understand, but he wasn't going to give her that chance.

'I can give you a ride somewhere if you'd like me to,

Zara?' Jasper stood with his back to Tomas, as if he knew he was risking the wrath of his employer.

'My car—'

'Is in the village,' Tomas interrupted. 'It's been fixed. Jasper can drop off and you can pick it up on your way through. It's been paid for.' He glanced at his desk. 'The Kilpatricks don't get back until Tuesday but I think I can cope alone for a couple of days.'

Zara winced; could he sound any more sarcastic?

'Is that okay with you, Zara?' Jasper asked.

She tried to hide her tumbling emotions. The older man was concerned, so she smiled. 'I think it's a good idea.'

She wanted time to talk to Tomas. To make him understand. But he wasn't allowing that. He was sending her away.

'You'd better pack,' Tomas muttered in her direction without looking at her. 'And you concentrate on getting those papers filed as quickly as possible,' he ordered Jasper. 'Leave everything else for me to sort out.'

He didn't speak to her again.

It took less than five minutes for her to put her clothes into her bag. She was so very cold. So hurt. And hopeless.

Tomas stood in the doorway, a forbidding expression on his face as he watched Jasper get into his car. She saw no way of breaking through to him.

She gazed up at him, at an even greater disadvantage height wise because she was on the lower step, trying not to slip in the melting snow.

But she had to take one last chance. One last risk.

'I don't want to leave,' she pleaded softly.

Finally he turned and looked directly at her, that dead look still dulling his expression. 'If you stayed, it would only be to have sex and I don't want you any more.'

CHAPTER THIRTEEN

It was always going to be just out of reach.

TOMAS COULDN'T BELIEVE the day had ended so horrendously.

For the first time since the accident he'd woken up happy. Yes, he'd had that moment when he'd remembered what he'd lost, but then he'd opened his eyes and looked straight into hers.

It wasn't just his body that had responded. His very soul had lifted. The loss had diminished, ebbing away like a gentle tide and taking the usual frustration and bitterness with it. It hadn't mattered because *she'd* been by his side. She'd smiled at him, her eyes luminous and—he'd thought—loving.

Waking up next to her had been the best moment of his life in so very long. He'd actually dared to think he might have found something he'd not thought possible. He'd thought he could hold onto it.

But it was all a charade.

She'd fooled herself into thinking she was in love with him. It was some hideous mix of pity and gratitude. And, yes, sexual attraction.

But not love.

It was as if the sweetest of cakes had crumbled to ash in his mouth.

And as for the veracity of her tale? He could well believe he'd played the hero in a moment of madness—one look into those dreamy eyes and he'd have done almost anything she'd asked.

But he was damned if he was going to shackle her to him and a life of servitude that she'd really only just escaped.

She'd done nice things for him because it was how she could show her appreciation. All those touches had been about saying thank you, more than anything else.

It hurt. He felt like a damned fool. A weak, vulnerable idiot.

Well, no more of that. He'd get back to work. Properly focus. Keep the company pushing forward.

He'd forget all about her.

But in the cruellest irony of all, his brain refused to block the memory of her with him. All he could think about was Zara. All he could see was the devastated expression in her eyes when he'd rejected her.

When he'd banished her.

He closed his eyes and willed himself to move forward. To concentrate. To do anything but ruminate over the last few days events. But it was futile. Time and time again his thoughts turned to her.

And the ache in his chest?

He pushed through, determinedly firing off email after email. Demanding reports come back to him sooner. Researching to find a new trend. Anything to occupy his mind.

It was almost midnight when he stalked into his room and slammed the door shut. Thank heavens he hadn't taken her into his own bed and tainted it with memories of her there.

But he couldn't sleep. At who knew what hour he found himself walking back down the corridor, to the room she'd slept in and walking into it. There was barely a sign of her presence. Only the faintest lingering lemony fragrance.

He sat on the edge of the bed and breathed in the pain.

Maybe she was right. Maybe it *was* pride holding him captive here. Maybe he was afraid of showing any kind of vulnerability because he knew this was such a dog-eat-dog world. Every man for himself and all that. He'd lived it, breathed it, built his empire on the rules he knew governed it. Money made a man. People had power over those who were poor and vulnerable and he wasn't putting himself at risk again. He couldn't when it had taken so much to claw his way out of that position.

And even if what she felt for him was genuine? Even if she really was in love with him?

His rejection of her wasn't about him at all. It was about what was best for *her*. He couldn't be the man she deserved to have. She didn't need someone who might let her down. He couldn't be everything she needed. He didn't know from one day to the next whether he'd wake up and remember anything at all any more. He wasn't lumbering her with that. Not when she'd fought so long and so hard to get herself free from the oppression and emotional burden of her uncle. She wasn't becoming his *caretaker*. It was never, ever happening.

He wasn't what was best for her. He never would be.

And he couldn't bear the thought of losing this too— these precious new memories.

At some point he slept—still dressed and on the edge of the bed he'd shared with her. When he woke, it was the worst moment ever. Furious with his inability to rationalise, he went out to the glasshouse, determined to maintain his daily routine. He worked out—longer and harder than usual.

Then he stomped to the kitchen. He hadn't eaten in hours. The lights were off and it was cold. There'd been no warm woman up baking at two in the morning making the whole house smell scrumptious and making him smile with her enthusiasm. And it was silent. She'd taken her phone and its relentlessly upbeat playlist with her.

But she'd left him reminders. He lifted the lid from the container he found in the fridge. There was a cake in there. A typically Zara, lemon-loaded, generously proportioned cake. He couldn't help it, his mouth watered. He cut a piece and put it on a plate and took a seat at the table that now held such significance. He bit into the treat.

As he'd known—feared—it was too delicious for anyone's good. And as he chewed, it came. That fleeting moment of familiarity—remembrance. But the returning memory remained just out of reach.

It was always going to be just out of reach. Eternally elusive.

Déjà vu again, tormenting him, because his brain now knew he'd met her before and it was trying to piece it together.

He was never going to remember any of that day he'd first met her. The day he'd married her. He'd done something so extreme and he couldn't remember a thing about it. He couldn't remember her at all. How was that *possible*?

He stood in fury and threw the plate into the sink.

The sound of it smashing echoed in his head as he stalked out of the room.

In his office the empty entries in his journal tortured him more. He flicked through the last couple of pages. Then he flicked back further, determined to remind himself of what was important.

His business. His privacy. Priorities, right?

Except as he flicked through the pages, he couldn't find what he was looking for. He tossed the journal down in exasperation. It was the most boring thing he'd read in months. He, who supposedly had an aptitude for identifying patterns, was only just seeing the reality now. His life had become so constrained and isolated—and boring. And he'd thought he was happy…but he wasn't.

He'd never been more miserable. Not even that day when the specialist told him his memory might never return was as bad as this. Because only now did he understand what he'd done to himself. And to her.

His fear of losing more had meant he was too afraid to live in the present.

It wasn't that he couldn't trust Zara. He couldn't trust *himself*. His worst fear was that he'd lose more of his memory and become a millstone around her neck.

He'd told himself it was just lust, just a case of having a beautiful woman under his nose for the first time in for ever—exactly the insecurity she'd once voiced. And as he'd replied, that idea was an insult to her. And to him.

It was only to her that he'd had such a reaction. It would only ever be to her.

And here he was afraid again—unable to trust that she hadn't done what she had out of some misguided sense of obligation and pity. But wasn't that insulting her all over again? Was he really going to believe that she didn't know her own mind? She'd told him as much herself—she hadn't given up her virginity to him out of pity. She'd wanted him. Plain and simple. And she'd had him. Exactly the way he'd wanted her himself. And he wanted more too.

Now he hoped she still wanted him—for more than just his body.

If he didn't earn her pity any more—by stopping hiding and starting to live—then maybe they could be together as equals.

But he had to stop hiding now.

Because he hadn't only lost his past. He'd stalled his present. And he'd lost his future too. He'd pushed her out of the door and slammed it after her.

He was an absolute idiot.

CHAPTER FOURTEEN

It was a lie.

ZARA GASPED AS she read the headline that dominated the online newspaper. She sank into the chair as her legs weakened and she squinted and leaned closer to the screen to read further.

> ### Galloway Investments CEO suffers
> ### severe memory loss
>
> *Tomas Gallo, millionaire CEO of Galloway Investments, was the victim of a near-fatal collision a year ago. Sources close to Gallo say the accident left his memory impaired with a temporal amnesia and there is no likelihood of full recovery. Yet the business has thrived, with Galloway Investments providing more than a twenty per cent return to investors in the last twelve months.*
>
> *Sources say his work output has not been diminished at all. The CEO, always known for his work ethic, has become reclusive since the accident, living alone in an estate in Buckinghamshire. He is rarely seen in public.*

She skimmed the accompanying fact box explaining his kind of amnesia and more about the company's stellar results but her gaze leapt back to that awful headline. Her blood iced.

This was terrible. This was exactly what Tomas hadn't wanted. And for it to have been leaked less than a week since she'd left him? There'd be no prizes for guessing who he'd suspect. Panicking, she grabbed her phone and hit Jasper's number. She'd not spoken to him at all in the five days since he'd dropped her into the village to collect her car. And the only conversation they'd had then was apology met with apology.

'How did they find out?' she asked as soon as Jasper answered. 'Who betrayed him?'

Who was the 'close source' who'd told all about his head injury?

'Have you spoken with him?' she added before Jasper had the chance to answer. 'Is he okay?'

'I haven't been able to contact him today,' Jasper finally answered in his usual cautious manner.

Zara pressed her hand to her forehead.

'He'll be all right, Zara,' the lawyer added calmly.

Probably, but 'all right' wasn't enough. He was unhappier than he'd ever admit. He was isolated and lonely and determined to believe he liked it that way and she feared this exposure would only drive him deeper into his seclusion. But he had so much to offer and she hated the thought of him being alone in that huge house all the time when he should be laughing and teasing and *loved*. There was so much in him to love.

'Are you going to see him?' she demanded.

'I can't. I'm en route to the airport now. I have a meeting to get to in New York.'

Jasper was going to the States *now*? 'You don't think checking on him is more important?'

'His company is important to him, Zara,' Jasper said firmly. 'It's what he's told me to do.'

'So ignore what he's told you and go check on him,' she snapped.

'I value my job and I respect Tomas. If he says he can handle it, he can handle it.'

That wasn't good enough. It wasn't okay to leave him alone when this news had just broken.

'I've already crossed the line with sending you there in the first place,' Jasper suddenly explained in a chastened tone. 'My job is to take care of the company, not the man.'

'But you care about the man.'

'Of course I do,' he replied. 'I care about him enough to do as he's instructed without argument.'

But what Tomas was asking was pure defensive reflex—putting his company ahead of his personal life as he'd always done. This was only going to drive him deeper into his isolated world.

'How are you doing, Zara?'

Her heart stalled at the gentle pity in Jasper's query. Of course he knew how she felt about Tomas; there'd been no hiding how devastated she'd been when he'd made her leave the other morning. She'd been almost silent in that car, but there'd been tears she couldn't stop from falling.

'I'm fine,' she assured Jasper quickly, glancing around her dreary little bedsit. 'It was a rough week and this was a shock, but I'm okay. I've been very busy getting back into my work.'

It was a lie. She'd spent the first two days crying. Then she'd pulled herself together and told herself to get on with it. But it was damn hard. She missed him with every fibre of her being.

She ended the call as quickly as she could, still angry and upset and still none the wiser about who had betrayed Tomas's confidence.

Jasper might be willing to say yes to everything Tomas wanted, but she wasn't going to. She was going to stand up and do what she knew in her heart was right.

He might not feel the same way about her, and that was fine, but she could check on him as a friend. And the only way she was going to know he was okay was to see him face to face. And she needed him to know she hadn't been the one to expose him. Honestly, she just ached to see him.

Decision made, she threw her bag into the car and locked up her small bedsit.

The entire drive down she mentally planned what she was going to say, envisaging how he might react. He'd probably changed the security code and she wouldn't even get past the gate. But if that happened she'd just have to climb it.

Almost four hours of non-stop driving later, she pulled up at the heavy gates. Her legs were stiff as she got out of the car and she stretched to ease them. She punched the security code and waited that half-moment.

'Miss, miss!'

She turned at the voice, startled to see a man with a large camera peering out from a gap in the hedge.

'Are you here to see Tomas, miss?'

As he asked he took photos of her as she stood, stunned and immobile. And then she heard that familiar creaking of the gates opening.

Galvanised into action, she dashed back to her car and drove through the gates, hoping the man wouldn't try to follow her in. Nervously she checked the rear-view mirror but to her relief saw he'd remained on the other side of the gates. But he was still taking photos of her.

Good Lord, it was horrendous.

She tried to pull her focus back and remember how she'd planned to greet Tomas, but all she could think was how relieved she was that it wasn't raining and that she wouldn't look as bedraggled as she had that first night she'd arrived here.

As she parked the car in front of the big house her heart sank. The beautiful building looked empty and cold and she knew he wasn't home. She wasn't surprised he'd left given there were paparazzi stalking him.

She knocked on the door regardless, hoping the house-keeper might be in, but no one answered. Deflated after driving all that way, she leaned back against the gleaming black door and stared down the driveway. She wasn't sure what to do next. She didn't want to drive back out past that photographer. She didn't want to leave without seeing Tomas.

She'd just have to wait. She slid down the door and sat at the base of it, wrapping her arms around her knees so she was in a tight little ball. She'd wait as long as it took.

But it was only about twenty minutes later when she heard shouting and the faint clang of the gates in the distance. She scrambled to her feet as a car came round the corner of the driveway. Without thinking she walked to the edge of the top step. Her breathing quickened as she recognised the vehicle as Tomas's big grey four-wheel-drive. As it drew closer she saw he was alone in the car, his expression hidden behind sunglasses. He parked it right behind hers, so it blocked her exit, preventing her from leaving in any great hurry.

She held her breath as he stepped out of the car. There were tired lines in his face, stubble on his jaw, yet there was energy in his leashed movements as he walked towards her. He removed his sunglasses and his gaze burned her skin with that hot accusation—like the time he'd caught her watching him from the window. He was heart-stop-pingly gorgeous. But her heart jack-hammered as she realised how angry he was.

'I—I didn't tell anyone—' she stammered immediately, thinking of the paparazzi hounding him at the gate. 'It wasn't me.'

'I know.' He stopped on the bottom step, meaning his face was almost level with hers.

'Honestly, I—' She broke off. He'd believed her?

'I know it wasn't you,' he repeated, his almost black eyes unfathomable and unwavering. 'Is that why you're here?'

'I—' She didn't know how to begin.

'You promised me you'd never come back.'

'How could I not?' She knotted her fingers together in front of her to stop herself from reaching out to him. 'I was worried about you.'

He studied her intently for a long moment. And she studied him—he seemed edgier, but as strong as ever. More strong, if that were possible.

'It is okay to break a promise because you care about someone?' he suddenly asked softly. 'Or to lie because you're worried about someone?'

'Some promises aren't right to keep,' she answered with a small shrug. 'And sometimes, yes, you think you're doing the right thing by lying. But generally I think it's better to be honest. Even if it hurts.'

She'd hurt herself, and him, by not being as honest as she should have been right from the start. But she just hadn't been able to be.

'I know you didn't leak my amnesia to the press,' he said decisively. 'I know that, because I did.'

'You leaked your own secret?' She gaped at him. '*Why?* Aren't you worried about how your clients will react?'

He didn't answer her directly. He turned and walked back to his car and picked up a manila file from the front passenger seat. He walked back to the foot of the steps and held it out to her.

'What is it?' she asked as she opened the cover. But it was obvious the second she looked down. It was the paperwork she'd signed less than a week ago.

'The annulment has come through?' she asked dully, not able to force a smile even though it would be the best form of defence. It hurt too much that it was all over between them.

'No.' He picked the pages up, leaving her with an empty folder. 'These haven't been sent in yet.'

'I thought Jasper took them—'

'I got him to bring them back.'

She stared at him, not getting where he was going with this.

'You were right, I have been lying,' he said. 'To myself. And I lied to you too.'

He tore the forms in half. Then he tore them in half again. Then he tossed them to the ground.

'What are you doing?' she shrieked.

'Why didn't you tell me we'd kissed before?'

She didn't answer; she was too busy staring at the shredded pages between their feet.

'When I asked you to tell me about the day we met, you left that out.'

'It wasn't relevant.' She drew breath and looked back into his eyes. 'It was only a minor thing.'

'Was it just a peck on the cheek?'

She froze.

'Or did I kiss you on the mouth?'

She simply couldn't answer.

'Surely you're not *still* shy?' For a split second he actually smiled—that gorgeous teasing, vital smile. Why was he teasing her about this now, when things were so tortured between them?

'I just don't think it's fair that you're a kiss ahead of me,' he added in a low voice. 'I'm going to spend my life trying to catch up.'

Her jaw dropped and she still couldn't get her head around what he was implying. But suddenly he spoke again, and she scrambled to follow what he was telling her.

'I got up early and drove all the way to Durham this morning to see you.' He shoved his hands into his pockets. 'I would have come last night before that story broke, but I had to pre-record an interview and it took longer than we thought. I didn't think you'd see it so quickly. I'm sorry because I wanted to get to you before you read it.'

'Why?' she asked, but the word didn't actually sound.

'When I got to your bedsit at lunchtime, you weren't home and your car wasn't there. I called Jasper and he thought you might be on your way to see me.' He sighed. 'So then I got back in my car and drove all the way home again. I guess I've been slowly catching up to you all day.'

She cleared her throat. 'Why were you coming to see me?'

Did she really have to ask? Tomas looked at her pallor, her wide eyes that revealed so much, and his heart ached.

He didn't want me that way.

He'd never forget the sadness that had sounded in her voice when she'd told him about her husband.

About *himself*.

While he understood the reasons, he hated that she was so insecure and he was so sorry he'd made her feel it all the more. He'd been cruel to her and he knew he didn't deserve her forgiveness. But he was damn well going to fight for it anyway.

'I've worked out what I hate the most about my amnesia.'

She licked her lips. He was mucking this up but he didn't know how else to say it all.

'I can't remember our first kiss,' he muttered, feeling hollow inside. 'That hurts me so much. I don't want to miss any more moments.'

'But—'

'I'm sorry I can't remember the first time we met. How can I not remember our first meeting?' The bereft feeling almost overwhelmed him. 'That's been stolen from me.'

She shook her head. 'I'm *glad* you can't remember.' Her eyes filled. 'You didn't want me then. You wouldn't have loved me then.'

'I kissed you, didn't I?' And that had only been the start.

'Only to say goodbye. Only because you were gallant.'

He almost smiled. 'I was never gallant in all my life. I might not remember much of that time, but I know that for certain. I might not have recognised it then, but there was some fundamental pull between us. I hardly knew you and yet I took one look and married you. That's not the kind of thing I'd do.' He shook his head. 'There was something, there was always something. There had to have been.' He caught her hand as she held it up to stop him. 'I know I can't make you believe me about that back then. But believe me now.'

'Tomas.' The tears trickled down her face. 'You didn't like what you saw in my uncle. In my situation. You saw a way to help me, so you took it. That was all it was. You would have done that for anyone.'

'No, I wouldn't. And even if that were true, then I finally have reason to be glad about the accident. Without this memory loss you might never have come back into my life.' He shook his head. 'That would have been the real tragedy.'

'No.'

He couldn't bear to see the tears spilling from her eyes. She was distraught and it was destroying him inside and he was so screwing this up. 'But I think if I hadn't had the accident I'd have tracked you down anyway. Why else did I get Jasper to delay filing for the annulment if I didn't have some other plan in mind?'

But she shook her head again.

Frustration welled up in him. He needed to make her understand how he felt—what she meant to him. But he'd never opened up to another soul in this way. Never felt this way.

A ring wasn't personal enough for them. Marriage wasn't personal enough—not for them. He wanted to leave an indelible mark on her—brand her as being his. Only his and always his. Because she'd burned her mark on his heart. He might as well tear it from his chest and give it to her on his knees because he was so totally, utterly hers.

Yet at the same time, he never wanted to hurt her or see her hurt again. She was too precious and he didn't know how to keep her close and safe.

He wanted to make her smile again, to make that dimple peep at him and that softly wicked look enter her eyes. But if he had any chance of making that happen, then he had to do the hardest thing and be completely honest with her.

'Tomas?' she murmured as he reached out and framed her face with his hands so he could see into her beautiful eyes and draw the courage he needed from the luminous emotion he saw shining there.

For a second he couldn't speak. He'd been alone all his life. Never more so than in this last year. And oddly, never more so than in this minute. He had only this chance to bridge the gap between them; he needed to do it right.

'I need to tell you the truth,' he confessed, holding her closer. 'I need you to listen. Can you do that?'

'Of course.'

And he needed her to believe him. 'I was horrible and I lied. It's not that I don't trust you. It's that I don't trust myself.'

He dug into his pocket and pulled out a black leather-bound book.

'Read it.' He handed it to her.

'It's your personal journal.'

'Read it.'

Zara nervously opened the journal, reading the entry on the page it had opened to. Dated from a few months ago, it simply detailed all the research he'd done that day. The decisions he'd made. Same with the next entry, and the next, and the next. What soon shone from the pages was the stark lack of interaction with other people. There were emails, occasional phone calls but rarely any meetings. Those there were were only with Jasper. She knew he barely met with his household staff. So it wasn't so much what he'd written, but everything that was *missing*. It was just as she'd feared.

'Incredibly boring, isn't it?' He reached across and turned the pages faster. 'Skip a few, they're all the same.'

But she didn't want to read the entries from the last week. From when she was there.

But when she turned to the pages there was only one word written under each date.

Zara.

'I couldn't capture it then,' he explained in a low voice. 'I couldn't face it myself, let alone write it. Turn to today.'

Apologise. Bring her back. Love her.

He closed the book and dropped it to the ground, stepping closer to her at the same time. 'I sent you away because I was trying to do the right thing but I did it horribly. I made you think I didn't care. I deliberately said things I knew would hurt you most because I wanted to drive you away. I wanted to hurt you so you'd hate me. So you'd turn and leave and never come back. But now here you are, back again.' He smiled sadly. 'Because you were concerned about me?'

She nodded.

'Because you love me?'

'Yes,' she whispered. 'But you don't believe me.'

'I don't deserve your love, Zara. But I'm going to take it. And I'm never giving it up again.' He held her so she couldn't step away. 'I'm never letting you go again.'

She pressed her hand to her mouth, trying to hold back

her sobs, because it was so important she listen and hear him. She ached to understand.

'I'm terrified of losing more. Of losing all *this*. The mornings are the worst. I wake up and then remember how much I've lost. Every day it's like a weight that gets dumped on me, dragging me down. But that morning I woke up with you beside me and it was the best morning that I can remember ever. It didn't matter any more because you were there smiling at me.'

She remembered his smile. The way he'd held her. She remembered the sheer joyous vitality pouring from his body.

'But then Jasper arrived,' she said.

'I felt betrayed.' He nodded. 'I hated that you knew all this stuff I'd missed. It crystallised all my worst fears. But most of all I was so bitterly disappointed. There was a part of me who'd wanted what I shared with you to be new and fresh. I hoped that you could accept me as I am now, that you'd never really know how broken I was. But you knew exactly how broken I was. You knew me from before. And I didn't want you lumbered with someone so...' He trailed off.

Her heart broke for him.

'You'd had enough of a rough time trapped in a horrible environment. You don't need a man who isn't one hundred per cent. Someone who...'

'Tomas—'

'But I'm selfish. I'm so selfish. And I want you too much. I don't want to let you go even when I know I should. I used to hope it would come back. I need to lose that hope. Just as I need to lose the fear I might lose more of my memory. I need to stop hiding and live now,' he said. 'You showed me everything I'm missing out on and now I want it all. I want you with me. I was afraid of waking up and not remembering you. But waking up now and not having you with me is a nightmare. I'm living one without you. I can't bear to wake up tomorrow morning and not have you be the first thing I see. Nothing is right when I don't see you first thing. I need you next to me.'

'Tomas—'

'I love you, Zara. I'm sorry I drove you away. I've never regretted anything more. It is the worst thing in the world when a person you love leaves you. I know this too well and I'm sorry I hurt you.'

But she needed to tell him the truth too. 'It's so awful of me but there's a part of me that's glad you can't remember that day. I don't want you to know how truly weak I was then. I *hate* how I was then.' She hated that she hadn't had the strength to leave of her own accord. That she'd needed his help.

'You would have rescued yourself eventually,' he said.

Would she? These things took a strength that was hard to come by. Hard when you'd been through years of being belittled. Undervalued. Unloved.

And people wanted love. People put up with all kinds of horrible for the paltry bit of love thrown their way. People clung on in the hope that it would get better. She'd been that person. She'd tried so hard for so long because she'd wanted that approval and that love.

She'd wanted what she'd lost when her parents had died. That security and safety and sense of belonging.

'You're more resourceful than you like to believe. Stronger than you know. But back then you were alone and unloved and a bit damaged.' He lifted a shoulder. 'But, you know, I'm a bit damaged too. That's okay. We're still okay.'

She looked into his eyes. He was so very right.

'Can you just hold me?' she begged.

His arms came around her and she cried. He held her close, rocking her gently as she let go of all the awful tension and doubt.

'I'm so sorry.' She sniffed. 'I've made your shirt all wet.'

'Never apologise,' he whispered. 'Stay with me now.'

She could finally smile. Finally believe it. 'Will you come back into the world more with me?'

'Haven't I already? The whole world knows the truth about me now.'

'You did that because of me?'

He nodded. 'I want to stop hiding. Stop being afraid. And I know you need more of the world because you were constrained for so long by your uncle. So we don't have to stay here at Raxworthy if you don't want to.'

Her jaw dropped. 'I adore this home and I'd love nothing more than to live here with you.' Frankly she'd live anywhere with him.

'You'll work on your business?'

'Just try and stop me.'

He grinned, the tension finally easing in his features. 'Thank goodness. I love being your guinea pig.'

She cupped his jaw with her hand. 'Maybe we could throw open the gates and show the gardens again. Just once a month.' They could let the world in, just a little.

'But how are we to bathe naked in the glasshouse if there might be people about to see?'

She laughed. 'One afternoon's abstinence will be a sacrifice, I admit.'

'We'll have to go somewhere for that weekend—Venice, New York, Paris...'

She couldn't stop the huge smile from spreading across her features. 'That sounds like a *really* good idea.'

'I've got another one.' He leaned closer.

'Full of them this afternoon, aren't you?'

'Uh-huh.' He nodded, but his expression turned serious. 'The gardens will be beautiful in spring.' He gazed at her. 'I think you would look lovely walking towards me in that garden.' He inclined his head. 'Maybe you'd wear a dress.'

'I get to be in clothes now?' she teased. 'Why would I be walking towards you in a dress?'

'For our marriage blessing,' he answered softly. 'And we'll reaffirm our vows so I can remember them this time.' He brushed his finger across her lips. 'I'll mean them differently this time. And I'll mean them for ever.'

She smiled at him. 'I'll say them every day to you if you need me to.'

'Yes.' He dropped to his knees. 'So will you marry me, Zara? Even though we're already married?' He smiled ruefully.

She loved that he could laugh about it with her. But more than that he was giving her that moment that she'd not had last time.

'Yes.' She bent and took his face in her hands and kissed him tenderly. 'And you'll make the most of the moments with me?'

'Zara. I love you,' he said simply as he stood. 'And I will love you every moment of every day for the rest of my life.'

She wrapped her arms around him tightly, unable to speak for the joy flowing through her. They'd both been alone but they had this second chance. They had each other. And then the magic was back—those long, luscious kisses that she couldn't get enough of. She leaned back against the door for support as he soothed her soul—then stirred it to new heights as their passion exploded.

'What are you doing?' she gasped as he unexpectedly broke the kiss and lifted her into his arms.

'I'm carrying my bride over the threshold,' he answered, tossing her a little higher, then tighter in his arms. 'It's a bit belated, but I'm taking the moment.'

'What other moments do you have in mind?'

'I'm going to close the door and press my wife up against it and have my way with her here and now because I cannot wait a second longer.'

'That sounds like a good moment.' She smiled at him.

'It'll be the first of millions,' he promised.

'Yes,' she vowed. 'Yes, yes, yes.'

* * * * *

If you enjoyed this story, why not explore
Natalie Anderson's fabulous duet
THE THRONE OF SAN FELIPE?

THE SECRET THAT SHOCKED DE SANTIS
THE MISTRESS THAT TAMED DE SANTIS

Available now!

MILLS & BOON®

MODERN™

POWER, PASSION AND IRRESISTIBLE TEMPTATION

sneak peek at next month's titles...

In stores from 9th March 2017:

The Italian's One-Night Baby – Lynne Graham *and*
The Desert King's Captive Bride – Annie West
Once a Moretti Wife – Michelle Smart *and*
The Boss's Nine-Month Negotiation – Maya Blake

In stores from 23rd March 2017:

The Secret Heir of Alazar – Kate Hewitt *and*
Crowned for the Drakon Legacy – Tara Pammi
His Mistress with Two Secrets – Dani Collins *and*
The Argentinian's Virgin Conquest – Bella Frances

Just can't wait?
Buy our books online before they hit the shops!
www.millsandboon.co.uk

Also available as eBooks.

MILLS & BOON®

EXCLUSIVE EXTRACT

Stefano Moretti wants only revenge from his wife,
Anna. When she reappears after leaving him, with no
memory of their marriage, he realizes that this is his
chance…for a red-hot private seduction, followed by a
public humiliation! Until Stefano realizes there's
something he wants more than vengeance—Anna,
back in his bed for good!

Read on for a sneak preview of
ONCE A MORETTI WIFE

Stefano pressed his thumb to her chin and gently stroked
it. 'When your memories come back you will know the
truth. I will help you find them.'

Her heart thudding, her skin alive with the sensation
of his touch, Anna swallowed the moisture that had filled
her mouth.

When had she given in to the chemistry that had always
been there between them, always pulling her to him? She'd
fought against it right from the beginning, having no intention of joining the throng of women Stefano enjoyed such
a legendary sex life with. To be fair, she didn't have any
evidence of what he actually got up to under the bedsheets;
indeed it was something she'd been resolute in *not*
thinking about, but the steady flow of glamorous, sexy
women in and out of his life had been pretty damning.

When had she gone from liking and hugely admiring

him but with an absolute determination to never get into bed with him, to marrying him overnight? She'd heard of whirlwind marriages before but from employee to wife in twenty-four hours? Her head hurt just trying to wrap itself around it.

Had Stefano looked at her with the same glimmer in his green eyes then as he was now? Had he pressed his lips to hers or had she been the one…?

'How will you help me remember us?' she asked in a whisper.

His thumb moved to caress her cheek and his voice dropped to a murmur. 'I will help you find again the pleasure you had in my bed. I will teach you to become a woman again.'

Mortification suffused her, every part of her anatomy turning red.

I will teach you to be a woman again?

His meaning was clear. He knew she was a virgin.

Anna's virginity was not something she'd ever discussed with anyone. Why would she? Twenty-three-year-old virgins were rarer than the lesser-spotted unicorn. For Stefano to know that…

Dear God, it was *true*.

All the denial she'd been storing up fell away.

She really had married him.

Don't miss
ONCE A MORETTI WIFE
By Michelle Smart

Available April 2017
www.millsandboon.co.uk

Copyright ©2017 Michelle Smart

The perfect gift for
Mother's Day...

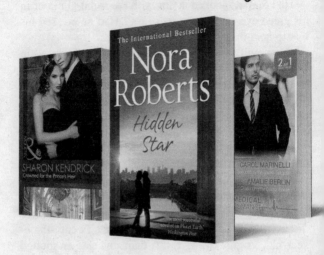

a Mills & Boon subscriptio

Call Customer Services on
0844 844 1358*

or visit
millsandboon.co.uk/subscriptio

* This call will cost you 7 pence per minute plus your
phone company's price per minute access charge.

MD16

MILLS & BOON®

Congratulations
Carol Marinelli
on your 100ᵗʰ Mills & Boon book!

Read on for an exclusive extract

How did she walk away? Lydia wondered.

How did she go over and kiss that sulky mouth and say goodbye when really she wanted to climb back into bed?

But rather than reveal her thoughts she flicked that internal default switch which had been permanently set to 'polite'.

'Thank you so much for last night.'

'I haven't finished being your tour guide yet.'

He stretched out his arm and held out his hand but Lydia didn't go over. She did not want to let in hope, so she just stood there as Raul spoke.

'It would be remiss of me to let you go home without seeing Venice as it should be seen.'

'Venice?'

'I'm heading there today. Why don't you come with me? Fly home tomorrow instead.'

There was another night between now and then, and Lydia knew that even while he offered her an extension he made it clear there was a cut-off.

Time added on for good behaviour.

And Raul's version of 'good behaviour' was that there would

be no tears or drama as she walked away. Lydia knew that. If she were to accept his offer then she had to remember that.

'I'd like that.' The calm of her voice belied the trembling she felt inside. 'It sounds wonderful.'

'Only if you're sure?' Raul added.

'Of course.'

But how could she be sure of anything now she had set foot in Raul's world?

He made her dizzy.

Disorientated.

Not just her head, but every cell in her body seemed to be spinning as he hauled himself from the bed and unlike Lydia, with her sheet-covered dash to the bathroom, his body was hers to view.

And that blasted default switch was stuck, because Lydia did the right thing and averted her eyes.

Yet he didn't walk past. Instead Raul walked right over to her and stood in front of her.

She could feel the heat—not just from his naked body but her own—and it felt as if her dress might disintegrate.

He put his fingers on her chin, tilted her head so that she met his eyes, and it killed that he did not kiss her, nor drag her back to his bed. Instead he checked again. 'Are you sure?'

'Of course,' Lydia said, and tried to make light of it. 'I never say no to a free trip.'

It was a joke but it put her in an unflattering light. She was about to correct herself, to say that it hadn't come out as she had meant, but then she saw his slight smile and it spelt approval.

A gold-digger he could handle, Lydia realised.

Her emerging feelings for him—perhaps not.

At every turn her world changed, and she fought for a semblance of control. Fought to convince not just Raul but herself that she could handle this.

Don't miss
THE INNOCENT'S SECRET BABY
by Carol Marinelli
OUT NOW

BUY YOUR COPY TODAY
www.millsandboon.co.uk

Copyright ©2017 by Harlequin Books S.A.